WISH

ANTHOLOGY

Wishes don't always come true.
When they do, they aren't always the way we want them.

Edited By

Blessing Egbekun

Written By

Olamide Agemo

Feyi Aina

Mobolaji Olanrewaju

Christiana Agboni

Temitope Omamegbe

Timileyin Okunlola

TABLE OF CONTENTS

INTRODUCTION

Everyone has wishes - tiny sparks of hope that dance through our minds throughout our lives. Some people make a dozen, others hundreds, each one carrying varying weights of possibilities.

In this anthology, six stories dive deep into the tangled web of desires and the unexpected ways they unfold.

In the realm of wishes, outcomes are not always as expected. Even though some wishes may come true, many do not always arrive the way we'd hoped or anticipated.

Yet, even when we are left picking the pieces of shattered dreams, we continue to churn out more, again and again, because to stop wishing is to stop living.

THE AWAKENING

A crystal practitioner falls for a boxer, discovers a need to break repeating cycles, and chooses the love she deserves.

By
OLAMIDE AGEMO

Dedication

To every girlie choosing a higher kind of love.

"You will not overlook these red flags again because you will not forget this feeling. You also have a better idea of what you want out of love, trust that. Trust that you know better now and forgive yourself for whatever you think you did wrong."

~gaiaelect

Circa 2002

"You must be born again!" The greying talking head at Love Baptist Church belts out in a baritone voice that spreads across the room. Hollow. Unfeeling. The spittle on the corner of his mouth makes an appearance from time to time, shy, yet not.

The choir has been exceptional lately, with Dame Esther promising wave after wave of musical excellence. Now, they are keeping up a particularly high note and Bishop smiles in approval towards her direction.

Dame Esther blushes shyly, adjusts the hideous blonde wig on her frail head and continues to conduct the choir.

I yawn. For the life of me, this charade tires me out and I absolutely cannot wait to return to the quiet of my room. But that has been taken away from me, too. My gaze falls on my old friend, Anu sitting at the back pew, but she averts her eyes.

Sigh.

Mama sits in the second row, shoulders raised high, back straight, hanging on to every word that Bishop says. She dons the blue flowery dress reserved for important occasions. The important occasions have been coming more frequently now since Papa left.

"It was a love story that changed the world." At least that's how she put it—Mama. This was before all the fights. Papa's visits have now trickled down to once a week. And on some weeks, he doesn't even come.

My diary is my best pal. It never judges me. In it, I sometimes write about the plays and art exhibitions Papa took Mama and me to. I remember the laughter in Mama's eyes and the mischief they got around to doing, running around the house, making cute and silly faces at each other.

Uhh.

Anytime I couldn't go with them, Papa would make it up to me by taking me to exotic bookshops when he had free time. I'd bury my head reading page after page of sci-fi and mystery novels, figuring out the whys and whens while enjoying another Popsicle.

I'd sometimes pull a tantrum when it was time to go home, and Papa would purchase new books for me. Oftentimes, after having read another great who-dun-nit, my thoughts took a darker turn, and my diary bled for it. Still, it held me close; a friend indeed.

Fun times.

It all finally went south during one Christmas holiday. Mama and Papa had been fighting more times than I care to remember. Doors kept getting slammed incessantly. The smiles turned into ugly scowls. Papa started staying out longer.

Mama soon began to barge into my room without knocking. "There's nothing on your body that's not on mine," she would mutter indignantly. "I don't believe in privacy." She'd then randomly go through my things, under different guises, looking for *contrabands.*

I could never figure out her deal, why everything and *everyone* seemed to be falling apart, but I thought it was one of those things that happen—and maybe families don't always see eye to eye.

I hear Mama crying when she thinks no one can hear. Papa has moved out now. He says it's because of work, but I know he isn't telling me the whole truth.

When the school bells ring, boy! Am I excited? At least I'd see my friends again and be rid of Mama's new crazy.

I spot my friends, Anu and Stephanie, standing by my locker, giggling and whispering to each other. We three have been great friends since preschool. Getting into trouble together and wriggling our way out of it in sync.

I walk up to them, a big grin playing on my face, but as soon as I get closer, their expressions turn sour.

"What's up?" I ask, surprised.

"Nothing," Anu says, with a smile that doesn't seem to reach her brown eyes. "We were just talking."

I shrug off the weird feeling and pry open my locker. But I don't see my diary in its usual corner. *Maybe I left it somewhere.* That's when I feel Matau, a sturdy-built Somali, pull me into an awkward embrace from behind. Matau shares a seat with me in science class, but we don't talk often—well, except that one day.

As soon as he lets go, I feel Anu's eyes on me.

"What was that?" she asks, her voice turning cold.

"Just Matau getting a little handsy," I say, putting the rest of my lunch into my locker. "And why are you—"

Anu dresses me up and down with her eyes in a non-respectable way and storms off.

The next day, the rumours started. I was the class slut, and was trying to steal all the boys in our grade. Anu had told everyone that I'd stolen her boyfriend, just like I had taken my father away from my mother.

Soon, everyone was laughing and pointing at me in the hallways. I could hear the whispers, the snickers, the cruel jokes. The bolder ones said it to my face.

It was like living in a nightmare.

I tried to defend myself, but no one would listen. How Anu had managed to instigate everyone against me, to the extent that they knew what was going on with me at home, was a complete mystery.

Just like those books I read in the book clubs.

Stephanie didn't say anything, but she didn't defend me either. Even our other friends didn't want to be seen with me. I felt like a pariah. An outcast, a freak.

With each day that passed, I became more invisible. Drowning in a sea of shame and humiliation.

Living someone else's life.

And worst of all, it wasn't even true. I'd never stolen anyone's boyfriend, neither had I tried to. But no one would believe me. The damage had been done, and there was nothing I could do to fix it.

"Let's share the grace!" the Bishop calls out from the pulpit, bringing me back into the present. The choir has taken their position to sing the Love Baptist Church theme song. Anu stands with them, in her soprano voice, singing to the highest glory.

And Mama raises her hands high, waving them. She's been blessed by the meeting of believers in one accord.

Of course, no one ever gives me grace when I need it.

1
Awakening Crystals

I stand amidst the mesmerising array of crystal stones in my sacred grove, lost in thought. Pulling out a blunt from the drawer next to me, I take a moment to marvel at its perfect cylinder shape, moulded with love. I then pick up the red lighter from my leather purse on the table and ignite the blunt; basking in its glow and feel.

Seeing everything as is.

With every exhale, the versatility of the universe calls out to me, and the souls that tango endlessly, oblivious, under its rhythmic watch, make me chuckle. My crystals, the ones that have held me dear, and called me friend these past years, sit in captivating heaps on the windowsill, with their diverse shapes and colours, each emitting their unique energy.

Just as I am wont to do on Tuesday mornings, I plug in the vacuum cleaner to do a deep cleaning of the floor of my crystal practice alongside some quick energy reading. *If I don't cleanse my soul to make room for the new, how would the old go?*

As I move towards the consulting room, I see some sugar ants lined up on the table before me in a cool procession.

Did you know that ants have special antennae that help them form queues in search of answers? They never think of resistance, only pathways.

My mind is constantly bursting with new pathways, and sometimes, I wonder if I wouldn't go into overdrive one day, mad, trying to help people find new answers.

Hmm.

It is 9:30 am, signalling the almost beginning of a new day. I shut down the vacuum cleaner as the neon sign on the grey walls comes alive, proudly proclaiming my sanctuary "Crystals by Felicity —Your Soul Doctor."

With a heart full of purpose, and a smile on my face, I take a moment to appreciate the tagline that perfectly encapsulates the essence of my life's work.

After my morning rituals, I light some sage, cleansing the space and setting the stage for the day's spiritual journey. The pleasant aroma fills the air, blending with the scent of my blunt as I change into a flowing black silk dress adorned with coral beads. The ancient energy of the crystals activates me to be the healer my clients need.

Sitting at my table, I say some words of affirmation, mentally preparing for the tasks ahead. The steady rain outside creates a soothing ambience that soon calms my mind and centres my spirit.

The chime of the entrance bell suddenly interrupts my thoughts, drawing my attention to the client who shuffles in. Not a regular, he is a man of medium build, dressed sharply in a beige suit. As he places his wet umbrella in the corner and collapses into the comfort of a yellow chair, I greet him with a warm smile.

I assist him in removing his suit, hanging it carefully on a cloth hanger in the consulting room. In a series of short dramatic spats, he shares the harrowing experience of fainting at a particularly tasking board meeting, leading to an emergency hospital visit. And after regaining consciousness, he'd felt compelled to seek my assessment having seen my ad earlier in his company's monthly brochure.

"Take off your shoes and wristwatch," I gently say to him. Instinctively, I run my hand through the back of his head, guiding him to wear a grey loose-fitting garment—symbolising a willingness to open up and shed emotional burdens.

Leading him to a restoration bed where he lies down, my voice takes on a soft and soothing note as I ask.

"What is your intention? What do you want?"

Placing a red crystal on his throat, I encourage him to share freely. He soon breaks down in tears, revealing his financial hardships—the sudden loss of funding for his fishery business and the need to liquidate painstakingly built investments.

As he speaks on, I learn that his son's troubling behaviour, coupled with the absence of his wife, further adds to his distress.

Moving the crystal slowly from his throat to his chest, I mutter, "Open up your heart chakra. Let me in." Flinching, he pulls away, as if too afraid to see himself for who he is.

Sensing the depth of his darkness, I intuitively select a green crystal and place it over his heart. I guide his hand firmly to it, as he shares his struggles. In this moment, as the heat from the crystals radiates, judgment does not exist. *Only presence.*

Once more, I ask solemnly, "What do you want?"

"Freedom... Forgiveness," he replies, his voice trembling with raw emotion. "I just want to... let go. Maybe I cannot have it all, but I need... something."

Applying gentle pressure to the back of his neck, I knead it tenderly, allowing the crystals' energies to harmonise with his. Slowly, he quiets down, feeling a sense of relief as his body assimilates the crystals' healing properties.

Taking his hands in mine, I stroke his fingers rhythmically. *"How can I they, if I already am?* All that you need, you have. You only need to go within."

"Breathe."

As he grasps the depth of my words, the man seizes my hands with fervour, grateful for his newfound revelation, not unlike a baby who's just taken his first steps. With a deep sigh of release, his lips find the back of my hands and he kisses them gingerly.

"What's my tab?" he asks moments later as he slides back into his two-piece, a crooked smile appearing on his oblong face.

"It's $555," I reply smugly, imagining how he eats oranges. "There's a partners' discount. I'll send the bill to your office."

"I'll do you one better," he says with a wink, taking out his phone and punching out some numbers. My phone beeps shortly, my cash app grateful for the abundance boost.

As he leaves, a spring returns to his step that wasn't there when he came in, and I am left with a profound sense of fulfilment and of course, something to chuckle about.

Later that evening, as I close my eyes breathing in the soothing scent of sage, I remind myself that my journey as a healer and *lover* is far from over. The universe has chosen me to be a conduit for healing, and I must embrace both the joy and the burden it brings. *Especially when my love sometimes feels a little too much for many.*

"I get the feeling that I'll be alone again tonight," I whisper as some jazz from my Vinyl in the corner serenades the air.

2
Bonds in the Garden

The flickering TV screen casts an eerie glow in the dimly lit room. Empty bottles of alcohol lie strewn on the floor, mirroring the disarray of emotions that swirl between my mother and me.

"Felicity Animashaun, why can't you ever do anything right?" Mama suddenly snaps, taking her attention from the soap opera she's spent days binging.

"I-I tried my best with the rice, but the gas ran out," I stammer, feeling several sizes smaller than my size 6 frame. Trying to avoid the heat oozing from her eyes, I stoop to pick the picture frames of Mama and Papa lying face down randomly across the room, but she slaps them out of my hands, furious.

"Just excuses! You're becoming so careless," she continues, anger seeping into every word. "I've told you times without numbers to check all your items before you start cooking. When you never stop burying your head in those books, how would you pay attention???"

"How you do anything is how you do everything!!!"

Brnggg.

The shrill ring of the landline phone suddenly pierces through the room, and for a brief moment, hope flutters within me. I make a quick dash to the corner, grab the receiver and slowly flash a grin.

"Who's calling?" Mama demands, taking giant steps towards me, before finally snatching the phone.

Silence greets her question as she puts her ear to the receiver, and her anger only intensifies. Her chest heaves as her face swiftly displays about 19 different emotions.

"I knew it! It's your father. He never answers or returns my calls, but he calls you!" she fumes, stamping her feet on the heavily padded floors, giving flight to the ants that have gathered around.

"H-he wanted to know my exam results," I admit, my voice shaking with fear as I shrink deeper into the corner. My heart pounds in my chest, and tears pool in my eyes as I brace for the inevitable storm. "And I don't think I've done anything that deserves this. Is it my fault that— "

"You smart mouth!" Her eyes blaze with fury, the back of her hand connecting with my face. She soon brandishes her slipper as a weapon. "I keep working hard for this family, and is this the thanks I get?"

"No one cares about what I think. No one even wants to—"

As each hit descends on me, I am again reminded of the peace we once shared at home and wondering how everything went to shit. It is almost ironic how people never take their own advice but always want to shove it down other people's throats.

Just like Mama and how she did *anything* now.

Feeling exhausted, I seek refuge in a nearby garden later that afternoon. Here, birds sing their joyful melodies and carefree children play, oblivious to the emotional turmoil that churns within me. But isn't that what life is about though?

Everyone feels their feelings differently, and that's just okay?

Clad in a faded t-shirt and a pair of jeans that have seen better days, I pluck two leaves and absentmindedly intertwine them, trying to soothe my frayed nerves. The gentle breeze brushes against my tear-streaked face, offering a moment of respite from the emotional tempest.

Suddenly, he appears, Matau, a classmate with whom I seldom exchange more than a few words. He dons a blue chequered shirt with a threadbare backpack slung over one shoulder and a small basket in his other hand.

"Hey. What are you doing here?" he mouths throatily, placing his basket of tinctures beside me. He then plops himself on the concrete seat I am sitting on, propelling me to scoot over.

"I should ask you too," I mumble, feeling a strange sense of knowledge as if meeting him truly for the first time. "Just needed some fresh air."

"Makes two of us," he replies, offering a small smile.

We sit in silence for a moment and then, he begins to open up about his struggles with his grandmother. He tells me how, after the death of his parents in a ghastly accident, he was consigned by his family to live with her. The journey so far had been fraught with many challenges as he couldn't figure out why he mostly *needed* to be the adult in their relationship.

"Look at these tinctures," he points to the basket on the floor next to him. "This is the 4th time I've had to go to the market to get them, despite the fact I told her this was the combination they had right from the beginning."

"My grandma's a stubborn old mule who simply thinks words from those younger than her mean nothing at all."

His words feel like a soft caress on my heart, and I chuckle. I find myself responding in kind, sharing my burden.

"I feel suffocated at home too," I admit, my voice barely above a whisper.

"See. Sometimes I wonder if I'm related to my grandma at all." Matau says after a moment, swiping a speck of dust from his shoes. Stifling a sneeze, I shrug.

"Right? I often ask myself this about my mother — 'if I can't relate to you, then tell me who it is I can relate to?'"

"It's tough, isn't it? When the adults can't handle their own emotions," Matau sighs, his empathy enveloping me like the green teddy bear I hug tightly at night, when no one's there.

"You don't know the half of it. It feels like I'm always stuck in the middle with my parents, with no one to hear me out," I confess, matter-of-factly, my hand becoming wrapped around my throat.

"Hmm. I get that. Sometimes I just want to disappear," he admits, his eyes mirroring my pain. "But it is what it is."

We share a moment of silence, our hearts intertwining in shared understanding. *Saying just enough. Nothing more.*

"I often come here to clear my head," I say, a silver of resolution in my voice. "It's like this garden understands everything I'm going through."

"Yes. I feel the same way too. She listens without judging. Just holding space," he responds, taking his calloused hands in mine, his gaze unwavering. It only lasts for a moment.

"I wish more adults would take a big fat cue and chill."

As we laugh out loud, our mirth mingles with the chirping of birds, forming a symphony of comfort amidst the underlying chaos.

"Thank you for being here," I say, feeling a newfound sense of camaraderie.

"No. Thank you. I don't feel so alone now," he says, a small smile tugging at his lips.

The golden sun begins to dip below the horizon, casting a warm glow over the garden, and I know it's time to head back home. Reluctantly, I gather myself together, grateful for the refuge this little corner of nature and great conversation has offered.

"I should probably head back," I say, my heart heavy with the thought that the chaos at home still awaits me.

Matau nods, realisation written on his face. "Yeah, I should too. Grandma won't be happy if I'm late again."

"Again??" I chuckle, my words steeped with understanding. Home was wherever one was loved, and if one didn't feel loved enough, *why would they want to go there?*

We laugh awkwardly, standing up, and brushing off stray blades of grass from our clothes.

Unbeknownst to us, Anu watches from afar, her disapproving gaze casting a shadow over our moment of connection.

3
An Enchanting Smile

Have you ever watched the sun rise in a person's eyes? As the smile dances on their face so alluring it almost outshines the stars during a full moon? It's how I feel about her—Halima. Watching her as she pulls out 5, no, 6 volumes of a really old text, her face scrunched in total concentration, as if too afraid to let the words down, I feel a thrill pass through me.

I observe her dreamy walk down the corridors with her headphones, the rhythmic beat of music guiding her steps. She carries a bottle of water and takes her chosen seat with her usual precision. The rose-tinted glasses she dons seem to hide secrets behind their tint, but it only adds to her allure.

This year, I take the courage to ask her out—if only I can manage to pull her attention from the books in the library and to me, a simple boy. My friends however remind me I'm anything but simple, as I build my muscles in preparation for the next college boxing tournament.

As soon as she's about to leave the library, I catch up to her. "Hey, I've seen you here quite often," I start, trying to sound casual, my biceps straining against my white tee.

"Whoa! This is creepy," she retorts, moving a few inches backwards, but her lips curl into a quirky little smile that makes my heart skip a tiny little beat.

"So sorry. I didn't mean to come off as creepy. It's just… you have this vibe about you that—" I stumble over my words, trying to explain. "You're so much prettier when you smile."

"Oh, 'vibe.'" She rolls her eyes. "I hear that word a lot. Anyway, I enjoy my solitude and books. I don't need the added burden of a relationship."

"Plus, you have no right to tell me whether to smile or not."

"I admire your spunk," I say honestly, watching her mouth purse with a fierceness. "And I'd like to take you out on a date." I get her desire for solitude, but it only makes me want to get to know her more.

"I appreciate the offer," she replies, tossing her long brown braids against her slender back, "but I'm really not interested."

"Besides, I'm already betrothed in line with our customs."

Her words sting and I feel a flash of anger, but I try to hide it. "Fine, you're not that pretty anyway," I blurt out, my anger fueled by the sting of her rejection.

She doesn't react as I expect, instead, she takes out her headphones and looks at me straight in the eyeballs, her voice tinged with a mix of shock and pity. "You don't even know me."

"What if I'm a serial killer?"

Her words catch me off guard, and I'm left speechless. I storm off, feeling an odd mix of embarrassment and regret for my outburst.

Later, I let my frustration take another form—I encouraged my friends to bully her whenever she passed by. Her strong, muscular calves, reminiscent of a boy's, become the target of our ridicule.

As the days pass, however, I find myself missing her presence in the library. I wonder if my actions have driven her away, or if there's something else going on in her life. Perhaps she was betrothed, as she'd said, and I was an unwelcome distraction.

One day, she's completely gone. I can't tell if it's because of my bullying or for some other reason, but I'm left with the lingering feeling of regret, knowing that I let my anger push away someone who could have been special, just like my father pushed everyone away.

You see, my mom passed when I was quite young, leaving me in the care of my father, a hotshot contractor who was always busy with work and never stayed home. His revolving door of girlfriends was a constant presence in my life, and I often found myself shipped off to boarding school, like an unwelcome burden.

Those women tried to win his affection by splurging on gifts for me, cooking for him, vying for his attention. But his first love was work, and they all faded away one by one, leaving me hurt and alone.

In time, I learned to keep my thoughts and opinions to myself, eventually retreating into bodybuilding to gain some semblance of control over my life.

Bodybuilding became my refuge—a sanctuary where I could mould and shape myself, both physically and mentally. As the weights lifted, so did the burden of my troubled past. The repetitive rhythm of pumping iron drowned out the echoes of loneliness and insecurities that had haunted me for so long.

In the weight room, I found solace and control. Each rep was a step towards reclaiming my identity, a defiance against the shadows that lurked in the corners of my mind. *Against the darkness of the world.*

With each muscle that bulged, I grew stronger not just physically, but emotionally too.

While my father's love remained elusive, the iron became my companion. In the gym, I didn't have to vie for anyone's attention or approval. There, I belonged to myself, and my progress was measured by the pounds lifted, not by the fleeting affections of the temporary visitors in my father's life.

Through bodybuilding, I discovered that I was more than just the boy my father's girlfriends sought to impress. I was a force to be reckoned with—a boy who could transform into a man of power and purpose.

I knew that as long as I kept pushing myself in the gym, I would continue to grow not only as an athlete but as a person.

Halima remains a mystery to me. I never got to know her beyond her love for books and her enchanting smile. I can't help but wonder what could have been if I had done things differently. *Perhaps I wouldn't have needed to go ask someone else what her name was.*

Life goes on, but her memory stays with me. I try to learn from my mistakes, striving to be more than a boy with muscles, determined to find my place in this cold world.

4
Shattered Dreams

My sitting room is adorned with portraits of legendary black boxers, like Muhammad Ali, Mike Tyson, George Foreman, and Sugar Ray Leonard, each a symbol of the greatness I aim to achieve. The TV murmurs in the background, filling the air with static as I anxiously await news from my promoter about my next match pairing.

Excitement courses through me as I perch on the edge of the new Ankara-infused couch that I just designed and built. The thrills of the upcoming fight, the potential surge of new fans, and the prospect of lucrative endorsements make me giddy. College boxing was great, but the real world is even more thrilling.

I pull out my mobile phone, intending to call my father for support to cover my upcoming expenses. Together, we run a textile furniture business, with him providing the funding and me handling the management. However, as I dial his number, my world is suddenly upended.

A voice on the other end informs me of a tragic event. My father, entangled in a web of gang violence, has been shot dead on his way back from visiting one of his lady friends.

Tears well up in my eyes, and for the first time in a long time, I break down in ugly sobs. My father's loss hits me hard, as I grieve the relationship we never had—a connection I thought our joint business would forge. I think of the many 'could have,' 'would have' and 'should haves' and I can't seem to stop the growing ache in my heart.

But grief is only part of my turmoil. The financial support I'd hoped for is now gone, and my promoter's long-awaited call leaves me stumped. Despite the heartache, I must muster the strength to go through with the scheduled fight, hoping to honour my father's memory in the ring.

***

Later that week as I step into the arena, the familiar sights and sounds of the boxing ring surround me. The crowd roars with excitement, cheering on their favourite fighters and the smell of sweat and adrenaline fills the air.

My opponent stands tall and confident, all 106 pounds of him, a lightweight boxer who looks poised to win. The referee gives us final instructions, and I clench my gloves, preparing myself mentally for the challenge ahead.

The bell rings, and the match begins. Adrenaline surges through my veins as we dance around each other, looking for openings to strike.

With Joe Frazier's famous left hook, I go all in, the sound of leather hitting flesh echoes in the ring as our punches connect with precision and force.

I feel a rush of excitement and determination, channelling my grief and frustration into each blow. The crowd's cheers and shouts blend into a symphony of support, urging me to fight harder, to push my limits.

But as the match progresses, my emotions get the better of me. Memories of my father, his absence, and the pain of our broken relationship swirl in my mind, distracting me.

My opponent senses my vulnerability and seizes the opportunity, landing sharper punches with accuracy and speed. My guard falters, and I take hit after hit, my body absorbing the impact like a sponge.

I try to regain my focus, to block out the emotional turmoil, but it's a losing battle. The blows keep coming, and I struggle to defend myself effectively.

The referee's voice becomes distant as he counts the seconds of a standing eight-count, and I find myself struggling to stand upright. The weight of my father's death and the fight itself pull me into a bottomless pit.

"You're better than this, Jamal!" Mekus, my promoter, shouts from the sidelines, his words cutting deep.

All I hear is a reminder of the disappointment I am.

Unable to find my rhythm, my opponent takes advantage, landing punches with accuracy and force. My body feels heavy, and each blow takes its toll.

Red welts mark my face from the blows, a show of my mental and emotional distraction. The crowd's cheers now blend with gasps of surprise and annoyance.

They see that I am not the fighter to pull their weight behind.

I push myself to keep going, to fight through the pain and grief, but my movements lack the precision and power they once did. My opponent sees my weakness and presses on, determined to cinch a victory.

As the final bell rings, I find myself still standing, but my spirit feels crushed. My opponent's arm is raised in victory, and I am left battered and bruised, with my mind in turmoil.

Mekus approaches, his natural dreads bouncing off the side of his shoulders, his disappointment palpable. "What happened, Jamal? I pulled big strings for this match, and this is what you give me?" he berates me, his words stinging, mixed with a putrid mouth odour.

Trying to hold back tears, alongside my disgust, I stammer an apology, unable to articulate the storm raging within me. I feel like a failure, not just as a boxer, but as a son who never got the chance to build a meaningful relationship with his father.

Of course, now I owe my promoter and his network. *Good showing.*

Dejected, I gather my sparse belongings and begin to make my way home. But fate has a surprise in store for me. A black Lexus pulls over, and the tinted window rolls down, revealing the face of— Halima, the girl I once admired from afar in the library.

Embarrassment washes over me again as I remember my past behaviour. "I'm sorry for how I acted back then," I say sheepishly, pulling my hoodie closer to my chin. "I was naïve and childish."

She smiles, her beauty as captivating as ever, and in not so many words assures me that she has forgiven me. As I ride shotgun with her to the next bus stop, she adds gently, "But you must learn to forgive yourself."

After offering her condolences for the loss of my father, she hands me a grey business card. "Go see this person," she says, her voice soft and reassuring, like a balm to my wounded soul, "and start your path to healing."

I find myself clutching the card tightly, my emotions a tumultuous mix of gratitude and confusion. Amid my grief and defeat, Halima had appeared again like a beacon of hope, pointing me towards a path of redemption.

Who knows what tomorrow will bring?

"Can I get your num—".

With tear-stained cheeks, I call out a little too late as she zooms off.

5

Embracing The Tides

The beach stretches endlessly before me, its golden sands inviting me to bask in its warmth and solace. The waves crash against the shore, a continuous rhythmic dance and the salty sea breeze caresses my skin. Seagulls soar gracefully overhead, their wings painting patterns against the azure canvas of the sky.

I sit there, vulnerable in my bikini, feeling the grains of sand beneath my fingers as I clench and let them fall from my hands. The cool touch of the ocean water brushes against my feet, a reminder of the ever-changing nature of life. It understands the turbulence that rages within me.

In this seemingly idyllic setting, I struggle to find peace within myself. The vastness of the ocean mirrors the depths of my emotions, and the crashing waves echo the storm of memories that haunt me.

I throw stones into the water, each one representing a memory that refuses to leave my thoughts. The weight of past decisions and regrets burdens me, just like the stones weigh heavy in my hand. The ocean takes them in, carrying them away, but I know that these memories will never truly disappear.

The laughter of children playing nearby fills the air, a joyful concert that contrasts with the heaviness in my heart. I watch them, envious of their carefree spirits, longing to feel that sense of innocence and lightness once more.

A little boy's ball rolls towards me, and he rushes over to retrieve it. He looks at me, his eyes filled with wonder and curiosity, and I ruffle his hair gently. "Suffer little children to come," I whisper, a fragment of wisdom that has stayed with me from church. His innocent smile momentarily brightens my heart before he scampers away to his mom seated not too far away with some other middle-aged women.

The wellness resort is a sanctuary of sorts, a place where the vastness of the ocean offers a glimpse of hope and possibility. Everyone comes in for something. For some, it's a place to unwind with family and friends after a hectic year, week, day or month. And for others like me, it is a place to remember.

It's the anniversary of Sarah's conception. My baby who never came to be. I vividly remember the pain in my body and mind as she was ripped out of me. *You know we aren't ready,* he'd said.

Yet, barely 8 months later, he was on his knees asking a woman he'd just met to marry him.

Was it something about me? Why did everyone want to take me for a ride? Was I not good enough to be committed to? Or was I just blind to see what was really good for me?

I hated myself for a long time, second-guessing myself for that painful decision and the silly ones I would go on to make.

I had never imagined I would be that woman who would throw away her own child. My mother had once confided her own intrusive thoughts about wanting to get rid of me before I was born, and that revelation had always haunted me. *Yet, I was in that dilemma.*

The evacuation process was excruciating, and even though I tried to muster love for Sarah's father, it never felt natural. The bond we once shared had faded, leaving a void that could not be filled. The loss of that innocent life scarred me deeply, and it was a wound that refused to heal completely.

And it was a pain only I felt and knew, as my supposed lover was caught up in his own life, not even stopping to acknowledge how much had changed within me.

***

"Beautiful day, isn't it?" Lost in thoughts, I'm momentarily startled by a baritone voice behind me. The words are accompanied by a warm, friendly smile.

I turn around to see a tall, dark, attractive man standing, holding a jar of snake oil in his hand. He looks like he belongs on the beach, with his sun-kissed skin and a relaxed feel about him. I manage a smile in response and nod, noting the angle of the sun on his bald head.

"Yeah, it is," I reply softly, my voice carrying a hint of wistfulness. There's something about him that draws me in yet, I find myself hesitant, guarded by the walls I've built over the years.

"Mind if I join you?" he asks, gesturing toward the space next to me on the sand.

"Sure," I say, trying to sound welcoming. What could go wrong?

I move over slightly to make room for him, and he settles down beside me.

"I'm Jamal," he introduces himself, extending a hand.

"Mystery," I reply, offering a playful smile as I take his hand. Somehow, it feels right to keep my identity hidden, even if it's for a moment.

He chuckles, seemingly intrigued by my choice of name. "Mystery, eh? Well, it's nice to meet you, Mystery girl."

The familiarity of his nickname for me catches me off guard, and I find myself blushing slightly. "Likewise, Jamal," I reply, hoping my smile doesn't betray the swirling emotions inside me.

"So, tell me. What do you have in your mystery chest that needs to be uncovered?"

He reaches for the now open jar, as if in answer to his own question, and I can't help but be curious about his intentions. I watch him intently as he rubs the oil on his skin, his movements slow and deliberate. The glistening sheen of the oil reflects the sunlight, making him look like a bronzed statue, an absolute sinful delight.

"Can you—?" he asks, holding the jar out towards me.

I consider his request for a moment. "Uh-huh. Sure."

As I apply the oil to his back, I can't help but feel a mix of emotions—vulnerability, curiosity, and a tinge of excitement. The scent of the snake oil fills the air, and it is strangely comforting yet deceptive.

6
A Meeting of Souls

The crackling fire casts a warm glow on Jamal and me as we sit on the sandy beach, sipping hot cups of cocoa. The ocean waves provide a soothing soundtrack, blending with the distant laughter of other vacationers. The resort's serene ambience envelops us, creating a cocoon of comfort as we trade stories and laughter.

During our budding conversation, something catches my attention in the distance—a mesmerising art rendering of a red door carried in a knapsack by a teenager. My eyes fixate on the intricate details, and I find myself lost in thought, reflecting on the various emotions it evokes.

"It's almost mysterious, isn't it?" Jamal's voice breaks through my reverie, and I turn to meet his gaze.

"You think?" I reply, my voice tinged with a hint of awe. "Look at those jagged edges around the corner of the piece. They stretch on and on endlessly as if hiding something."

"How do you mean?"

"You see… when I meet people, my first inkling is to look into their eyes, to take a peek into their souls to know who they really are."

"And somehow, I can see what the artist saw in this moment as he painted this."

Taking a deep sigh, Jamal crunches his nose and then chuckles. "I don't really get it. I'm just a learner."

"Okay. Visualise this.

Every human is gifted with a unique perspective. And those jagged edges are reminiscent of a mind who sees too much, yet says too little; thus—"

"Hiding something!"

"Exactly!" I nod, "And now, the artist hides behind the safety of the red door, too afraid to let the light in, yet scared of the dark."

"Hmm. A wonderful conundrum." he says, "Maybe he's not hiding anything." Jamal adds as he reaches for the whiskey bottle in a satchel that has magically arrived by his side.

"You think?"

***

"Have you ever wondered why sex often ends the moment a man cums?" I say, switching up the vibe not long after we fall into a comfortable silence.

"And almost no release for the pretty lady!" Jamal concedes.

As the evening progresses, the whiskey loosens our inhibitions as we laugh, play, and squeal, allowing us to delve into deeper emotions and thoughts. Our conversation flows effortlessly, weaving through intimate topics with ease.

The ocean breeze caresses our skin, carrying the scent of the salty sea and the sweet notes of whiskey.

"Would you like to see my space?" I suddenly ask. The twinkle in his eyes, as he nods, reminds me of a time when I was a little more carefree and spontaneous.

I take his hand and lead him to my hut, smack in the middle of Eden Villa, the mental wellness resort that has brought us together, and show him to a padded mat.

He lies down gingerly, surrendering to the moment like Abraham's Isaac once had. I take out two sweet-smelling oils from my pouch in the corner and kneel to massage his shoulders with gentle strokes. The rhythmic sound of the waves blends with his soft moans of pleasure as he surrenders to my touch.

It lights a fire within him, and he reaches out, wanting more. "Handle your pleasure," I whisper fiercely, brushing off his hands. I need him to be fully present in the moment, to experience the blissful sensations without intrusions.

As my hands travel slowly throughout the length of his body, our energy intertwines, and our connection deepens. I retrieve a citrine crystal from the pouch and place it on his back. I playfully tease him with my tongue. He responds with shivers of delight.

Soon, passion takes over, and we give in to the intoxicating chemistry between us. Our bodies move in harmony, and pleasure washes over us in waves, resulting in an explosive climax that leaves us breathless.

Spent, we lie on the mat, basking in the afterglow of our shared experience. Jamal gazes at me, his eyes full of gratitude and— something deeper. He tenderly brushes a braid away from my face and leans in to kiss me, conveying a depth of emotion that words can't capture.

"It's been so long since I felt this cared for," he finally admits, uncertainty in his voice as he goes on to speak of how lost he felt after his father's death. His words resonate within me, and I understand the weight he carries, having experienced loss myself.

"Grief is a complex journey, to be honest," I say when he's done."It takes time to heal, and it's okay to feel lost and unsure right now. Just give yourself the space and time to process everything."

"And do everything from love."

Jamal nods, seeming comforted by my words. "Thank you for saying this, Mystery girl. I'm grateful."

I smile shyly."My name is Felicity. And thank you for sharing your thoughts, feelings and ahem… body with me."

"The pleasure is all mine."

"Presence is everything, you know?" I say softly, after a while, my gaze locking with his. "As long as we stayed in that moment, and felt our feelings, it became easier to reach bliss."

He smiles knowingly as I return the oils and crystal to the pouch and take a sip from my now cold cocoa.

Laughing, Jamal suddenly grabs his wallet from his back pocket, his eyes widening in realisation. "You will not believe this," he says, pulling out a well-worn business card. "An old friend gave me this a while back, referring me to a crystal healer. I thought it was a crazy idea, but now I realize… it's you!"

I chuckle at the serendipity of the situation. "It's so funny how the universe plays its little jokes. We are only the 'unwitting' actors."

"Your friend must have been an old client," I add, taking the card from him with my already outstretched hand, examining its jagged edges and older design.

"Right? I only saw her by chance." Jamal replies, a hint of wonder in his eyes. "Maybe a crystal healing session would have helped me deal with my father's death back then. Or even make better choices. Who knows?"

"Well, it's never too late to explore the journey to healing and self-discovery," I wink and return the card to him. "Ready when you are."

Jamal looks thoughtful as he puts it in his wallet. "I'll keep that in mind."

As we continue our conversation by the crackling fire, Jamal looks at his watch and sighs, a wistful note in his voice.

"I hate to break this beautiful moment, but I have a boxing match in two nights. I should be training and preparing for it."

My heart sinks a little, not wanting our time together to end so soon. "Oh. I understand," I chirp in a voice that nearly betrays my disappointment. "Work is important."

I want to ask him to stay or at least exchange numbers, but I hold back. If he wanted to, he would.

7
Aching Hearts and Unuttered Longings

The scent of burning sage fills the room as I prepare for another session with a client. The crystals glisten under the soft glow of candlelight, casting a soothing aura over the space. But no amount of healing energy can dispel the ache in my heart, the longing for a stranger I only just met.

My client, Rachel, enters the room, her face etched with worry. She sits down, fidgeting with her hands, and pours out her feelings about her obsession with a certain ex. As she speaks, I can't help but see a reflection of myself in her words.

The need to be needed, to fix someone, to fill the void of loneliness.

"It's like no matter what I do, I can't stop thinking about him," Rachel says, her eyes searching for solace. "And even when he says hurtful things to me, and pushes me away, I still find myself wanting to help him."

"To be there for him."

"Am I broken?"

She breaks down in tears, and I place a hand on her shoulder, offering a comforting squeeze. "Breathe.
Obsession can feel all-consuming, but it's important to remember that you are more than this fixation."

"It's also very likely that the other person has certain traits you're supposed to embody as well. You're not actually obsessed with them but with your own potential for growth."

"Focus on that, and you'll find the strength to let go and the courage to choose better."

Rachel nods, her eyes filled with tears. "Right? But it's just so hard. It feels like he's snatched my soul."

I give her a reassuring smile that I don't quite feel. "I understand. You have to remember though, that healing is a journey, and acknowledgement of the pain source is the first step."

"So what can I do now?"

***

After the session, I take a walk to the garden to clear my head. No matter how many forgetting rituals I carry out or important tasks I try to focus on, my mind keeps circling back to him, Jamal...

Just as I'm lost in my thoughts, my phone buzzes, bringing me back to reality. It's a text from him —*"wya, I'm at your spot."* My heart skips a beat, and I hurry back to my office.

At the entrance, he stands, holding a bouquet of lilies in one hand and a bag of marijuana in the other. The contrast in his offerings almost makes me laugh. "I thought I'd never see you again," I manage to say.

He grins, his eyes locking with mine. "Don't think you can be rid of me that easily."

The realisation dawns on me as with a flourish, he pulls out the card his friend had given him, then returns it to his wallet. A smile spreads across my face, and I feel a mixture of excitement and nervousness.

Jamal shrugs, non-committal. "I was just passing by the neighbourhood and decided to drop in."

As we sit in the open garden later, sharing a blunt, I sense that something has shifted. The easy connection we had that night is now shrouded in tension.

His phone keeps buzzing with notifications from different women, and I can't help but feel a pang of jealousy. And anger. *The bouquet in the corner long forgotten.*

"Why are you here, Jamal?" I find myself saying. "I can't deal with these mixed signals."

"Are you coming, or are you going?"

"Hey, chill out, mama." He laughs in his most 'don't-take-me-serious' voice as he passes the blunt to me. "We had a good time. But I never said we'd be anything more."

The words hit me like a punch to the gut. In the days that had passed, I had let myself believe that there was something special between us. I take a deep inhale from the blunt, puff out the smoke and stub out the fire.

"You didn't bother to reach out for weeks, and then you show up out of nowhere. It's really confusing."

"I'm sorry if you got the wrong impression. I'm just a young man trying to make my way on these streets." His fingers graze my chin as he smiles. "But I like your vibe. No lies."

The air around us feels heavy with unspoken words and unfulfilled desires. His meaning is clear.

"Hmm. Maybe it's best if we keep things casual then. No strings attached."

"You are right." Jamal nods his bald head a little too excitedly. "I think it's for the best."

But deep down, I know it's not what I truly want. I want more than casual encounters and mixed signals. I want a connection that goes beyond physicality, a love that is present and true.

As he leans in for a kiss, I feel myself break apart a little more.

8
A Moment of Clarity

"We are not even a thing." The words echo in my mind like a resounding bell, stirring up a mix of feelings within me. I sit in my consulting room, the weight of Jamal's words sinking into my mind.

We've only just returned from a cousin's birthday party, and I can't count on one hand the number of ladies he flirted with shamelessly, bolstered by the flowing alcohol.

Why did I think anything would change?

Why did I think I was THE ONE to make a leopard change its spots or a snake shed its skin?

Why did I constantly build castles in the sky, pretending to accept things I didn't like just because I didn't want to be alone?

Just when we were leaving the party, my cousin came to find out what his deal was, and Jamal pretty much laughed in our faces and said to my chagrin, "We are not even a thing."

I died a little inside.

You see, I've realised that I often attach myself to anyone who shows me the slightest interest and attention, seeking validation and affection without questioning their intentions.

And getting to truly know them.

But this time, something within me shifts.

I want someone who truly sees me, values me, and chooses me every day without hesitation. I know how much love I have to give, and I deserve to be more than an afterthought in someone's life.

As I shake off my thoughts, I tell Jamal to leave and inform him that I have a client coming soon. He then proceeds to mock my work, questioning why I don't pursue a "real" healing profession like being a medical doctor or nurse.

I feel a flicker of irritation coming on, but choose not to match energies. It's already been a particularly hectic day, and I know it's up to me to discern what is in my control and what's not—then act accordingly. *Barely.*

"Just because I don't wear a white coat and carry a stethoscope doesn't mean my work isn't legit," I spit out, my voice shaky as I open the blinds to let the light in.

"Healing is not about treating physical ailments; it's also about addressing emotional and spiritual pain. My clients come to me seeking solace and guidance, and I'm very proud of the work I do."

"In fact, I should do a ritual cleansing of this space now, you're totally contaminating it."

Jamal seems taken aback by my response but quickly brushes it off, claiming he was only joking. He goes on to say he doesn't understand why I was making such a big deal out of the situation back at my cousin's shindig. "I'm good with the current flow," he adds.

But I'm not. I'm done settling for casual flings and temporary connections. And I don't want someone who doesn't support or at least acknowledge my chosen line of work. In my experience, that always spells the beginning of the end for any partnership.

"See. I don't want your crumbs anymore. It's not nearly enough for my big needs." I say out loud, my gaze unwavering as I shoo him towards the door.

"You need to come correct, or hit the road."

He looks at me with a mix of confusion and exasperation. "Where's all this coming from? I thought we *was* cool!" Jamal protests, his voice sounding petulant. I almost want to smack him.

I take a deep breath and find a seat, trying to find the right words to express myself without becoming a prison inmate. "Cool?" I say in my best Kevin Hart intimation.

"No. I haven't been cool with any of these from the beginning. I haven't been cool with the way you flaunt all of your women without considering how I feel."

"I definitely haven't been cool with all the money you've been getting from me under one guise or the other. I may seem lonely or desperate to you, but I'm not dumb."

"And I'm done pretending that I'm okay with the way things are," I finished, my voice tinged with sadness and resolution.

"Felicity, you don't mean—"

"Yep, I know," I say wistfully as I look at his bulging crotch. He has placed his perfectly manicured fingers on it and is rocking it slowly back and forth. I force myself to look back at his face.

"The sex has been awesome, the vibe and adventures lit. I mean, who knew bungee jumping while fucking could be so much fun?"

"But if I don't feel safe and secure in my partner's presence, what's anything worth?"

"Partner? What do you mean partner??"

Laughing almost derangedly, I feel the remnant of my self-control slip away.

"Yeah, that's the thing. I probably should queue up to get the world award for *Miss Delu-lu.*"

Brrrgg! My phone rings loudly, interrupting us. I grab it hastily and see a video call from my ex, Animba.

Whoa.

It feels like the universe is sending me signs, reminders of the patterns I make over and again, and how stupid I can get when I think I'm in love.

"I have to take this," I say, my emotions raw from the conversation. I head to the loveseat in the garden, press the green button, and launch to the talking head that is Animba.

***

As the call ends, I return to the office, and Jamal stands in the same spot I left him. I take a moment to take in all the sights, sounds and feels.

"You know what, Jamal? You're right. We are not a thing," I say finally, shutting the door, my heart feeling both heavy and light at the same time.

9
Two Dinners of Reflections

"The hardest thing I had to learn in break ups and heartbreaks was taking accountability for the shit I stayed through, for the things I allowed, for the times I didn't get up and walk away."

~Author Unknown

As I step into the opulent restaurant, Animba's eyes light up as they settle on me. He is dressed in a three-piece suit, and I notice the faint mark on his ring finger. The restaurant is a sight to behold, with chandeliers casting a warm glow over everything and a breathtaking view of the ocean. The waiters, all impeccably dressed, move gracefully through the space.

"You look happier," Animba says as I approach the table. There is a certain déjà vu feel to the whole thing.

"When you said you were here, I wasn't sure—"

"You weren't sure what?"Animba gesticulates with a flourish and clucks his tongue in that ear-grating way he used to. "That I could pay for this??"

"Well, you're looking at the owner of one of the oil blocs allocated by the Governor last year."

"Oh wow."

He smirks and takes a sip of his wine, bursting with pride, "Ah yes, the Governor owed me a favour, and I thought, why not get a little something for myself?"

I gush with feigned enthusiasm, "I'm so happy for you. And how's your wife, by the way? Does she know you're—"

"Tonight is about us." He waves his hand around and clucks his tongue. "Not anyone else." Suddenly, he stretches his hand to touch the tattoo on the side of my neck, the infinity symbol.

"You eventually got the tattoo…"

Feeling exposed, I chuckle and quickly wrap my shawl across my neck. "You can't touch me like that.

"You lost your rights when you decided to walk away after making me take out our baby."

The waiter arrives with our food, a beautifully presented dish that looks like a work of art. My appetite wanes as the awkward silence between us lingers. I finally gather the courage to speak. "You know—"

"I—" Animba starts to say, but I nudge him to go ahead. He declines, insisting I go first.

With a deep breath, I let my words flow freely. I confront him about our toxic past, and how his hurtful words cut me deeply every day. I express how his self-absorption and need to be in control was suffocating, and how I became entangled in the role of trying to fix him.

His attempt to interrupt me only fuels my determination to be heard.

I admit that when he left, it was a relief as I realised I would never have found the courage to let go of him myself. But seeing him flaunt his marriage pictures on social media felt like a festering wound, a reminder of my past mistakes.

"What kind of mistake? We weren't ready for that child, and you want to put it all on me. And it's not like you wanted to fuck me again after that day."

Animba signals to our waiter to pour him some wine, nonchalantly sipping it as if he hadn't just dropped a bombshell. Deflated, I sigh.

"Sarah. Her name was Sarah."

"Oh, you even named her." Animba bursts into uncontrollable fits of laughter, and I contemplate emptying the rest of the wine in my glass on his tailored suit. "How did you know it would have been a girl?"

"You don't get it, do you?" I whisper, my voice tinged with frustration. "It's not just about you. It's never about you! You're so self-obsessed, you can't even see beyond yourself."

He leans back in his chair as if seeing me with new eyes. I slam the table with my palms.

"You always thought everyone else was the problem, that you were this perfect, blameless individual."

"You know what hurts most? You knew my trauma, and you weaponized it."

"Plus, you never refunded any of those 'loans!'"

He pats down his pocket square, seemingly unbothered by my words. "Well, maybe I am perfect now.
"Thanks to all the fussing you did, my wife is getting the best version of me. And I can repay you now if you want."

"Whoa. Touché."

I swallow hard and proceed to pick up my purse from the table. Animba guffaws loudly from behind his glass then winks. "I won't say no to a good time though."

"I'm sure those hands of yours still work their magic."

Suddenly, Olamide's *Infinity* blasts from the speakers and I flinch. Animba laughs hard, finding a wicked amusement in the whole situation. Infinity was *our* song when I was still thinking about forever.

Yep. Totally déjà vu.

***

Moments later as I walk through the giant glass doors, I can't seem to be rid of the haunting feeling that I never really knew him. But how could I have, when we'd all but started our 'relationship' as a situationship?

Feeling drained, I hail a cab to pick up a rain check for a dinner date with my mother, who now resides in a retirement home. One more 'bad' dinner today can't hurt, right?

The place is filled with the scent of fading memories and ageing wood. The reception area is adorned with family photos, and I spot a picture of my parents together, a pang of nostalgia hitting me.

As I enter her room, I find my mother sitting by the window, lost in her own world. Her once radiant beauty is now replaced by the marks of time and struggle. We exchange pleasantries, but as we head to the cafeteria to have a simple sandwich, the conversation quickly takes a steep turn.

Our conversation is real, raw, and long overdue. I confront her about the past, how she didn't believe me when I said our Bishop was inappropriate with me, and how she implied my father was. I express how her lack of support turned me into a people pleaser, always seeking to fix others.

She waits for me to finish before she squeaks, her throat cancer getting the better of her.

"Your diary! How could you write such vile things?"

I pause, mildly surprised. "What do you mean?"

"Anu gave me your diary."

"You see, I always wondered why your father would buy you those books without thinking twice and anytime I asked him for a purse I liked, he'd say no!"

"Mama!"

"It was those dirty dirty thoughts, Felicia Animashaun.

"How could you think about going on 'romantic' walks with your father, not to talk of writing it down?"

"And the girls you were crushing on too. Don't even get me started."

"Plus, Bishop did the best that he could. You were such a wayward child. And even now, you've completely abandoned the Christian way!"

"Mama!"

My mind goes to that day nearly 21 years ago, when my diary disappeared. I'd searched high and low, but for some reason, it remained elusive. At least now I know why.

That diary had housed every bit and part that my crazy brain had managed to conceive. If I wasn't writing an alternative ending to a mystery novel I'd just read, I was thinking of the next way to make the girl I liked like me back.

And sometimes, it was just wishes of what I thought and hoped could be.

"Mama, I was only 13!"

My heart aches for my mother, sensing that her own wounds run deep. But I can't ignore the pain she caused me too. I also recall Anu's recent puny attempts at reconciling by sending unsolicited voicemails while refusing to do the inner healing work and I sigh.

"Papa's love was never a competition."

"You may have been hurting, Mama, but that doesn't excuse how you treated me," I say, my voice firm. "You even treated a stranger better than your daughter."

"Well—"

"I was only a teen with an overactive imagination and you," I pause for effect, "instead of taking me under your wings to properly guide me, became an active op.

"I had to look outside for guidance, so much I made many mistakes, you won't believe even how many."

"Yes. Why won't you make mistakes when you were thinking of the next way to seduce your father."

"And the Bishop too, while ditching the friends that were looking out for you."

"Mama!"

"I didn't understand why you couldn't be happy for me, Mama," I say, my voice filling with sadness. "Every time I had brunch with Papa and his new family, you'd act like I was betraying you. But he was my father, and I needed him too."

My mother avoids my gaze, staring out of the window as if searching for the right words. "You were his favourite," she says, her voice tinged with bitterness. "He always made time for you, even after he left."

"He made time for me because I reached out to him, Mama!" I reply, fighting back tears. "He may have left, but he still cared about me. Unlike you, he never made me feel like I was a burden or a mistake!"

"I did my best, Felicity," my mother says defensively. "You just never appreciated it."

"You didn't show up for me when it mattered," I sigh. "Even through the rape incident.

"When I needed support, you were not there. Instead, you turned to alcohol and pushed me away. And yes, I found a different religion—*love*. Do you know how to do that? Love me? Love yourself??"

My mother's face crumples with emotion. "I didn't know how to be there for you," she says, her voice barely above a whisper.

"I was fighting my demons. Besides, I didn't have the best parenting examples, too, so being a mother was the farthest thing from my mind."

For the first time, I see her helplessness, and it tugs at my heartstrings. "You didn't have to figure it all out on your own, Mama," I say softly, reaching out to touch her frail shoulders. "I wish you had let me in, allowed me to be there for you too.

"You don't know half of the things Anu got up to doing. And you always believed her over your own daughter."

"I know I messed up, Felicity," she admits, her voice shockingly filled with remorse. "I pushed you away because I was afraid of losing you, just like I lost your father."

"I'm still here, Mama," I say, my voice gentle. "And I'll always be here for you, but you need to begin to take responsibility for your healing."

She looks at me with a mix of gratitude and sorrow. "You've grown into such a strong, compassionate woman," she says, her voice filled with pride.

"I'm sorry I couldn't be the mother you needed, but I'm proud of the woman you've become."

She reaches out a bony hand towards me, but I step back, needing some distance from the woman who had broken my heart into tiny pieces. "I need to heal, Mama," I say, my voice increasing a notch. "And that starts with acknowledging the truth and setting boundaries."

"You hurt me."

She nods, tears streaming down her cheeks. "I understand," she says, her voice choked with emotion. "I hope you can find it in your heart to forgive me one day."

"It's going to take time," I say, my heart heavy with the weight of the past. "But I'll try."

~

10
A Private Party

"You've had you since birth. You'll have yourself forever. And you're putting yourself to the side to accommodate keeping someone else that's replaceable? I don't think we realise the message this sends to ourselves. We speak of loyalty, but we rarely show it to us."

~ Zoraya

"After the doctor/nurse conversation, we had the other day, I've had some time to rethink how I really should've answered you," Felicity starts.

The sun hangs low in the sky, casting a golden hue over the serene beach. An artist with dreadlocks sits close to the water, strumming his guitar and singing from the depths of his heart, creating a soulful atmosphere around them.

Jamal, donning a big brown jacket, matched with beige shorts and a pink slip-on, looks at Felicity intently. His bald head reflects the sun's rays, making him appear both strong and vulnerable. They take a leisurely walk close to the water, feeling the coolness of the waves beneath their feet. And the sun in the sky.

It's a few days after Felicity's 34th birthday, and she's been unwinding at Eden Villa, reconnecting with nature after a Christmas shindig with her father, stepmom and their kids.

It had been a day filled with roller coaster events, skiing, yoga, paintballing and other fun stuff. She'd even managed to get herself two stylish boots to match the flowery dresses in her wardrobe that never seemed to get much airtime these days since she didn't go out as much as before.

But that had to change.

This was one of the reasons she reached out to Jamal today for this long-awaited conversation to get all their issues sorted out once and for all.

"You were so angry," Jamal replies, thrusting his hands into his pockets. "It was almost like I didn't know you anymore. All your sweetness just—"

Felicity sighs, her emotions still raw. "But of course, I would be angry," she trails off, her eyes glistening with unshed tears.

"It's the thing, you know?" Jamal tries to explain, looking down at the sand as they walk on. "I never meant to hurt you. I didn't know how to handle it all.

"The intensity of your love was not a feeling I was used to. I got scared."

Felicity stops and turns to face him. "See. It was not just about you," she says, her voice steady but filled with emotion. "It was about me too. I needed to find my own path, my sense of fulfilment. And I couldn't do that if I was constantly trying to fix someone else.

"Especially one that was not paying for my crystal healing services."

The artist's song reaches a crescendo as Felicity takes a deep breath, feeling the weight of her decision. Enjoying her private joke.

"For so long, I put my feelings aside, what mattered to me, and pretty much died inside," she confesses, looking into Jamal's eyes. "If I were to count the number of folks that I had to cater to their every whim as their own passions took centre stage, I'd run out of fingers.

And you, I unwittingly took you as a project to fix, not unlike the subject of The Cavemen's *Saviour* tune."

Jamal's shoulders slump, and he looks pensive. "I didn't mean to make you feel that way. I was just looking for a good time," he says softly, regret evident in his voice.

Felicity smiles sadly at him, feeling a mix of emotions. "I know," she replies. "I deluded myself for so long.

"I foolishly thought I was the one to make you finally hang your bad boy boots. That I could love you into loving me."

"Just like I did the others before you…... Merely wishes."

"See, I–"

Felicity puts up her hands and goes on. "The thing is, there are different paths to the answers that we seek and the problems that come for us in life, but we all want to face the same direction.

"Why are we always trying to put square pegs in round holes?" she continues, a zen look in her eyes. "You go be you, and I'll be me!"

The ocean breeze disturbs the all-white see-through dress that Felicity wears, and her purple bikini underneath makes a brief appearance.

"Uh-huh," Jamal grunts, understanding the gravity of her words yet pulled to Felicity's milk skin and the many shared memories behind them. "I guess I never really saw it that way."

A firework goes up in the sky to display the words, "You are Safe in Eden," followed by some *ukulele* music all through the wellness resort. Some seagulls have gathered to play close to the beach, and their quiet procession only accentuates the vulnerability at this moment.

"It's okay," Felicity says, reaching out to take his hand. The gentle sea breeze caresses her skin, and the sound of the waves crashing against the shore forms a soothing backdrop to their conversation. "We both have our own journeys to take."

She takes a moment to collect her thoughts, her heart still heavy with the weight of her decision.

"You deserve to be happy," Felicity adds, her voice softer now. "So do I. But I don't think we can find that happiness together.

"And sometimes, letting go is the best thing we can do for ourselves."

Jamal nods, grasping the gravity of her words. "I guess I didn't realise how much I was holding you back from true expression," he says, his voice sincere.

They fall into silence, the music from the distance providing a poignant soundtrack to the moment. Felicity takes a deep breath, and drops his hand, feeling the weight of her decision lift slightly.

"I truly wish you all the best," she smiles, her voice filled with sincerity. "And I hope you find what you're looking for in life."

Jamal looks up at her, his eyes searching her face as if trying to find the right words to say. "Thank you," he finally says, his voice soft. "I'll miss you, Felicity."

Felicity's heart twinges at his words. "No. You don't deserve the view, but I'll remember you.

"At least, now, I know what I'll settle for and the red flags to look out for in myself and others."

"So, I'm truly grateful for this experience."

India Arie's *Private Party* booms from a speaker in the distance as Felicity turns and walks away barefoot, taking in the beauty of the world around her; feeling connected to the earth and to herself in a way she hasn't felt in a long time.

She slowly makes her way to her tent, takes off her glasses, and pours out a glass of palm wine for herself, blissfully ignoring Jamal's presence. In a slow tease, she strips to her bikini and sways from side to side, the wine and the haunting lyrics of the song, her ancient guides.

Jamal meets Felicity's gaze from afar. The words hang in the air, unspoken yet understood.

"Can we start over?" he finally says, his voice hopeful.

11
Redeeming the Time

"Love is the easiest thing when it happens by accident, but it doesn't get real until you do it on purpose."

~ Entergalactic

I step out of my crystal practice, my heart filled with a sense of fulfilment after a third session with my client, Rachel. She winks at me, ecstatic to be finally healing, as I walk towards the BMW that Jamal has sent for me.

The driver opens the door, and we head to a quiet spot adorned with flowers, a serene sanctuary for our conversation, Jamal and a picnic waiting.

"It didn't help that I had to be the mom to my mom," I begin, feeling a rush of emotions. My mind wanders to how many timelines ago I shared a simple bond with a Somali boy in a garden just like this. "I think I'm talking too much."

"No, you aren't," Jamal responds, gently taking my hands in his. "You haven't even begun to say anything, and I absolutely love to hear you talk."

My heart warms at his words, and I continue, "During my alone time, I finally came to understand why that situation unwittingly made me into a worrying mom.

"I always wanted to fix those I thought were lost, not stopping to consider that everyone has their journeys to take."

"And on their own timelines."

"I'm sorry I was such a jerk most of the time," Jamal sighs. "It took me a long ass time to recognize that special thing in you, and I was gonna let you slip away."

"Oh. I'm not your mama."

"And I'm not your daddy," Jamal teases back. We both laugh, feeling the weight of our past misunderstandings slowly shift.

"You know, I was attracted to auras for so long but I eventually didn't know what to do with it."

"How do you mean?"

"So for me, it was like, I meet this very amazing girl, be drawn in by her vibe, but as soon as she let me into her heart, or showed me kindness in any form, I would disappear.
"Or try to bully them."

"Just like you did to Halima," I retort, taking a bite of the cheese in the basket and helping myself to some white wine.

"Ouch!" He laughs as I continue. "It's not enough to be drawn in by a person's light. We must not be afraid of their darkness too."

"Uhh?"

"Yes. One could say that a person who's always trying to absorb auras without giving anything positive back is simply an energy vampire who doesn't even know what they want."

"I think you're right. Life's all about giving and taking. The ying in the yang. Hmm. I still have so many lessons to learn from you, *sensei*."

"You bet, learner." Laughing, I lean to wipe off some crumbs from the side of his lips.

"I'm glad we took that time off to get to know what we wanted," Jamal confesses his soulful eyes doing a little number on me.

"Now I understand that to really love a person, one must love what they do too, how they poop, how they pop their zits, and all that."

"While also genuinely loving and forgiving oneself."

"Intentionality and value sharing is everything. *Starting on the right note too.* I cannot wait to love and experience you over and again."

"W-wait, go back," I interrupt, noticing and taking a certain relish in Jamal's confused expression.

"You said, 'love.'"

His face turns bright pink as he admits, "Yes, Mystery girl. I'm in love with you."

"And I won't mind if you made me an honest man."

I can't help but laugh, "Is this a proposal?"

"Cos I don't see you on your knees and all that."

"Don't worry, my love." Jamal winks mischievously as he empties the rest of the wine in his glass. "You won't even see it coming."

Feeling a newfound sense of ease and courage, I say. "You know, we don't have to like the same things. That's why we'll do it differently this time."

"Oh yeah?"

"Let's have our different me-times and our collective us-times. I also think we could build two houses with a connecting bridge. I'm not sure I can deal with your snores for the rest of our lives."

"I'll come to your boxing matches though."

"W-wait. I hope I'm not doing too much."

Jamal's laughter fills the air, and he shakes his head and says, "I actually like the sound of that. 'The rest of our lives.'"

"And no, you can never do or be too much."

Smiling sheepishly, I continue, getting caught in my own little universe. "It will be our place, where we make all the rules.

"You'll be mine, and I, yours."

"No more staying stuck in the old way of doing things."

"Oh, absolutely ma'am," Jamal says as he plants a wet kiss on my forehead. "You'll be my undoing, and I'm totally here for it."

Feeling a small thrill pass through me, I manage to pull myself together and ask. "So, what's your plan for the next 5 years?"

"Learning to love the heck out of you, of course." Jamal smiles as he proceeds to feed me some croissants from the basket. "You, Felicity, are an experience I can't quite get enough of."

My eyes water from joy and something else in me waters too.

"And I'm truly sorry for denigrating your work. I guess that's on the long list of things I need to do penance for." Jamal states clearly as he cups my jaw in his hand, his eyes reaching into the depths of my soul.

Crumbling with emotion, I say those five magical words, "Let's build an empire together."

"Oh, how I love you, Felicity."

"The feeling is mutual, Mr. Jamal Akanbi." In response, he pulls me close and kisses me deeply, holily, the croissant getting lost in the feel.

At this moment, I feel like I'm truly born again. Not the nominal façade the Bishop and his cronies sold us over the years.

True awareness has never felt this good.

I proceed to hit play on my phone, and Ella Mai's voice booms through as she sings her song, *Naked*, our lips and hands rediscovering each other.

Epilogue

It is Jamal and Felicity's partnership ceremony 2 years later at the beachfront in Eden Villa. The party is in full effect, and everyone is getting jiggy with the music.

In the months before, they've taken time out to write and discuss the specifics of their planned partnership together; including vacations, values, income streams, dreams, ideologies, faith, family, culture, fantasies and even vices.

And now, their disagreements have dwindled to a trickle.

Somewhere in the back, Felicity's mom and dad are having a small tete à tete with Jamal's auntie on flower rearrangements and whatnot while some children are running around in circles, doing backflips.

It's a particularly great day for love and blended families.

Felicity stops to say hello, then struts down the beautifully adorned beachfront, onto the DJ's stand and hands him her playlist on a small USB.

The DJ chuckles as he realises on plugging the USB in that on the list is Beautiful Nubia's *Eleko 'Dere*, closely followed by DoTTi the Deity's *Akoya*, some of his favourites.

He gives her a fist bump before returning to his turntable.

In her simple lilac silk outfit, Felicity looks divine as she heads back to Jamal, who's helping himself to some of the doughnuts in the ring circle.

The carbs never seemed to show on his body, no matter how many he consumed, much to Felicity's pretend annoyance.

"Bobo, my back hurts."

Sighing, Jamal abandons his half-eaten doughnut and stoops to apply a little pressure to the bottom of Felicity's spine with his knuckles.

"Sorry mama, it is giving 30+ vibes."

"Want some doughnuts?"

They both burst out laughing as Felicity compliments his well-tailored blue blazer, observing that it nearly competes with the colour of the sea. She links her right arm to his.

"You know you can't bully me much longer, eh?" She flexes her fists to show her muscles. "I'll soon be bench pressing 150kg."

"Of course, of course. You're my student. Gotta be able to teach you something, too."

"Yeah, right. I still prefer yoga though."

"Uh-huh, when you eventually get the hang of it." Jamal teases.

Felicity tiptoes and pinches Jamal's nose, and they both laugh. "So, what do you think of the colour we want to paint the bridge for our twin apartments?"

Thinking momentarily, Jamal bops his adorned head as DoTTi the Deity's *Akoya* hits the airwaves. "Hmm. Light purple, for forgiveness, wealth and …possibilities? I think it's perfect."

"You, my darling, are a genius."

Felicity winks and leans in for a kiss. With a twinkle in his eyes and a swagger in his gait, Jamal unlinks his arm to take her hand. He kisses every manicured finger, before waving to the manic crowd. "Ready to make the next 5 years count?"

"Absolutely, partner."

"You?"

"Definitely."

"Well, just like I said at our last reconciliatory dinner," Felicity pouts her purple-stained lips and bats her eyelashes at Jamal pointedly. "You can't ever use the same format with me that you use for your other girls."

"Oh. I'll be foolish if I don't let you indulge me."

THE END.

"I have loved men unconditionally and loved their beauty and their pain, when nothing was being offered to me in exchange for it. Because they aren't difficult to love. I have no regrets. All I can say is that most of them don't know what to do with love."

~Sofia Barbosa

About the Author

Amongst other things, Olamide Agemo is a Soul Coach and Music Therapist. Through art and narrative therapy, she takes words and weaves them in ways that appeal to (and impact) her intended audience.

She is the Head of Creative Expression at her recently founded holistic creative agency, FQue Thirt3 Media. On days when she isn't putting together branding and strategy solutions for her clients or herself, she's planning intimate business, art and therapy events.

Olamide runs Lami's Memoirs, a brand that caters to the ghostwriting, scriptwriting, art reviewing, web copywriting & art descriptions, and editing & proofreading needs of her clients.

She has two other stories with the Black Female Authors, **Hell Hath No Fury** a Dec 2020 anthology and **Nights at Club Nova**, an early 2021 release. She is also the author of a 2021 memoir, **The Girl in The Mirror: How 2020 Became the Year of My Grand Shift,** a book she aptly describes as the compass on her path to enlightenment. Olamide writes other pieces on mental health, and critical thinking, as well as mysteries, psychological thrillers, crime and biopics.

The Awakening is her first completed fiction book project since 2021.

Also known as L.a.m.i, Olamide is a yoga instructor and has learned to find holistic ways to rid herself of this little back pain that people over 30 tend to have, just like Felicity's.

You can catch up on the rest of her story at linktr.ee/olamideagemo

A
CRASH
AFFAIR

A Valentine weekend sightseeing trip is gate-crashed by an ex-boyfriend who Anike is still madly in love with.

By

FEYI AINA

1
The Crash

Anike!

The voice was that of the boy who had loved her in secondary school.

Anike!

He'd chased her all the way from there to university, finally capturing her heart during the one-year, national youth service program where he made himself indispensable to her life.

Then he'd been a promising, young, final-year medical student. And she, a shy, new business admin graduate, not more than twenty-two years of age. Life had been simple. Love had been sweet. And their future—in her head—was etched in numerous shades of glittering gold.

Anike!

She'd fallen fast. First, for his upright nature. Next, for his gracious manner. She'd fallen for him with all of who she was and everything she had. And his smile was all that lit her heart for days on end.

Wake up!

The cold words made the darkness real. Darkness, and tiredness. Why was it so dark? Why did the world feel so empty all of a sudden? Why did he want her to wake up?

Open your eyes for me, please.

He was insistent. Separating her from the gloomy dimness. Pulling her back into an awareness that demanded the judicious use of brainpower. But she didn't want to think about anything or respond to anyone, she was comfortable with the shadows. Happy with the peace that came with being in it as she calmly floated around in—in where exactly?

Where was she?

Confusion enveloped her. She wasn't sure where she was. Only that she was content with lying there. Weary, and wondering what it was she had been doing before she began floating.

Anike! Breathe, baby! Breathe for me, please! Oh, please sweetheart, breathe for me.

Breathe! Breathing.

She remembered what that was and how to do it. Dragging air in through her nostrils and pushing it out through her mouth.

It was the one thing she had lost the ability to do—pre her current state of floating. An art that she had practised every morning before she got out of bed.

It centred her, gave her tranquillity, and supplied her with enough courage to help her get through the day without breaking down.

I think we need some space.

Space. That dreadful word. It sparked a glimmer of recollection in her memories because it was the reason she was struggling to breathe. Why she had been practising breathing for weeks.

We need some space!

The four words that had pinned her heart to her stomach and thrown the floor right out from under her.

He'd said it, she'd freaked out, and her breathing had bottomed out for a few seconds. She'd silently gulped in air, so she could deal with the crazed panic that ravaged her mind at the thought of losing him. Then she'd thought about what the words meant.

Space.

He wanted it, but they had lots of it. Too much, considering that they were supposed to be a couple in a love relationship. However, could he want more space?

Why would he need it?

Anike!

Why was he calling her when he wanted some space?

Anike!

Why are you calling my name? You said we were over.

Baby, please!

Pain, coupled with a pressure that squeezed her heart against her ribcage spread through her insides. She was being crushed, more like, the way she was feeling. Short, sharp, and painful thrusts that compressed her chest, chimed in time with the words 'We—need—some—space', one after the other.

Anike!

Space. Wasn't that where she was? Wasn't that what they had? Wasn't he happy with it? She'd given him space. So, why was he calling her?

Sweetheart, please open your eyes.

The pain came and went in regular bursts. Quick and consistent. Sharp. Crushing. Overwhelming.

Don't do that. She wanted to tell him. *It hurts!*

But he wasn't listening. She tried to breathe but her chest felt like dead weight. She couldn't breathe.

'We need a little bit of time apart to figure things out?' he'd said.

'It's over between us,' she'd heard, and she'd agreed.

Now he was hurting her, and she didn't know how to make the hurt stop.

Tears slid down the sides of her face from underneath closed lashes. The pain was brutal. It was sitting on her chest like an elephant, refusing to budge till she acknowledged it. A strange chill followed and she wanted to welcome it, much like she'd welcomed his words and the meaning of them.

'We need to take some time out to figure things out.'

He was right. It was time to stop thinking things would improve. Time to accept the inevitable conclusion that had been staring her in the face the last few weeks before he'd said the words. It was over. They were over. Why hadn't she accepted the fact of it and moved on?

Warm, moist lips straddled hers at that moment.

They were his lips. She knew the taste of them. She would know it even if she was deep in sleep and he roused her. She wanted to kiss him back, but she couldn't. She couldn't move her arms or her legs or her face. She could only lay back and accept whatever was coming.

It's over. Why am I hearing your voice and feeling your lips against mine? WHY? Why— are you kissing me?

She felt nothing but warm air pushed—no, forced—down her throat, through her mouth.

What is this? What are you doing?

The pain came back all of a sudden. Hard, fast, and directly aimed at her heart. It felt like a punch in the gut. She was rapidly sucked upwards, hurled through a deep vortex of blackness into a light that woke her up and left her a little disoriented. Pressure and pain were what came next. The pressure of hands on her chest pushed her into the hard ground beneath her body in regular spurts of time.

Aching pain from everywhere imaginable descended with a rush of confusing blurry images. She coughed.

"Anike? Oh, thank God!"

Slowly, her eyes opened and settled on an animated face.

"You've just been in an accident, don't try to speak." Fingers brushed away the scattered strands of hair across her damp brow. "I'm so glad you're okay. Just stay still."

Accident? Her mouth made the movements, but no sound came out.

"Yes. Can you squeeze my arm?"

She blinked and felt the firm muscles of his forearm beneath her weak right arm. She reached out slowly and squeezed it in response.

"Great," he said. "Squeeze once for yes and twice for no. Does your neck hurt?"

She closed her eyes briefly from the increasing intensity of the pain in her left leg as her awareness of her surroundings grew. Then she squeezed his arm twice.

"Good. You've been injured. You have a deep gash on your leg, but I suspect it's just soft tissue. Please lift your arms one after the other as gently as you can. I need to be sure you can move your feet too."

She kept her eyes on him and tried to mouth the word *pain.*

"Sweetie, do you understand me?"

As his mouth moved, she heard the words, but all she could see was the bus in the air and the frightened faces of her companions. In that terrifying moment, it was his presence that soothed her and made the realisation much easier to bear.

They had been in an accident, and they had survived.

"Dola! I need you back here!" someone screamed from behind them.

His forehead creased between his brows as he stared into her eyes. "Nikki honey, can you hear me? Can you take hold of my arm with your left?"

Nikki? Honey?

She replaced her hand on his thick forearm as she tried to find words within her numb brain to explain how glad she was to see him, but he was more interested in checking her lower eyelids than in that.

"DOLAAA!"

"I'm coming!" he yelled and leaned back so he could shrug off his shirt. "I need you to move your feet for me. There's a big gash around your thigh. I'm going to try and bandage it up as much as I can. I just need to know that you can move it."

That was when she noticed she had no shoes. What had happened to her shoes? Her toes were hugging the warm, prickly air around them, but she still couldn't look down at her feet. All she wanted to do was stare at his face and commit every feature to memory.

He had a jagged rip on his forehead above his brow, and blood was seeping down his sideburns and dripping onto his white singlet. She wanted to wipe it away, but it was the worry in his eyes that caught her attention. It was such a relief to see. She hadn't seen any emotion other than anger or indifference in his face for months. It was odd that it took an accident to bring out the softer side of him.

When he was done wrapping her leg in his shirt, he stared down at her.

"Move your feet for me, sweetie. Wriggle your toes."

Sweetie?

His voice was tender. She was not imagining it. She flicked her big toes back and forth twice, then moved the others weakly.

"That's good, sweetie, that's good."

He touched her thighs, ran his hands up her sides, and felt her hips and abdomen. She watched his face. It had been long since he held her hands or even looked at her, let alone touched her. She knew he was checking for other signs of injury, but it was a welcome touch. One she'd ached for, for weeks.

She winced when he palpated her abdomen.

"That hurt?"

"A little," she mouthed, but she wasn't sure he heard. The pain in her leg had doubled, and every other part of her body was hurting. Especially her back.

"Hey, does it hurt anywhere else?"

Her lips were dry as she lifted her left arm and grabbed his singlet.

"DOLA! Help!" The voice came again, insistent and demanding. Someone else needed help, and he had to go.

"Just lie still and don't move. I'll be right back."

He made to stand, but she grabbed his arm tight.

Please, don't leave me!

"I have to *help others*. I promise I'll be back soon to check on you."

After he let her go, her eyes followed him as he moved into the blurry distance.

Please, stay with me, Dola. I don't want the space anymore.

<h1 style="text-align:center">2
Two Hours Earlier</h1>

Anike Lamidi couldn't remember the weather ever being so capriciously hot.

Sweat poured down her face and neck into her armpits, and her shirt was sticking to her back despite the creaking fan above the rectangular waiting room. Tilting her head backwards, she emptied the last few drops of the liquid in her water bottle into her parched throat. It did little good.

The heat was brutal. Draining. Frustrating.

Cindy had joked that it was the summation of all the fiery, romantic feelings the month of February usually brought to every new year. Aside from the North-Western and South-Western air masses blowing in from the Sahara Desert and the Atlantic Ocean, the love month always cranked up the heat.

Bimbo had insisted it was punishment for their enjoyment of the harmattan season a few weeks prior. Maybe for the pile-up of the whole world's sins.

Regardless, it was stated by environmental experts that the heat was caused by global warming. And that the rains would soon follow. Something about warm air rising and condensing to form storm clouds. The planting season would make way for the incoming showers, and the cool air would bring in a tolerable atmosphere.

Everyone was looking forward to it, but Anike wasn't feeling particularly optimistic. Amid all that ravaging heat and drama, Dolabomi Desalu had broken up with her.

After two years of stringing one another along, suddenly, there was so much distance between them, that a third party could build a house in it and have a swimming pool and gardens.

The detachment happened gradually. Anike hadn't noticed. Then it quickly became a gulf. Afterward, they couldn't look each other in the eye anymore. Neither party was willing to build a bridge, and neither was interested in sliding down the sides of the gulf to meet up somewhere in the middle.

So much for the famed month of love and ardour.

Anike picked up the wooden hand fan that Cindy had thrown on her lap before marching angrily out of the waiting room to look for their ride to Abeokuta. She opened it up and flipped it back and forth, hoping to cool the air around her a little. But the air was still and warm and not planning on yielding to reason anytime soon. Cindy had been right to take a walk.

She had also been right to have been angry. Perhaps it was time to make another phone call to the trip organisers to determine exactly where they were and when they were hoping to arrive.

In truth, it was already past noon—the proposed pick-up time for their relaxing expedition to the city under the rocks. Their transport providers, Dare and Halima, were nowhere in sight, and her initial excitement had faded into irritation with the tiredness that came with sitting around doing nothing. Cindy had chosen full-blown anger over impatience. Anike had simply just sat in her chair and stewed.

So far, seven of them had shown up for the trip.

Well, eight, if one was to count the stubborn stowaway currently seated opposite her.

She glared at him across the corridor's wide pathway, wondering which one of her friends had extended him an invitation. He certainly hadn't taken any liking to any of them at any point in time during their relationship. Nor had he bothered to learn their proper names.

Dolabomi Desalu, her egotistical ex-boyfriend, had somehow bought himself a seat on the bus and was coming along for their trip. There was nothing she could do about it.

Crossing her right leg over her left knee, she leaned back onto the bench and let her eyes make contact with his face. The jerk wasn't giving her the time of day. Not that it mattered anyway, they were over and done. As closed a case, as they had both agreed to be.

Yet, she was bothered by it all. Disturbed by the heat in the waiting room and by the fact that the man she was trying so hard to pretend like she didn't care about, hadn't -- for one moment -- looked up to acknowledge her.

She waved the hand fan some more to find what little cool air she could in the room, then thrust her nose back into the book she'd brought along to pass the time. She was having no luck getting into the story. The gigantic ass of a man seated opposite her was the distraction.

She didn't want to look at him, but her eyes strayed upward and across the corridor often enough to study his calm, hard-lined facial features. His alluring, slanting eyes and thick lashes made up for the delicate frown between his brows, and his reclined posture on the chair was deceptive. He was an extremely well-trained and hard-working doctor with boundless energy, and he never failed to exhaust her with his zest for life.

And, she still liked him.

A lot.

Proud as a cock and as aloof as a lone tree on a rock, Dola was in a class all by himself. Handsome and brilliant, he was all the right shades of smug whenever he wanted to be. And that had turned out to be a lot, especially in the last few days till they'd broken up.

Anike figured that the smugness had been an add-on from medical school. Six years of cramming remedial information and being told that his course was at the top of the medical courses' leaderboard, had done that. She had only started to notice it in him a year into their relationship. Right after he and Grace won the grant to carry out their research work.

He took his hand away from his mouth to swipe his index finger across the surface of his device, then began to type furiously, his fingers hardly pausing for breath on one key.

Anger brewed a storm inside her. Fierce anger, mixed with a fair amount of yearning.

She thought about yanking the notepad right off his knees and hurling it across the corridor. What in the world was he trying to prove by accompanying them on the trip? She knew how taxing his schedule usually was. How on-call duties were back to back. How patients were like two hundred to a doctor, and how the limited hospital equipment connived with the unsatisfactory health facilities to make being a doctor in a Nigerian general hospital, difficult.

He was supposed to be busy!

'Supposed' was a word she now had to throw out of her dictionary. The reason why he had decided to come along was a mystery to her.

Was he planning on tagging along to show off how close he and Grace had become? Was he planning on hanging around so she could see what she was missing out on and get jealous? Was he simply just monitoring her, to ensure she didn't end up with anyone else on that trip?

And why—oh why—couldn't she keep her tortured eyes off of him?

She hated that he had decided to ruin her Valentine's weekend get-away, by putting his unwanted *'yummy'* self in the picture. And she couldn't do anything about it. Yanking the notepad off his knees was foolish. It wouldn't heal her fractured heart or put them both on the pathway to reconciliation. It would only earn her his famous freezing look. This was the hospital where he worked. He had more right to be there than she did, and the right to go anywhere that he wanted to, to take a break from his life and hustle.

She had needed—no craved—that time with the friends she'd pushed away when she'd made him her sun and moon. Everything had come back to bite her in the face. Their relationship had collapsed, her friends had moved on to other things, and she had become a lonely, old-soul, with no boyfriend and no goodwill left with anyone to command any respect.

Only the blessed connection to Cindy had kept her in the loop of things. When they had asked if she'd like to come along on their proposed trip, she'd readily agreed. Without asking who and who was coming. Being at home alone on Valentine's Day would be dangerous. It would put her one phone call closer to the very person she needed space from.

The person who had decided he wanted space from her. The person, who was now in her personal space, on her private trip with her friends, being a silent ass.

When he suddenly stood from the chair opposite her and started to walk towards the exit with his things, she closed her eyes so she wouldn't look at him. Yet, her heart followed his heavy footsteps as they emptied out of the corridor. Her head soon followed the movement, her eyes tracing his broad back in the blue, button-down shirt he was wearing. Her look had turned into a full-on stare and she mentally kicked herself for letting it show.

As mad as she was at him, he still made all her bells tinkle. He was still the best-looking thing that walked the face of the earth in her opinion. Their break-up wouldn't change the fact of that.

They had been the most envied couple amongst the resident doctors in the quarters where he lived, but she was sorry that their love had not been enough to withstand their differences. There were moments when she had wanted to call him and apologise. Tell him how much she missed him and how sorry she was for not trusting him. But those moments were few, and far between, and gone before she could even make sense of them.

He'd made it clear that he needed time to focus on all the other things in his life. There was no time for her. She had to move on. Besides, it didn't look like he wanted her anymore.

3
One Hour Earlier

"They're here! Ogun state, here we come!" Cindy's cheerful voice jolted Anike out of her sadness.

She sprang to her feet in response, glad to get out of her head and out of the sweltering waiting-room heat.

Grabbing her travel bag backpack and empty water bottle, she stowed her novel away and followed Cindy. Whatever story wasn't breaking the defence wall of her wandering attention could live to fight another day. It would be good to get out into the fresh air and then into the comfortable, air-conditioned insides of the eighteen-seater bus.

At least, she hoped, it would be as big and airy as Cindy had promised.

Pushing all her melancholic thoughts about Dola aside, she scrutinised the people in the room on their way down the same path he had taken earlier on. On one hand, she had hoped they'd run into him again. On the other, she was glad that they hadn't. The sad faces of the ill-looking patients and their relatives as they walked through the emergency room did more to depress her than her thoughts about Dola did. She uttered a silent prayer for a quick and total recovery for them all.

The heat was worse when they got outside. Cindy promptly took the pathway underneath the shaded walkway and Anike followed. There was no point getting sunburnt all in the name of rushing to catch a bus.

"Nikki!"

They looked up at the sound of someone waving excitedly.

Bimbo was ahead of them in a green and yellow polka-dot sundress, her trolley travel bag stowed in front of her long, shapely legs. She was looking good for a mother of one, and even better for a wife in a three-year-old marriage.

Anike glanced down at her simple, cream, short-sleeved top and three-quarter jeans.

'No wonder Dola doesn't find me attractive anymore,' she mused as Cindy's off-shoulder yellow top on black, knee-length slacks caught her eye. 'I seriously need to update my clothes.'

Dola had always loved her petite five-foot-four frame and dark skin, as well as her simple way of life and manner of dressing. Her job at the Insurance Company meant she often wore skirtsuits and formal dresses which she found uncomfortable. Dressing down at home and on outings with her friends was her means of relaxation. Cindy and Bimbo however made it mandatory to appear like they were walking down fashion runways every day. A fact which a year or two ago, hadn't fazed Anike.

In hindsight, she wondered if Dola had only pretended not to mind.

Bimbo and four others were hiding from the bright sun under the canopy of an ice-cream pavilion, sucking on lollipops. Most of them were watching the bus drive down the long stretch of road leading toward the medical emergency building. Only Bimbo was looking in their direction.

"You made it!" Cindy squealed.

"I did o!"

"I'm so glad you changed your mind."

"I just figured you both would be so lonely without me to make you laugh and show you around the famous *Itoku* tie and dye market."

"Peacock!" Cindy hissed and rolled her eyeball upward for a length of time. "That poor bird doesn't have enough coloured feathers on you."

"Parrot! I think the bird gets more credit for talking than it deserves. When we have you around. Anike, dear, I haven't seen your dimpled cheeks in three weeks!"

Anike laughed and grabbed Bimbo in a bear hug. "It's so good to see you."

"I'm so happy to be with you guys too. Glad to get away from my child and his dad for a change, regardless of how much I love them. I hope this *amebo* has not been boring you with tales of who is dating who, and who is two-timing who."

"All that and more!"

"Don't worry, I'm here to take care of you."

Anike grinned. Bimbo was her favourite person, and she was happy to discover that her husband had released her to come along with them for the trip.

Valentine's Day was three days away, and it was going to fall on a Monday. Thomas, Bimbo's husband, had been looking forward to spending the weekend quietly with his wife and son. Anike had begged for him to let her come along. To her surprise, he'd agreed.

So long as they'd be back on Sunday morning.

"I got you both ice cream," Bimbo was saying as she signalled the seller to bring them out of his ice box. "This diabolical heat will melt us before it melts it, but you people should gobble it up immediately."

"My personal person!" Cindy hailed as she grabbed an iced lolly from her. "*This heat serious no bi small. Be like say na village people send am. See as e wan suck ma bodi dry!*"

"True talk! I'm so fatigued, it feels like someone beat me with a drumstick."

"Don't worry, once we get to the hotel and shower, we'll all feel much better," Anike assured them as she collected a chocolate-coated ice cream from the seller, and tore off the wrapper, tastebuds watering in anticipation.

"Bus is here!" Ridwan, the conveyor of the trip, called out. "Everyone, gather around."

It was an ash-coloured Toyota Hiace with more than enough space for all eleven of them, including the driver, and their bags.

Anike bit into her icy confectionary with relish and finished it in four large bites. She paid half attention as Ridwan laid out their itinerary for the trip and Dare loaded all their luggage together into a pile for transfer into the back of the bus.

As Bimbo and Cindy chatted with Halima and the other two girls, Anike subconsciously looked around for Dola. It was tough to realise that her heart was still searching for him even though they were now apart. He was nowhere around the bus.

She exhaled. It could be that he'd had no plans to come along with them and she'd jumped to a conclusion from pieces of the conversation she'd heard him having with Cindy.

'I don't care,' she told herself. She hadn't wanted him to come along in the first place.

They had all agreed to meet at the hospital grounds because it was central to where everyone was coming from. Cindy had met up with her at home, and they had both taken an Uber to the hospital.

When they had wandered into the waiting room corridor to chill and wait for everyone, they'd seen him seated with a duffel bag beside him, his notebook open on his lap.

Anike's heart had slammed into her chest at the sight of him. Then it started a hundred-metre race on its own. They hadn't seen each other in a month since they'd broken up, and it seemed he had gotten better looking in that short period.

His fresh-skinned face dignified his fine features, but his broad-shouldered, athletic look was deceptive of his bookish nature. He had a genial face. One that people bared their hearts to without hesitation.

It wasn't a wonder why he was such a great doctor, or why she had entrusted him with her heart and soul.

He'd been two years ahead of her in secondary school but they had parted ways when he left for Medical school. He had tried to keep in touch, but Anike hadn't given him the time of day. Then they met again at a mutual friend's birthday party while serving together in Calabar. The odds had been so random. She had been unable to say no to his request to take her out afterward. Something about him had screamed trust and stability.

Now that they were fully broken up, all the things she'd always wanted to say to him pre-breakup, rose to mind but stayed at the base of her throat. Including, and especially the fact that missing him gave her sleepless nights. It was why she had often bickered with him. She'd been too scared of losing him to someone else.

But he'd completely ignored her and spent the time talking to Cindy.

As he and Cindy exchanged pleasantries, Anike had found herself a seat on the only empty bench opposite the armed chair he was sitting on and slid into it. Pressing her earphones into her ears one after the other, she pulled out her novel and flipped it open. She didn't switch the music on though, and she wasn't able to read a word either. She'd been too bothered by his presence to concentrate.

Then she heard references to Abeokuta and the bus and froze. He was joining them. His duffel bag hadn't been for on-call duties only.

Anike hadn't even wanted to think about it or ask Cindy any questions when the girl came over to sit beside her. Dola was free to go wherever he wanted. Who was she to stop him? There were many possibilities to his reasons for going to Abeokuta, chief of which was to hitch a ride along just for the journey there and nothing else. He had a family in Abeokuta. Family, she'd met. A family who adored her.

"Climb aboard!"

The sharp call made Anike look up, squint, and cover her eyes.

Behind her, Cindy burst into a scream. "Joshua! You made it."

Joshua grinned from the open doorway of the bus and waved at them all. "Halima made me come," he said, pointing out the dark-skinned, Kanuri girl. "She complained that it's been long since we all got together."

"Oh, my goodness, she's so right!" Cindy leapt at Joshua's six-foot frame.

Joshua was her male best friend, or—as Anike and Bimbo suspected—her secret crush. Whenever the guy would meet up with another girl, Cindy would grumble and complain until she was sure they weren't dating. Bimbo had told her severally to ask him out, but Cindy had denied anything being between them. Besides, she hadn't wanted to ruin a good friendship based on feelings she didn't think he had.

"I guess you are not sitting with me," Anike said to her.

"Not after she has seen Josh!" Bimbo nudged Anike towards the bus. "Come on, let you and I sit together. We have a lot to talk about."

Cindy smiled; her left arm linked to Joshua's elbow. "I'm sorry. We also have a lot to catch up on too."

"Yes, but I need to be of help," Joshua replied before he extracted his arm out of Cindy's elbow to go and help the other guys with loading all the travelling bags onto the bus. "Go sit on the bus."

Anike settled with Bimbo in the middle seat while Cindy hugged the window seat on the other side of their line, hopeful of keeping the stowaway seat linking the whole row together, for Joshua.

The bags were still being arranged in the back, so Anike and Bimbo chatted with Halima and Tolu who had taken seats in front of them. She had almost forgotten that Dola was coming until she saw him at the open doorway of the bus.

Their eyes had met and held for an instance that felt like minutes before she turned her head to look out through the window on her side of the seat.

"Hi," she heard him say, in his characteristically civil voice. "Ladies."

"Hey, Dr. Dola, long time. So glad you made it. Your HOD gave you time off?"

"In a manner of speaking. I'm not on call over the weekend so, I can be here."

"Well, I'm so happy you're here." Halima beamed at him and Anike caught it.

Halima. Halima had been the one who'd invited him and neglected to tell her. She turned her face away and heard all her friends waving accolades at her ex-boyfriend, asking how his day had been and what his work was like at the hospital.

"Hey Nikki," he finally threw her way.

She turned her head to look at him and felt the silence steal around the bus for a moment. Everyone was waiting to see if she'd respond.

"Dr. Desalu!" she replied and squirmed under his cool gaze. He absolutely hated it when she called him that.

"How are you doing?" he continued.

"I'm good," she replied. "And you?"

"Great."

There seemed nothing more to say, so she turned her face back out of the window, and he climbed into the bus and made his way to the seat directly behind hers.

She reacted to his nearness. It upset her that he was physically near her, and she couldn't touch him. She folded her arms and rearranged her handbag on her lap to starve off the stream of nervous energy that had suddenly engulfed her. He was going to be with them throughout the trip. It was going to be awkward, and painful.

Bimbo reached her hand out and grabbed one of her clasped hands. "Relax," she whispered. "I've got you."

Anike turned to look at her. "Thank you," she mouthed.

4
Half an Hour Earlier

The bus loaded up and left the hospital at about 1 pm. It was carrying eleven people and one driver. Spirits were high as they headed for the Conference Hotel in Abeokuta, Ogun state, said to be the best hotel the state could boast of.

The occupants of the bus were all full of excited chatter as they discussed plans for visiting the presidential library and the famous *Olumo* rock, but Anike closed her eyes. The idea of Dola so close yet so distant saddened her.

She missed him. She missed his goofy smile and brilliant suggestions for her numerous work problems. She missed sharing instant noodles with him and cradling his head in her lap while he read his medical textbooks. She especially missed date nights where anything could happen, from taking turns giving each other massages, to quirky game night shows with other couples.

How everything had ended in this state of funk was a mystery to her. They had agreed to keep away from each other for a month.

Time apart, he'd said, to figure things out.

She'd gone along with it because he had become unbearable to be around. Cranky and cold, on the few days they'd managed to snatch time out of his crazy schedule to be together. Way too busy, on the nights that she was alone and needed someone to talk to.

And there was the matter of his best friend, Grace, the diva doctor.

Dola had spared all the time for Grace and none for her. Even now that they were figuring out the 'space' as he'd called it, Grace was with him every waking moment. Anike knew. Cindy and Bimbo, her best friends, had become her unsolicited spies. Cindy was a pharmacist at the same hospital where Dola worked. Bimbo, a public health advocate, had lots of doctor friends working with Dola. Every move that Grace made was reported; whether she cared to hear about it or not. And Dola was not innocent in all those shenanigans. As the stories that reached her ears showed.

He had only suggested a break, but she'd taken it to mean the end. It was the end for her anyway, being there didn't seem to be any solution to their problem. He didn't seem to want to change anything about his life the way it was except for her presence in it, and he hadn't said once in all their time of bickering, that he loved her.

Their last conversation had been tough. It had shown her a side to him that had scared her and made her wonder if any part of their relationship had ever been genuine.

"You know what about Grace? She's stressless. She doesn't whine or grumble about me missing her calls. And she doesn't compare herself to you or try to make me feel guilty about all the time I spend with you."

"Why should she? She's not your girlfriend, I am."

"She's a work colleague and a friend, but you've been so jealous—"

"Well you are always with her and I never can be sure what you're doing."

"What in the world did you think we were doing?"

"I don't know. Having meals with her at your break times, or giving her a massage when you get tired of reading."

"What are you accusing me of? Cheating on you with Grace? Are you serious, right now?"

"What else will you say?"

"We've been doing research work together and you would know that if you even bothered to listen to me. I told you about the grant and the work that it entails. It wasn't and has never been a date with Grace!"

"Really? Do you know what upsets me about this whole matter? You don't even want to admit that you dropped the ball. You forgot me in your rec room for hours while you were getting comfy eating Chinese rice with her. What did you expect me to think? I was patiently waiting for you, and hungry too by the way, but you forgot all about me and you expect me not to talk about it. Do I mean that little to you?"

"I'm sorry but I had a project on hand, more patients than I could handle, and plenty of literary review deadlines to meet up with. I was up to my neck in work, and I sincerely forgot you were around. I made a mistake and it was not intentional, or because I have something clandestine going on with Grace. I simply forgot. When are you ever going to let it go?"

Anike had stared at him with hurt. He'd been shouting at her. It didn't feel like he was sorry about anything. "Whatever is happening between us has nothing to do with Grace. You've been distracted and dismissive, and I don't know where I stand with you any longer."

"What's that supposed to mean?"

"Exactly what it means. I realise now that I'm not important, so forgive me for always wanting to be with you."

"This—this is what you do all the time! Make me the bad guy. Say things that are not true to curry sentiments and prove your points!"

"I do not make you the bad—talk to me! Why do I feel like every time I tell you how I feel about our relationship, I'm making you the bad guy? I don't feel like I'm in a relationship anymore. I don't feel like I am being heard."

"You are always talking, and loudly, and I hear you."

"I'm always waiting for you to show up all the time. You forgot my birthday. You forget our date nights. I can't call or talk to you because your work is so much more important than anything else going on in your life. I'm here, and you're never there. And the worst thing is that we can't talk about it."

He exhaled and put his hands on his waist. "I'm never there because I'm busy. I expected that you would understand that at the very least."

"I don't have a problem with your being busy. I have a problem with you acting like I don't have a right to complain about being neglected. There is no point in you stringing me along if you don't have time for me."

"You know what, you are right. This that we've become is not healthy for either of us and— I can't keep stringing you along."

She stared at him and folded her arms. "What does that mean?"

"I think we need some space. We need time to—figure things out, I dunno. I have a lot on my plate right now and sincerely, I don't have time for—" He'd looked at her.

'You don't have time for me—say it!'

"I'm sorry Anike, I don't have time for this."

The tears that had filled the back of her eyes at the finality of things had been blinked away with gritted teeth. She'd hoped that she'd have been able to make him understand and that they'd talk, and they'd look at his schedule a bit more, agree on dates and times that they could meet up, and maybe figure out the long picture but— he'd wanted space instead.

She exhaled. "Sure."

He hadn't said anything more, and she had lost all the will to fight him into changing his mind.

He'd found it difficult to look at her afterward. She had simply turned around and walked away from him, every step a prayer that he would call her name. When he'd offered to drop her off at home, she'd declined. She'd been too distraught.

Just twelve months prior, they had been so happy. She had felt so lucky and he'd been the best boyfriend. Valentine's Day had been a pleasurable affair because Dola hadn't wanted something cliché. He'd filled up the tank of his fifteen-year-old Toyota Corolla and loaded the back seat with pizza, chicken, cans of fizzy drinks, and provisions for the less privileged. Then they'd driven all over Lagos looking for unpopular orphanages to hand the gift items out to.

They'd ended the day lying on the windscreen of his car holding hands and staring at the starless indigo sky. They'd talked about everything and planned the future, but nothing had prepared her for the rocky year that had followed.

"Hey," Bimbo whispered, suddenly nudging her into the present. "What are you thinking about?"

Anike opened her eyes and turned her head to the right so she could look at her friend. "Nothing," she mumbled.

"Awww," Bimbo said with a smile. Then she leaned over and whispered. "He's right behind you. Why don't you talk to him?"

She shook her head and turned it so she could stare out of the window. Talking hadn't done much good then. She didn't think that it would now. Even though she'd been finding it difficult to move on. Theirs had been a crash affair, peaking quickly and fizzling out on time management issues.

"If he wants to talk, I'm right here," she said, and she knew he'd heard her.

He readjusted his position in the chair behind her and she closed her eyes. She could feel the stream of energy emanating from him. She wasn't just struggling to move on, she was still in love with him. She would always love him.

"A–Anike."

She heard his soft, subdued voice call to her from behind her chair and a glimmer of hope rose in her. *Please tell me you made a mistake.*

"I—"

That was when the truck hit their bus.

5
Moments After the Crash

Anike turned her head to the right-hand side and saw the forests.

Her eyes dimmed for a moment as images flashed before them. The bus tumbled harder and faster than she could endure. Terrified screams renting the air all around her, and bile, rising in the middle of her throat as they flung as a group through a ripple of timeless space. The hissing sound of deflating tyres, the whine of metal grinding against metal, and the thick cloud of smoke and heat unearthed themselves from her memories.

She shut her eyes and heard ringing in her ears for a few seconds.

What was it that he'd said to her? Lay still. Lie on your back. Relax, I'll be back to check on you.

Anike remembered the last time he'd told her that he'd be back.

He'd put her in the resident doctors' break room while he finished his shift. Then he'd forgotten all about her until she'd stumbled out of the room after a three-hour wait, watching doctors come and go. Someone had pointed out where to find him, and she had followed the directions to their main office. He'd been there, relaxed, butting heads with Grace over a sheaf of papers. An open pack of Chinese fried rice, and a carton of pineapple juice on the table in front of them.

She'd been too angry to be sad.

In his defence, his eyes had featured a semblance of horror for a second, then had been full of regret, and then they had hardened in response to the slew of angry words that had burst forth from her mouth. A week after that they had both gone on to have the painful conversation that would define their relationship.

And eventually, break it.

When she opened her eyes again, she was still lying on wet grass. The sky was full and blue above her and howls for help surrounded her. The pain in her leg had subsided somewhat and her mind had cleared, but she was in too much shock to appreciate the horror of what had happened.

There was a body lying half a foot away from her with the neck turned at an impossible angle. That person needed help. She couldn't just lie there and wait to be helped when she was sure she could get up. When she could be of help to someone who seemed to be in a worse condition.

She rolled like a block unto her side and tried to raise herself to her right elbow. Then she began to drag herself across the grass towards the bloodied, fallen body. Who had been with her on the bus? Halima, and Dare and Ridwan, and Cindy, and Bimbo. Her eyes widened. *Bimbo!* She'd begged Thomas to let her come. Promised to have her back home on Sunday morning. *Oh, dear Lord!*

It was easier now to see that the person on the floor was not female in any way. And not Bimbo. Bimbo had been wearing a green dress with yellow polka dots, this body wore brown pants.

She turned over to her belly and pulled herself into a crawl position. The voices were louder now. Dola and Dare were trying to heave something up, maybe the bus.

One! Two! Three! They grunted out loud as more voices pooled into the crash site and metal whined under the force of their push.

Anike was more concerned with reaching the body. Each movement forward came with pain till she reached the body and flipped it over. The lifeless form rolled onto its back, and a large gaping wound was visible on the right side of his neck.

"Jesus!" she screamed and drew back. "Ridwan!"

"Nikki!" Dola's concerned voice was followed by running feet. He reached her in moments, crouched low and pulled her to himself. "I told you to stay put!"

"I couldn't. I couldn't!"

He slid into a sitting position on the floor beside her and wrapped his arms around her from behind. Then he clung to her as she screamed uncontrollably at the reality of what had happened to them. "Ridwan, oh, Ridwan!"

Ridwan had planned the trip. He'd gathered everyone together and ensured that the invitation was extended to her.

Dola held her tighter. "Calm down. Help is on the way."

She turned her face into his dirty, white singlet and burst into more tears. He held her close for a bit and let her cry. Then he pushed her away from himself so he could look into her face.

"Baby," he said softly, "you're okay. You're going to be fine. Some people are still trapped inside the bus and I need to get back to help them. I need you to stay here and keep calm. Don't look at anyone. Please."

"Cindy…"

"Cindy's still on the bus. We'll get her out."

"I want to help."

"No. You'll help me by staying right here."

"Okay. Where is Bimbo?"

"Anike, we are checking on everyone but I can't do anything if I'm here holding onto you. Every second counts. Please, lie down and stay still. I promise you I'll be back."

She shook her head and held him back. "No, don't leave me."

"Nikki, get a hold of yourself! Stay here!"

It felt like her heart was being torn in two as he unhooked himself from her arms and left again. She didn't lie down though, she sat where she was and stared around at the wreckage that had been their happy journey to Abeokuta.

Two unidentified men carried a body through the debris and laid it on the floor ahead of her. She frowned and tried to make out who it was.

Halima! Halima had been wearing a red dress.

She took in deep breaths of air and tried to calm herself. It was possible the girl was still alive and had only just fainted. Bimbo would be all right. Cindy would too.

When she looked up, she saw more people arriving at the crash site. They had been able to get more victims out of the truck, the bus, and the other two cars involved. Dola and the driver, Dare, had done most of the work, joined by Victor who had only sustained a few scrapes himself. A few motorists had also stopped to help. They were lifting victims into cars and willing to take the injured to nearby hospitals.

Anike got to her feet as soon as she felt she was able to. That was when she saw him again. Dola!

He was kneeling beside someone, with his arms fully extended, elbows locked, fingers locked and hands on top of one another performing chest compressions. She stared at the person he was working on and stopped in her tracks, frozen to her feet.

Bimbo!

Bimbo had a husband and child waiting for her at home.

"Is that Bimbo?"

His head lifted, and his eyes locked onto hers as he pushed down hard and fast over Bimbo's chest without stopping.

"What are you doing up?" his voice came at her, harsh and brusque as he focused on his task. "I told you to stay put. You just came out of an accident and you were unconscious. Go and lie down."

"Save her please!" she pleaded as her eyes sought his eyes.

"She's going to be fine!" With that, he lowered his face to the girl beneath him and kept right on pumping. "One-one thousand, two-one thousand, three-one thousand…"

She had never seen him look so determined.

Adrenaline lit his eyes, and his shoulder and arm muscles glistened with sweat and strength as they did their job working to keep Bimbo alive. His mouth had the determined set of one who wasn't going to give up, but still, Bimbo lay unresponsive. There was sweat pouring down his face but he was still pumping.

"Come on! Come on, Bimbo!" he muttered. "Come on!"

Fear gripped her. That was her friend lying motionless on the floor.

"Go and lie down, Anike!" he barked at her.

'I want to do that, but I'm sick of us not talking to each other. I can't talk to you in the morning, I can't talk to you in the evening, and I sure as hell can't talk to you in the middle of the night because you're on call duty. Too busy with your patients to take a call. I'm just that girl who's disturbing you. When, ever, will the time be right for us?'

'How about when we're out of this crazy situation and I'm not pumping someone's heart, trying to get them to stay alive long enough for a rescue!'

She stared at him with sadness. She couldn't fault him. He was performing chest compressions on her unconscious friend, for goodness sake, and there she was, thinking about a fight. This was not the best of times to talk.

"Anike?"

She snapped out of her dazed dream and blinked. He was still pumping away.

"Go and sit down!"

She'd been dreaming. She'd been daydreaming about fighting with him while he was working hard to save Bimbo. What was wrong with her? She knew everything that was happening in his life and how real his challenges were, advancing his career. Yet she had wanted him all to herself.

At that moment, she saw how selfish she had become, and how selfish she still was. Dola was the most amiable, the most giving, the most selfless person she knew, and she'd given him hell because she'd been too focused on herself and her needs to notice how divided his attention had to be to juggle everything going on in his life. She'd blamed him for their breakup, but the fault had been as much with her, as it had been with him.

She recalled the many arguments they'd had, the explanations he'd given, the sincerity in his voice when he'd told her that it had just been research work that bound him and Grace together. She recalled with pain, the resignation in his voice as he asked for the space. He hadn't rejected her; he'd just needed a breather. She'd been throwing all manner of emotional fire at him the past six months and he'd just been juggling it all trying to keep himself afloat.

Bimbo coughed just then, and relief washed over her. The girl was alive. She looked weak and helpless, but a second later she was screaming.

"Over here! There is bleeding. The abdominal area, I can't make out what," Dola shouted and raised an arm. "Help!"

Anike looked up at the sound of running feet and two LASEMBUS emergency workers ran towards them with a stretcher. The dizziness hit her just then. It was happening. It was all happening. Halima was dead, Bimbo was injured and Cindy was missing. The crash site had become a busy hub of activity. Vehicles were piling up. Latsma officials were on site. She moved about in a daze, unable to take it all in anymore.

Cindy! She still had to find Cindy. She staggered towards the bus amidst the activity and got there just in time to see them lay yards of brown material over three bodies. The fourth was behind her. Ridwan. He was dead too.

"Madam, what are you doing here? Are you part of the crash? Do you have an injury?"

A Latsma official was asking her questions, but she couldn't hear him. She was looking at a broken window within their bus which was lying on its side.

"Madam?"

Everything was going dark. She reached out her hands and found herself falling.

"Hey, Madam, catch her!"

She had just found out why Dola had wanted her to lie down. Why he had been trying to keep her away from the bus wreck?

Cindy was strewn halfway across one of the bus's broken windows, on her tummy, blood dripping from her abdomen.

6
One Day Later

Anike, half lying in bed, was staring miserably at her casted left leg. It turned out that her injuries had included a hairline fracture of one of the bones in her left lower leg. It had been the main reason why Dola hadn't wanted her walking around.

The open wound on her thigh had been dressed as well, and she was waiting for her parents to come and pick her up from the hospital. They had been notified of the accident moments after their arrival the day before and were billed to arrive soon.

She had woken up the day after the accident on a hospital bed, scared out of her wits and hungry for news of her friends. Joshua, who had survived the accident with a broken collar bone and a sprained wrist, had popped in and out of all the rooms where each one of them had been admitted, giving news to everyone. Anike had been glad to hear it, but she'd wanted news of Dola. All she'd heard was that his quick thinking and basic life support techniques had saved most of them.

She brooded at the thought of a Valentine's Day forever ruined for all who had survived. Halima and Ridwan were the only casualties from the event. The other two victims had been from the truck whose brake had failed. Every other person had sustained minor injuries. They would remember though; they'd remember Halima and Ridwan every Valentine's Day.

Anike sighed. The reality of a life without Dola had been easier to process with Cindy and Bimbo around to cheer her up now and then. With Bimbo yet to wake up from surgery and Cindy hooked up to machines in an ICU, life looked bleak and unreal.

The door opened and she looked up, expecting family.

"Anike."

Dola!

Her back straightened. "Dr. Desalu."

He had a bandage wrapped around his left wrist and his forehead had been adequately stitched up.

"How are you doing?" he asked, shutting the door to her room.

"I'm all right," she replied and watched him approach her bed.

"Thought I'd give you news of your friends. Bimbo is awake and doing fine, but Cindy is still half-conscious with a head injury and hip fracture. I believe they will both make a full recovery anyway, so don't worry."

She nodded and just stared at him. There was so much that she wanted to say, starting with the words *I'm sorry.*

"Thank you for the news, and for being there and saving all of us."

He nodded and gripped the handle of her bed's footrest. "I'm glad you're okay. Let me check on the others." He turned to leave.

"Dr. Desalu—"

The words stopped him in his tracks. "Dr. Desalu?" he said with a sigh as he turned back to look at her. "What happened to Dola?"

She stared straight ahead at him and took her time responding. "It got swallowed up in the space between us."

He was quiet for a moment at the words. "You know how much I hate you being formal with me!"

"We're not together anymore, what does that matter?"

"It matters to me. I wanted us to take a little break from one another so we could stop fighting and you took it to mean the end."

"What did you want me to think? I didn't see any other way around our issues, Dola."

"You were always angry and raising your voice. I didn't want to talk to you when you were in that mood."

"I'm sorry you felt that way but it didn't feel like you wanted to talk at all, it felt like you wanted everything to be over."

"But I only wanted a breather—"

"I wanted you!" she yelled. "But I gave you what you wanted—space!"

He sighed with tiredness. "You are doing it again, raising your voice."

"I am not—" Anike caught herself with clenched fists and realised at that moment that he was right. She'd been shouting. She took in a deep breath and unclenched her fists. "I'm sorry."

"I'm sorry too."

Staring at him made the longing in her heart double. She had missed him for weeks. The last thing she wanted was to fight with him again.

"All I wanted to say was that staying away from one another doesn't solve anything. Sitting down and talking about our issues, that's what does. Making plans and mapping schedules and making everything clear… that's how I wanted to solve our problems."

"I realise that and I want things to change."

She looked down at the bedspread. "I'm sorry. I'm sorry that I wasn't understanding enough or caring enough to be your support system. You were handling a lot but I was plying you with stress. I didn't see what it was doing to you—what it was doing to us."

"I'm the one who's been a selfish jerk. I've treated you like you didn't matter as much as my career did but it took this horrible accident to make me realise how devastated I'd be if I lost you."

"I was jealous. I enjoyed being with you so much, I didn't want to share you with anyone or anything else." She fingered the bedspread. "The truth is, you deserve a girl who is comfortable in her skin and on her own even when you are not there. That's the reality of relationships."

"You're right, but I want us to get back together. I love you, Anike; I don't want to be with anyone else."

Anike's mouth turned down at the corners, seeking to hold back the tears. "You don't know how long I waited to hear you say that."

"Nikki, I've wanted to say that since the day we broke up but you wouldn't let me. From now on I want you to talk to me. Say everything that you want to say to me, I will listen."

She looked up at him, not caring that he could see the tear sliding down her face. "I missed you. I'd been missing you long before we broke up. I'm scared of losing you for good. I don't want the space anymore."

"I don't want the space anymore either."

"If you hadn't been there—" She sunk her face into both her hands and wept with exhaustion and fear.

He walked over to sit on the bed beside her and drew her into his arms. She clung to him and cried. Tears of joy, tears of relief, tears of loss, and tears of fear. The fear of what could have been for both of them.

"I was so insensitive."

"Honey, it's okay."

"Don't ever leave me again," she said when she was done crying.

"I won't. I promise."

He handed her a handkerchief from his pocket. She took it and wiped both eyes gently.

"Why did you come with us? You are always so busy. What made you want to come?"

"I heard a rumour," he said and managed to give the first smile she had seen on his face in twenty-four hours. "That someone was thinking of shooting his shot at *Olumo* Rock, and I was scared. I was scared you'd say yes to him."

"He already did before the trip," she said, looking up at him. "I turned him down."

"You did?"

"He doesn't—didn't compare to you."

"I'm glad to hear that," he said and grabbed her hand. "Do you think we can start again?"

She released a nervous breath. "Yes. I want to start again."

Eyes on hers, he raised the back of her hand to his lips and kissed it. "Thank you for giving me a second chance. I cannot promise that I will never neglect you in favour of my work again, but I will listen whenever you prompt me, and I will make the necessary adjustments where I should."

She nodded and squeezed his hand back. "I will try to be understanding."

"Valentine's Day is the day after tomorrow, do you want to go dancing?"

She looked down at her leg. "With this cast and the crutches?"

He laughed. "Why not?"

"Halima…."

"I understand." He leaned across, cupped her neck, and kissed her on the cheek. "I'm glad you're alive. I'll never take this for granted again."

"Me too."

She smiled at him.

Anike knew their love would not always be rosy, but that they would start again with a better expectation of one another.

And less space between them.

THE END.

About the Author

Olufunmilola Adeniran writes as Feyi Aina, a Christian author and poet crafting contemporary inspirational women's fiction as well as historical stories infused with an African fantasy flavour.

She started off publishing e-books in December 2017, most of which can be found on Amazon, and Bambooks. Her stories feature strong male and female lead characters in 'what if' scenarios created to epitomise good moral conduct while showing off the beautiful process of falling in love.

Feyi won the RWOWA 2019 Author of the Year Award for her novel Love's Indenture. She is also the author of **Love Happens Eventually,** and **Ayanfe** which are both in print and can be found at Roving Heights, Patabah and the Book Nook bookstores. She is also a member of the Black Female Authors collective with stories in several anthologies including **Hell Hath No Fury** and **Roses Aren't Red**.

Learn more about Feyi from her website www.feyiaina.com.

HIS
LUCKY
CHARM

Everyone desires love, no matter how elusive the right kind seems to be.

By

MOBOLAJI OLANREWAJU

ONE

Olamiposi

Women were bitches.

Wives were the most deceitful being in the world and marriage was nothing but a playing field for them. Why was he even thinking that he could make his marriage work when his parents' own was a failure, despite his Mama's best effort? Thank God for his only sibling, Akintunde, who brought a semblance of normalcy into his life while growing up.

A snort escaped his mouth, and a lump filled his throat. He picked up his glass of gin and gulped down his drink in one swallow. It burned a fiery path down his throat and seemed to open a wound in his stomach lining. His eyes watered and he clutched his stomach.

He wasn't a drinker.

He had never had the stomach for harsh dry drinks like whiskey but he would rather take it than commit murder. If he hadn't walked out of his matrimonial home, the one he shared with Miriam, the woman he married 5 years ago, the way he did a few hours ago, dead bodies would have littered that house. He was that furious.

His eyes watered. He wasn't sure if it was because of the drink or he needed to break down and have a good cry. His life was a mess right now and he didn't know what to do about it. He poured the amber liquid into the wine glass blindly.

Miriam was the love of his life. They had been through thick and thin together before they got married and even, after the marriage. He practically worshipped the ground she walked on. He couldn't believe she could do this to him. He gulped down the drink and he swore he could feel his innards tearing apart. The dark joke brought a weary smile to his lips.

"Good evening. Please can I join your table?" A solemn, barely audible voice jolted him out of his misery.

His head snapped up and he stared into the most innocent face he had ever come across. Her catlike, hazel-coloured eyes were shy and smiling. She lowered her gaze the moment their eyes connected and her fingers tangled and untangled her purse straps. She looked like an angel.

Had he died and gone to heaven? Oh God! He didn't want to die now.

His eyes snapped open again. She was still there, waiting for his consent. His eyes perused her almost modest outfit of jeans and tank top and he felt his groin swell with arousal. The flowery tank top stopped in the middle of her flat belly, showing off bare, glowing caramel skin that made his mouth water with desire and a high waist black jeans moulded long, slim legs which ended in a pair of colourful, feminine sneakers. A small purse rested on her flaring hips. There was nothing remarkable about her oval-shaped face with its high-cheek bone except for her cupid-shaped lips painted in light pink and begging to be kissed. He crossed his legs and shifted uncomfortably in his chair. She would need to find another place to sit down.

"Please let me join your table. I think you need my company as much as I need yours. I have been watching you for a while from across the bar, over there." She pointed towards the bar, still avoiding his direct gaze.

It was as if she could read his mind. He shrugged. He had nothing to lose. After all, they would be sitting on different chairs. He waved her to the vacant seat and she sank into it with a murmured, 'Thanks.'

He continued drinking while she ordered a chilled bottle of water and pepper soup. When she was done with the pepper soup, she continued sipping her water and looked everywhere except his face.

"What is your name?" he blurted out but his voice was slurred and he winced. He was drunk and wondered how he was going to get himself home.

"Sandra." She smiled at him.

"Sandra is a beautiful name. If it is your real name." She chuckled at that but didn't deny or confirm it. He was pressed and needed to use the loo. He got to his feet and swayed heavily.

Oh my! He was in trouble.

"Are you all right?" She was by his side, supporting him and he couldn't help but lean on her.

"Should I be wary of you? I am beginning to get scared." His tongue was heavy and the words felt tangled in his mouth. He stepped towards the loo and she guided him to the entrance of the men's restroom.

"Be careful," her murmured caution followed him into the restroom and he took a step at a time because the floor was suddenly too far from him. He walked slowly but steadily and found himself looking forward to her presence. She was waiting for him at the entrance and he felt warmth suffused him.

"You have had enough to drink for the night and you are in no position to drive tonight. You are driving right?" He nodded as he staggered along her side and noticed her warm curve nestled into his side.

She stopped to collect a key at the reception and led him into a room. The room was dark but before she could turn on the light, he had turned her into him and kissed her soft cupid-shaped lips. She

hesitated briefly before she started responding shyly at first and then
her screams filled the room. It was music to his ears and they were all
over each other as if they weren't two strangers who just met a few
minutes ago.

*****

Sunlight was filtering into the room, poking its fingers into his eyes
and his heavy eyelids flew open. He shut them immediately as he
reached across the bed and his hand met an empty sheet. His eyes
opened fully and completely, looking around the room. He was alone.

His head was banging and his mouth tasted like cotton bud but he sat
up in bed and looked around. Had he dreamt the whole event? No,
he hadn't. There were two pillows on the bed and both had
headprints on it. The other side of the bed was also rumbled and the
bedsheet was almost off the bed. No, he hadn't dreamt it.

Where was she? Who was she? Oh God! He hoped he hadn't had sex
with a ghost. Not only had he had sex with a ghost, but he also just
put himself in the same space as his cheating wife. Disgust filled his
gut, and he kissed his teeth.

He fell out of bed and banged his shin on the floor. It was then he
realised he was butt naked under the sheet.

"Oh my God! What have I done?" His hands cupped his manhood
protectively as if he wasn't alone in the room and snatched the sheet
off the bed to cover himself. "Hey! Hey!" What was her name again?
The cloud of haze over his brain lifted and her name along with her
face floated into his mind. "Sandra! Sandra!" He felt foolish calling
the name because he knew instinctively it wasn't her real name.

He peeped into the bathroom and came back into the room. All his
belongings were folded neatly on the single sofa in the room. His gold
wristwatch, wallet and everything was intact. At least, she wasn't a
thief. He picked up his wallet and opened it. That was when a note, a

receipt for both his own orders and her own, and a wad of cash fell out. He didn't carry cash on him, so they weren't his.

He picked up the note which reads, 'Thank you.'

That was all.

He turned it over and over as if willing other words to appear but nothing. Just that.

He sank onto the edge of the bed and stared into space.

TWO

Omotara

Oh my God! She was pregnant!

She stared in awe at the two lines on the stick. Her heart beat in excitement and she did a fast jig on the tiled bathroom floor.

He would be happy. There would be peace in this house finally and he could look at her with love in his eyes again, rather than contempt.

Would he? He takes joy in bullying you around.

No, it wasn't like that. He was not happy with the situation and now that she was expecting a baby, things would change.

But the baby is not his own. Why are you shielding him from his own problem?

She was not. She wanted him to be happy, she wanted them to be happy. She wanted her husband back.

Cloud of sadness threatened to overcome her newfound joy but she pushed it firmly away and held on to it. She couldn't wait to break the news to her husband. She disposed of the kit and went into the bedroom to change into casual wear. It was time to prepare dinner.

As she opened her wardrobe, she came face to face with the tank top and jeans she wore that fateful night. Memories assailed her and moisture dampened her panties. Her husband, Joshua, was her first man and with him, sex was lukewarm at its best. She had never enjoyed it but if he was satisfied with it, then all was well in her world.

Hence, she wasn't prepared in any way for the experience she had with the stranger. She felt ashamed, guilty and unbearably aroused whenever she remembered which was every second of the day. She was sure her husband wouldn't have recognised the screaming woman who was thoroughly ravished in that hotel room weeks ago. She didn't recognise the loud vixen she turned into. She couldn't believe she was that woman or that part of her existed. She had been avoiding her friend's calls all this time because she didn't want to face her shame and guilt.

Remembering the conversation that led to her shameful act made her cheeks flame with embarrassment. *"I need to fix my marriage, Linda." She had paced her friend's sitting room in agitation.*

"The responsibility for your marriage falls on you and your husband's shoulders," Linda had countered as she sat on the single sofa in her sitting room and filed her nails. She was her childhood friend but still single and didn't understand her dilemma. She hissed but her friend continued anyway. "The fact that your husband is infertile is not your fault and you shouldn't be the one to fix it."

"Joshua has changed. He wasn't like that when we first got married but the few times we sat down to have conversations, he admitted he was always angry because I couldn't give him a child. I want my man back, Linda, and I will do anything to achieve that." Her voice rang with determination as she lifted her chin and squared her shoulder.

"And that is why he insults and bullies you at every opportunity?" Linda unfolded her long legs and sat forward. She didn't wait for her response. "How do you want to give him a child? I am curious."

"I am not sure yet. I really don't know but I will find a way around it."

"Don't go and do anything foolish, Tara. Talk to your husband and you guys should visit a fertility hospital, instead of this foolishness you are cooking in your mind." Linda warned with a stern face.

"He didn't even want to go for a fertility test. It is a dent on his ego. It is a woman's job to give a man a healthy child and that is what I am meant to do."

"When did you turn into this foolish woman, Tara? I thought you were smarter than this?" Linda glared at her but she had only stared back unflinchingly until

the latter subsided and sighed in exasperation. "Now that you have heard from his family that he is infertile from a childhood accident, are you still going to solve that issue for him?"

"Linda, you don't understand. I only stumbled on that conversation by accident. Joshua doesn't know about it and it is my duty to protect him as well." Her mother-in-law and sister-in-law had visited them some weeks back and Tara left the house to the street market to get crates of eggs and other ingredients for breakfast.

When she returned, she went into the kitchen through the back door and unknown to her mother-in-law and sister-in-law that she had returned, they began to discuss her husband's inability to have children. It was a stroke of luck from her end to stumble upon such a well-kept secret.

"I give up on you, Tara."

Afterward, she followed her instinct and did what she had to do. The memory of that night would live with her forever.

"Tara! Tara!" Her husband's bellow jolted her out of her reverie, and she nearly jumped out of her skin. She quickly pushed the clothes to the back of the wardrobe.

"I am coming. I am coming." The man behaved like a caveman sometimes. Why was he shouting her name for crying out loud? Hopefully, there would be peace when she shared the good news with him.

Her heart lifted a bit as she hurried into a casual t-shirt and shorts and ran out of the bedroom.

Tonight was going to be different from other nights and hopefully, she could recreate what she had with the stranger with her husband.

She chuckled to herself at the mere thought. If wishes were horses.

THREE

Olamiposi

It had been over 6 years since the night his home began to crumble like a pack of cards and their marriage would have been eleven years old today. He couldn't believe how much he still missed Miriam and was hurt from her betrayal. At least, she was happy in her new home and that was all that mattered.

A sad little smile danced around Olamiposi's mouth as he stared at his wedding ring. It had been sitting in a corner of his office desk since the divorce was finalized. He couldn't bring himself to dispose of it. His investment company was growing in leaps and bounds and she should have been part of this success but she decided to sell her shares to him. The fact that she was severing all ties to him cut him deeper than he expected and the heartache never went away but it had dulled with time. Anyways, it was for the best. There was no need hanging on to the past.

There was a light knock on his office door and he dropped the ring into the corner of his office drawer again.

It was time to focus on work. Maybe he wasn't lucky in the game of love but he could always pick his choice in the game of lust and sex. He only needed to wriggle his little finger and women would tumble into his bed, willingly. Nancy was his latest and most recent conquest. They were still at it but he was getting tired of the fling and something about her didn't sit well with him. He was getting too weary and old for this game.

"Come in." He sat back and turned on his laptop.

The door opened and Jason walked in. He was a junior executive in the Human Resource department.

"Good morning, sir. I am here to introduce your new personal assistance. Can I bring her in?" He stood at a respectable distance, waiting for his approval.

"I would have preferred a man though." He sat back and sighed. He had started off with a woman P.A, Daisy and she had done a great job while she was with him. She got married two years ago and relocated out of the country. The Japa syndrome. Arrgh. Her predecessors were complete disasters and they were both men. "Don't remind me of the past failures, though."

Jason's lips twitched with the urge to smile or laugh, but he only nodded politely and inclined his head, "Can I bring her in now?"

"Yes, please. Let's see what she has got to offer." He picked up the pen and rolled it between his fingers.

Jason went out, and came in with a young woman. She was dressed smartly in a brown skirt suit and white blouse. The colour did nothing to flatter her caramel skin and he wouldn't have spared her a second look if he had met her on the road except for her eyes. Before he could take a second look at it, she had lowered them and was staring at the floor.

She looked vaguely familiar. Had they met before? He frowned when she lowered her eyes and the simple gesture rang an alarm bell in his head. Where had they met before now? He had had too many women in his bed since his break-up with Miriam that he wasn't sure if she was among them.

Jason's voice brought him out of his reverie and he shook himself out of his thought, "Sir, meet your new Personal Assistant, her name is Omotara Jacobs. This is the Managing Director of Global Wealth Investment Limited, Mr Olamiposi Adewunmi."

"Good morning, sir. It is my pleasure to meet you sir." A shy smile spread over her innocent-looking angelic face as she met his probing gaze briefly before lowering it. He wasn't ready for the jolt of awareness that slammed into his gut or the lust that made his flesh rise against the zipper of his pants.

Oh Jesus! Is this the one he would be working with?

"How are you, Omotara? Are you ready to work with me? I have been called a few unpleasant names such as workaholic, mean boss and the likes." He rocked in his chair as his gaze dropped to her hands and noticed they were fiddling with the straps of her handbag. She was nervous.

He could bet his life he had seen that movement before but couldn't place it.

"Yes sir. I am ready." Another shy smile and he nearly groaned.

"That is fine. I have a management meeting in the next one hour. I will forward the files to your desk. Meet me in the boardroom in 45 minutes." He tapped a key on his laptop and it came to life. "And call me Olamiposi. That is my name."

"Okay si…. Olamiposi," she corrected herself on time, curtseyed slightly and followed Jason out of his office.

He released the breath he wasn't aware he was holding and sat back. He was fairly sure they had met before now but his brain refused to remember where or when and he was almost certain the meeting was sexual in nature. She seemed to have a reserved nature. If he couldn't remember her face, that only meant the meeting was fleeting or brief and she didn't strike him as the casual one-night stand type. Do women even have types? Bunch of green snakes under green grass gender…

A short humourless laugh escaped his pursed lips as he swivelled his plush leather seat from side to side with his fingers linked in front of him. He wasn't aware he was staring into space, lost in thought until his intercom phone shrieked loudly and he nearly jumped out of his seat.

He swore loudly before he snatched the phone off the cradle and barked into the mouth piece, "Who is this?"

"Sorry sir. This is Omotara. The management team is in the boardroom, waiting for you sir." Her hushed, smooth voice came over the line and he felt blood rushing downward again. He swore under his breath again as he adjusted his pants. "What did you say sir?"

"Do you have issues obeying simple instructions?" He tapped a finger on his keyboard and the laptop lit up, then he sent out the files he needed to her.

"No sir."

"Call me Olamiposi. Why is that so hard for you?" He growled, delighting in the fact that he had rattled her.

"Okay… Okay. I have received the files. Is there any other thing I need to have before going into the meeting, Olami?"

Olami? Wow.

The shortened form of his name rolling out of her lips pleased him immensely and he didn't want to explore the reason behind it.

"That is all for now. I will meet you in the boardroom in the next 10 minutes. Apologise on my behalf." He dropped the phone and exhaled loudly. This was going to be interesting.

FOUR

Omotara

Oh my God!

What kind of game was fate playing on her? Why did he have to be her boss? The man who had been haunting her dreams and her waking hours since that fateful night six years ago?

What was she going to do? She stared into the restroom mirror with eyes wide with fear and realized her body was shaking. It was a matter of time before he remembered her and she was worried he would fire her instantly once he did. Her first instinct was to turn around and leave the premises but she needed this job desperately. Ah! They would go hungry. Life had been tough since her husband sent her and her boy out two years ago. Getting a job hadn't been a walk in the park.

She only had a degree and diploma certificate to boast of. No professional experience except for her National youth service as a teacher and 3 month experience as a secretary to the meanest, most lecherous man she was unfortunate to work with. She had practically ran out of the office building one evening when he nearly succeeded in raping her.

 Fortunately, she didn't need to work when she got married. She was content being a full-time housewife and then a mother until even that wasn't working any longer. She sighed loudly.

She was lucky to get this job. She had brought her A game to the interview and luck had shone on her. Now, nemesis had to catch up with her this way. She needed this job desperately and would hold on for as long as possible. Her son's last term school fee was pending and if this man booted her out today, she honestly didn't know what she would do. She had better start giving him every good reason to let her stay from now on.

Olamiposi! Olami, my wealth! What a beautiful name!

A smile tugged at the corners of her lips and spread to her eyes. He was a fine man. He had grown even more good-looking than the last time they met and his well-trimmed beard, sprinkled with white added character to his striking face. He was a fine man indeed and she had no business fantasising over him or remembering the way he fitted perfectly between her thighs those years ago.

Oh my! She stared down at her puckered nipples in dismay and knew she had to tame her line of thought. It was time to get back to work. She adjusted her blouse and went out to do her duty.

The meeting went well and they attended several others after that. With the aid of a phone as a recorder and her notepad, she was able to capture the essence of the meetings and retired to her space to transfer it into the computer. She was glad for her short-hand skills now more than ever.

She was busy typing away on the keyboard when her phone rang sharply and she was startled. She gave a nervous laugh as she picked it up and gasped on realising it was past 5 p.m.. Her stomach growled loudly, reminding her she hadn't eaten all day. She still had a lot on her desk.

The after-hour center where her son, Ebunola stayed, would close by 6 p.m. and she hadn't made preparation for extra hours. Extra hours meant extra cost. She sighed. She really needed this job and hoped her secret would not be exposed anytime soon. The phone rang again and she picked up. It was one of his nannies, Mrs. Fabiyi aka Mama Ibeji.

"Mommy Ebun, Good evening. You are late today. Hope there is no problem?" The older woman's voice came through the line.

"I am so sorry, mama twins. I just got a new job and I didn't want to leave at the closing hour on dot."

"Ah! Oluwa seun oo. Thank God. Congratulations!" The woman was obviously dancing and she laughed out loud. The woman was aware of her recent struggles with finance and job-hunting.

"Thank you ma." She was grinning. "Please, I will pick him up a bit later than usual but I will make it worth your time."

"It is all right. I will be waiting. Come quick." The woman disconnected the phone and she did the same as she exhaled. Her stomach growled again. She needed to eat something but she couldn't afford to buy anything right now. She had to pay Mama Ibeji for her time. Every penny counted at this time.

"Did you go for lunch today?" Her boss's voice jolted her out of her thoughts and she schooled her face properly before turning to face him. Her heart was racing but even she didn't know why.

"No si…" She swallowed the rest of her sentence when he frowned at her. "No, I didn't go for lunch. I have a lot on my desk."

"I didn't go for lunch either and I am famished. Can we go to lunch together then? It is past closing hours so the canteen would have closed but there is an eatery close by." He was looking at his wrist-watch and didn't see her look of surprise.

"Thank you for the offer but I still have a lot to do." She glanced at the cursor blinking on the excel sheet on her computer.

"If you say so. Shut down and go home then. There is nothing urgent you need to do right now." His eyes were almost expressionless as he turned away to go back into his office but he paused with his hand on the door knob. "You have a kid, right?"

Her eyes widened in horror. Had he heard her side of the conversation with mama Ibeji? Was he averse to kids?

"Yes. Will that be an issue?" Her voice was almost a whisper.

"Will it be an issue?" He repeated with a raised eyebrow.

"No, it won't." She crossed her chest like a solemn oath.

"Good. Shut down and go home. That is a direct order. " He opened his office door and went in.

"Thank you, God." She completed the report, saved and shut down. She freshened up in the restroom and left the building in a hurry. She couldn't wait to see her boy. She had missed him badly. Finally, there was light at the end of the tunnel for them.

Traffic wasn't too bad on her way home and she stopped at the mini market at the bus-stop to get groceries before heading to the school. She was late and could as well make use of her time well.

Ebunola was outside, pretending to play with his toy gun but she knew he was waiting for her. She was grinning as she opened the gate and he came charging towards her but stopped a few steps from her.

"Mommy, you are late." His eyebrow winged up with accusation and her heart literally came to a stop. She just witnessed that single act on an older version of this little face. She stared in disbelief until the accusation turned to confusion. "Are you all right, Mommy?"

"I am fine, baby. Come here." He didn't need further prodding before he flew into her arms and she enveloped him in a bear hug.

She would do anything within her power to protect her secret.

FIVE

Olamiposi

She had a child? This could only mean there was the father of the child and invariably a husband or boyfriend somewhere.

He wasn't sure why the thought filled him with anger and spoiled his day that had been going so well. He was impressed with the way she joined his team seamlessly and continued from where the others left off as if she had always been part of the company. He had even dragged her into meetings that she didn't have to attend and her contribution had been enlightening. She hadn't disappointed him so far and he was aware of her presence throughout the meetings, even when he wasn't looking directly at her.

The way she bit on the corner of her cupid shaped lips when she was thinking or the way her eyes narrowed to a slit in concentration? Damn! Who was she and where had they met in the past? She wore no ring, even though there was a faint mark on her finger. He knew because he had checked out her fingers and ... he needed to remind himself that she was his personal assistant, not a potential date or sexual partner.

All he needed to do was to request for her data from the Human Resource department and he would have all the information he needed but he wasn't ready to stoop so low. No, there was time for everything.

He shut down his laptop, locked up his drawer and proceeded out of his office. Her office space was right in front of his but it was empty now. He was about to walk past it when he saw a sheet of writing pad on her otherwise clean table. He picked it up and studied the list of things she wanted to do at home. A smile of admiration tugged at his lips. She was cleaning up the mess left by his former assistants. If she kept up this momentum, she would turn into a workaholic.

He dropped the note in his backpack and proceeded to the car park where his driver was waiting for him. His first point of call was his favourite fish joint.

*****

Six months later, he was proven right. Tara was an organised and highly efficient workaholic. She planned every aspect of his business unless he wasn't directly involved in it. She reminded him of appointments and went into meetings on his behalf sometimes, then always proceeded to give him well detailed feedback. He had no complaint about her but knew no human could be that perfect.

His staff were well-paid and their welfare was well taken care of. He was amazed at the transformation in her in the short time she had been with the company. Apart from the fact that she had become curvier in all the right places, her taste in dressing had also improved tremendously and he couldn't help but admire her whenever she was in the room with him.

That sense of déjà vu still hit him whenever she turned those sexy slanted eyes on him and his third leg would recognise her presence but his brain refused to kick in. Where had they met before? The fact that she had a child still bothered him because he wasn't sure she was in a relationship or not.

His phone beeped with a message and he brought it out of his bag as he strolled out of the elevator. A heavy sigh escaped him as he stared at the message that just flashed across his phone.

I have a surprise for you tonight. Hurry home, baby.

It was from Nancy, his present girlfriend. He had kept her for too long and now, she was turning into a big-time nuisance. It had started as a casual affair with no strings attached but now, she was changing the rules of the game. She wanted to move in as his live-in girlfriend but he had refused point blank. He wasn't going to start living with a woman he wasn't married to. She went behind him and duplicated his house key to have unrestricted access to his home. It had caused their first real fight and he assumed he had gotten rid of her finally but he was obviously wrong.

"Good morning Tara. How are you this morning?" He smiled as he walked into her office.

"Good morning, Olamiposi. How was the virtual meeting with the artist, Aristo, last night?" She smiled as she opened her organiser and leafed through it. She wore a tomato red lipstick this morning and it made her lips inviting.

He shifted on his feet and transferred his backpack to the other hand. He needed to escape before his body betrayed him. "It was great, even though the guy is too pompous for my liking. He insisted on talking to me before he would sign anything with the company."

She chuckled at that. "But you worked your magic on him and got him on board, right?"

"Well, we are almost there. I will share his contact details with you shortly. Our accounting team will be meeting his own so we can finalise things and sign on the dotted line."

"That is a great one. I will inform Peter and the rest of the team to prepare. Congratulations to us in advance." Peter was the company secretary. With a tap on the keyboard, her organiser had opened and she was typing in it.

"Thank you, Tara. I need a personal favour from you." She turned her head, with a questioning look on her face. "I need to change the locks in my home and tighten up my security. Intruders have been invading my privacy."

"Hope you are all right? Are they people you know? Do I need to call the police or something?" There was concern in her voice. Did she really care for him? As a boss or a man she was interested in? He needed to get his head out of the gutter and focus on their professional relationship.

"No need to call the police. I am all right. I can handle it for now. Thank you for your concern." She studied him for a while until she seemed to believe him and smiled. Damn! He could fall for this babe.

"Please send me your house address. It will be done and completed before the end of the day."

"You are a lifesaver. Thank you. I will send it as soon as I settle in the office." He grinned as he marched towards his office door. "You deserve a raise."

"I will hold you to that, boss!" They both chuckled at that and he was whistling when he went into his office. His day just started on a good note.

*****

An irate Nancy was waiting outside his apartment, dressed in his house robe and that angered him more than anything. He alighted from his car, collected the car key from his driver and sent him home. He didn't want to be the object of grapevine gossip in his office the following day.

"What is going on here?" He kept his voice low as he approached her. His gateman, Emeka, was a few metres away with his ears on alert.

"I should be asking you the same question. I went out to get groceries for us, spent a few hours at the nail and hair salon, then came back to find out I have been locked out of the house." She spat at him.

"Well, that obviously serves you right because you should have called me before coming uninvited into my home." He moved to deactivate the new security installed, opened the door and strolled in. She charged after him and almost collided against his back.

"So, you did this deliberately to humiliate and embarrass me right? I can no longer come into my fiancé's home any longer without calling first? Are you cheating on me?" She blinked rapidly and tears filled her eyes. Oh, man! What was this for crying out loud? He hated dealing with crying women.

He stood upright and refused to allow her tears to get to him, "Nancy, I am not your fiancé. We had an agreement and if you are no longer comfortable with it, I think you should leave." He turned away and realized his sitting room was a mess. There were female magazines littered everywhere and other female articles he didn't want to inspect too closely. What had he gotten himself into?

"You are definitely cheating on me. Is she the one who gave you this for fucking her so well?" There was a sneer in her voice and he turned round with a dreadful feeling in the pit of his tummy. She was holding wads of cash and the single piece of note that had given him nightmares for a long time.

"Where did you get that?" He moved with the speed of lightning and snatched the items out of her grasp before she could blink.

"Who is she? Is she prettier than I am? What is she giving you that I can't?" Desperation coloured her voice as she moved closer and he stepped away. He didn't like the look in her eyes at all.

"Nancy, I am giving you 5 minutes to get out of my house. Otherwise, I will call the security to bundle you out." He turned on his heel and almost ran into the guestroom. She was a crazy woman. Time to run for his dear life.

He locked the door after him and sank into the unmade bed in the room. His heart was racing but he couldn't relax until he was sure she had left his home. He waited with bated breath, staring at the door. He heard her footsteps approaching and tension filled every cell of his body.

"I have planned a special dinner to celebrate us and treat you like a king but you messed up big time, Olamiposi." Her breathing slowed for a while and she laughed lightly. "When I want something badly enough, I will pay any price to get it. I want you and I will be right back." There was a pause, then he heard her receding footsteps and complete silence afterward.

He exhaled deeply as his shoulders slumped in relief. His eyes fell on the old wad of cash and piece of paper in his hands. Who was she? Olamiposi stared at the note intently, something about it niggling at the back of his head. He dropped it beside him on the bed and reached for his bag. He needed to make an urgent call. He remembered dropping the phone somewhere in the bag immediately he saw Nancy, standing in front of his apartment.

Instead of locating his phone, his hand came across a writing pad and he brought it out. A smile tugged at his lips. It was Omotara's to-do list on her first day at work. He intended to give it to her the following day but he forgot. Staring at it now, a frown replaced the smile on his face as he realized the handwriting was the same as the one on the piece of paper his mystery one night lay left behind almost 6 years ago, saying, *"Thank you."*

He picked it up and laid the papers side by side. There was no doubt about it. The handwriting belonged to the same person! He stared in absolute astonishment. What the fuck!

SIX

Omotara

They just secured a deal with another new client, Olive Estates and Properties. It was a big one for them. However, the company's headquarters was located in Abuja and they had to travel for a final meeting with the Board of Directors. She was one of the team members going to Abuja and they had only a day to prepare for the journey. The jitters hit her and she ran into the restroom immediately after the meeting.

She stood at the sink, running the water and staring at the mirror. Why did Olami insist that she should travel with them? Fair enough, she had worked her butt off to make herself indispensable to him and the team. Her probation days were over and she had been confirmed with a raise in her salary.

It made a huge difference in her and Ebunola's life. The company also had a great welfare package for the staff and it was a huge relief to be able to take her son to the hospital without being scared of the bills. He always got sickly whenever a new school term began. It was as if he came home with all the infections the other kids had accumulated over the holiday break.

Where would he stay when she was away on the overnight trip to Abuja?

She inhaled and exhaled softly as she relived the short intense conversation between her and Olamiposi shortly after the meeting. The expression on his face was what she remembered the most. Come to think of it, he had been giving her this weird, smouldering look whenever he thought she wasn't watching since...her face scrunched up as she tried to remember the day. It was the day after she changed the lock in his home and updated the security. Why did he need to do that anyway? Crazy girlfriend or mad neighbour? She was curious but not brave enough to ask him.

"Omotara, I need you on that team going to Abuja," He had told her when she protested after the meeting ended.

"But there is nothing for me to do there. Someone needs to be here to manage the company when you are not in."

"That is why there is a Vice President and the rest of the investment analyst team. They will do just fine. You are my personal assistant, and you should be wherever I am." The way his voice lowered on the last sentence and the look in his eyes made her heart flutter in her chest. Was she reading too much meaning to his words? Their eyes met and held for several humming seconds before she mumbled an excuse and hurried out of the room.

Her phone rang, and she was startled out of her reverie. She had forgotten the damn thing was inside her pocket. She whipped it out and stared at it. It was her friend, Linda calling. Just the woman she needed right now.

"Hey, PA Omotara." Her friend's laughing voice hit her the moment she picked up the call.

"You are not well, I swear." She hissed but there was no sting in her voice. Linda laughed heartily. "I need your help jor. There is fire on the mountain." She lowered her voice as she peeped into the two female toilet stalls to be sure she was alone.

"Superhero Linda to the rescue. Tra la la."

"Can you be serious for once?" she reprimanded her, even as she laughed too.

"The serious ones are in Yaba left." They laughed at that. "I am on leave, so I have all the time in the world." Her friend was a workaholic and rarely went on leave unless there was a family emergency or she was going on vacation outside the country.

"Are you all right, babe?"There was concern in her voice.

"Another relationship just hit the ceiling and I am back to square 1. Unfortunately, his company is one of my best clients. I need a few days to cool off and put myself together. It is always a bad idea to mix business with pleasure." Her heavy sigh, tinged with misery, reached Omotara over the phone. Linda was a corporate banker and was steadily climbing the success ladder to the top but her love life was zero. She always ended up with the wrong men.

"I am so sorry, babe. You know what? I and Ebunola will come over after work and we can talk better."

"That would be great. That is exactly what I need right now. I miss that young man. Better still, prepare for a sleepover and I would be glad to host you." Her cheerful voice was back. Almost.

"Deal. See you soon, babe." Omotara clicked off, took a deep breath and walked out of the restroom.

*****

"Oya, enough of my sour love story. Spill everything right now." They had just put Ebunola to bed in Linda's spare room and were tip-toeing out of the room.

It was always great, to connect again. They talked mostly on the phone and rarely had time to see physically. They had a hearty meal of garri and rich seafood Afang after which Ebun dozed off on Linda's lap.

"I need to be away on a 2-day trip to Abuja with my boss and the rest of the team. I am not comfortable with Ebun staying overnight with Mama Twins but it seems I don't have a choice now." Omotara sighed as she pulled the door closed and headed to the sitting room.

Linda went to her mini wine bar in the corner of her sitting room and joined her friend with a bottle of red wine and wine glasses, "He can stay with me while you are away. He will keep me busy, and take my mind off my woes."

Both she and Ebunola had stayed with Linda overnight several times and Linda had babysitted him during the day if the need arose as long as she was available.

"You are Godsent, babe. I swear. You always come through for me." She leaned over and planted a kiss on her friend's face.

"Get away, Lesbo." Linda jerked away, with a grimace and she burst into laughter. "Now, tell me about that sexy boss of yours."

Omotara stared into her wineglass for several seconds before lifting her eyes to meet her friend's expectant own and lowering her voice, "My sexy boss is Ebun's biological father."

"Jesus! Say that again!" Linda's whispering voice belied the bulge of her eyeballs as the wineglass dropped to the tiled floor and she jumped. "Shit! Shit!" She ran into the kitchen and came back with a sweeping brush and dustpan.

They both cleaned up the room and settled down for their gist.

"Are you for real?" Linda frowned at her. "But he was a random man you met at that hotel that night, nah?"

"Yeah, he was but I recognised him because I took the time to study him that night. I was in the bar before he came in and it was obvious he was bent on drowning his sorrows in booze. That was an advantage for me. I didn't want a man who would be lucid enough to recognise me." She shrugged but a reminiscent smile was playing around her lips.

"Why him? Why did you choose him amongst all the men who were in that bar that night?" Linda watched her curiously as she swirled the freshly poured drink in her glass.

"I honestly can't say. I was at the bar, not really drinking but watching the entrance of the club for any suitable candidate and of course, doubting my sanity. The moment he strolled in, I knew he was the one and went to join his table when he was inebriated." Her smile was self-deprecating.

"Hmmm." Linda sipped her drink, her gaze locked on hers. "If he hasn't recognised you over 6 months that you have been working for him, I sincerely doubt that he will now. You didn't leave anything behind that could point to you, right?"

Omotara brought out her phone, flipped through the gallery and gave it to her friend, "One of the pictures we took during one of our victory periods. He is big on celebrating every little win. He is the one holding the bottle of wine and …."

"Laughing. Ebun is his spitting image." Linda ended as she stared intently at the picture. "Babe, you will be in a big pot of trouble if he finds out. IF. In my opinion, you are still safe."

"Yes, if he finds out." She swirled her drink and took a long sip. "We are going to Abuja and I am hoping to God we won't be in any sort of proximity."

"Ah! Do you still have a crush on him? Oh wow." Linda clapped her hands with glee. "This got even better." They both laughed.

It was past midnight when they staggered to the bedroom and fell face down into bed.

SEVEN

Olamiposi

She was nervous.

She did her job efficiently and he appreciated her contribution at the meeting which finally sealed the contract. She avoided being alone in the same room with him or holding eye contact with him for too long. She was either twisting the pen in her hands or the straps of her handbag if it was close enough.

The latter transported him back to that fateful night years ago which he had put a lid on. The memory of it sent blood to his nether region and his pants were suddenly too tight. He had no business thinking about this in the middle of a business meeting but each time he looked at her which was almost throughout the meeting, he couldn't help the excitement coursing through him.

How he had survived the last 6 months that they had been working together was a miracle. The more he studied her, the more he respected and liked her. Her outward calmness belied the fire and passion he knew was locked beneath, waiting to be unleashed. It had helped them win over a few annoying customers when the team would have thrown in the towel.

Her weird sense of humour was also refreshing and entertaining. She would make a joke out of a dark situation, even in the most tense moment and the whole boardroom would dissolve into laughter. Damn!

The woman was a marvel. She also loved her food. She wasn't a glutton by any standard but she always cleaned her plate the few times they were out on official lunch or dinner dates. He loved women who eat well. Remembering the way she broke chicken or meat bones to pieces stylishly made him want to burst into laughter and he coughed slightly to hide his amusement.

She glanced at him as if she knew he was thinking about her and he pretended to write on his notepad. He didn't want her to note the amusement or admiration he had for her. Could this meeting end already? He sighed silently as he brought his mind back to the present and glanced subtly around him until his gaze rested on her slender fingers flying over her phone's keypads as she typed rapidly.

Who would have thought such a professional woman was also a single mother? He tried to drop her off at her bus stop or asked the company driver to do so whenever it seemed she was running late to pick up her child. For reasons best known to her, she seemed to prefer the company driver to him. A frown marred his face as he doodled on his notepad but shrugged off the confusion. They would have a chat very soon.

Who was that idiot who left such a strong, yet beautiful and smart woman to take care of herself and her child alone? It was his loss anyway and another chance for him to get to know her. Oh, man! You were a goner. His lips curved in a weary smile but he felt no regret and that surprised him.

The meeting took almost all day and after signing the binding contract, the team declared an impromptu party. An hour break was declared to freshen up and change clothes, then everyone would convene at the hotel's lounge.

He took a cold refreshing bath and changed into casual pants and an open-neck t-shirt. He picked up a fancy crossbody bag and left his room. He had a mission to accomplish, and it would be done tonight. A short walk down the tiled corridor, he paused and knocked on a door to the third room to his own on the right. There was a clatter and a swear. His lips curved in a smile, then she responded with a polite, "Who is it?"

"It is Olamiposi. Can I have a few minutes with you urgently please?"

"Sure." There was a rustle, a click and the door slid open. She held it open narrowly and stood in the gap with a questioning look on her face. It was obvious she had no intention of letting him in. "Hope everything is all right? The team is still meeting right?"

"Yes, we are. You are part of the team. Can I come in please?" His voice was polite.

"Okay." Her voice was reluctant but she opened the door wider and stepped aside for him to walk in. She locked the door and folded her arms across her chest as she faced him. She wore a robe and her short braids were packed on top of her head.

He looked around as he gathered his thoughts. Her room was similar to his but she had added a little feminine touch to hers.

"I am almost ready to go downstairs but I need to call home in case I am unable to make the call tonight."

"How is your son?"

"He is fine. Thank you for asking." Her brow winged up in surprise. He had never asked about him before.

He gave a tiny shrug, moved to the dressing table and brought out the contents of the bag. He turned around with it and watched the blood drain from her face as her gaze landed on it. Her legs seemed to give out and she dropped down like a stone. Fortunately, the bed was right behind her and her bum connected with it.

He didn't take his eyes off her as he moved closer. Her pulse was beating fast in her throat and her lips were parted in shock.

"Oh shit. I am in trouble. How long have you known this?" She didn't look up.

"Not quite long ago. Are you my mysterious beautiful woman?" His voice was a whisper, but it drew her attention, and she raised her gaze to meet his own.

"Have you been looking for me? Please don't fire me. My life depends on this job." There was desperation and something else in her voice. He drew closer and dropped beside her on the bed. She didn't move away but he could see the rapid beating of the pulse in her throat and the rise and fall of her boobs above the robe.

She smelt like jasmine and sunshine, and he paused slightly before nuzzling her throat. Her smell made him want to cuddle and hold her forever. Bullocks! This was nothing but lust. He took a mental step back. She inhaled sharply and didn't push him away. He nipped the side of her neck and her lips parted in a moan. He knew he was a goner already.

"Does that mean you knew who I was when you started working for me?" He dropped his souvenir and framed her face. He watched as fear replaced the budding desire in her eyes. "Please don't lie to me."

"Yes, I recognised you the moment we were introduced on my first day at work. I didn't know your name or the place you work or who you were when I approached you that night." She tried to move away but he increased the pressure slightly around her face.

"No, you don't get off so easily. So I was just the one-night stand to you, right? Hmm." He licked her lips and felt a shudder go through her body. "I have been wanting to do that since the moment you walked into my office. Your lips are so sexy." He mumbled almost to himself as he watched her lips shudder apart.

"It wasn't like that. Please let me think." She raised her hands to his shoulders to push him away but held onto him when he buried his head in the curve of her neck and nuzzled. Another moan escaped her lips, and it enraged the beast, struggling to be free from him.

"Don't think, babe. Your brain is one of the things I admire about you but at this moment, I want it this way." He rained kisses on her face as he murmured dirty sexy words that seemed to stoke the fire in her restless body while his hands wandered and he swallowed her moans.

The next moment, it was as if something snapped in her and transported them back to that sizzling, fateful night years back. They were all over each other, struggling to remove all barriers between them and trying to catch their breath as they pleasured each other with their hands, fingers, and lips.

Their bodies and souls eventually joined in an explosive climax that had them panting for breaths.

EIGHT

Omotara

She couldn't believe they barely made it back for the party. He had the guts to suggest that they ditch the party and go for another round but she refused. It was bad that she was ruining her reputation. Her life and work were at stake. If Olamiposi decided to let her go now, she didn't know what she was going to do. She wasn't comfortable with the fact that she hadn't had time to speak her mind and find out what he had decided to do about them. Of course, he still wanted the cookie he had years ago.

Could she blame him for wanting what she was eager to give again? That was not to talk of the fact that she hadn't told him about the real reason she approached him years ago and what came out of it.

What was it about him that always made her lose her home training? The moment he touched her, she was mindless. Her self-deprecating thought was replaced by confusion when he joined her in the bathroom, bathed her with a mischievous glint in his eyes and helped her get dressed. He also packed the thank-you gift she gave him years ago and put it back in his bag.

"Won't you return those to me?" She wanted to trash the reminder of her foolishness years ago.

"The souvenirs were mine and they will be in my custody always," he responded as he ushered her out of the room. He went to his room to put the bag there before they proceeded to the party. All these times, he held her hand loosely in his and refused to let go. Each time she tried to move away, he moved effortlessly with her and got himself glued to her side.

It earned them curious looks from her team members, and she began to feel uncomfortable. They hadn't had time to sit down and talk and she wasn't sure of his reaction when he knew the reason behind her wayward action years ago. She dreaded his reaction when he knew. As it stood, she wasn't sure of what he wanted from her and why he was glueing himself to her side.

After the party, he came to the room with her and wanted to spend the night with her so they could talk but she knew as long as they were in the same room together, alone, no decent conversation would take place. She claimed to be tired and shooed him away.

However, the memory of the afternoon tryst between them kept her awake and her body craved more of it. She blamed the craving on her state of long abstinence. That was why she was craving his body like a loose woman. She was cranky as she prepared for their morning flight to Lagos the following day and refused to sit beside him, in his business class cabin.

On landing in Lagos, they were given the rest of the day off and she went straight to Linda's place. The latter was not around and Ebun was still in school. She dropped her bag in the room, went to take her bath and dropped into bed.

*****

She was woken up by the clatter of feet and laughter from the sitting room as Linda and Ebun went about their business in the house. She stumbled out of bed, pulled on a t-shirt, went into the room and found them wolfing down snacks and cold drinks. A frown of disapproval formed on her face and the two looked startled to see her but it was Ebun who recovered first.

"Mommy!" he squealed as he jumped onto his feet and ran to give her a bear hug. "I missed you so much."

"I don't think so. You know this junk you are eating is not allowed in my house," she chided as she hugged him back and planted kisses on his face. He giggled with delight and stepped back to finish his snacks. She turned to her friend.

"I know I am a bad aunty but we are entitled to snacks once in a while. It smelled and tasted so good, right? Ebun." She turned a sheepish smile to Ebun who nodded vigorously as he stuffed the last of the bite into his mouth.

"Yes, Aunty Linda," he mumbled around a mouthful.

"Horrible aunty indeed," Tara chided before hugging her friend. "I missed you both."

"We missed you too and now, you guys will leave me in my misery again." Linda made a puppy eye at her.

"So you can be feeding us with junk? It won't work. You will be all right." She gave her a playful push and went into the kitchen.

"Ebun, change your uniform and do your homework," Linda was saying as she walked into the kitchen behind her and stood watching her for a moment. "Did something happen apart from the business meeting?" Her voice dropped to a near whisper.

"Geez! Is it written all over my face?"She slapped her palm over her face in exasperation.

"Well, I know you so well. Who is the lucky dude who popped the cherry the second time?" Linda grinned from ear to ear.

"You are not serious. I am not exactly a fan of sex except with…well, sex wasn't one of the things I missed in marriage." She shrugged as she moved to the sink to wash the dishes. Linda wasn't a fan of domestic chores.

"Except with a certain young man who gave you the best sex of your life." Linda moved to stand beside her to peer into her face. "Is he the one again?" There was disbelief in her voice.

"He found out who I was. I don't know how he put two and two together, but he confronted me with the souvenirs I left for him that night." She turned to face her friend.

"It is a lie." Linda's jaw dropped in surprise. "Tell me how it happened." She did.

"It is as if that man has my mumu button. I went wild over him just like that night. Instead of us having a decent conversation like two grown adults, just a touch, Linda, and I turned into a wanton woman." She was confused and filled with self-loathing. "Even after I turned him away that night, I couldn't sleep. My body refused to settle down and behave itself. I nearly lost my manners and was tempted to crawl to his room, begging him to have me all over again." Tears filled her eyes.

"Did he use protection?" Linda was blunt as usual.

"You mean a condom?" She nodded. "Yes…No…I can't remember. I don't know. Am I all right like this?" Omotara was almost wailing.

"Keep it down, babe. It is not too late. It is still under 48 hours. We can still get an after-sex tablet tonight. As for the possibility of STD, you may have to go for a test."

"Thank you, Linda. What will I do without you?" Her shoulders sagged with relief.

"There is nothing wrong with you. You are physically and sexually attracted to the man plus he is good in bed. Every woman wants a man who can bring out that part of them but very few end up that lucky."

"Am I supposed to be relieved by your words?"She frowned at her friend.

"I don't know. I am just stating a fact here. The attraction has been there right from the first time you met him and it never went away.

Now, you are both single and available. Why don't you explore the possibility of building a relationship with him?"

"You seem to be forgetting something here. He is my boss."

"So? Is it today that office romance has been in existence?" Linda arched her brow.

"No, but I have my reservations. If it backfires, I have a lot to lose. My job will be at stake unless I want to start looking for another one now. I also have a secret I have yet to tell him."

"This is the opportunity to tell him if he asks you out properly. I think you should push for that, rather than falling on his dick whenever he snaps a finger." There was mischief in Linda's voice as she took a step back from the venom in her friend's eyes.

"You are a goat, I swear."

"Mommy, your phone is ringing." Ebun came in with her vibrating phone moments later.

"Thank you, darling." It wasn't a call, it was a message from Olamiposi. He was asking her to hang out with him tonight. She held up the message to Linda and the latter's face broke into an excited grin.

"Go for it, girl. There is no harm in trying."

"Thank you, babe. I will."

NINE

Olamiposi

Nancy was stalking him.

The shit was beginning to scare the living daylight out of him as he stared at the latest love message from her. She had been sending gifts to his house, ranging from a set of briefs to pam sandals, a gold wristwatch and a wallet. He didn't allow his security to bring it into his home before he gave him a sound warning and a threat to his job if he ever received any such gift on his behalf from the woman or her messenger.

He blocked her from his contact and all his social media accounts but she was relentless in her pursuit. He had lost count of the number of mobile numbers she had used to call or text him, begging for a date or at least a hangout. He swivelled his seat from side to side, rubbing his clean-shaven jaw as he stared at the text message. Should he report her to the police? Knowing Nigerian police well, they would likely laugh at him for running from a willing woman. She hadn't hurt him in any way yet, but he was scared she was capable of violence if she realized she wouldn't be getting what she wanted. What kind of problem had he gotten himself into?

There was a light knock on the door before it opened and Omotara strolled in with a wrapped gift. His chest filled up with warmth, even as his loin responded to her presence and peace replaced the anxiety in his heart. She was good for him. Their hangout weeks ago had been surprisingly devoid of the usual white-hot passion but filled with easy banter, laughter and meaningless gist. They went to the movies and took a stroll afterward before he dropped her at home later that night.

They were officially dating for almost 4 months now and he would have preferred to go public but Omotara wanted to keep it low for now. In the office, she would go all official on him until he decided not to be official and delighted in ruffling her professional façade.

"You have a package." There was curiosity in her voice as she dropped the wrapped package on his desk.

"From who? You didn't even check if it was a time bomb," he teased as he got to his feet and came around his desk. He made no move to touch the package. He knew where it came from.

"Really? You want me to die, right? Your plan will not work." She raised an eyebrow at him.

"Nah, no one will die. What will it benefit me if you die?" He snatched her off the floor and planted her ass on his desk. She caught her breath as her hands settled on his shoulders to balance herself. He fitted snugly between her lap and pressed his bulging hardness against her lower tummy.

"Won't you open your gift?"Her voice came out breathlessly.

"No, I know where it came from and I have no need for it but I'm still thinking about what to do with the sender though." He nipped at her neck, and she moaned.

"The door is not locked. Anyone can come in ….oh." Her voice ended in a moan when he nipped at her nipple through her shirt. He made love to her mouth while he moulded her boobs through the cotton shirt and loved the little tremors coursing through her slim frame.

A finger trailed from a poking nipple, down her belly and settled on her exposed thighs. He stroked the puffy lips of her pussy through her lacy panties and her breathing quickened, causing her boobs to rise and fall rapidly. Moisture soaked the seat of her panties and her body jerked when he finally slid a digit into her warm, wet, wet coochie. Her arms tightened around his neck and she deepened the kiss. She was so responsive to his touch and it was one of the things he loved most about her.

"Hmm…" He crooked his finger inside of her, hitting her G-spot and turned her moans into one high-pitched orgasm. She shuddered against him and her legs trembled around him. It unleashed the beast in him. "I want you now."

Their mouths merged and mated while they both struggled to unbuckle his belt and zipped him down. His pants and white briefs came down halfway, freeing his hard pulsing manhood. He slid in smoothly and they gasped in satisfaction. He began to move and her world tilted.

He started with a low tempo, waiting for her to adjust to his increasing girth as each thrust dug him deeper into her core and he hissed through clenched teeth. Her jasmine scent wafted into his nose and he groaned.

His thrust grew in momentum, his hips shooting in and out of her like a piston and she clung to him as her moan increased in pitch. He tried to shush her to keep her voice down but his balls tightened in anticipation and he groaned as a climax ripped through him. Her own followed almost immediately and their breath seized as the aftermath of the sexual marathon settled between them. Their eyes met, held for a few sizzling moments and both burst into laughter.

"You are a crook, I swear." She slid down from the desk and her legs threatened to dissolve beneath her but he caught and held her until she regained her balance. "Get away from me." She pushed away from him and walked into his ensuite restroom/ bathroom to clean up.

He cleaned himself up with a tissue and gave a glance at the package on his desk. His mouth twisted with displeasure as he sighted Nancy's name on the package. He called the security and told him to come and pick up the package.

"Sir, you have a meeting in the next ten minutes," Omotara announced in her most professional voice as she came out of the restroom and sashayed out of his office with a mischievous smile on her face.

"Yes ma'am." He grinned and was still grinning as he sauntered into the conference room for the meeting.

***

He was on a call with a client later in the day when the door opened abruptly and Omotara came in. She looked worried and frantic but was obviously trying to pull herself together.

"Excuse me, Prof. I will give you a callback." He ended the call as he got to his feet. "What is the problem?"

"My son…" She gulped and linked her fingers together. "He had an accident on the playground and broke his arm. I need to leave now please."

"I am so sorry about that. Have you spoken to him yet?"He placed his palm over her hands and squeezed, then pulled her in for a hug. "He will be all right, babe."

Her arms went around him and she held onto him until her shaky breath evened out, "Thank you. No, I only spoke to his class teacher. He lost a lot of blood because he and his friends were trying to manage the situation until a teacher noticed them. He has been taken to the hospital."

"We are leaving together. I will call my driver to get ready now."

"No!" Her voice was abrupt and full of panic. He paused as he was about to call his driver. "Don't bother, please. I have everything under control." She smiled but the smile didn't reach her eyes.

"No, you don't have things under control. You are scared and worried and all you want right now is to be by your son's side. That is fine and normal but you are my woman, Omotara. We are not on one-night stands or in a casual relationship. Whatever concerns you, concern me, so we are visiting that young man together. The meeting is long overdue anyway."

"But...okay." She subsided and turned away as he called his driver's number. He watched her back as he spoke to him.

Why didn't she want him to come along? She still didn't trust him? If he had his choice, this relationship would have gone further than this but she kept slowing them down. All this hide-and-seek was getting on his nerves and they would have a discussion soon. It hurt badly and he realised she had the power to hurt him much more.

He should have learnt his lesson from his first marriage and now he was heading eyes open into another heartbreak. It was time to take a step back.

TEN

Omotara

She was in trouble.

Her son was somewhere in the hospital, hurting badly and all she could think of was the fact that she was about to hurt this man terribly. She knew she should have summoned the courage to tell him the truth but each time she wanted to, her courage failed her. She still remembered their conversation about the reason his first marriage failed and she cringed inwardly.

"I wasn't man enough for her, Tara. I couldn't even father a child. She only needed to cheat on me with one man and she got pregnant. She got the one thing we had been trying to achieve all the time we had been together." He'd said reflectively as he swirled the wine in his glass but she could see the pain lurking in his eyes and her heart hammered in her chest.

She wondered if this was the right time to tell him her secret but she didn't want to spoil the moment or see hatred for her burning in his eyes. She couldn't stand it and decided another opportunity would come when she would bear her mind to him.

"Don't say that, please. You are probably not destined to be together." She had reached over and put her hand over his. *"Every marriage has its ups and downs."*

"Come here." He had pulled her to his side and wrapped his arms around her. *A sense of contentment wrapped around both and they sat like that for several minutes, soaking up each other's warmth.* She could fall in love with this man.

Guilty conscience didn't allow her to sleep that night. She turned and tossed, thinking about the best way to break the news to him. In the end, she lost her nerve again and postponed the inevitable until it was too late. *Oh God!* How was she going to deal with this?

She glanced furtively at his face as the driver pulled up in the parking space of the hospital premises. His face was cast in stone and he refused to look at her. He was probably angry because she didn't want him to come along. She missed their conversation, his comforting touch and humor but it was just as well. She jumped out of the car the moment it came to a stop and rushed into the hospital. Ebun's class teacher, Mrs. Oduwole, was waiting in the reception and she came forward immediately after she sighted them.

"Good afternoon, ma. You are welcome." She greeted politely before turning to Olamiposi who was right beside her and gasped, "Are you Ebunola's dad? It is so nice to meet you."

Omotara could cheerfully strangle this nosey woman as she stared daggers at her but the latter was oblivious to her impotent anger.

"Thank you, madam. How is he doing now? How bad is it?" There was concern in his voice and her eyes shot to his face. Was he really concerned about a child he had never met?

"Please come along." Mrs. Oduwole introduced them to the nurse on duty who took them to the emergency room where Ebun was.

All thought flew from her head when she saw her son's arm wrapped in a cast that was beginning to get soaked with blood. He looked pale and worn out but awake. His eyes lit up when he saw his mother and Omotara rushed to his side.

"Oh, my baby!" She hugged him as much as she could and dropped kisses all over his face.

"My arm hurt so much, Mommy." Tears filled his eyes and he clung to her with his good arm.

"I am so sorry, baby. The nurses and doctor will make you feel better, okay?" She dropped a kiss on his forehead and turned to realise Olamiposi was in deep conversation with the nurse and the class teacher.

"He needs a pint or two of blood to replace what he lost. Otherwise, he will be fine. He is a healthy young boy and will heal faster than you imagine. Please go and see the doctor now."

"Thank you, nurse Chiamaka. We will do that right away." He smiled at both women and resentment bubbled in her. Who was he to be interfering in her family business? The nurse was supposed to be talking to her and not him.

Your son doesn't belong to you alone, A voice reminded her but she stamped it down and concentrated on the present event that was fast spiralling out of her control. How could he just come on board and jump into her personal affair as if he owned her life?

"Thank you, Mrs. Oduwole. You can go now. We will take it up from here." She smiled at the middle-aged woman.

"Okay, ma. On behalf of the school management, we are deeply sorry for this negligence. The teacher on the playground went to ease herself for a few minutes and it happened before she came back. We will gladly bear all the hospital bills." The woman raised her hands in supplication as she looked pleadingly from one face to the other.

"It is all right. Kids will always be kids. I will appreciate it if an adult is always around to supervise them."

"This is noted ma. I will keep calling for an update. Bye ma, sir." Omotara saw him squeeze a wad of naira notes into the woman's hand and a big grin spread over her face. Money made the world go round. The woman would worship Ebun till he left her class.

"Hey, young man. How are you feeling?" Olamiposi sat on the other edge of the hospital bed and smiled at him.

"Better. Good afternoon, sir." There was a shy smile on his young face as he looked at him under his eyelids.

"Brave, brave boy. If I am the one, I will be crying like a baby. I am sure it is awfully painful." He touched the cast with reverence, with the look of hero worship on his face.

Ebunola giggled, "Really? You will cry?"

"Yes, I will. You are such a brave young man."

"I cried. A little. It is still hurting me." His voice lowered as he swallowed hard. "Does that still make me a hero?" His eyes sought validation from the older man.

"Yes, you are. I am super proud of you. My name is Olamiposi." He reached out his hand and the little boy put his smaller one in his.

"Ebunola. Are you my mom's boss?"

"Yes, son. I am glad to meet you. We need to go and see the doctor now." He bent and whispered into his ear. "Do you like chocolate? I love them."

Even though Omotara didn't hear Olamiposi's questions, the mischievous look in Ebun's eyes gave her the answer and she rolled her eyes skyward. The identical look in their eyes made her heart constrict and she prayed her secret would be saved for a little bit longer.

Ebun nodded vigorously and whispered back, "My mommy doesn't like chocolates. Don't let her know,"

"Cross my heart." Olamiposi crossed his heart with a solemn look and Ebun giggled again. "How old is Ebun?"

"I am five!"

"Wow. You can't be. You are such a big boy" Olamiposi high-fived him but she observed the tiny frown on his face. Was he doing the maths already? Oh, Lord! She was in trouble.

"We need to go and see the doctor now. We will be right back, okay, big boy?" He winked at the little boy and strolled out of the ward, closely followed by Omotara.

"You don't need to come with me. I can handle this myself. I am truly grateful for your support." The words came out in a hurry.

The moment they rounded a corner, a few steps from the doctor's office, he grabbed her arms and held her against the wall, "Is there something I need to know?"

Oh No! Not now. "No… why do you ask?" She swallowed hard and smiled but she knew it was a grimace. Her doomsday was here. No more hiding place for the wicked.

He watched her for a while, obviously not believing her but released her and put his hands in his pocket, "That is fine then. Let's go and see the doctor. That boy needs our attention."

The word, "Our" caught her attention and her heart thudded in her chest. This was the perfect opportunity to spill the beans and she cleared her throat. It was at that time that the nurse from earlier in the evening walked passed and Olamiposi beckoned to her. Omotara clamped her lips together and bolted to the doctor's office. Of course, luck was not on her side. He was right behind her as she went into the doctor's office.

"Good evening sir, madam. You must be Ebun's dad. The resemblance is so striking." Doctor Fabiyi was smiling as he got to his feet and stretched out his hand.

"Good evening, sir. Thank you for your help." Olamiposi was already shaking the doctor's outstretched hand firmly with a friendly smile that got nowhere near his eyes. Omotara knew the game was up and felt as if the ground should open and swallow her.

"You are welcome, sir. He was brought here just in time and the minor surgery was successful but we need to replace the lost blood as

soon as possible. You will go to the lab now and run some tests, sir."
Doctor Fabiyi was typing in the system in front of him before picking
up a notepad, scribbling on it and giving it to him.

"Thank you, Doctor. We will be right back." His hand circled her
wrist in a vice-like grip and pulled her out of the office.

"That is the second time I have heard that statement. Why does your
son look like me, Omotara?" he gritted through clenched teeth as he
glowered down at her, caging her in his arms. Her tongue felt heavy
as she stared at him and her fingers entwined in a vice-like grip on his.
It was now or never. "It is almost 6 years since we had unprotected
sex in that hotel room and Ebun is 5 years. Tell me what I am
thinking is insane." His whisper was filled with anguish.

"It is true. Ebunola is your biological son," she blurted out and felt as
if a burden was lifted off her shoulders.

He turned around and walked away from her.

ELEVEN

Olamiposi

A vein stood out of his neck and his head pounded as he stared at the test result. Their blood group and genotype were a match. He would still have to carry out a DNA test, but he was almost sure the DNA would be 99.99 % positive. Once again, he had fallen victim to another woman's deceit. Would he ever learn from his past mistakes? The other one followed another man because she believed he couldn't father a child. This one used him to get a child and fostered the child on another man. Why was he so unlucky in love and relationship?

Just when he believed he had found the woman of his dreams, she turned out to be a liar, a cheat and a whore. What kind of woman fucked a random man anyway? To his horror, tears filled his eyes and he walked briskly to the back of the hospital to avoid meeting anyone. He had donated his blood and his son would be all right.

His son? Talk of a silver lining at the edge of a cloud. A weary smile curved his lips as he stood at the edge of the flower beds and watched a teardrop fall on his palm. So he could father a child? What a horrible way to find out!

What had he done to deserve these kinds of women anyway? He had never treated a woman carelessly in his entire lifetime. Even in his teens when his peers were experimenting with different women, he had always respected them. His brother, Akintunde, was his direct opposite when it came to women.

The only time he was ever promiscuous was after his divorce and he stated his terms before they got into any kind of relationship. Unfortunately, each time he tried to be faithful to a single woman, they ended up betraying him. Was he cursed or something? Was he destined not to have an everlasting love? His body craved and his heart yearned for a woman to call his own and he assumed Omotara was the ultimate answer.

His chest burned and he rubbed it continuously with his right hand. He wished this pain would go away. She used and lied to him and still had the nerve to continue sleeping with him. He clenched his teeth in anger and hid his balled fists in his pockets.

"Olamiposi." Her jasmine scent reached him before the quiet lilt of her voice washed over him like warm wine. His heart picked up a race at her nearness and warmth surrounded his heart, despite the anger in his mind. He hissed under his breath. Even in his furious state, she still had a calming effect on him.

"Go away." His voice was low, ladened with pain and anger. He swallowed hard and his throat burned with unshed tears.

"I am so sorry, Olamiposi. Please give me the chance to explain myself." He didn't see her move but knew she was closer.

"Don't come any closer. I am not ready to listen to you right now. Just get away from me." He cleared his throat and moved away.

"Okay." Her voice wobbled slightly but he hardened his heart against her. She wasn't getting away easily this time around. "Ebunola is asking about you. He said you promised him something."

Oh! He had totally forgotten about that. He wasn't starting his relationship with his son by breaking his promise. His son? Olamiposi's heart soared at the mere thought. There was a rainbow at the end of the storm. He needed to get the DNA done as soon as possible and then, they would sit down and talk.

"Okay. I will see him soon." He still didn't turn around until he heard her footsteps recede. He released a shaky breath. It was time to face his demons.

He went to collect the chocolate from the nurse and went to Ebun's ward. He was on the blood transfusion and was sound asleep. Omotara sat on one of the plastic chairs and was watching the little boy. He placed the box of chocolate by his pillow and shot a glaring look at Omotara, daring her to antagonise him. A little smile formed around her lips but she said nothing at all and lowered her gaze.

He was spoiling for a fight but if he knew Omotara well and he did, he would get no reaction from her. She was one of the calmest women he knew and when she reacted, she would have planned it well before she took any action. That was one of the reasons her betrayal cut deep.

"Go home and change. Freshen up and come back with anything he might want. I will stay with him while you are gone. It seems he will be here for a while." His voice was blunt.

"Are you sure you want to do this?"She looked up at him.

"Yes, I am. I can always call you or holler to one of the nurses if I need help." His eyes didn't leave Ebunola's face as he spoke. The boy was so cute. Was he that cute when he was little? The thought made him want to smile but he suppressed it.

"Okay, then. See you soon. I will be right back." She picked up her purse and left the ward.

***

"What happened to my favourite Godson?" A loud bright voice was saying as the door to the ward swung open and a slim, beautiful lady entered the ward. She was formally dressed in a pencil skirt and white blouse. Her heels made a click, click sound on the terrazzo hospital floor. She carried her handbag in one hand and a fancy bag of provisions, fruit and goodies in the other.

Ebun was still sleeping but he stirred at her voice and opened his sleepy eyes to smile at her. Several nurses and the doctor had visited in the last hour and his cast had been changed. The cut on his arm looked nasty and Olamiposi felt dizzy, just looking at it but he was assured it looked nastier than it really was. "Aunty Linda, Good evening."

Olamiposi turned his head to look at the lady, their eyes met and the woman stumbled on her heels. He shot out of his seat and held her before she fell. Her eyes didn't leave his face as her jaw dropped in shock or amazement, he couldn't place which one.

"Oh my God! Oh my God!" She kept muttering under her breath.

"Are you all right?" His eyes ran over her in concern.

"Thank you, sir. I am fine." She smiled as she steadied herself and went to the boy's bedside. "How is my lil one doing?"

"I am fine, Aunty Linda. Is my cast beautiful?" He lifted it slightly with pride in his voice.

Kids would be kids. Imagine taking pride in the cast that was holding his young bones together while they healed.

He chuckled silently as he watched the easy camaraderie between the two of them. They were obviously close. He picked up his phone and tried to do a little work from his work tablet. How did Omotara juggle work and childcare alone and so effortlessly? The father or husband was no longer in the picture. She had never made an unnecessary excuse because of her son. He had to give that to her.

She was a strong woman…he put an abrupt stop to his line of thought and was intentional about not thinking about her. She had lots of explanations to do and he was not ready to listen.

Linda left about an hour later when Omotara came back. She saw her out and persuaded Olamiposi to leave.

*****

It became a routine between them for the next two weeks while Ebun was in the hospital. The little boy had grown fond of him, and they became fast friends. Ebun told him all about his day from the moment he left till the time he came back to relieve Omotara and he discovered he had a fascinating way with words, despite his limited vocabulary. He was a great storyteller. Olamiposi found himself growing attached to the little one and looking forward to the time they spent together..

Both adults rarely stayed in the same room for too long. They were civil to each other for the sake of the little one but they still managed to find a balance between them and worked as a team. It was the same in the office. Between both, they kept the work at the office going. How they did it seamlessly between the two of them never ceased to amaze him but he refused to dwell on the implications. They were being mature and responsible and doing what needed to be done. Simple.

He missed her. He was shocked at how much he missed their friendship, her laughter, her smell, and the way she organised his life …work life down to the minute detail. She still did the latter, but it wasn't the same. It kept him awake at night and when he eventually fell asleep, his sleep was filled with images of their bodies locked in an erotic embrace. He walked around with semi-aroused wood and it made him even angrier.

Ebunola was discharged. His bruises had faded, and his broken arm was healing nicely but it was still in a sling. His classmates visited him and wrote all sorts on his cast. He carried it with pride.

Olamiposi shook his head in bafflement as he went to settle the hospital bill while Omotara cleared up the private ward. He could never understand kids completely. How could anyone be proud of his injury for God's sake? He couldn't blame the boy though. He had been the centre of everyone.'s attention since the accident and had gotten lots of gifts. Who wouldn't be proud of such elevation?

He was at the door to the private room when Ebunola's voice stopped him.

"I wish Uncle Ola was my real dad. I like him better than my daddy."

"Don't talk that way about your father. He took care of you when you were small."

"I still don't like him, Mom, because he used to beat you. I know, Mommy, don't lie to me again."

His back went ramrod straight as he stared into space. Was she in an abusive marriage? That man should be killed. His hands tightened into fists.

"I am not lying to you. All those mornings that I had bruises on my face, I honestly had little accidents. Enough of that anyway. It is time to go home." Her voice was low, and he knew she just lied again. Some men were truly bastards.

He took a few steps backward and came back noisily to meet them halfway.

"Hey, big boy." Olamiposi tweaked his cheek and Ebunola giggled happily.

"Hey, Uncle Ola. The doctor said I must come back again for a checkup until my arm is healed. Will you bring me to the hospital?" He skipped on his toes as he held onto Olamiposi's hand with his good hand, looking up at him.

"Uncle Ola is a busy man, Ebun…" He cut her sentence off with a withering look and turned back to the little boy with a smile.

"Yes I will. That is a promise."

"Yay!" He jumped up with glee and Olamiposi caught him before he fell.

"Stop doing that. I don't want to spend a night more in this hospital please," he warned and they both laughed.

He dropped them at her apartment, gave Omotara the day off and proceeded to the office.

*****

As he was driving into the company premises, the security man on duty, Fred, greeted him as he waved him to a stop. A feeling of premonition hit him but he shrugged it off as he rolled down his window. Hot air rushed into the cool interior of the car and he winced slightly. Ebunola had loved riding in the car and he couldn't wait for the opportunity to take him on another ride. The smile forming on his face froze as he spotted the envelope in Fred's hand.

"This is for you, sir. A lady came to deliver this to you but she refused to tell me her name." The young man curtseyed as he gave him the package.

"Thank you, Fred." He dropped it on the passenger seat as his windows went up and proceeded to the car park. He tore open the package with a bored look and the look turned to shock when distant photos of him, Ebunola and Omotara slipped out from the package. He turned one of the photos over and read the message scrawled across it:

"When I want something badly enough, I crush all obstacles in my path."

His blood ran cold with dread, and fury. Nancy had struck again and this time, she hit him below the belt. It was time to strike back before her blow turned fatal.

TWELVE

Omotara

He was a better father than Joshua.

It was obvious from the way he related with Ebunola, even before she blurted out her secret like a teenager with a loose mouth. She could have waited for a better opportunity to do so. She had always been an idiot when making decisions about anything that concerned her boss. He cried. Dear God! She saw his wide, strong, shoulders heaving in sobs in that lonely part of the hospital premises and was alarmed at first before she realised what was happening. Men were not supposed to cry. That was what she knew both as a child and an adult.

Each tear drop was like a knife wound in her chest, knowing that she was responsible for his pains. Had she hurt him that much? She couldn't fathom what level of hurt could make a grown man cry like a baby but at that moment, she realised she had fallen in love with this vulnerable strong man.

 She wasn't sure what she was going to do with this new found knowledge but she knew she would fight for him with her last breath unless she was absolutely sure he didn't want her again. That would hurt terribly but she would cross the bridge when she got there.

Even Linda had been shocked by the striking resemblance between her son and her boss, "I nearly fell, babe, if not because he caught me. It was like looking at Ebunola in a decade or two. How have you been handling being in the same office with him?" she had asked as she followed her to her car.

"Well, I don't have much choice. Karma is a real bitch." She shrugged with a little smile.

"I take it he knows Ebun is his now, right? It is difficult for him not to know or for people not to comment on it." Linda's assumption had been right and she nodded. "I noticed the strain between you guys but if he is still hanging around you, and Ebun, there is hope. Don't give up please."

She had no intention of giving up.

***

It was a quiet evening in her home as she prepared her son for bed. He had retired to bed without much argument tonight after several yawns and early dinner. His medications were still making him drowsy. After their nightly prayer rituals and bedtime story, Omotara got to her feet and made to leave the room.

"I miss Uncle Ola." Her son's quiet voice stopped her in her tracks. Her heart lurched suddenly in fear but she turned around with a smile. How would she tell him that Uncle Ola was his biological father when the father hadn't accepted the truth yet? He refused to acknowledge her statement or discuss it, despite her best effort.

"I am sure he misses you too, honey." Her smile was brittle and forced. She went to sit beside him on the bed.

"Why did he stay with me in the hospital? Is he going to be my new daddy?" There was excitement in his voice as he turned sleepy eyes to look at her. Oh my! Her eyes widened in shock.

"What gave you that idea? Your daddy is your daddy. No one can have a new or old daddy." She chuckled lightly but she knew what he meant.

"My friend, Collins, has a new daddy. His daddy went to heaven and his mommy got him a new daddy." His lips trembled but the sentence ended with a yawn.

"Can we have this discussion tomorrow, honey? You are sooooo sleepy." She patted his head soothingly. The lilting voice of Beyonce singing 'Halo' filled the room and it was then she realised her phone was still in the pocket of her baggy jeans. She also knew who she allocated the ringing tone to and her heart skipped a bit. Talk of the devil.

Her son looked at her with curiosity as she brought out the phone and slid aside the green button. Her lips wanted to curve up in a smile, but she suppressed it and schooled her features properly. They were not on good terms and she needed to remind her heart of that.

"Hello, Olami. Good evening."

"Good evening, Tara. Are you all right? How is Ebunola?" There was concern in his voice with a hint of panic and she frowned.

"Yes, of course. We are all right. Is everything okay?" There was a sigh of relief on the other hand and a heartfelt, "Thank God."

"Did something happen? Do you want to talk about it?" She got to her feet.

"Not now." There was a momentary pause. "Can I talk to Ebunola, please? I can't believe I missed that dreadful hospital because of him." He said it so solemnly that she burst into laughter.

He laughed too.

"Hold on." She turned to her son and found him grinning from ear to ear. "I am giving you only two minutes. It is his bedtime."

"Yes, ma." She could hear the smile in his voice. Were they on good terms now? Or was he looking for a way to bond with his child? The latter thought dimmed her smile a little bit but she gave the phone to her son.

She stood by the side while her boy talked to the man who was fast becoming one of the most important persons in her life and she had no clue how to bridge the gap between them. The conversation was brief but when the call ended, Ebunola fell asleep with the biggest smile on his face.

****

Omotara went to take her bath and had just settled down in her favourite settee to watch a Netflix movie when she heard a knock on her door. She paused the movie and cocked her head to the side. It came again. Who could be looking for her at this time of the night? She looked at the wall clock. Well, it was just 9 p.m. People were still moving around but she wasn't expecting anyone.

Unfolding her long slim legs encased in her cotton pyjamas, she moved to the door and looked through the peephole. It was an unfamiliar face that belonged to a woman. She couldn't see the rest of her face but she looked angry and impatient. A trickle of unease ran down her spine.

"Who is it?" She checked to make sure her door was properly locked.

"I have a package from Mr. Olamiposi Adewunmi. I am so sorry for coming this late. I was delayed in traffic." The smooth voice belied the grimace and ugliness on her beautiful face.

A package? She just spoke to Olamiposi and he didn't mention anything about a package. She remembered the concern and panic in his voice when he called earlier that evening. Something was going on and she would get to the root of it.

"I am sorry. Please take it back. I don't want any package from him." Her voice was firm, even as she continued watching the woman. Her eyeball hurt from the continuous strain from peeping through the thin hole.

"Madam, please let me deliver it. I don't want to go back to him again after the stress I have been through today." The strange woman had moved closer to the door, as she glanced up and down her corridor.

Omotara couldn't see her face again but could see the rapid fall and rise of her ample chest. She was breathing fast as if she was angry or stressed.

"Please, go away. You can keep it to yourself or return it. Either way, the choice is yours." Omotara moved away from the door but her hands were clammy with fear. Who was she? Why did she want her to open her door so badly? Were she and Ebunola in danger of any kind? Could it be her ex-husband? What could Joshua possibly want with her? After all, he knew Ebunola wasn't his before he gave her the final beating of her life that landed her in an emergency ward in the hospital.

Her mind raced with several thoughts while her heart thudded in her chest with fear. She looked around with wide-eyed panic.

"Madam, will you please open the door before …."

"What is going on here?" Linda's strong authoritative voice cut off the woman's voice and relief flooded Omotara's body. She nearly sagged against the wall.

"Nothing ma'am. I have a package for Mrs. Jacobs…"

"She is a lying bitch. She was threatening me to open my door by force when you come along." Omotara began to unlock her door with speed but before she got out, there was a tussle and the woman fled. "What happened, Linda? Thank you for coming." She ran to her friend who was holding one of her spike-heeled shoes in her hand.

"I wanted to nail this on her ugly head. She went around me and fled. Stupid bitch." Linda removed her second shoe, picked up her handbag and followed her inside the room.

After locking the door securely for the second time that night, she sat on the sofa while Linda went to get a cold soda from the fridge before joining her in the sitting room. Omotara told her about the night's ordeal from the moment Olamiposi gave her a call.

"We can't go to the police station because all we have is suspicion. Be careful and vigilant and ensure Ebunola doesn't talk to strangers at any time. Only God knows her intention." Linda stared into her drink thoughtfully.

"But she mentioned my boss' name. That means she knows I have a relationship with him one way or the other." Omotara frowned.

"You mean your sexy boss/boyfriend? That man is fyneee." Linda grinned at her and she rolled her eyes in exasperation.

"I should have known you came because of aproko. Amebo. Why are you not hanging out with your friends this evening?"

"I missed my bestfriend and Godson. How is he by the way?"

"Ebunola is fine. Still in a cast sling but should be out in a couple of weeks. Otherwise, I am sure Ebun is having the best time in the world. All the attention and gifts are going to his head. Let me warm the leftover dinner for you. I will add grilled chicken wings to the firewood jollof rice for you."

Linda screeched with excitement and did a fast jig with her bare feet. Omotara laughed as she headed to the kitchen and her friend followed her. They sat at the kitchen table as Linda wolfed down her meal and her friend brought her up to date with her life.

"I doubt if tonight's incident has anything to do with Olamiposi but call him tomorrow or have a heart-to-heart talk with him on Monday when you resume. When are you guys settling your fight nah? He knows the truth now and only needs time to accept it but don't give him too much time to overthink abeg."

"He is still furious with me and he has every right to be so. All I have ever done is deceive him. He doesn't deserve that from me." Misery filled Omotara's voice.

"Well, you didn't do that intentionally. You have been hurt by a member of his gender and it is a pity that he got caught in the crossfire. All you have been doing is to protect yourself and your heart." Linda threw the last piece of the grilled chicken in her mouth and chewed noisily. She didn't look like a high profile banker at the moment and the thought made a fond smile spread over Omotara's face.

"This is why you are my best friend. You still have my back, even when I am being foolish." Sentimental tears filled Omotara's eyes.

"I don't know where else to dump your sorry ass. So I have to manage you like that." Linda spread her hands with a pitying look and she flung the discarded can of Fayrouz at her head, then they both laughed.

"He cares for you. He could have walked away but he didn't and he still called tonight to check on you and his son. I think he is worth fighting for, babe."

"You are right. What should I do? I am not sure how to bridge this gap between us." She knotted her fingers together.

"Right now, I have no idea but we will think of something before the weekend runs out. Thank you for a beautiful meal, girl." She sashayed out of the kitchen, leaving the remnant of her meal behind.

"Remind me again why I adore you please, because you are nothing but a pig." Omotara glowered after her but Linda only laughed heartily from the sitting room.

By the time Omotara was done cleaning up her kitchen and clearing her stuff from the sitting room, Linda was fast asleep in the bed they would be sharing tonight.

THIRTEEN

Olamiposi

"She hasn't struck yet, right?" Akintunde asked as Olamiposi ended his call with Ebunola.

"No, she hasn't and now, Omotara is suspicious that something is going on." Olamiposi was pensive as he dropped his phone on the coffee table beside him.

"She has a right to know. Her life and her son's lives are in danger because you can't keep it in your pants and don't have the sense to at least frolic with sane women. This one deserves to be in Yaba left." He paused as he lit a cigar stick, inhaled deeply and blew smoke into the air.

Olamiposi sighed heavily as he rose to open the window to the coffee room. His only sibling, best friend and confidante was his older brother, Akintunde Adewunmi. He was a chain smoker, a drinker and he suspected he smoked weed or other illegal substances but had never done it in his presence. His only other fault was the fact that he loved him to distraction and would do anything to protect him from all sorts of evil.

"I know. You don't need to rub it in my face, nah. Kolomental is not written on the face. How am I supposed to know some nuts are missing in her head?" Akintunde laughed so much he began to cough but Olamiposi didn't crack a smile. It wasn't a joking matter. "I will talk to Omotara on Monday when she resumes work."

"The kid's matter apart, you really like her right? She is different from Miriam." Akintunde studied his face and he jammed his hands in his pocket as he stared out of the window. "I have always known Miriam will mess up. I ran a check on her and she has always been in contact with her ex. It is easy to go back when problems struck in her marriage."

"Why didn't you tell me, Akin? That was totally selfish of you." He glared at him. Akintunde was a lawyer and investigator with several other business deals by the side, both legal and illegal ones. He was also well known on the street and he used his connections well whenever it was to his advantage.

"No, that was me looking out for my kid brother and hoping your ex-wife will change for good. I also persuaded her to leave your company alone. We don't deal with cheaters and betrayers in our family." He raised his hand to stall him as he opened his mouth to counter his brother. "You are the loverboy, Olamiposi. You crave a relationship and try your best to make it work. I have never believed in it but whatever you want, I will always support you. I will do anything to help you get what you want."

Their parents' marriage was a toxic one. As their parents drew apart amid violence, physical, emotional and sexual abuse, the bond between the two boys grew stronger and his older brother tried to shield him from the worst of it. As a result, he craved love, warmth, emotional bond and commitment in his relationship with women but it was the direct opposite with Akintunde. He fled from any form of commitment and Olamiposi was beginning to fear that he may never settle down.

"You know how to insult and flatter me at the same time, Akintunde. I will sort out my issue with Omotara. How do I deal with this mad woman before she gets to the one thing I have wanted all my life?"

"You have run all the necessary tests and he is yours?"

"Yes, I was with them in the hospital. He is biologically mine."

"Does the mother know you ran a test behind her back?" There was a mischievous glint in his eyes.

"What point are you trying to prove, Tunde? She was with my child for 5 years and even had the guts to date me without telling me the truth."

"Don't bite my head off, nau. I am not the culprit here." Akintunde burst into a deep-belly laugh and he was tempted to join him. "You are all frauds, I swear. How can a relationship work when the foundation was built on deceit? If you want this woman badly, take her out and clear the air between you and then begin on a fresh note."

"Thank you, my relationship expert, who can't hold one successfully." His voice was heavy with sarcasm and he laughed again.

"Don't worry. I have your woman and son covered. Nothing bad will happen to them on my watch."

"Now, I can sleep with both eyes closed. Mtcheew. I need to go and find something to eat in this big, for nothing house." Olamiposi left the room but his brother was right behind him.

"Let's wake Timilehin. That is why he is being paid." Timileyin was Akintunde's cook, one of the litters he picked up from the street and the guy was a badass cook.

"At this time of the night, Tunde? Have mercy nau. I am still a better cook than you are. I will whip up something." He opened the freezer and whistled long and slow. There were different sizes of bowls of assorted soups and food. "Your cook is a genius. I have to borrow him soon." He brought out bowls of meat and ogbono soup, garnished with assorted seafood and made eba.

A few moments later, they sat at the kitchen table, wolfing down morsels of semo, well coated in the delicious ogbono soup.

"I wish you have more women problems so you can visit me more. I miss your annoying ass." Akintunde swallowed a morsel and winked at him.

"You are a goat. Just say you are feeling lonely and need a companion." Olamiposi hissed at him as he opened a bottle of cold water and gulped it down.

"Please leave me out of the relationship palava. I am fine the way I am. Free as a bird."

Olamiposi snorted in derision. "How is our business doing?" He was a major shareholder in his brother's investment company.

"You will know when you attend the next shareholder and management meeting." Akintunde burst into laughter again.

"Man, I really miss you, kiddo." Olamiposi grinned at that. Underneath his brother's rough surface, he had a soft spot for his only family.

***

Olamiposi paced his office as he waited for Omotara to come in. It was the best time to do away with his past and start afresh. He just finished clearing his desk, his wedding ring had gone down the toilet drainage and everything that had to do with his first marriage. It was fun while it lasted with Miriam but the time she had occupied in his mental space and mind was enough.

He was uncharacteristically nervous and anticipation was killing him. He told himself It was because it had been a long time since they were in the same office space. He stood at the window, looking down at the car park but saw nothing. Nancy had sent him several messages over the weekend with different numbers and they contained subtle threats but she made the mistake of leaving her name at the end of each message. It was either he belonged to her or belonged to none. What a nerve! He didn't even know where she lived.

There was a movement outside the door and he had just a few moments to compose himself before the door slid open. Omotara walked in and his heart came to a literal stop. Her slim curvy body was balanced on a 4-inch heeled strap sandal and the short formal dress that hugged her like a second skin stopped mid-thigh. The white blazer she wore on top added elegance to her outfit and made his mouth water with desire.

Her scent was a bit different today. Her jasmine scent was mixed subtly with vanilla and amber and it sent blood to his nether region. If she was trying to seduce him, she was succeeding royally. Their eyes met across the expanse of the room and held. Awareness cackled between them, strong and thick and he knew he had lost the battle before it even began. He was in love with this woman and may not survive another heart break from her. He swallowed hard. His legs moved but he wasn't aware until he was a few feet from her.

"Hi, Olami. Thank you for taking care of Ebunola." Her smile was shy again and she twisted her fingers together. He was not the only one who was nervous and the observation relieved him a bit.

"You are welcome, Omotara. He is my son too, right?" He searched her eyes and saw distress mixed with regret in them.

"He is. I am so sorry I kept it away from you for so long. Joshua was the only man I knew as a woman until you and he seemed like the perfect one for me. The excuse he gave was that I played hard to get and didn't allow him to sleep with me until we got married. He blamed me for everything that went wrong in that marriage including his infertility." She gave a sad smile as she moved around his office, unconsciously arranging and rearranging things on his office table. His eyes followed her movement and her vulnerability touched a soft spot in him.

"Fortunately, I stumbled upon a conversation between his mom and his sister, discussing the reason behind his infertility. He was ignorant and I wasn't brave enough to tell him without medical evidence to back it. I wanted to save my marriage and believed if I could get pregnant, he would be happy with me and everything would be all right in my home. It was the greatest mistake of my life." Tears welled up in her eyes and rolled down her face. She sniffled and he smiled. She looked so cute, almost like a child.

"That was where I came in, right? The sperm donor. The irony of it was that I couldn't get my ex-wife pregnant. Yet, it took one night with you and I have my spitting image right in front of me. Aren't you my lucky charm?" He smiled at her.

"Oh?" Her lips formed an 'O' in surprise and he moved to gather her against him. She didn't resist him as he tilted her face up and devoured her mouth in a deep, toe-curling kiss that left both panting for breath.

"I have been wanting to do that since you came in." He kissed her forehead and settled her head on his chest. "What happened to the bastard? When did you come to your senses and run for your life?"

"Our home was normal for a while until I gave birth and the child looked nothing like him. He returned to his old ways of physical and emotional abuse and I was getting tired of it. My mother was a divorcee and wouldn't hear anything about me leaving my matrimonial home for any reason. Linda, my friend, was the only one I had in my corner. The last time he beat me and I landed in the hospital, she reported it to the police and had him arrested. It turned into a family battle and it was during the family meeting that his mother declared that I was nothing but a whore because her son cannot father a child. Her son was shocked and embarrassed and I was publicly disgraced. I and Ebunola never went back to that house again. The rest they say is history. Linda sponsored my divorce lawyer." She moved away from his embrace and started moving around again. Restless.

"Please remember to introduce us properly the next time we meet. I need to thank her properly." He crossed his heart. She smiled but it didn't touch her eyes and he began to get worried. "What is the problem? You don't want to be with me any longer?" Something close to panic was trying to rise in his throat but he shut it down.

"I want to. I want you, Olami. I miss you. I am in love with you." Her eyes lowered at that but his heart soared with joy. A smile was threatening to spread over his face but he felt an obstacle coming and swore on his life he would do anything to crush it.

"But?"

"I know you have wanted a child all these years and I have yours with me. I can't be sure you are with me because you want me or because you want your child." There was uncertainty in her voice.

"I have known you before I met Ebunola and …" He was cut off by the ringing of her phone from her office and he swore under his breath but followed her out of his office anyways. Even though he hadn't taken her out on a date as he had planned to before they could clear the air between them, he would like to do so as soon as possible and was ready to use any opportunity he could get to do so.

She brought the phone out of her handbag. It was Mrs. Oduwole, Ebunola's class teacher and they exchanged glances, their thoughts mirroring one another's. What was going on again, God?

"Please call her back."

She did and put the call on speakerphone.

"Good morning, Ma. I am so sorry to disturb you on Ebun's first day back to school but we have a situation on ground. There is a woman here who is holding the whole class hostage. She wants to talk to you." There was panic in her voice as she tried to compose herself.

His blood ran cold. Could Nancy go to the extent of holding little kids to ransom because she wanted the father of one kid? He remembered she had an unscrewed nut in her brain and she wouldn't think like a normal person.

"Who is she? Why me? What is her name?"

He could hear the puzzlement in Omotara's voice and a guilty conscience threatened to engulf him. *She targeted you because you dared to love me; I will do anything in my power to ensure you don't regret it.*

"Good morning, Madam Omotara. It is your boyfriend or the father of your child I have issues with." It was Nancy quite all right. He knew that voice and anger suffused him. Omotara glanced at him in confusion and he nodded solemnly. There was no sense lying over it or omitting it as the case maybe.

"Hello, Nancy. How are you doing?" He collected the phone from her and mouthed to her to get his phone. It was time to call his brother. Omotara removed her sandals, pushed them under her desk and changed to a pair of low heeled sandals, then she rushed into his office and was back within seconds with his phone. He ran a hand up and down her spine in soothing motion.

"Olamiposi, why have you refused to pick my calls? Is it because you have a kid and a wife stashed somewhere?" There was a whine in her voice. Mental case. He took deep breaths severally and neutralised his voice so the anger bubbling in him would not reflect there.

"I am a divorcee, babe and you know that. I got to know about my kid probably around the same time you do too. If you do your findings well, you will know that." There was silence at the other end while he held gaze with Omotara, conveying his feelings to her. Her arms went around him and she rested her head on his shoulder. She trusted him and that was all that mattered right now.

"Okay. You are right. Where are you now? I want to see you desperately."

"Stay where you are and don't do anything I won't be proud of. I am coming right away."

"Okay, baby." She giggled and he felt like puking his gut out. The call ended.

FOURTEEN

Omotara

"I know her voice. I think it was the woman who came to my house shortly after your call on Friday." They were on their way to Ebun's school and Olamiposi took the company's car. According to him, he didn't want any of Nancy's goons to recognise his car, wherever they were.

"Really? I have never seen a more desperate person in my life. It was supposed to be a casual fling between us but she turned it into something else. I am so sorry for risking both your lives this way." He reached for her hand and squeezed it in assurance.

"Hmm. Your brother is calling back." She was scared out of her pants but the fact that she wasn't alone in this battle gave her strength, even though he was the one who put them in this spot in the first place.

"Answer the call and put it on speakerphone." She did and his brother's booming voice filled the cool interior of the car.

"Hey, kiddo. I know she is in your kid's school. We have calmed every other part of the school except his class. Just play the perfect loverboy to her until we can safely move in. Apologies to your lady love."

Omotara's lips twisted in amusement. He knew about her? That was interesting.

"Okay. She can hear you." She glared at him and he grinned at her.

"Good morning, sir."

"Hey, sweetheart. We will talk better when the situation is saner. Bye for now." The line went dead.

"Your brother is…funny in a weird way."

"I know, right. You will like him. He is the only family I have except for you and Ebunola." He navigated the last turn that led to Ebun's school.

"I am not your family," she mumbled as she looked out of the window.

"Yet." Arrogant bastard. She crossed her arms across her chest and huffed. He laughed and pinched her cheek. She swatted his hand away and glared at him.

***

Her heart lurched as the gate came in view. Today would have been one of her happiest days if not for this situation. She prayed for her boy and everyone in that school. What kind of woman went after a man like that? Definitely a madly desperate one. He parked two buildings away from the school.

"Our kid will be all right. Nothing bad will happen to any of us. It is me she wants, not you or Ebun and I have given her the impression that we are not together." He turned to look at her and fear gripped her anew.

"I am scared, Olami. She doesn't want to see me but her kind will crush any obstacle on her path. What if something happened to Ebun or to you? I can't live with it." She gripped his hands urgently.

"Nothing will happen to Ebun as long as I am alive. If I am unable to protect him, my brother will do so and he will take care of you." He cupped her face and looked earnestly into her eyes. "I love you, my ladylove. Don't ever forget that." Her smile came at that nickname but it was watery.

"Don't allow anything to happen to you. I will never forgive you. In fact, I am coming with you." She reached to open the door but he stopped her.

"No, that is not wise. We can't allow Nancy to see you. The loose screw in her head will drop immediately. If you are coming, wear my jacket and disguise yourself in any way you can." His phone rang as if on cue and an unknown number flashed across the screen. "She is the one. See you soon, babe."

Her heart was heavy as she watched him saunter towards the school gate, receiving the call and she bent her head to pray hard. If there was anything her mother taught her, it was to pray hard. If there was anything she learned from her best friend, Linda, it was to take action towards what she wanted. She put on Olamiposi's hoodie, searched his car and found a sunshade and baseball cap. She put it on and left for the school compound.

Everywhere was unusually silent. It would be difficult to believe she was in a school premises. She could feel eyes on her but couldn't see anyone except for the head of the school children, all gathered in a class. The block of class where Ebun's class was situated was at the end of the school and she looked around furtively as she approached. Her heart hammered in her chest and her palms were clammy with sweat.

Omotara wasn't sure what she would do when she got there but it was taking too long and she couldn't leave her child's fate in other people's hands. She hid her hands in the pockets of the hoodie, gripping her phone tightly while the other hand held a pen. As she got close to the door of the classroom, the door opened and two people came out, wrapped around each other. It was Olamiposi and Nancy.

She was surprised at the lance of jealousy that went through her, even as her mind reminded her it was an act on his side. She made to turn around before the mad woman would recognise her but it was like something about her pulled Nancy and her piercing gaze caught her own like a deer in a car's lamplight.

"You, bastard. You tricked me. She is here." Nancy shrieked in fury as she clawed at Olamiposi.

"Calm down, Nancy. She is here for her kid. I told you there is nothing between us." Olamiposi tried to calm her but she escaped his grip and came after Omotara with a gun.

"She has a gun!" Omotara shouted as she ran for her life and the woman chased after her. Olamiposi tried to catch her but she was surprisingly fast for her chubby body. The school was thrown into pandemonium but fortunately, no one came out or stood in her way. There were screams and cries from frightened school children but none came out.

"Get down, Tara. She is about to shoot." Omotara glanced backward for a second and saw Olamiposi tackle Nancy from behind. His hand caught her right foot as he went down and dragged her with him. In fury, Nancy turned around and raised the gun to him.

"Oh, no." Omotara turned around and headed towards him as fast as her legs could carry her. This mad woman dared not shoot the father of her son and her future husband. She dared not kill her first ever chance at real happiness.

Two gunshots followed simultaneously and Omotara saw blood. Her world tilted and she bit her lips as she staggered towards Olamiposi who laid on the sandy, uneven ground. She tasted blood and was reminded she was still alive.

'Olami, did she shoot you? Are you hurt?"she whispered as she fell on him and shook him. She didn't dare glance at the other woman who was sprawled lifelessly on his other side, the gun she held a few feet from her.

"Yes, she did but I am fine." He sat up cautiously, lifted his bleeding arm and she muffled a scream as she held it gingerly with her hands. "Don't panic. It is just a graze." His grin was reassuring.

"You could have been killed. That was a close call." Tears filled her eyes.

"Well, I am a lucky man." He looked around tentatively. "My brother is here. I could feel his presence."

"Yes, kiddo. I always got your back." Omotara looked in the direction of the tall, lanky man, striding towards them and her mouth opened in awe. He was drop-dead gorgeous. He was also holding a smoking gun while his long blazers billowed behind him.

"Oh my God!" She stared at him until Olamiposi nudged her with a glare. Akintunde laughed heartilly. "I am sorry. He is so gorgeous. He looks like a rock star. Pardon me, sir." She curtsied in respect.

"I have that effect on women." He reached out his hand and pulled her to her feet. "Nice to meet you, sweetheart."

"Thank you for coming to our rescue." She glanced at Nancy's crumbled body a few feet away and shuddered. " Is she dead?"

"No, she is not. I only incapacitated her. She will soon come around and will never bother you again. I will see you around. Talk to you later, kiddo."

He put his two fingers between his curved lips and gave a shrill whistle.

Men trooped into the school compound in police and military outfit and Nancy was taken away, even as she began to stir.

***

"Mommy! Mommy! Uncle Ola."

Ebunola was running towards them as they approached his class. The police were around and they had finished writing their report in the proprietor's office.

Olamiposi had been tended to by the school nurse and his arm was lightly bandaged. Even though it was a graze, Omotara could see the pain in his eyes. It must hurt like hell.

Olamiposi met his son halfway and kissed the boy's forehead before lifting him onto his good arm. Ebun giggled with excitement and sobered when he saw his father's bandaged arm, "What happened to your hand, Uncle Ola?"

Olamiposi battled with either telling him the truth or lying and glanced at Omotara for help. She took pity on him. He just took a bullet for her which could have gone fatal. For that alone, she would always love him. "The lady criminal shot him and he was so smart that he dodged it, then brought her down. The police have taken her away."

"Wow." Ebunola's eyes were round with admiration and awe. Olamiposi nodded solemnly but his lips were twitching with amusement. Omotara coughed slightly to hide her own hilarity. "Did you bleed a lot? Was there lots and lots of blood?"

Trust boys and blood. She rolled her eyes but answered all the same, "Yes, it has been cleaned up by the nurse. He will be fine, baby."

"Sorry, Uncle Ola. Does it hurt you a lot?" The little boy stared at the wound intently.

"A little bit but I will be fine." Olamiposi juggled him until the boy raised his eyes from the injured hand and looked at him. "I love you, boy. Don't ever forget that."

'Are you going to be my new daddy?" There was anxiety in his voice.

"I am not your new daddy. I am your real daddy."

"Really? Mommy, is that true? He is my real real daddy. Everyone said I look like him." He looked at his mother.

"Yes, honey. He is your real daddy."

"Hurray!" He threw his good hand in the air and bounced in his daddy's arms. "Are we going to live together like a real family?"

Omotara looked at Olamiposi, her heart in her eyes and he grinned as he bent to kiss her parted lips. "Yes darling. We will live together like the family we are if your mom will accept me."

"When you ask properly, I will give you my answer." There was mischief in her eyes but she looked deadpan serious.

"I love you both. You are my world." He pulled her into his embrace and felt his world settled.

They were his home.

THE END.

About the Author

Mobolaji Olanrewaju is a Travel Management Consultant, CAC (Corporate Affairs Commission) registration and training consultant, and a writer/author. She is a Lagos basaed storyteller who's romance tales are sprinkled with doses of suspense, thriller, steam and everything in-between. She lives and works in Lagos. She is the author of, **Twists of Fate** and **Rapture**, A Twin Bliss Resort novel.

She is also a co-author of anthologies such as the African Christmas anthology titled **Hell Hath No Fury**, and an erotic romance titled **Nights In Club Nova**. Her stories in the anthologies are titled **Hidden Desire** and **Whispers Of Pleasure** respectively.

Her novels can be found on Bambooks, Selar, Pabpub and Amazon. She loves to blog on her personal blog http://mobolajiolanrewaju.com.

THE
WISHLIST

Perfect love casts out questions and uncertainties, and ticks more than any requirement we can think of, and, or imagine.

By

CHRISTIANA AGBONI

Prologue

21 August 2008.

My name is Ufedo Okpanachi. I am 12 years old, and I will marry at 22 years old. My future husband must be:

1. A born-again Christian.

2. Tall, handsome and have skin the colour of coffee seeds.

3. A Master's degree holder and have plans to get a doctorate.

4. Confident, caring and patient.

5. The owner of a trendy car, a decent four-bedroom house, and a nice paying job or business.

6. A sharp dresser and loves to wear suits.

7. Not more than 5 years older than I am.

One

June 17, 2023.

Ufedo sat as still as a statue as the clipper went 'kkhheeerrr ssshheerrr' on her hair. Chunks of hair fell and landed on the floor at her feet, and on the cloth the barber had wrapped around her shoulders. She had her eyes tightly closed as cold air rushed at her exposed scalp and she felt like a figment of her own imagination.

Her hair had been her pride, her mother's pride too. Her heart beat with trepidation at the thought of Mama's reaction when she found out that she had cut her hair. Daddy would not mind but she was going to make sure Mama never found out until it was absolutely impossible to hide behind wigs. She had to heavily invest in wigs now. She sighed.

The last time she cut her hair, she was eight years old. She was tired of the pain of hair plaiting. A pain she went through every Saturday, plaiting the hair styles the teacher gave at school. So, she devised a plan one evening when Mama sent her to the store to get something for her, she had gone to the neighbourhood barber and told him her mother sent her to have her hair cut.

The barber had done justice to his trade. Ufedo had gone home, took one look at Mama's face and hid under her aunt's bed until Daddy came and fished her out, with a stern warning to never lie, or go against her mother's wishes again.

Mama took it upon herself to tease out her hair painful by painful inch, from threading it in little tomato style, to digging her fingers in to plait two hands style, and then tiny weaving, her hair had grown back, fuller than before, longer, thicker, darker, and stronger. Ufedo had come to love her hair too, and had tried to care for it, she did try, but she was tired of the hair and the effort that went into its maintenance.

That was why she found herself seated in a chair in a barbing salon while a huge silent barber cut off her hair.

"Hair is a woman's glory. God has blessed you with an abundance of it," Mama used to say.

Well, Ufedo's glory was now in question, no doubt. She was almost 27 years old and dreaded having to tell her mother she had cut her hair. She also had Victoria, her one and only friend to contend with as well. But she had resolved to cross the respective bridges when she got there.

The icing on the cake was last Saturday. The new hair stylist recommended for her had said with bold confidence, "Don't worry, your hair cannot burn in my hands. Those other people are doing it wrong. Your scalp is sensitive but I know what to do." Ufedo nodded and admired her long peach gown. She looked like Mama, and she submitted her head and hair into her hands.

For most of her life, her scalp had always itched and had become sensitive and painful over time. Treatments had helped, but never for long. She had gone with loose braids and left her hair combed and flowing around her shoulders most of the time. She had washed her hair with rice water, poured a sachet of Omo and Klin in it, she had even used raw eggs once, and all the anti-itching shampoo, conditioner and hair creams had drained her money and her joy. Itchy, sensitive, painful scalp stayed. All the relaxers she had ever used had burned her scalp.

She had changed hairdressers over and over until last Saturday. She explained all these to the woman as she cut her hair into sections and applied the relaxer to her hair.

The woman with the peach gown did her thing and washed her hair. Ufedo felt a telltale tingle but the hair stylist brushed off her complaints. Ufedo went home and the next morning, her head shot off pains and when she raised her hand to her hair, most of it was matted to her head. She cried. Then she poured oils and creams on it and went to the woman with the peach gown. This time, she wore a royal blue velvet pantsuit. She had a good sense of style, Ufedo thought surly. She knew it was not the woman's fault her head was doing its thing but she needed to blame someone.

"Once the wounds dry and you wash the hair, you will be fine," she had said matter of factly.

The wounds dried, and Ufedo washed the hair and found her way to the nearest barber's shop a week later.

"You are all done," The barber said and in one movement, removed the cloth from her shoulders. Ufedo opened her eyes and stared back at the person staring at her from the big salon mirror. She rubbed at her head, almost bald and sighed. Her eyes appeared bigger and rounder than before, fortunately, her forehead did not seem as big as she had feared. Her cheeks were sunken in, and her head felt so small. She had thought she had a big head, but it was quite a normal size.

"I will recommend the products you can use to treat your scalp and grow back your hair in no time," The barber said to fill the silence as Ufedo kept staring at the mirror and rubbing at her head. It felt so fragile, and it hurt.

He went ahead and wrote the names of the products on a piece of paper and handed it to her.

Ufedo paid her bills and went home, trying not to think but failing.

*   *   *

"Ufedo, what have you done to yourself? Ufedooooooo....," Victoria screeched as she came face to face with Ufedo in her apartment.

Ufedo had totally forgotten the home cell fellowship by 5 p.m. every Saturday. Victoria hadn't forgotten. Unlike Ufedo who had cut off her glory, Victoria's was intact on her head, braided in tiny lengths that cascaded down her back with black attachments.

"What happened?" Victoria asked again.

Ufedo shrugged. "It was time." She sat on a plush cushion chair.

"And me, your best friend was never informed of this situation? No heads-up?" Victoria said as she sat on Ufedo's slate grey sofa.

"You knew I had hair issues."

"Yeah. But we were treating them. You just needed to be patient."

"I'm tired of being patient. My name is Ufedo."

"Don't be sarcastic, all right. What will Mama say?" Victoria said.

"Mama can't say anything about what she is not aware of. And Mama will not be made aware, right, Vickie?" Ufedo pinned Victoria with a look.

Victoria shrugged.

"You're so full of surprises, girlfriend. And you do not even have a wig, what are we going to do now?" Victoria asked.

Ufedo didn't bother with an answer. Victoria was her closest and oldest friend since they were 10 years old. Their parents were friends, they attended the same church, and now worked in the same real estate company. Victoria would come up with a solution, possibly a wig from her own collection.

"Let's go to the cell meeting first. We'll stop by my house and get a wig for you. We must go wig shopping soon." She stood.

"I do not feel up to it, Vickie."

"I reject that feeling on your behalf. First, you cut off your full head of hair, now you're opting out of cell meetings. What will you do next?" Victoria raised her hands in frustration.

"God! Stop already. You're my best friend."

"Fine." Victoria capitulated with a pout as she sat back down. "Let's go to my place. For a sleepover. You'll come back to your place after church service tomorrow." she amended.

"Okay." Ufedo dragged herself up. She felt a headache coming up.

Two

"Hey, Ufedo, nice wig," Ojochide commented when she walked into the office on Monday morning. Ojochide wore a leaf green skirt with a white blouse and thin strap heels. There was something about Monday and white shirts with heels.

"Thank you," Ufedo said and patted the wig self-consciously. She had opted for wide-legged red pants and a white chiffon blouse with black two-inch heeled sandals. She knew she looked beautiful but her mind ran to her almost bald head covered by a thin cap hidden under the wig. She smiled, showing a perfect set of small white teeth.

"When did you start wearing wigs?" Urah strode over to touch the curly wig Victoria had said was a perfect fit for her. As always, he was immaculately dressed in a suit. Today, it was a navy blue suit with stripes.

Ufedo's heart skipped a beat. Urah was tall, had skin the colour of coffee seeds and when he spoke, his voice sounded as sweet as real coffee drink, with a little bit of sugar and cream. Urah was always tugging at her long hair and while he had not openly said anything to her yet, she was waiting. Patiently waiting. Victoria had said Urah was such a show off. But why wouldn't he? With such skin, and that perfect dress sense.

"Meeting's in five!" Victoria announced. She wore a royal blue knee-length straight dress with a shiny gold belt around it. With her hair let down and skin as ebony as Ufedo's and tall heels, Victoria looked like she was about to go for a fashion photo shoot.

Mrs. Ajuma sat at the end of the table and they sat at both sides of the table with Victoria at the other end, directly opposite Mrs. Ajuma, the director and owner of Ujenyu Properties. Two not-total strangers sat amidst them.

After the opening prayer, Mrs. Ajuma started speaking.

"Well, people, it's no longer news that 'Ujenyu Properties' have added a new area of focus to our Anyigba office. We will be dealing in residential homes from now too, alongside what we're used to. Our other offices have been doing that for a while, it's time for us in Anyigba to step up. And in light of this development, some roles have been shuffled and familiar hands have been moved in."

She moved to introduce the two not-total strangers. Philemon and Loveth were from the Lokoja office and they had been transferred to the Anyigba office due to the upgrade. They had always communicated. As colleagues working for the same organization, so were a little familiar with each other, via meetings, seminars and phone calls.

Ufedo looked over at Loveth and smiled. She had on fashionable pink glasses to match the sleeveless pink blouse she wore and her straight long hair looked so lustrous and soft. She knew it had to have been human hair.

She knew Victoria would know the name and price. She looked at Philemon and gave him a small smile, Philemon had a smile on his face as well. He was dressed in a sky-blue long-sleeved shirt and black pants and he wore glasses that looked medicated. But still, what was it about Lokoja colleagues with eyewear?

Philemon looked to be about Urah's height, but he was slimmer and his skin was dark brown. His whole appearance exuded calmness and Ufedo found herself looking at him again, she caught herself and frowned. What was wrong with her?

"After the meeting, you will be notified of your new roles and new partners. To success." Mrs. Ajuma said and lifted her cup of tea in a toast. She was an attractive woman in her mid-fifties and was decked out in a blinding white shirt tucked into a blue suit pants and her jacket was stylishly draped over one shoulder. The woman had no intention of looking her age.

"To success," they all chorused with their cups raised too. They had quality tea and doughnuts fresh from Thoria's cakes and pastries at Monday morning meetings.

"Here are our letters," Ojochide said as Victoria walked towards their spacious office, letters clutched in her hands. The cubicles were separated by curved transparent glass, except for Mrs Ajuma and Victoria's offices. Victoria was her personal assistant as well as the secretary.

"Well, I'm in commercial and industrial properties!" Loveth announced.

"Me too. I guess that makes us partners." Urah said with a huge smile on his face. Ufedo was happy when Loveth didn't smile back.

Ufedo opened her letter and sighed. Her new role was in residential properties and estates. She was quite fine with being a realtor for the sale of undeveloped lands. Nothing beats tramping around in boots and jeans as she looked over large expanses of land with a prospective buyer or even the occasional developer. So long, she thought.

"I'm in residential, who's my new partner?" Ufedo looked hopefully at Victoria. Her friend shook her head and she turned to look at Ojochide.

"Nope, I'm on land, still," Ojochide said.

"Same as me," Sandra said as she stood beside Ojochide. Sandra always wore pleated materials. No matter what it was, there was sure to be a hint of a pleat on it, somewhere. Today, it was her skirt. It was fully pleated in bold orange. She had on a white ruffle blouse and sturdy Mary Jane shoes.

"Ufedo, I am your partner." Philemon came towards her with his right hand extended. Ufedo took it and shook it. He smiled at her and she couldn't help looking at his eyes. *Why does he have such tender eyes,* she wondered as she released her hand from his grasp. He had a firm grasp and his palm was not as smooth as she had thought. It was strong but without calluses.

"I am still in the personal assistant/secretary ministry and I love it," Victoria said.

"I hoped to work with Ufedo. I guess Mrs AJ knows best, though." Urah winked at her.

"Philemon is like a veteran in this real estate business. You'll learn a lot with him." Loveth said.

Ufedo agreed with that. She had met Philemon when she came in, and she had been around for almost three years. She turned to Victoria. "You knew about this all along. We spent the weekend together. No hint from you."

Victoria shrugged. "We had our hands full over the weekend. Remember?" she said as she casually adjusted a strand of hair that needed no adjusting.

"Lame," Ufedo mouthed and returned to her desk.

Three

Ufedo and Phil sat in a tight silence as the driver navigated his way to the first house on their list. Mrs. Ajuma had mandated them to familiarise themselves first with any property they were to show a client. Ojoagefu, the office driver cranked up the volume of the music playing on the car stereo. He nodded his head to the beat.

"Ojoagefu, please reduce the volume. I don't care for this thing you think is a song this afternoon." Ufedo told him.

"Sorry, Miss," the driver said as he lowered the volume.

"What songs do you care for?" Philemon asked.

"Well...not this," Ufedo said. She was not about to let him in on her musical preference. It was enough with Victoria making fun of her.

"Okay. I'm hoping you'll tell me some other time." Philemon said amicably and leaned back against the car seat. He looked so calm and collected. Ufedo wondered if his confidence was a facade or part of his personality. He wore a pair of ash-coloured chinos pants and a white short-sleeved shirt with black boots. Not a suit wearer and is comfortable in his own skin and style. Ufedo's head itched under Victoria's wig and she resisted the temptation to hit her head a few times.

"We're here, Miss, Sir," Ojoagefu said and stepped out of the car. They stepped out after him.

The four-bedroom house boosted a parking garage for two cars, a full fence topped with jagged pieces of broken bottles and a gate that slid into itself when pushed. It was a new building and the light grey and off pink paint told the story of the newness with its freshness.

"Shall we look inside?" Phil said as he led the way in. He had majorly been into the residential aspect of the real estate in Lokoja, and so was in his element. Ufedo trailed after him.

"I'm a complete novice at this," she admitted.

"Not for long. I was too." He told her and turned to grin at her. He had a narrow face with deep-set eyes and a chin that she had to admit was not bad to look at. His grin lit up his face.

"We'll look around, know what the house contains and its condition, and we'll take some pictures which will go on our website. When a client comes knocking, we will be able to sell the house to them with our eyes closed."

Ufedo nodded. This was the longest she had heard him say. His voice was smooth and he seemed to weigh anything he said so it came out sounding perfect and necessary. She tried to imagine Urah's voice and shook her head at the absurdity of her thoughts. *Abba help me,* she whispered under her breath.

"The house did not come furnished. Just the standard furnishing of the bathroom, sink and shower, kitchen sink and cabinets and the wardrobes in the bedrooms." Philemon continued further.

"Is that good?" Ufedo asked.

"The buyers will know. Some buyers prefer to furnish their own place as they like, and some do not want to go through that whole stress, so they just want to come into a fully furnished house."

"Choices. And money."

"You got that right. Your budget and your taste determines what you'll go for." Philemon said.

"Budget apart, I'd prefer to furnish my own house."

"Right? Imagine meeting sturdy brown chairs when what I want is dark black or pale red." He winked at her.

She burst out laughing. "Dark black? Pale red? Are those Lokoja colours?"

"Well, the lady can laugh after all."

"Of course, I can laugh. What do you think I am?" she asked him.

"I'm still thinking," he said with all seriousness as he rubbed at the not-too-bad-to-look-at-chin and strode into one of the bedrooms.

Ufedo followed him and watched as he moved to a position in the room where he could get a good snapshot of the room including the beautiful mahogany brown wardrobe.

"So you like sturdy brown chairs?

"They're sturdy and brown," he said with a smile. "Why don't you make a video of the kitchen and the bathroom and the sitting room? I'll do the bedrooms. We can sync them together, edit and upload later."

"Great," Ufedo replied as she went to do just that.

Residential properties were so different from the undeveloped lands she had dealt with before. This was an interesting challenge. And Philemon with all his gentlemanliness and simple appearance was turning out to be an interesting personality.

She smiled as she angled her phone to make a video.

*   *   *

Victoria curled up beside Ufedo on her bed as they looked at pictures upon pictures of wigs.

"So, you're going for a bob, a straight one and which?" Victoria asked.

"Just the bob and the straight one."

"Girl. Nope. You need to select at least one more. I say a curly one. Yes. It will frame your face quite beautifully."

"Vickie, I don't really care for wigs. I'll soon start moving around with my head as it is. It's not as if I'm completely bald or not good-looking with the haircut."

"Not on my watch. Ufedo, get serious, please. I see how Urah looks at you these days…," she started.

Ufedo rolled her eyes. Since Victoria's engagement to Onuche, her fiancé, she had not allowed Ufedo a moment's rest. She was forever trying to hook her up with guys from church, and Onuche's friends. To date, Ufedo had managed to hold her ground.

"Ufedo. We're more than friends. You're like my sister. I want you to find the same happiness I have found with Onuche. But you're not even giving guys a chance. And Urah who you seem to like seems fine with just flirting with you. And many other ladies."

"Vickieeee, can you please let me breathe? Last time I checked, it is not a crime to be single. I am waiting on the Lord. Need I remind you?"

"Hmmm. I get that. But it seems like you may wait forever even when the Lord gives you a go-ahead."

"We'll see."

"Philemon is a nice guy," Victoria said out of the blues.

"What? He is. So… "

"And…"

"And nothing. Girl! We're partners. Colleagues, same office."

"You wouldn't say all this if it were Urah."

Ufedo shrugged. How did their conversation get to this point? She wondered.

"Ufedo, you have resigned yourself to the fact that you might not see a man that meets your requirements. Because of a childish wishlist. You'd better throw it away and face the real world."

"I am facing the real world. It's sitting on my bed in a yellow shirt, ordering expensive wigs for me and haranguing me about relationships. You're the real world Victoria. Like I said, I am waiting on the Lord." Ufedo moved towards the kitchen. She was not ready to discuss her checklist just yet. Victoria followed her.

"I suggest you take out that your list and do an update. An adult update. And while you wait on the Lord, I also hope you listen to what He has to say too, because I feel He is ready to renew your strength. And what do you have against the colour yellow?" Victoria said as she opened the freezer and took out a plastic container filled with the stew Ufedo made the night before.

"I think it's time I start charging you for the food you eat here," Ufedo teased her. Victoria did not like cooking and relied on Ufedo and takeouts. And sometimes her lawyer fiancé, Onuche, cooked and brought some to her.

"You should be grateful I came around to eat your food. Helping you avoid waste." Victoria replied.

"We're a perfect match." Ufedo smiled. It was true that cooking soothed her, but eating what she cooked was another story. A cook who did not like to eat what she made, and a food lover who did not like to cook.

"I and Onuche are a perfect match, as you and the 'one' you're waiting on the Lord for will be too," Victoria said with a laugh as Ufedo began to tickle her.

* * *

Ufedo looked up from her seat to find Urah striding towards her. She smiled at him and touched her wig to be sure it was in place. She had worn the straight one today. The one Victoria ordered at an astronomical price. Money Ufedo had had difficulty paying, but pay she did, and now she was grateful for that.

"Hey there, how have you been?" he asked as he plunked himself down on the wine and blue-coloured swivel chair in front of her desk.

"I'm good. You?"

"You look good. These wigs you wear these days, wow!" He kissed a finger and pointed it in the air, which made Ufedo smile and her heart skipped. She thought of her almost bald head under the wig and what he would say if she came to work without a wig.

"How has work been?" he asked.

Ufedo gave him an amused look. True, they were pals and all, but this show of intentional attention was a bit off-pattern. She smiled again, she couldn't stop smiling, maybe he was ready now, she told herself and straightened in her seat.

"So, what's your evening like?" he asked in a rush, tugging at the coral tie he wore with his white shirt. He sounded nervous as he gave a slight cough. Ufedo wondered why. This was Urah. Handsome, confident, playful Urah.

"My evening, today? It's good and free," she answered quickly.

"Good. I was wondering if we could go out later. Just to have dinner, you know..."

"Yes. No problem." Ufedo answered quickly. If her behaviour surprised her. She didn't think too much of it.

"Good then. We can leave from the office," he said.

"All right," Ufedo agreed. She would have loved to go home and change her outfit. Oh well, she didn't look bad in her gold belted maxi gown and pencil-heeled shoes.

The moment Urah left, she rushed to meet Victoria.

"Victoria! He asked. We're going out this evening."

"What? Wow! Okay." Victoria answered as she guided Ufedo to take a seat.

"Tell me the whole story," Victoria said and Ufedo proceeded to do so.

"That's a good development. Be guided, please. I love you, and Urah is fine as a colleague but...I don't know."

"What don't you know? Vickie, can you be happy for me without being judgmental?" Ufedo countered.

"Ufedo! I am the last person to judge you, you know that." Victoria sounded hurt.

Ufedo felt bad as she hugged her best friend.

"Sorry, Sis. I'm a bit nervous. You know I don't do this often and I like this guy. You know."

"I understand. You look good. I know you're not a fan of makeup but I could touch up your face a little. Come around when you're ready to leave."

"You're the best. Love you." Ufedo all but sang as she went back to her seat.

***

"You look really good, Ufedo," Urah said softly as he reached for her hand across the table. They had finished their dinner and were sipping the last of the Valetta wine that was served with their meal; jollof rice and peppered turkey.

"Thank you," Ufedo responded. She waited with bated breath. She knew Urah was going to ask something of her.

"Would you like to come home with me for a while?" he asked.

"What?" Ufedo jerked her hand out of his. She found herself at a loss for words.

"Look, babe, I do like you. Really. And I had the feeling you did too. Let's spend some sweet moments together at my place." He reached for her hand again.

Ufedo got up, placed some naira notes on the table and hurried out of the restaurant as she struggled to hold back her tears.

*   *   *

"He wants to sleep with me." Ufedo sobbed as she fished out some tissues out of a box. Victoria had her arms around her.

"You can't be sure of that, Ufedo."

Ufedo turned red-rimmed eyes at her friend.

"We had dinner at a restaurant. Does having sweet moments at his house look like another dinner to you?"

"Thank God you're fine and back in one piece. Your eyes have been opened to the kind of person he is now. He never even met all the requirements in your list."

"I wanted to have a compromise. You said I may not see the man on my list. He came close."

"You should review that list, Ufedo."

Ufedo sighed. She had no words tonight.

Four

"Babe!!!" Loveth screeched when Ufedo entered the office on Wednesday morning. "You look so good. Never thought of it, but girl you're so rocking this style." Loveth continued as she adjusted her purple-rimmed glasses to get a better look.

Ufedo was in a fire engine red dress topped with heels of the same colour, she carried a medium-sized multi-coloured Turkish handbag. She had also ditched her wigs and was rocking her now growing closely cropped hair in all its jet-black beauty. Her large round multi-colored earrings swung as she moved to her cubicle. Her dark skin seemed to shimmer in the daylight.

"Thank you," Ufedo said as her female colleagues gathered to compliment her.

"That bag is to die for. You have such a good eye." Ojochide commented.

"The haircut suits you," Sandra said as she reached out to touch Ufedo's head. Today, Sandra was dressed in a wine-coloured pleated flounce gown.

"Well, you pulled it off. You look so good, baby girl." Victoria told her with a smile and gave Ufedo a big hug.

She was bent over her keyboard when Philemon sauntered into her cubicle and stood still for some seconds. He removed his glasses, put them back on and looked at her again.

"Good morning to you too," she said as she looked up at him.

"Yes. It's a good morning. You look..." He touched his head and pointed at her.

She laughed, she didn't believe he could be at a loss for words. She felt happy and full of life. She was going to review her list, maybe even throw it out, and she was not going to let Urah or his attitude bother her again. It was time she let God have the pen to her life chapters again.

"My hair has been cut for a while now. The wigs were to avoid self-consciousness and any awkwardness, but no more," she told him as she waved him to sit down. He was dressed in brown chinos and a T-shirt.

"You look beautiful no matter what you wear, Ufedo," he said softly.

"Thank you, Philemon."

"You do. Really," he said

"Okay...." Ufedo cleared her throat.

"I'm sorry. You took my breath away for a moment there."

"Oh wow! Is your breath back now?" Ufedo teased, her insides were churning with emotions she couldn't fathom yet. What was going on here?

"Sure. We need to be at a property in 20 minutes," he said.

She had completely forgotten. She scrambled to her feet and picked up her bag.

On their way to the car, they met Urah coming in. Ufedo's back stiffened.

"Ufedo, Babe, look, I am sorry about yesterday. I didn't mean to..."

"That's past and over," Ufedo said as she got into the waiting car.

"Are you okay?" Philemon asked her as he got in beside her.

"Of course," her answer was curt.

"I do not want to pry, but you looked shaken there. Dinner didn't go well?"

She turned sharply to him, "How did you know?"

He shrugged. Their office walls had large ears. They both knew that.

"Did he hurt you? I can go beat him up for you," he said as he patted her back.

"My knight in chinos." She smirked at him as she imagined his lanky frame taking on Urah's muscled one.

"Glad to see that smile," he said.

"Well..." She smiled again. What was it that made her smile so much around this guy? She sneaked a peak at him. He was confident, calm and gentle. He was tall and handsome in his own way but his skin colour was a dark brown. She sighed. She needed to say something that would bring them both to solid ground.

"We need to sell this house. We have received promises for all the ones we've shown and no payments. I pray we sell this one." she said.

Philemon took her hand in his immediately. "Let's pray then." And he said a prayer while they were still in the car. Ufedo was moved. He took her seriously, and from the look of things, he took God seriously too. She felt a flutter in her heart but left it unacknowledged.

The house was impressive. A row of duplexes separated by high-walled fences and wide compounds. Most of the duplexes had been bought as the owners wanted buyers and not tenants.

The couple were waiting by the house when Ufedo and Philemon arrived.

"Apologies for coming late please," Philemon said as he shook hands with the couple.

Ufedo did the same.

"Not at all. We haven't been here long." the young woman holding onto the arm of her husband replied with a smile.

"Yes," her husband said as she looked into his wife's eyes. They smiled.

"You're such a lovely couple. The house will suit you just fine." Ufedo found herself saying to her own greatest surprise.

"Well, we will see," the man said with a smile as Philemon opened the door and they went in.

It was a fully furnished three-bedroom duplex with two sitting rooms, a dining room and a kitchen that was as big as Ufedo's bedroom and sitting room combined.

The young wife rushed towards the kitchen cabinets and rubbed her hands over the polished golden wood.

"It's so beautiful honey."

"I can see that, babe," her husband replied as he stood at the sink and fiddled with the tap.

Two of the bedrooms were painted in soft grey and the bed and coverings were in muted blues and blinding white. Ufedo could not resist sitting on one of the beds. It was so soft but it had the right amount of firmness.

The wife squealed when they got to the master bedroom, the huge poster bed was dressed in red and black bedspread with gold coverings and the large wardrobe stood in a corner. The wood sparkled.

"Impressive," the husband murmured in a voice that was trying to stay aloof but was failing.

"I'm sure you will love this house. The neighbourhood is quite cool and safe." Philemon said.

"I like your confidence young man, but have you seen the price of this house?" the husband asked.

"This house boasts a terrace, a parking garage, a sizeable backyard, comfy rooms and lots more. You won't get it better anywhere else, Sir." Ufedo said.

"You both are evenly matched against me, but no problem, we're here to look. So we will look," he said.

"And possibly buy it?" The wife said as she hugged her husband. "It's so beautiful. What better place to start a family than here."

"Let's check the sitting rooms," the husband said as he walked out of the bedroom hand in hand with his wife.

*   *   *

"To success," Philemon said as he lifted a can of malt. Ufedo raised another and laughed.

They were having celebratory drinks at Philemon's cubicle. The couple had driven back to the office with them and paid for the house. Ufedo had been over the moon and Mrs Ajuma had commended them for a job well-done.

"Between you and his wife, the man didn't know what hit him," Philemon said.

"Oh, we all did our part. I'm sure he loved the house, he was just being macho about it."

"Sure he did. I do love the real estate business. Providing budget-fit properties for people, watching the pleasure on their faces as they make payments, move in, develop it or even resell it later. What's not to love? I would like to start mine soon."

"Me too," Ufedo said.

"What? Wow! Okay. That's cool."

"Why is it okay for you to have a real estate business and then you raise eyebrows at me for wanting to do the same?" Ufedo said as he stood.

"What? What? Wait, Ufedo." Philemon moved towards her and pulled her back to the seat. He leaned against the table and faced her. He touched the sleeve of her dress lightly.

"Must be all this red you're wearing today. You're on fire. Can we backtrack again?"

She shrugged.

"I didn't raise eyebrows at you for wanting to start your own real estate business. Why do you think that?" he asked.

"The tone said it all." Ufedo looked at him with her head cocked to the side, as if daring him to deny it.

"Ufedo, I would be the last person to do that. I was a little surprised you'd want to start a real estate company. Not many women are in the business. They can be shareholders and stuff, but to build it from scratch? Hardly. Even our Mrs. Ajuma didn't. Her husband owned it first before he died. Though she's doing a good job, it's quite a lot of work. I am impressed." Philemon said

"What did you think my interest would be?" Ufedo asked.

"You have this keen eye for fashion. Everything you wear is a hit. Even with your haircut, you still exude that class and elegance. And you walk like a model." he said.

"Wow! Fashion business? Modelling? Okay." Ufedo laughed, not knowing what to say and her mind fluttering at the thought that he had looked at her long enough to notice how she walked. Abba! She didn't know where to look. His sizable cubicle suddenly seemed confining.

"Now I know better." Philemon shrugged.

"So when do you want to start yours?" she asked.

"Maybe in two years' time. Been making plans for a while. I'd like the woman I marry to join me in the business too. It will be more comforting as we can take our wins and losses together. What about you?" Philemon asked.

"Definitely not in two years' time. Still got some major adjustments to make. So when are you getting married?" she asked.

"Can't say for sure. But I know it won't be long now. Maybe a year from now. If the young lady I have my eyes on is the one and if she agrees to marry me of course."

"You mean you haven't even asked her out yet?" Ufedo didn't know what to make of him.

"Well, Ufedo, would you like to be my partner?"

"What? Why are you changing the topic? Partner in what exactly?" Her head was reeling. Philemon looked so simple and cool, now she wasn't sure what to make of him. And why was her stomach fluttering like she had a butterfly in there?

Philemon sighed.

"Ufedo. This may not be the best time or situation, and it may not be ideal, but I know you know what I mean. No pressure. Please pray, and do think of it. I will keep doing the same."

"What is the prayer point?" Ufedo asked. She wondered if she was the same girl that walked into the office that morning. She daydreamed a lot and was sure she was in one of her dreams.

"If it's okay for Philemon to be your real estate business partner and your life partner too," he said calmly, touched her hand and settled into the seat opposite her.

"I see," Ufedo replied as she got up on shaky legs and walked out of his cubicle.

Five

"I don't know what my feelings for him are," Ufedo said to Victoria.

"Are you sure? Ufedo, you can lie to the world and even Philemon, but do not lie to yourself. And you cannot lie to me, for I already know." Victoria said smugly as she swept into Ufedo's kitchen.

"You know nothing. Absolutely nothing. That you're in love does not mean I should be in love too. Our umbilical cords are not tied together. We do not share one heart." Ufedo followed her to the kitchen where half of her friend's body was inside the freezer.

Victoria came up with a big plastic bowl that contained Egusi soup.

"Ufedo, let love in. Do not fight against your own self. Why are you suddenly avoiding him if you're not scared of anything." she said with eyes full of an expression Ufedo did not want to qualify.

It wasn't as if she was some frigid lady scorned by love and was therefore being careful about who she let in.

She was just a church and a career girl who had a list of requirements she wanted in a man.

She did not know what she was scared of exactly. Philemon was the most non-threatening male she had ever met.

During a visit to a house last week, Philemon had quietly come up behind her and asked what she was scared of.

She was quick to tell him she was not scared of anything. At that moment, she thought he looked ready to slay whatever dragon he thought she was going to mention. He had then asked, in a soft voice,

"Then tell me, what is it that stands between us? I need an answer, Ufedo."

She nodded, unable to look into his eyes.

He had such expressive eyes and she had avoided him since then.

*   *   *

"Abba, that I may know your will. I do not want to ruin this season of my life. That I may know your will, dear Lord." Ufedo sat on her bed as she prayed.

Her mind wandered to all sorts, she dragged it back and prayed again. She kept at it. She knew her working at the real estate firm was not a mistake. She knew Philemon coming there, and them getting on well, even before then, was not a mistake either. But she knew that the fact that these were not mistakes did not mean she should jump into a relationship with him. A marital relationship.

"God, must I be married?" she asked.

But the answer was obvious. If she didn't want to, she wouldn't; but she wanted to, she had her list to prove it. Ufedo wondered how fair that list was now though. She didn't have a car or a house. Ufedo had no plans for a doctorate, and she had just one piece of suit. She didn't even meet her own requirements. She gave a dry laugh.

For long she had dreamt of a prince charming, a knight in shining armour. She grew up watching Barbie and Cinderella, and Hallmark movies but she knew life was not as easy and pretty as Barbie and Cinderella made it seem. Life was difficult. Choices were complex. She could even die, lose her eternal life if she made a wrong one.

"Oh, God, that I may know your will." She prayed again. Her facts were that Philemon was a born Christian and he had a job and was kind. Did he even love her? He didn't know her that much, she didn't know him that much either. Diverse thoughts welled up in her again.

The Lord keeps in perfect peace those whose minds are stayed on Him.

The scripture came to her and she held that in her heart as she prepared for bed all the while trying to keep her mind on God.

"Abba, the entrance of your word gives light and understanding. Help me to see, help me to understand." she whispered as she fluffed her pillows and as her head touched the pillow, a verse came to her, *"the steps of the righteous are ordered by the Lord and He delights in their way."*

*   *   *

Ufedo glanced at her wristwatch and sighed. It was 20 minutes already and Philemon was nowhere to be found, and neither were the buyers. They had agreed to meet there as they both had other appointments.

She had no key to use and gain entrance into the house so she paced as she waited for him.

The house had no fence and stood on a narrow strip of land. The owner had built the house on most of the land. If he ever built a fence, the buyer would have to park his car by the road, unless he didn't plan to have one.

"Hey, I'm so sorry." Philemon came up behind her and touched her shoulder lightly.

She turned around sharply.

"Okay."

"Ufedo, I'm sorry."

"Okay."

He smiled and opened the door. She walked in after him.

"Maybe I should have my own keys," she said tightly.

"Ufedo, I had a family emergency. My Dad collapsed at work yesterday. I went to Lokoja last night and the car didn't take off on time."

Ufedo was shaken. She covered her eyes.

"God, Phil! I'm sorry I didn't know. How is he now?" She moved to take his hands.

"He's stable now. God is always good."

"I didn't know. I assumed your other appointment was work-related."

"It's okay. Enough of apologies. Let's see the house." He squeezed her hands. Ufedo had forgotten she had her hands in his. She slipped her hands out of his.

"I don't bite, you know. This feels quite good." Philemon said as he took her hands, raised them and brushed his lips lightly across her knuckles.

Ufedo shivered. She was at a loss for words. Philemon stood silently beside her, saying nothing. It unnerved her. This perfect patience of his. This quiet confidence and strength he exuded from within, she didn't know what to do, so she cleared her throat.

"Well..." she started.

"How are you?" he asked.

"Fine."

"What is it?"

"We don't know much about each other." She pointed at him and herself.

"Okay. I am a born again Christian, the first of 3 boys, and I'm 33 years old and have worked with Ujenyu Properties for 8 years."

"Okay. Basics. It's a start." she said.

"Yeah. And you're an only child and 27 years of age. Been with the company for 3 years now." he said and laughed at the shock on her face.

"How do you know that?" she asked nonplussed.

"I made it my business. Here." He dipped his hand into his pocket and handed over a slim package to her.

"Chocolates. Thank you." Ufedo gave a surprised laugh as she unwrapped it.

"Here." she held it to his mouth. He shook his head but she held it there until he took a bite.

"Happy?" he asked.

"Yes. Let's check out the house," she said and moved into one of the rooms. It was a simple four-bedroom bungalow.

"Whatever you say, my Lady," Philemon said and followed her.

"Where are the buyers?" she asked.

"Co-asking my dear. Let's give them a call."

He called and called but no one picked up. When Ufedo tried the phone numbers, she got 'number busy' which later became 'switched off'.

"Been a while someone did this to me," Philemon said.

"Me too. But all is not lost. Let's get some pictures and make a video." she suggested.

"Great, you do the bedrooms and I'll take care of the rest."

The house was freshly painted and that was all. No single piece of furniture was in it. And the kitchen just had the sink and the cabinet. Same with the bathroom. The bedrooms had no wardrobes and the living room had no single piece of furniture. Just the fresh paint and beautiful tiles in an intricate ash design.

The verandah of the house was roomy enough and was walled in a little. They sat on the little walls opposite each other to compare pictures and videos.

"Please send me the pictures and videos you have," Philemon said.

Ufedo raised her head after sending the pictures to see Philemon with his phone raised and the light pointed at her.

"What? Are you taking a photo of me?" she asked.

"Yes ma'am. You look so good today. So put together. What is the secret, young lady?" he asked.

Ufedo laughed and tugged at the sleeve of the lilac coloured cutwork blouse she had worn, tucked into slim denim jeans and Chelsea boots. Oh, this guy was getting to her all right. She smiled again.

"I love that smile."

"Stop already," she said.

"Ufedo..." He came to sit beside her and took her hands.

"This morning, in a conversation with my father, I told him about you and he gave his fatherly Christian advice, then he said something from the scripture 'The steps of the righteous are ordered by the Lord, and he delights in their way.' Isn't that comforting? To know our steps are actually ordered, and therefore the Lord himself will not let His righteous ones end up in terrible situations?"

Ufedo was moved. Her heart stilled for a moment and picked up again. Oh Abba! Her mind cried.

"I received that scripture last night too. But what if our steps are not ordered towards each other?" she asked.

"Oh, Ufedo! Do you delight in tormenting me? Why are you evading what is right in front of your eyes? I've known you for a while now. Though we didn't interact much and meet physically as often as we do now, I've known you, and I've been praying about you. You may think mine and Loveth's coming to Anyigba office is just an official redeployment, it is more than that. Loveth's family are here, and I know you're here. Our steps have been ordered my love. Mrs. A.J could employ any staff she wanted or even redeploy somebody else, but why us who didn't even ask for a relocation, even though we needed it?"

"Ordered steps?"

"Ordered steps, my Lady," he said and squeezed her shoulder a little.

Ufedo knew she had to say something to dislodge whatever it was that was in her throat.

"So, you and Loveth have known each other for a long while?"

"Ufedo!" His eyes opened wide in surprise.

"Really, all you deduced from my long speech is that?" he asked.

She shrugged.

"Well, is somebody jealous?" he asked with a smile.

"I'm never jealous," she announced.

"He that stands, let him take heed, lest he..."

"I won't fall," she said and they ended up laughing.

"Do we have a yes, or a no, Ufedo?" he asked quietly.

"A maybe," she croaked out.

"Okay. Could you put your hand on my shoulder please?" he asked.

"What? Okay. Why?" she asked as her hand moved its way to lie quietly on his shoulder. He raised his head, cleared his throat, and gave her a light kiss on her forehead before she could react.

He sat looking at her face with her hand on his shoulder. "I love you, Ufedo."

She sighed.

She had the words but they were far from her at the same time. Her mind was a forest of thoughts.

"Hey, no pressure my Lady. I'm here for you," he said and took her hand from his shoulder. He held both of her hands in his. "Dear Lord, teach our hearts to trust in you and to never lean on our own understanding. Direct our paths and may Ufedo and I have reasons to continually rejoice at your feet, O God." He prayed and squeezed her hands.

"Amen," Ufedo said and laid her head on his shoulder. Her mind was still and she needed no other words for the moment.

Six

Ufedo strolled into Tasty Castle, a plush restaurant in the heart of Anyigba in a red long-sleeved blouse with a cinched waist, blue jeans, low-heeled black sandals and a black mini pebble Mary bag. Philemon had his eyes plastered on her face as she approached his table.

She smiled at him as she sat opposite him.

"Classy place," she commented as she looked around.

The sitting arrangements were such that all tables were enclosed in a half cubicle that gave customers privacy. Dainty looking flowers were placed in pots and little ceramic vases around the whole place. The silvery curtains swayed in the air-conditioned atmosphere. Strains of quiet conversations and scent of good food lent the place a tranquil air. Philemon had chosen well and Ufedo told him so.

He smiled.

"Phil." He had not said a word since she sat down. "You okay?"

He cleared his throat. "You always dazzle me, Ufedo. So beautiful both on the outside and within. God took his time to send you to us beloved."

"Philemon. You should be a writer. Your way with words is something else. Thank you for your kind compliments. You look good yourself."

He was dressed in dark blue jeans and a short sleeved ash shirt with a collar and three buttons he had all buttoned up. She reached over and unbuttoned the first hole.

She smiled at him. He smiled back.

"Thank you." He caught her hand in his and laid a soft kiss on it. Put his hand behind his back and brought out a single, long, red rose flower. He handed it to her.

"Philemon! This is so beautiful. Thank you." She caressed the rose as she brought it to her nose to inhale the sweetness. She laid it carefully on the chrome topped table.

A waiter came to take their orders. They both ordered fried rice and chicken. She opted for bottled water while Philemon requested for fruit juice.

She fiddled with the straps of her bag and gulped down water as she looked everywhere but at him. She had prepared a little speech. But she could not recall a word now. He pried the bag from her hand.

"Ufedo, talk to me."

"I wanted everything to go my way. I had this list. I'm going to discard it now. I wanted a man who had all what I wrote on that list; I wanted to be the one to write my own story; but I've come to discover the peace and joy that permeates life when we let God write our story."

"You're right, my love. Thank you for yielding."

She nodded.

"Have I told you how good you looked today?" he asked.

"Yes. You have." She rolled her eyes.

"I'm telling you again. You look so good. How you always manage to pull off these looks is a gift." he said.

"Thank you." Ufedo felt warm all over.

"Can I see the list?"

"No!"

"Ufedo. Just satisfy my curiosity. I know you have it with you."

"I'm not showing it to you. And are you psychic or something?"

"I'm a son of God. Can I see the list?"

"Fine." She pulled it from her bag and handed it to him. She felt silly.

"Okay. I am a born-again Christian," he said as he held the paper with all seriousness.

"Phil! Noooo." Ufedo said weakly.

"It's fine. Let's just look at the list to the end."

"I'm tall, I know I'm not so bad looking, and my skin, oh well...which one is skin the colour of coffee seeds?"

She shrugged. She couldn't be more embarrassed.

He continued, "I do have a master's degree, but have no plans for a doctorate. I have taken business courses though, and will continue to do so. Gentle, calm, patient and a gentleman? What do you think, Ufedo?" he asked.

"Oh, you are such a gentleman," she said.

He beamed and continued, "Well, no car, no personal house yet, but we will get them, at the right time. And a nice paying job or business. Well, Mrs. A.J is not doing so badly in terms of remuneration. Been with her for eight years."

Ufedo nodded. She wanted him to stop already.

"You're a wise and faithful employee," she said.

"And good fashion sense, love to wear suits? I've just got one. You'd do the dressing up for both of us my dear. And I'm six years older. Oh well..." he said, folded the list neatly and pocketed it. She raised her eyebrows at him. He smiled.

"Hey." he took her hands. "Don't be embarrassed. You always impress me, you know that. I'm proud that you're not willing to take anything and anyone that comes. And I know that if God says a yes, you can say a no, but I'm happy that you're saying yes, to your father in heaven, and to me, Philemon on earth."

"Oh Phil!" Her heart was all gooey. He was funny too.

She was glad her requirements were not met, but rather refined and exceeded.

"Phil?"

"My Lady?"

"About being partners?"

"Yes?"

She extended her hand, "You've got yourself one, for life."

Before she could blink, he moved to her seat and had her in a bone crushing hug. She hugged him back. With all her strength. He lifted his head to look at her, when she lifted her head, he kissed her forehead and hugged her again. She hugged him back. They pulled apart to smile at each other.

"It's a public place, Phil." Ufedo found her voice as she tried to wiggle out of his arms. Philemon's arms were like boulders. She stayed caged in, watching him smile at her as she smiled back.

"Maybe I should stand on this table and shout about my good fortune. And please keep calling me Phil," he told her.

"You don't dare," she said with heat.

He laughed. "Fine. I am just happy."

"Did you think I would say no?" she asked.

"I prayed you wouldn't. Choices you know. I mean, my skin nowhere resembles coffee seeds. I love you, Ufedo."

"I love you, Phil," she said, sincerity ringing in her voice.

He finally released her, but stayed beside her.

"Do you hear the Angels singing my love?"

"Is it rapture already?" she asked with all seriousness.

He burst out laughing. "The heavens rejoice with us. Don't you know that?"

"Well...are we weird?" she asked.

"Never. We are just who we are."

"We are a love ordered by God."

He put his arm on her shoulder and she leaned back against him.

Today was not the day for fried rice and chicken. Its day will come.

About the Author

Christiana Agboni was born and brought up in Nigeria, where she currently lives. She writes Christian romance and literary fiction. Her short stories and flash fiction have been published in numerous literary magazines like Writer Space Africa, the Kalahari Review, Loana Press, amongst others.

She is also one of the authors of **Hell Hath No Fury,** an African Christmas anthology. Her story in the anthology is titled, **Yuletide Sparks**.

When she's not writing, Christiana can be found working as a Client Service Officer.

She can be reached on her following social media handles
Facebook: Christiana Agboni
Instagram: Christiana Agboni
LinkedIn: Christiana Agboni
X: Christiana Agboni

TANGLED

HEARTS

What a tangled web when we weave when, in the name of love, we first practise to deceive.

By

TEMITOPE OMAMEGBE

1
SUNDAY LUNCH

"I want a divorce." Regina listened to coughs, choking and cutleries clattering at the announcement she just made. It was as expected, after all, she had just dropped a bombshell at a family gathering. She gently put her spoon down before looking up at the faces of her family seated at the dining table with her.

Almost everyone was staring at her, everyone except for him, her husband. He continued to eat. Calmly taking one forkful of rice after another. She stared at him for a few more seconds before looking away.

"How and why did you think this was the right place to make such an announcement?"

She turned to her mother and smiled. "It's something that needs to be done, Mom. I am sorry I am breaking the news like this but I didn't think there was any better time," she looked around, still smiling, "or place."

"What did he do to you?" Her brother's voice boomed over the gathering. He pushed his chair away from the table and in seconds had jacked up her husband by the collar of his shirt.

Raymond, in his usual manner, did not react one bit. Instead, he stood there, held up by a man he would have easily handled, and stared down at him. Most of the people at the table were on their feet including Regina who ran forward and held her brother's arms.

"Please don't do that. We don't need all this. He did not do anything, I promise." They stood there in silence for like three seconds and Raymond was let go. In a flash, her brother fist connected with Raymond's jaw and Regina rushed forward as her husband fell to the ground, unconscious.

Shock reverberated through the room and silence descended. Regina knelt to check on him, and when she noticed blood at the back of his head, she raised an alarm.

"Richard! Why did you do that?"

"He hurt you. For you to want a divorce, that's what it means."

"And anyone that chooses to hurt an Ajiwe will feel the pain too." The words of her father, who up till that moment had remained seated despite the chaos, were spoken in utmost calmness but laced with venom. Getting to his feet, he approached the semi-circle of people looking down at the unconscious Raymond.

"This boy has been nothing but a problem and if it's a divorce my daughter wants, it is what she will get, with all the necessary compensation." He was speaking to her father-in-law, Raymond's father, who remained seated at the dining table behind them. "Name your price."

"Will everyone please just stop!" Regina shouted, flailing her arms in the air. She had started crying by the time she stood up. "Just stop. Asking for a divorce has nothing to do with Raymond. It's all me."

"How?" her mother, Rose, asked as she moved from her husband, Reginald's side to her daughter's, and held her hand. "What happened?"

Regina stared into her mother's eyes, pain etched on her face as more tears flowed freely.

"It's all me, Mommy." Her declaration surprised her audience and not wanting to give space for any more confusion, Regina quickly added, "I am so sorry. I was desperate."

"What are you talking about? Go straight to the point." Richard's statement was interrupted by a groan and everyone's attention turned to Raymond, who was starting to stir. Sitting up, he held his head and groaned again.

Visibly uncomfortable, the gathering dispersed, and using that opportunity to get closer, his sister, Ronke, helped him to his feet and up the stairs.

When they were out of earshot, the rest of the gathering turned to Regina. She had returned to the dining table and sat facing her father-in-law, Robert, who, like everyone else, was waiting for her to speak.

"First, I want to apologise," she started. Taking a deep breath, she looked up at her brother sitting on the other side of the table from her. "You all defended my honor when I did not have one. I have lived with this guilt for six years and it has only increased daily."

"What guilt are you referring to?" Robert asked as his wife Ropo came to sit beside him. Soon everyone else had pulled up a chair and were seated, albeit scattered, around the table, with the abandoned food lying about on the table, totally forgotten.

"Regina, what is happening?" Ropo asked, "Or should I say what happened to get to this point?"

"I lied," she paused, "About everything."

Silence.

They all sat frozen. Some sat staring at each other and then at Regina. Others stared at nothing in particular while trying to understand what they had just heard. Richard was the first to snap out of his shock. Turning to his sister, he raised a finger at her.

"What exactly did you lie about?" Richard's question got his father to speak up as well.

"Regina, please go straight to the point. We came here for a normal Sunday lunch but this is beginning to look like a confessional."

Ropo laughed lightly at her daughter-in-law. "Were any of these lunches normal in any way?"

Ropo and Rose, Regina's mother, exchanged glances before Ropo hissed and looked away.

"As I said, I lied about everything, from the beginning. It was all a scheme to get my way and I have regretted it multiple times over. I have not dared to say the truth because I hoped things would get better."

"Don't you think Raymond should be here to listen in on this?" Ronke said. She had returned and was standing at the bottom of the stairs.

"How is he?" Ropo asked. Her last born eyed her before stepping into the kitchen without another word. Ropo absentmindedly glanced up the stairs and then back at her husband.

Ronke emerged from the kitchen, carrying a bowl of water with ice. "I don't know if Raymond slept off or passed out again. He needs a doctor because his nose looks broken and he may have hit his head when he fell."

"I caught his head when he slumped," Regina stated.

Ronke looked her sister-in-law over, restraint evident on her face. "I don't think it's wise for him to be alone so I will head back to the room to stay with him."

"I have messaged a doctor and he will be here soon or he will send someone." Robert stated.

"Thank you, Daddy. That's more than you have done for him in recent times." Ronke retorted, walking up the stairs as she spoke.

Her words stung. Ronke was Raymond's staunch supporter and Regina was glad he had his sister's support.

"Regina, you were saying?" Richard said when Ronke was out of sight.

Regina nodded. "I know what I told you was that Raymond intended to jilt me after I told him I was pregnant but that was a lie. He didn't have anything to do with me. I set him up."

Ropo let out a little whistle. She leaned forward on the chair, resting her elbows on her laps while resting her chin on her hands.

"More details o! Dear daughter-in-law, tell us more."

Regina swayed her head from side to side, stray tears streaking down her cheeks, smearing her makeup even more. It was going to be a Sunday of revelations, a confessional just as her mother-in-law had said.

"He never touched me at the party where I said we had done the deed. He was vested in Royal, his then-girlfriend. He kept declaring his love for her throughout the party." Regina picked up an empty glass and filled it with water, taking a sip before she continued her tale.

"Royal didn't make it to the party that night. Raymond was upset about this and drank his sorrows away. He was soon out of it, drunk and staggering around. We were using a flat for the party and a friend of his took him into one of the rooms to sleep it off. I took advantage of the situation and went in."

"You," Rose started, looking around the room in panic, "Please don't tell us you did something to him in that state?"

"Use the right words, Rose. Ask your daughter if she took advantage of my son." Ropo frowned at Rose.

"Please let her continue. We need to get to the root of all this." Robert was visibly irritable. Reginald looked over at his friend of many years and recognized the despair in Robert's eyes.

"Regina, please continue. I am keen on understanding how far you went." Her father's words hurt.

"Even as inebriated as he was, he did not accept me. I lay there half-naked and embarrassed as he slept. Even in his sleep, Raymond had Royal's name on his lips." Regina shrugged. "I should have given up there and then but, for some reason, I decided to take pictures of us in such a way that would imply that something happened.

"When I returned to the dance floor, I met Rapu. He was a friend who liked me and gave me solace that night."

At that, most of the people listening to her threw their hands in the air. Rita, Raymond's twin sister, who had been quiet, let out a low cry. She got to her feet and started pacing.

"So you pinned your pregnancy on Raymond and this Rapu is your son's father?" she asked. When Regina did not answer, Rita took a step towards her.

"That's what you did right?" The anger in her voice startled Regina a little. She shut her eyes and took a deep breath. Rita was the opposite of her twin brother. Their temperaments were stark opposites of each other as much as they were twins of the opposite gender.

"Answer her, Regina," Ropo said. She turned to her daughter Rita, "Calm down. Let her speak."

"What more is she going to say? We all know what the outcome of her actions was." Rita said over Regina's head. She was almost yelling as she spoke and Ropo, a slender woman in her mid to late fifties, had to get up and physically drag her daughter away.

"Calm down before you blow a gasket. We need the whole story." She led her back to another chair and forced her to sit.

"I am sorry. I know what I did was awful."

"You think?" Ropo said. She grabbed a bottle of water from the table and looked over the mess that was their abandoned meal. A light sigh escaped her lips as she returned to her seat.

"So, what happened after that?" Richard asked. Regina looked over at her brother and watched him flex his hand. He sat staring off at nothing in particular and then down at his feet.

She was the reason for his regret.

"I informed Rapu when I found out I was pregnant and he told me he was going abroad for his master's degree and that we could not tell anyone. I was at a loss for what to do. One day I came across the pictures on my phone and the idea to pin it on Raymond popped into my head."

"What was your end game, Regina?" Robert asked. "Everything was going downhill for him. Raymond was maltreated and berated. But you kept quiet for over six years."

They were interrupted by a knock on the door that Rose got up to answer.

"Welcome, Doctor," she greeted.

As the man stepped in, Robert met him with a handshake.

"Good day, everyone. I am sorry I came later than promised."

"It's okay. As long as you made it." Reginald added.

"Erm, where is my patient?" The Doctor asked.

With that, Ropo gestured at the stairs and led the way. While gone, no one uttered a word as though afraid to speak. Everyone sat quietly before Rose looked at the messy dining table and got up. She started to clear up and was joined by Regina a few seconds later.

In the kitchen, Rose stood by the sink and started to cry. Regina stared at her, unsure of what to do.

"I am sorry, Mom."

"Over six years, Regina. Do you know how much damage you have done?"

"I know and I am trying to do right by him."

"But why now? Why are you choosing to tell the truth now?"

Regina leaned on the kitchen island for a minute before she turned to face her mother.

"When my baby was sick, Raymond refused to donate blood. I watched him get tongue-lashed. It was upsetting to watch." Regina confessed.

"He was stripped of his MD position, his cousin replaced him and he got demoted by two levels," she continued, smiling sadly at her mother. "Whenever he comes home, he heads straight for the bar to pick his poison before retreating to the room. No words. It's not like he had anyone he could talk to when his wife was his jailer. He was isolated from everyone for something he didn't do."

Rose nodded as she stepped in front of her daughter. She stared at her daughter's face and observed that tears had washed away most of her makeup, exposing wrinkles at the corners of her eyes.

"The truth is always best. Now, we can only wait and be hopeful for the best possible outcome."

"Hopeful? I don't know about that mom. I have done too much evil to think I have hope."

Regina's words carried a lot of weight. Rose feared what more there was to unravel and if she could cope with more truths.

2
REVELATIONS

"He has a concussion but it's not too bad. I will prescribe a refill of the drugs I administered so you can get them but for now, he is asleep."

The Doctor returned to the living room. He could not help but notice that it looked cleaner than when he arrived earlier. It was not his business and he didn't make it a habit to interfere in the matters of his clients but he could not help but be a bit curious.

"I thought I caught his head as he fell," Regina mumbled. The Doctor nodded.

"You may have but he hit his head on something. Maybe on the edge of a table or the ground before you caught him, preventing more damage."

The man shrugged as he spoke and he watched Regina's shoulders fall.

Checking his watch, he started to excuse himself. "I have to leave now. I told his sister to keep an eye on him. There may be some confusion when he wakes up and he will have a bad headache but if all that doesn't clear up by tomorrow afternoon or at least improve, please call me."

Minutes after the doctor left, they moved to the sitting room. Regina looked up the stairs longingly.

"I asked a question before the doctor came in," Robert said as he sat down. "I would like to pick things up from there."

Regina nodded. She sat on one of the side tables and leaned forward, arms on her laps and hands clasped.

"I was a stupid girl who wanted to be able to tell her friends a riveting tale of how my man and I fell in love." A sad smile flashed on her face. "I was enthralled by the stories of hate at first sight and love in the face of adversity."

"You chose to ruin a life to fulfil your fantasy," Rita chipped in.

"I was so certain that Raymond would come to love me over time. A baby in the mix made it even better. I imagined that at our anniversary parties, he would give a toast and talk of how we arrived at true love." She laughed lightly at herself, at her folly. "We were family friends. Who better to fall in love with than someone you grew up with?"

"What changed?" her father asked.

Regina looked over at her mother and answered the same way she had in the kitchen.

"I thought I knew you and what you are capable of. I defended you, Regina." Reginald scolded.

Robert laughed. He looked around the room before fixing his gaze on Reginald.

"Reginald Ajiwe once called me the father of a monster. How do I address you now?" he said bitterly. Turning to Ropo, he gestured for her to get up. "Let's go check on Raymond before we leave. I don't know if we are even worthy to do that but I am afraid of what I will do if I stay here much longer."

Rose buried her face in her hands. Rita, having lingered for a few seconds after her parents left, soon followed them upstairs.

Alone with his family, Reginald got to his feet and started to pace before turning to his daughter.

"Is that all? Or is there more you want to say?" He stood pointing at her.

"I am so sorry, Daddy, Mom. Please, I just want to have an amicable divorce. I will not ask for anything and will refund the eight million his father paid me, with interest. I don't want any more trouble for him."

"That is not the answer to my question." Her father's firm statement made Regina swallow hard.

"I paid off anyone who could have proven him innocent. I got someone to help me fabricate some evidence that proved we were in a relationship. All the pictures and chats were fake." She wiped a tear as she continued. "I begged him to agree and even offered him a way out after a few years if things did not work. He was so stubborn."

"Who are you?" Rose asked. She shook her head in disbelief. "Did I raise you? How did you become like this?"

Reginald sat down heavily, suddenly exhausted. Richard got to his feet and walked to the bar in the corner of the sitting room. He poured himself half a glass of vodka, paused, and proceeded to fill the glass.

***

"How is he?" Ropo's question was met with silence. She and Robert had entered the room to find their son sleeping. Their daughter, Ronke, did not acknowledge their presence.

Ropo stood beside the sleeping Raymond while her husband stood at the end of the bed.

"How is he?" When she still didn't get a reply, Ropo moved to the other side of the bed where Ronke sat. Looking up at her mother, Ronke sighed.

"He woke up briefly after the doctor left. He was confused and asked if lunch had started yet and he was out like a light." Ronke responded nonchalantly. Ropo nodded and looked at her son.

"He must have felt so alone. I can't imagine what he would have been going through."

Ronke laughed a little. "Funny you care now after that witch's confession."

"Do not be rude, young lady." Normally, her father's stern voice would have silenced any further retort from Ronke, but she was far from done.

"You didn't flinch when he was assaulted." Her tone was laced with venom.

Robert frowned. "I will not let them get away with this. I am going to take this up legally."

"Seriously? Wow. What good would that do?" Ronke asked. She threw her legs off the bed and sat up. "You are talking about what she did to him but what about what you did?" She paused. "Using him to grow your business, belittling and mocking him at every opportunity. You refused to let him earn his salary, instead giving it to Regina. And to crown it all, you put Reuben in charge."

"All that will be rectified," Robert stated.

"The damage has been done." Ronke pointed at her brother, "Do you know how messed up he is? How warped his psyche has become?

"He barely eats. He suffers from insomnia and stress ulcers. Why do you think I insisted on coming to live here?" Ronke added, counting off her fingers. "Maybe by now, Regina would have been confessing over his grave instead."

"What do you mean?" Ropo asked. She looked from her daughter to her husband and back. "Talk nau."

Ronke got up, edged past her mother, and stood facing her father. She was the spitting image of the man save for the fact that she was female.

"He did not make it to the meeting you scheduled after ousting him and replacing him with Reuben. You never bothered to ask why. Did you even notice he has not been to work?"

 She crossed her arms and eyed her father.

"And you know why?" Robert hesitated, his body stiffening at the possibility of more bad news.

"He tried something and ended up at the hospital." She put up two fingers for emphasis. "His stomach had to be pumped two times and then he was unconscious for over a week."

Robert's brow furrowed.

Ropo sank into the bed and buried her face in a pillow as she wept. In seconds, Robert was out of the room, quickly followed by Ronke.

As he ran down the stairs, he called out Reginald's name as though it were a war cry. Reginald, scared and fearing the worst, jumped to his feet.

They came face to face at the base of the stairs and Robert, still raging, stood poking his chest before pointing over his shoulder at Regina who had come to stand behind her father.

"Did you try to kill my son? Did you try to eliminate him first before this confession?"

"What are you talking about?" Reginald asked. Seeing a genuine look of confusion on his face, Robert looked over his shoulder, turning his attention to Regina.

"Ask your daughter. Ask her why she kept my son's attempt a secret from us."

Reginald whipped around to face Regina. "Attempt? What attempt?" As realisation dawned, his eyes widened. "Is that true?" he asked in a hushed tone. Regina nodded. "When?"

"After his demotion," she replied.

"That was months ago. Why did you keep quiet?" Rose stated.

"Maybe she intended to kill him to bury her secrets and lies?" Ronke added. Regina shook her head repeatedly.

"Your friend got married around that time," Richard's voice trembled as he spoke, "You attended the wedding. You dined, wined, and danced while your husband was near death?" he added in disbelief.

"I felt I needed to maintain a happy front. I paid the doctors well. I didn't want anyone to know of his condition. I wanted him to recover and to treat his addiction as well."

"Addiction?" Everyone except Ronke echoed.

Regina's eyes widened at her slip-up. The cracks were widening.

***

Rita listened quietly from the doorway and watched her father run out of the room before walking in. She felt filthy with guilt and regret roiled in her belly as she walked up to the bed where her twin slept.

"He looks so skinny," she stated in a near whisper.

Ropo stopped crying after her husband and other daughter left the room. She caressed her son's brow and was startled when he opened his eyes, a small smile on his lips.

"Hey, son," she said softly.

He mouthed something she didn't get and she leaned in to listen.

When she pulled away, Rita saw that he had slept off again.

"What did he say?" she asked. Ropo sat up. Her eyes were filled with tears again, her shoulders slumped dejectedly.

"Mom," she said. Looking up at Rita, she shook her head as she repeated herself, "He called me Mom."

Ronke returned to the room and eyed her sister at the doorway. Ropo looked up at her.

"Why didn't you say anything? You could have come to us and exposed all this." She asked, wiping her tears. Ronke scoffed.

"You didn't want to hear anything about him. So I chose to help him get through it."

"Thank you for that, Ronke. Thank you for choosing to believe in him when no one else did." Their mother's words hung in the air, making Rita visibly uncomfortable. Ronke did not acknowledge her mother's gratitude.

"I didn't do it for you," she spat.

***

Reginald was in shock at the worsening events of the evening. He could not shake the feeling that there was still a lot left to be uncovered and was overwhelmed with what he would need to do to remedy the situation.

In a way, he felt guilty at the fact that it was a habit of his to strategize how he would cover up issues and problems. Regina had taken after him in that regard. What he once saw as strength had become a deadly trait in his child.

3
TEARS AND REGRET

He did not want to wake up. The pull to stay under was strong and the buzzing in his head every time he tried to open his eyes did not help. Neither did the fact that his name was repeatedly being called from somewhere.

"Please stop," he whimpered, "Just stop."

"Raymond? Raymond?" The name-calling persisted until he responded. Slowly, he opened his eyes, frowning as he came face to face with his tormentor.

"I was trying to sleep."

"You have been at it for about ten hours. You need to wake up now."

Raymond squinted and blinked several times, struggling to focus on the face before him.

"Ronke?"

"The one and only. Welcome back."

Raymond closed his eyes and groaned. His head hurt much less than the last time he was awake, and for that, he was glad. Sighing, he opened his eyes again and looked around. They were alone and it was quiet.

"Has the storm passed?" he asked cautiously, fearing the answer would not be what he wanted to hear.

Ronke smiled. "For now, at least. Your wife is downstairs crying. The in-laws are also there but our parents and Rita left."

His memory was instantaneously flooded with the events from earlier in the day, culminating in the unexpected punch. Everything after that was a mix of sparsely placed glimpses and blanks. Ronke helped him sit up and when he flinched, she frowned in concern.

"Are you okay? Should I call the doctor?"

Raymond shook his head. "I am okay."

"You should stop saying that. You haven't been okay in years."

Raymond let out a pained smile. "Where is everyone?" he asked, "I vaguely remember people coming in and out of here."

Ronke sighed. "You remember I answered you a few minutes ago?"

Raymond frowned and shut his eyes.

"Sorry. My head is a bit fuzzy."

"The doctor told us to expect that. I am happy you are awake."

"Thanks."

She broke out in a smile and retrieved a covered tray from the side table. He accepted it wholeheartedly and they were soon laughing light-heartedly over the slightly over-salted beef.

At the door, Regina stayed out of sight before returning downstairs to the sitting room where her parents and brother were still seated.

"It's getting late," she said from the foot of the stairs. "You guys should get going."

Rose looked up at her daughter and nodded. Richard sat staring at the floor.

"So how do you want to proceed with the divorce?" her father's question startled her. He was sitting still, his head thrown back and eyes closed.

"I am going to speak with my lawyer," she said, "I had hoped that I would have been able to sort all that out with everyone present but everything went haywire."

"No, thanks to your brother," Rose chipped in.

Richard looked up at his mother and then at Regina.

"I stood up for my sister," he said, with a look of defeat. "How was I to know there was no honour to defend?"

Rose looked away and Reginald shook his head.

"To think my family would be reduced to this after one meal," he said. Turning back to Regina, he smiled but Regina could see the pain in his eyes. "Your selfish act ruined a friendship and a business partnership of over two decades."

"I am sorry, Daddy. I had silly aspirations and I kept pushing, hoping. I thought that my effort would make it better, that it would end the way I wanted."

"Everything I did was for nothing," Richard said. He hung his head again and let out a bitter laugh. "I'll be waiting in the car."

A bit confused by her brother's statement, Regina shrugged it off after he left, and turned to her father.

"I am disappointed, Regina. Back then, I asked you if you were sure it was wise to marry him even after all you said he did. I should have suspected when you insisted and justified marrying him." He waved a finger at her. "I should have been wary when you said it was the right choice. We would not be here if you had restrained your fantasies."

Rose placed a hand on her husband's arm.

"Let's go. It's been a very eventful day."

She watched her husband leave before coming to stand by her daughter. She sighed deeply, shutting her eyes for a brief second.

"I don't know what more to say. Why didn't you think to talk to me?" The hurt in her eyes brought tears to Regina's. "I don't know where this is heading, or how it will end, but be ready." She gathered up her things and continued to speak as she headed for the door. "I hope to the heavens that you are ready."

Seconds later, Regina was alone.

After clearing up the sitting room and the kitchen, she grabbed a cup on the way upstairs. Stopping outside the main bedroom, she hesitated before knocking.

"May I come in?" After a while, a female voice beckoned her in. Regina opened the door slowly, peeping in before proceeding further.

Raymond was asleep again while Ronke sat on the two-seater as though on watch.

"I came for my things and some beddings," she said. Ronke shook her head.

"I didn't ask."

Regina quickly picked the items she needed and moved to the side drawer. Just as she bent over, Raymond turned over and she found herself looking into his face.

She took in his wrinkles, eye bags, and grey hair as though she were seeing him for the first time.

"What are you doing?" Ronke asked. She was on her feet, watching Regina.

"I won't harm him," Regina stated as she picked what she needed and turned to face her.

"You have done a lot of that already so excuse me for being cautious," Ronke said smiling.

Regina took a deep breath. "I am glad you stood by him. You saw him for who he truly is. You backed him up."

Ronke scoffed. "You would have preferred it that way, right? For him to be alone and maybe your plan would have succeeded."

Regina shook her head. "Far from it. I could see that he was fading and struggling because of me. His alcohol intake alone doubled." she paused and glanced at Raymond. "He was dying slowly and if I wasn't careful, his blood would be on my hands. That's why I started trying to make things right."

"Are you trying to get me to feel sorry for you?" Ronke asked. She pointed at her brother. "He went through hell because of you." She moved closer to Regina. "Regret is not enough, Regina. What do you think will make up for everything? Where do you want to start from?"

"Somewhere, anywhere," Regina said, raising her voice a little. She paused, cautioning herself before continuing. "I may not be able to undo all I did. I can only try."

"He could have died."

"I know," Regina said. She turned to Raymond again before gathering her things and walking to the door where she stopped, her back to the still-fuming Ronke. "All I can say is, I am so sorry. I will live with regret all my life."

"I don't trust you," Ronke said. Regina could feel the venom in her words and the hatred in her. "I hate you, Regina. With every fibre in my being. If Raymond or anyone else won't hate you, fine. I have more than enough and then some."

Regina shut the door quietly behind her when she left.

In the guest room, Regina sat on the bed heavily. She retrieved the picture she picked from the side table by the bed. It was of her and Raymond on their supposed wedding day.

In hindsight, she had been the only happy one on that day. The dead look in Raymond's eyes would haunt her for the rest of her life. She tore up the picture, ripping it right down the middle as though symbolising their pending separation.

The tears soon followed, flowing freely again. It was only the beginning.

Every drop represented everything she held in since the day she decided to let him go. The day she decided to face the consequences of her actions.

She cried for the life she ruined, for the ones she had hurt, and for the hate she was sure to get. She deserved it but she did not look forward to it.

If she faced the same isolation that Raymond had lived through, she knew she could not survive.

Her phone rang and Rapu's name flashed across her screen. Regina threw her hands in the air and fell back in bed.

Her world was coming down around her and she had been the one that had taken the first sledgehammer to it.

4
NEXT STEPS

Raymond stretched as he got out of bed. The absence of his sister allowed him to move about, albeit carefully. His pounding head reiterated its presence with every wrong move.

It had been a few days since the whole debacle that was Sunday lunch. He had not seen Regina and had not heard from either his parents or hers.

It felt strange. He frowned, trying to find the right word to describe what he was experiencing. When it popped into his head, it took a few more seconds for him to acknowledge it.

Peace.

No wonder it felt strange. He had not felt that way in a while and it was awkward even.

A knock pulled him out of his thoughts.

"Erm, when did you start knocking?" After another round, he smiled softly, "Okay. Come in."

Regina opened the door slowly and subconsciously Raymond took a step back.

"I didn't know it was you."

"Sorry to bother you. I saw that Ronke stepped out and I needed to speak to you." Regina lingered by the door while Raymond, turning his back to her, started to fidget with the hem of his t-shirt.

"Sure."

"I will be moving out."

Raymond turned around. "You don't have to. I can move out instead."

"No. I don't want to inconvenience you any more than I already have." Raymond watched her shoulders fall and noticed that she had lost weight. For a second his heart seemed to ache for her.

"Where will you be staying? With the folks?"

Regina had moved to the wardrobe and was gathering her things. She laughed at his statement, shaking her head while she folded her clothes into the box on the bed.

"That would be dangerous for me. I rented a flat that's big enough for myself and Ralph."

"Have you explained things to Ralph?"

"How much would a six-year-old understand?" Her voice cracked when she spoke about her son. Sighing deeply, she sat on the edge of the bed. "I explained as much as I could and my parents want him to move in with them. I am considering it. I am not cut out to be a single parent."

Raymond nodded. "I'll excuse myself till you are done."

As he made to leave, Regina cleared her throat. "We have not had time to talk. Sunday was not meant to go that way, at least not in my head."

"You mean about the divorce?" Raymond answered, his back turned to her and a hand on the door.

"Yes. I am working on it with my lawyer. Once I have it drawn up, I'll get it to you. I was thinking you would want to talk beforehand."

"I am not ready for that," Raymond replied flatly.

Regina nodded, her heart thumping heavily. "Whenever you are ready."

She watched him nod again and he was gone. Embracing the quiet around her, she continued packing.

***

"Sir, you have not addressed my concerns."

Reuben was Robert's younger sister's son and had been in his care since he was eight. He could not think of any other time he had been more irritated with him. But then again, could he blame the boy?

He had been made the MD of the company over his son and, only months later, was being told there was a likelihood that the ousted son would be reinstated.

"That what, Reuben? Your concerns seem rather selfish to me. I expected you to ask how Raymond is faring but here you are only thinking about yourself."

"Do you blame me? I worked hard to make sure I was worthy of the position and responsibilities given to me. Only for me to get there and now it is a different story."

"Nothing has been decided yet. There is still a lot to be considered."

"But it will be the eventual decision, right? Is that being fair to me?"

Robert slammed his palm on the table. "Is it fair to Raymond? I hear he could have died and you are here nagging."

Reuben hung his head. "I am sorry sir. It's all a bit overwhelming." He took a deep breath and shook his head. "I have not been good to him either and I am ashamed of that."

"I know that feeling, believe me. My wife has not stopped crying, Ronke is not speaking to us, and Raymond? I don't know how to face him."

They fell silent, both lost in thought. After a few more seconds, Reuben shuffled forward on his chair.

"Uncle, maybe if you speak to him one on one. Pick his brain a bit and figure out how he is, then we can take it from there."

Robert's arched eyebrow made him smile. "I am not heartless even though I am not happy with what it means for me."

Robert eyed him before sitting down and crossing his arms. "Thank you for that. You and I will talk again."

"I will not doubt it but please don't expect me to go down without a fight."

Robert laughed and Reuben left.

 A sense of dread filled him, bile rising in the back of his throat as the thought of what lay ahead because of his rash and harsh decisions.

***

The house was eerily quiet. A stark contrast to the previous Sunday. It was the Friday after the eventful lunch and the first time he had set his eyes on his son.

Now they were seated across from each other in the sitting room, an untouched glass of red wine in front of the Father and a bottle of water in front of the Son. The tension around them was thick enough to cut with a knife.

Robert cleared his throat. "You look much better. I am happy to see that."

Raymond nodded. "Thank you."

Robert's face was laced with worry. "How are you?" When Raymond looked up at him in confusion, he pressed forward. "Ronke told us all that happened and the addiction."

Raymond smiled, raising the bottle to his lips. "Hence the water instead of wine. I have started therapy even though it's more of a staring match with the doctor."

Robert nodded, clenching and unclenching his fists. "I do not know where to start but I am sorry for everything. You must hate us so much and we deserve it."

"I do. I hate you, Mom, Regina's parents, her brother, my twin. I hate all the so-called friends I thought I had. I have so much hate that I don't know what to do with it." Raymond stopped, stopping himself from shouting. He smiled a little before continuing. "But I am grateful to Regina. In all this, I got to know my supposed family better."

"We aren't horrible people, Ray."

"I have always wanted to ask why. Why were you all so willing to believe everything you were told?" When his father didn't answer, he continued. "You did not question the narrative. It was as if you were so happy to jump on the bandwagon."

"Honestly, in hindsight, I don't know," Robert muttered, "It looked like there was no way to believe otherwise. It all fell into place without much effort." Robert threw his hands up, "And here we are."

"You just got here, Dad. I have been here all along. Yes, it feels good to be vindicated, but of what use is putting out the fire when it has burnt everything to the ground."

A while after Raymond left him in the sitting room, Robert dejectedly left the house. The anger and sadness in his son's eyes broke his heart.

In his room, Raymond collapsed onto the bed. He felt an anxiety attack coming on and soon was struggling to breathe. Sinking to the ground, he took deep breaths as he had done with Ronke several times before.

The fear of falling unconscious, with no one around, filled him. Soon he was covered in sweat. Raymond crawled into bed and was soon fast asleep.

5

FRIENDS AND FAMILY

Mother and Daughter sat across from each other at a café not far from their family house. Regina knew she was not forbidden from visiting the house after all her son had been moved there. She felt it was not wise to do so. Her mother, Rose, agreed.

Sipping on a cocktail, Rose savoured the feel of the vodka in her drink as it filled her and gave her a familiar fuzzy feeling she had missed.

"I know of the comfort Raymond found in alcohol," she said, opening her eyes and smiling a little. She caressed the glass before looking at her daughter. "The numbness that alcohol offers is a momentary relief from the troubles in one's life. One drink turns to two, then ten and more so that the numbness can last longer."

Regina nodded. "I drove him to it. I am grateful he didn't end up with a health problem."

Rose looked her daughter over, leaned forward, and rested her elbows on the table.

"How have you been?" she asked. "Your boy has been asking for you and I promised him that you would visit."

"I don't know if I can face Daddy yet."

"Let me know when you want to come over and we will find a way around that."

"Okay. To answer your question, I am fine."

"Have you spoken to your brother?" Rose's question elicited a sigh.

253

"Yes. He has not been in touch since he dropped us off. We are worried, even though his wife says he is okay and just brooding." she continued. "He has the right to brood. He wanted to fight for his sister and he ended up assaulting an innocent man. I disappointed him."

Rose laughed dryly. "It's more than what he did on Sunday though."

Regina frowned. "What else is there?"

When her mother did not respond, she leaned forward. "Mom, what did Richard do?"

***

"I need to talk to you." Regina was standing by the car when Richard closed from work. He had ignored her calls all day and was surprised when he found her waiting in the car park.

"You are the last person I want to speak to right now."

"I know that but Mom told me what you did."

"Dad allowed you into the house? And you are still standing?"

"I did not meet up with her at the house. Stay on topic." She grabbed his arm when he turned away from her. "Guy, you kidnapped Raymond?"

Richard flinched.

"What were you expecting Regina? What did you think I wouldn't do for you?"

"But not to the extent of kidnapping and threatening to kill him," Regina said, throwing her hands in the air. "I had expected a little more fight from him back then. Instead, he accepted and I foolishly saw it as a good sign that he was finally going to give into the love I had for him."

"So, you are saying I am to blame for your delusions?" Richard's tone was defensive.

Regina shook her head.

"Of course not. I am worried that Raymond could take legal action now."

Richard calmed down and leaned on the car.

"That has crossed my mind."

"I am so sorry for getting you involved in this mess."

"Anything new?" Richard's question was laced with concern.

"The divorce papers will be ready next week."

"You have not spoken to him?"

"I do not think I could or should face him without having the papers ready. It is best to save him the stress of an interaction."

Richard nodded. "Need a ride."

Regina nodded and they were soon on their way.

***

"I will not be relinquishing my position to Raymond. The board should decide and I will abide by it." Reuben's stern tone surprised Robert.

They sat in Robert's office with a few other staff present. No one dared to interrupt the discussion between the chairman and the MD. No one made any move to leave either.

"The choice to put you in that position was not made by the board so why should the reverse be the case?"

"Yes, you asked me, on a whim, to fill the position and I did. Now, you want to pull the rug out from under me after I have put in so much work."

Robert dismissed everyone before responding to his nephew.

"It's been less than eight months, Reuben. I do not doubt that you added to the bottom line of the company but seriously?"

Reuben faltered a little before responding.

"Please, don't dismiss my hard work. The board should vote 'cos that way there is no nepotism involved."

"You seem to have forgotten it was nepotism that got you that position, Reuben." Robert laughed.

After a few seconds, Reuben left without another word.

Alone, Robert picked up his phone and made a few calls. He recognized that Reuben, who had been a good option in a moment of anger, was quickly becoming a potential problem that he needed to nip in the bud.

***

"How will I cope when you decide to leave?" Raymond's question was directed at Ronke who was setting the table for lunch. She laughed as she placed a bowl of rice on the table and watched her brother immediately start to scoop some onto his plate.

"Don't worry, it won't be any time soon and even then, we will find a way."

A knock interrupted their banter, causing them to exchange puzzled glances.

It had been weeks since anyone visited and both lingered a bit before Ronke decided to answer the door.

Minutes later, Ronke led Regina in. She was followed by her mother and a man that neither Ronke nor Raymond recognized.

"I am sorry. I should have called or sent a text before coming over," Regina said. "We can wait until you are done eating."

"Not to worry. I don't have much of an appetite anymore." Raymond got up and moved to stand a few feet from the visitors. "How can I help you?"

Regina nodded. "I came with the divorce papers and to introduce my lawyer for future interactions." Regina gestured at the man they had come with. Rose, visibly uncomfortable, excused herself, returning to the car.

"Thank you. You can put the papers on the table. I haven't gotten a lawyer yet but I will be in touch if he includes his card."

"Yes, my card is in the envelope," the man said, holding up an A4-sized envelope before placing it on the table. "I will be expecting your call."

With that, and after a sad glance from Regina, they were gone. Raymond slumped into the nearest chair and let out the breath he had been holding. Ronke glanced at the table and decided to get him a glass of juice.

"Here." She handed him the glass and watched him empty the content in two gulps.

"Are you okay?" she asked.

"No. Far from it."

"Does seeing her cause that much anxiety for you?"

"According to my therapist, all the pent-up tension is coming to the surface now that I don't have alcohol to use as a coping mechanism."

"Did she say anything about how you will get over it?"

"Time and patience."

Ronke set before her brother the plate of rice that he had served for himself before their visitors arrived.

Sticking a spoon in his hand, she nudged him.

"Eat," she pleaded, "The last ulcer episode you had raised my high blood pressure."

Retreating to the kitchen, she mulled over the visit.

She pulled out her phone from her pocket and sent a text. Even though it was not what she wanted, it was what Raymond needed.

She would not allow him to face that next phase alone as he had been in the past.

***

"So what do you want from me?" Regina had no answer to her friend's question. She looked her friend square in the eyes and struggled to hold in her emotions. She wanted to nag and wail, to cry woe and lament but Ruby was not like her other friends who had left her to her antics.

Ruby had been the only one who ever spoke her mind. The harsh truth was never far from her lips. It was a no-brainer that she was the one to run to, even though they were estranged.

Regina sat cosied up in her friend's boutique, surrounded by her many designs and receiving a stare-down.

"I am waiting for you, Regina. You are not one to not have a comeback."

"Things changed, Ruby." She had been kind enough to offer Regina a drink and a smile escaped her lips when she saw that it was her cousin that served her.

"I can see your cousin is in charge," she added, "I wonder what the story is 'cos I recall you and her mother did not get along."

"Regina, what do you want?"

"I needed to talk to someone," Regina replied. Her face fell as she looked on, taking in Ruby's fixed stare. "You are my best friend and I felt I could come to you for advice."

"I have not been that to you in years. You had others to fill that position for you." Ruby crossed her legs. "Seeing you here, like a cat let in from the rain, is surprising."

"More like a thunderstorm." Regina looked up at her again and drew a deep breath. "I am sorry. I come with my tail in between my legs because I messed up, Ruby, and I am scared."

"I am not your mother confessor, Regina."

"I know but I don't have anyone else. I need advice."

When Regina walked into her shop, she had fought against every fibre of her being that wanted to scream and leap for joy. Ruby could see the look in her former best friend's eyes and she knew something was eating at her.

"Say what you want to say, Regina."

Regina's face fell. She stared at nothing for a few seconds before turning back to Ruby.

"I need to know how to handle Rapu. He has been threatening me since he came back to the country. He says he wants his son and will expose me."

"Was that what prompted you to confess?"

Regina shook her head. "Not entirely but it is part of it."

Ruby continued, "He is your son's father. What is the issue? He doesn't have that much of an upper hand now that the truth is out, so how is it a problem?"

"Rapu isn't the boy's father."

Ruby's eyes narrowed at first, then widened at the gravity of the revelation. "How?" she whispered. "You slept with someone else?"

Regina shook her head, sighing deeply before moving closer.

"I lost the pregnancy. I started faking it while hoping and wishing for something to happen. Then someone approached me with a proposition," she paused for a few seconds, "and a baby."

Ruby let out a little yelp. "Mo gbe! Regina! You bought a baby?" When Regina shook her head again, Ruby threw her hands in the air. "Then what?"

"Not just any baby, Ruby. That was why I jumped on the opportunity."

Ruby froze, sat back, and cocked her head. Regina watched her shut her eyes and frown before opening and squinting at her.

"Regina? What the heck did you do?"

Regina, gearing up for a possible hail of insults, took a few deep breaths before sitting up and closing her eyes.

"I timed my supposed birth with that of the boy's real mother and brought him home as mine. If he was ever tested, he would be confirmed to be Raymond's and we would be one step closer to our beautiful love story."

"Regina, whose child have you been claiming as yours for six years?"

"Royal's," Regina continued despite Ruby's increasing look of shock. "She found out she was pregnant and her parents insisted that she have the baby, so she came to me. She wanted nothing to do with Raymond so I paid her and took the baby."

Ruby placed both hands on her head and let out a cry that attracted her cousin. Looking both of them over, the girl checked the time before turning around to tell the two attendants to close up. It had been a slow day so closing early would not be an issue and given the look she had just seen on her older cousin's face, it was the right call.

"Regina Ajiwe, you are mad." Ruby jumped up and Regina did the same. She stepped back and watched as Ruby started to pace. "You are mad o, you are not normal at all."

Regina made a face as she nodded. It was a statement of fact. There was no doubt whatsoever. Some form of madness had indeed gotten a hold of her back then. There was no other way to put it.

6
MAKING AMENDS

Reginald paced the sitting room, visibly upset and muttering to himself. Rose eyed him multiple times from where she sat sipping from a glass of wine.

"The last heart attack you had scared me senseless," she said softly, "If you intend to repeat that, I am telling you ahead of time that I will not stick around."

Reginald turned to his wife, an incredulous look on his face. "How can you be this calm, Rose? This has hit the news and is going," he paused, trying to remember something. "What's that word again?"

Rose rolled her eyes. "Viral. It's going viral."

"Yes, that." Reginald snapped his fingers and sat down. "Do you know the implication of this on my reputation?"

"What about your friend's reputation back then? You dragged him to court and granted interviews when this hit the media, didn't you? Why are you angry now?"

"Whose side are you on? I was standing up for my daughter. Our child."

"I am just saying that you did the same thing to him. Maybe the news hitting the media now is in retaliation for your actions and a move to clear his name." She was a bit upset at what she felt was an act of selfishness on the side of her husband.

"Yes, all that crap supposedly went down between our children and your friend of over three decades asked you not to make it public and to settle it between the families, but you refused." she continued.

"So you are saying I deserve this? That all this is fair?" Reginald asked. Rose shrugged.

"If the shoe fits. Besides, have you called him? Have you spoken to him since that day?"

"I have not. I haven't had the guts to think about it. Would he even want to?"

"Maybe your lack of action is what made him lash out? Who knows, he may not be the one that leaked it."

Reginald stared at her for a few seconds, blinking rapidly at the thought.

"How?"

"Robert has always been the level-headed one between the both of you. I would not put it past him because he too has his pride but there are many ways news can be leaked in this day and age."

She watched Reginald spring to his feet and grab his keys from the coffee table. After he left, Rose mulled over how her friendship with Ropo had fallen apart despite Ropo's attempt to maintain a semblance of the bond.

She recalled the harsh words she had said and the actions she had taken. There was a lot to be done to make amends for everything and that was only if there was any friendship left to salvage.

***

"I do not recall scheduling an appointment to see you, Reginald." Robert's tone was flat and cold.

Maintaining his composure, Robert dismissed the secretary who had followed the man in. After she left, he continued to stare at Reginald while fighting the urge to call for security.

"I am not aware that I am supposed to book an appointment to see a friend," Reginald said as he sat down.

Robert arched an eyebrow and sat back, "Are we friends?" He continued to look Reginald over. "What do you want?"

"Did you have to go as far as going to the press?" Reginald's question made Robert smile. "I was hoping it wouldn't get to that."

"Like you did the last time? There seemed to be a set pattern to follow."

"Robert, I agree I mishandled things but we could have learnt from the past." Robert could hear the worry in his old friend's voice.

"Whatever," Robert hissed. "I am not like you. Reuben did that, thinking he could sabotage any effort to remove him as MD."

Reginald relaxed a little, sitting back and sighing deeply. "That's your nephew right, the one you raised?"

"Yes. One would have thought the fact that I raised him would have instilled some sort of morals in him. But I guess not." Robert picked up his phone and proceeded to send a text. "Anyway," he continued, "I will handle him and his indiscretions. I need to correct the impression that he is wise."

Reginald nodded and relaxed a bit more. The silence between them weighed on him and looking at his friend made him long for the level of closeness they once had.

"It can never be the same again but I want to ask if we could try."

Robert looked up at him and frowned.

"If the recent events had not played out, would you have thought of trying?"

"Yes. I had that in mind and planned to return the business I took away. I was never going to allow it to continue the way it was going." Reginald's words got to Robert. He had also missed his friend.

They stared at each other for a few more seconds before Robert stood up and walked to the mini-bar. He returned with a glass of his friend's favourite drink.

"Or have your tastes changed?"

Reginald smiled, accepting the drink and taking a sip.

"Can a leopard change its spots?"

Minutes later they were drinking in silence, enjoying each other's company.

***

Rita walked into the sitting room and sat in front of her twin brother. The look of determination she had deterred her brother from trying to get her to leave. Shocked at her sudden appearance, he quickly recovered and sat back.

"What's this, Rita?"

"Where are the divorce papers? I need to read through and make sure that lying rat does not cause more damage."

Raymond shook his head. "Ronke."

Rita nodded. "We may not be on good terms but she knows I am good at what I do."

"And if I say I don't need you?"

"You would have to drag me out of here kicking, screaming, and cursing. I am here for you, please let me help."

Raymond looked away and Rita's heart broke.

"Look bro, I am not asking for absolute forgiveness. I messed up and I know. I am asking you to let me protect you, starting with this." She watched Raymond bite down on his lower lip. He was afraid and it hurt that she was part of the reason he felt that way.

Slowly, he reached under a side table and passed her a brown envelope.

"I have not looked at it yet so I don't know what's in it."

Rita collected the envelope and emptied the contents in front of her. She proceeded to scan through the papers before picking up the business card that fell out. She reached for her bag, whipped out her phone, and made a call.

"Hello. I am going to send you a text and I need you to find out all you can about the law firm. Get back to me soonest."

"Is that needed?" Raymond asked. Rita smiled.

"I am curious to know about them. It gives me a mental picture of how to prepare."

"How to prepare for what? Do you mean court?" His voice quivered a little. Rita leaned forward and placed a hand on his knee.

"Not necessarily court. There may be a need for mediation." She looked her brother over. "I will try to avoid that if you don't want to face anyone."

"Yes, please try to. I do not want any further interactions if it can be avoided."

Raymond smiled and got up. When she was alone, Rita could not help but wonder how damaged her brother had become. She was glad that he let her in and that she was able to help.

She quickly sent the text before returning to the documents. She needed to be thorough. No one was going to cheat her brother more than had already been done.

***

"Was what you did wise?"

 Reuben had no response to the question his uncle posed.

He had gotten backlash from friends and extended family alike regarding the actions he had taken. Foolishness had him as its brand ambassador.

"I do not know what you are talking about, sir?" Even he knew that answer was stupid.

Robert laughed lightly, hanging his head and hissing. "Trying to be smart?" He leaned forward and stared pointedly at his nephew. "I raised and nurtured you. I treated you better than my son by choosing to trust you when the board wanted someone else and you decided that this is the best option you had?"

"What else was I expected to think or do, Uncle? You people were going to remove me from the position I had just taken up. Would that have been fair? I did not want to be cheated and decided to stand up for myself."

"I expected you to come talk to me. I expected you to ask us, your family, how we were doing, considering everything that was happening but no. Instead, you decided to bite off the hand that fed you, Reuben."

Reuben sat up. "I am sorry, uncle. It was a rash decision. I felt I did not have any other choice."

"You wanted the board to decide so why could you not wait?" Robert was genuinely concerned about his nephew's thought process. "Or did someone advise you to do this?"

"I made the choice myself."

"Well," Robert tossed a letter at him and waited for him to open it. "The board has approved your suspension. Someone else of their choosing will take over pending their final decision."

Reuben read the letter in silence. Folding it back into the envelope, he looked up at Robert with pleading eyes. "This can't be it, sir. The last eight months should mean something."

Robert got up and walked over to where Reuben was seated. "You thought that you could work against us because you were MD. I would not have removed you like that. I am not cruel."

Reuben hung his head, unable to bear the weight of his uncle's gaze.

"You chose to drag us in the mud again, as though what happened six years ago was not enough."

"Look at it this way, I did that to expose the Ajiwes."

"You should be smarter than that, Reuben. That story won't work. Anyway, you should head back to the office and clear out your desk."

Robert returned to his seat. He seemed to freeze for a few seconds before looking up at Reuben as he was leaving.

"For what it's worth, I am sorry. If you felt used in any way, it was not my intention."

Reuben stalled at the door, his back to his uncle.

"I was foolish and I got carried away, I agree. I hope I get a chance to make it up to you."

Robert nodded. "I will hold you to that."

***

Regina sat across from her mother and Ruby as though facing a panel. The look of shock on her mother's face mirrored that of annoyance on Ruby's.

Ruby, her chosen mother confessor, had dragged her to her mother's place the day after her revelation. She should have known what was on her mind when Ruby had asked if her parents still lived at the same address. But then again, did she think she could escape telling the whole truth?

"So if your father had not gone out, this is what he would have had to listen to?" Rose asked, a dry laugh escaping her lips.

Ruby shook her head. "Regina, what were you thinking?"

Regina managed a little smile.

"Truth is I wasn't thinking, Mom. It may have seemed like I was but, in hindsight, I was not."

"What I want to know is how?" Ruby asked.

Regina took a deep breath. "Royal came to me and coincidentally, it was after the miscarriage. I saw it as providence. She said her parents asked her not to give the child away. So, she came looking for me."

Regina felt unburdened as she shared the last of the secrets she was holding on to.

"I did not tell her I had been pregnant. I confirmed how far along she was and realised I would have to lie a little more because she was a month further than I had been."

She took a deep breath, holding back tears as she continued. "We arranged for where she would give birth. I paid some nurses, and proceeded to set up the events that led to my supposed delivery."

"Who are you, Regina? I mean, when did you morph into this?"

Her mother's words broke her and the tears flowed freely. Ruby's hiss filled the room just as a loud bang reverberated through the walls.

All three of them looked up in the direction of the doorway only to find Reginald and Richard standing there in shock.

"Did I just hear what I think I heard or were you gisting about the plot of a Nollywood blockbuster?" Rose met Reginald mid-stride, placing a hand on her husband's arm in a bid to calm him down.

Both Regina and Ruby had gotten up, the latter instinctively stepping in front of her friend whose crying had devolved into full-fledged weeping. Richard stared at his sister as though he dared not move.

"Regina, how many more secrets do you have?" he asked, a thin sheen of sweat breaking out on his forehead.

"I am sorry," was all the object of their ire could utter. What more was there to say? Her father looked from his wife's pleading eyes to his daughter's.

"Why? Why have you done this?"

"I was desperate. I was overly eager, stupid, and wishful."

"Wishful is when you want to buy a car but have no savings," Reginald yelled. "Wishful is when you want to head to Victoria Island from Ikorodu and you are still at home by 6 a.m. What you have done is disastrous and purely cruel. Wicked even."

"Reginald, please calm down. What's done is done. We need to talk through the next steps."

"Next steps? How do I go back to Robert to tell him there is still more he needs to hear because my darling daughter was not done?" He held Rose's shoulders, putting her at arm's length. "I just managed to re-establish a rapport with him, just today, and now this."

"How do we go back to that family and tell them there's more?" Richard's question made Regina flinch.

"Please, let's sit and talk. We need to figure this out as a family." Rose pleaded, near tears herself. Ruby made to leave but was stopped by Reginald.

"Please stay. She has dragged you into this mess and you are somewhat family anyway," he said soothingly. "Is this why your friendship degenerated to practically nothing for years?"

"Yes, sir. This was the reason. I did not know how bad it was." Ruby glanced at her friend as she spoke, side-eyeing her as she continued. "Her confession was as shocking to me as it is to you, sir."

Reginald nodded, sitting down heavily in the nearest chair. "When you were skimming and scamming, you did not bother to involve us. Regina, you can kill!"

Ruby turned around to watch her friend sink to the ground crying. She needed it, Ruby thought to herself, because what lay ahead needed a clear head and dry eyes. Tears would not work for what needed to be fixed.

7
WISHFUL THINKING

When Rita walked in on her brother, the look on his face scared her. He was engrossed with something on his laptop and she panicked.

"What is it?" she gesticulated.

Raymond looked up and sat back. The look on her face startled him. His gaze drifted around the room. "What's what? Did something happen?"

Rita put her bag on the sofa, placed her hands on her hips, and stared at him. "I thought you got some bad news. The look on your face was scary."

Raymond smiled and Rita's heart skipped. It had been a while since he interacted with her like that. His smile made her day.

"It's nothing. I was trying to update my resume and it is proving to be a chore."

Rita laughed and shortened the distance between them. Turning the laptop around, she glanced at the page and shook her head.

"Get one of those resume writers to get it done for you," she said, before returning to her bag and sitting down. That was Rita. Always one to look for the easiest way out. Raymond could not help but smile again.

"To what do I owe your visit today?"

"Do I have to tell you when I am coming?" Rita asked, throwing him a side-eye.

"Well, you have been coming here regularly and I am still getting used to having people over." Rita's face fell and Raymond scampered to salvage the situation. "Not that I don't like it. I have missed you loads. It's just that it's taking some time to get used to it again." He moved to sit by her and she reached out to hold one of his hands.

"I have a lot to make up for. You did not deserve what was done to you, even if you were guilty."

"Really?"

Rita nodded. "You didn't commit murder nor did you start a war," she added, shrugging as she spoke. "We should not have handled things like we did."

With that, and with Raymond's relaxed demeanour, Rita pulled out an envelope from her bag.

"It looks fine and she has signed her part. She addressed several things, including custody."

"Custody of who?" Raymond's puzzled expression made his sister smile.

"The child, of course."

"Why would she do that when the boy isn't mine?"

Rita shrugged. "I guess she is sticking to her story that he is. This might lead to mediation if you do not agree to take him. It also says that she will refund all the monies paid to her as compensation, with interest."

"Honestly, I don't care about all that. I am just glad it's over." he paused and looked away, staring off into space. "It's all over."

"You haven't said anything about the social media uproar on all this."

"What's the need? The only difference is that I am not on the receiving end. I don't have any energy to react or respond."

Rita looked away and sighed as she sat up. "And our parents? When are you going to have a sit down with them?"

Raymond sat back, grabbed the remote off the ottoman near his legs, and flipped through TV channels. "I don't have the will to do so. I don't think I can cope."

"Dad is preoccupied with handling Reuben and the damage he has caused. Reuben was suspended."

"I hope he does not think I will be coming back to the company?"

"Would you rather job hunt?" Rita asked. "It would be easier for you than most but I don't think you should stress yourself."

"It's not like I am looking to start work immediately. I am still good for up to a year and by then I am sure some things would have worked out." She could see he was a bit anxious and she was quick to change the topic.

"Whatever you decide, I have your back." She smiled reassuringly and passed him the envelope. "As for Regina's terms, a DNA test would sort things out."

Raymond nodded at the idea. "I did not think of that. Good one."

Ronke came in and eyed her older sister before she passed a bag of snacks to Raymond.

"Come on nau, Ronke. You can't be like that to her forever na." Raymond said. Rita jumped up and grabbed Ronke in a tight hug.

"I am sorry, sis. Sorry." Rita repeated as they tussled.

Raymond laughed when Ronke took their sister's wig off and used it to beat her. Rita in turn pulled her to the ground and pinned her there.

Raymond missed the laughter that now filled the house. It made his heart sing. The house finally felt like home.

***

"I need to hear you tell me why you did this," Ruby asked. "You explained it before but I am still trying to wrap my head around it."

They were in her room in her parents' house and Regina was lying on the bed, staring at the ceiling in silence.

"The more I say it, the more I realise how stupid it was. Way worse than wishful thinking."

Ruby laughed lightly from her spot on the single chair by the bed. "I am more concerned with how your latest revelation will be received by Raymond. It's not looking good, babe."

"How do I even present it to him? I have no idea."

"I think you should leave that to your parents. Seems like that's what they were discussing downstairs when I came in earlier and it looked like they had been fighting. They only stopped because of me."

"They are ignoring me. I should have gone back to my place instead of staying here."

"They wanted to keep an eye on you," Ruby added. After a few seconds of silence, she sighed. "And I agree with it. You shouldn't be alone."

Regina shrugged where she lay.

Ruby looked her friend over before tapping her and gesturing for her to sit up. When she did, Ruby leaned forward in her chair.

"Your fairytale love story has turned into a nightmare and you ran to me, the one who told you not to try it. Where are your other friends,

Regina?” When Regina tried to speak, Ruby put a hand up, shutting her down.

“I need to get this off my chest because I have been kind enough not to say anything in the last three days.” Regina nodded as her friend continued.

“Not one of them is here as you face all the backlash, but you felt it was okay to come to me. You have not asked me how I have been. Do you even know I am married and I have a child?”

Regina’s eyes widened and a tear rolled down her cheek. Unfazed, Ruby continued.

“You came to me as though I had no other choice than to accommodate you. Rather selfish, don’t you think?”

“My selfishness brought me this far. I was so self-absorbed and I am so sorry, Ruby. I do not deserve your support but I am eternally grateful for it, believe me. I do not take you for granted, babe.” Wiping her eyes, Regina edged closer to her friend and smiled. “So tell me, a boy or a girl? Who did you marry? Is it the same guy you had a crush on back then? The one that bumped into you and spilt a drink on that silk dress I liked? I want to hear everything, Ruby.”

After a little silence, she reached out to Ruby and took her hand in hers.

“I have missed you, bestie.”

“I have missed you too, Regina. Not the person you became but the person I knew you were deep inside. Too deep sef.”

Rose listened with joy to the light laughter coming from her daughter’s room. She had intended to inform them of her husband’s decision but that could wait. The girls needed to catch up.

An additional day would not change the outcome of the storm that lay ahead. As she walked away, she hoped it would be the final storm for her family and that afterward, they could attempt to return to a semblance of a normal life.

***

"You want to invite them here? To this house?" Richard stood, staring at his parents. He avoided eye contact with Regina, uncertain of how badly he would react. "How do you want to manage that?"

"There is nothing to manage. The outcome will come one way or the other. We cannot avoid it." Reginald's voice was filled with anger. His wife sat apart from him, a visible indication that all was not right between them. Regina looked from one parent to the other and was about to speak when her phone rang.

The caller ID displayed her lawyer's name. Excusing herself, she stepped aside to receive the call.

"That was the lawyer. He says that Raymond is asking for a DNA test on Ralph."

Rose sat up. "Why is he asking for that? Could he be suspecting something?"

"I delivered the divorce papers to him with clear terms on refund of compensation, payment of compensation, and custody details."

Reginald frowned.

"Again, you went ahead with this without informing us," he shouted, "What is the matter with you?"

"I wanted to handle things. Maybe I did not think it through properly but my intentions were pure. I am trying." Regina looked over at her mother and then she looked away.

"Stop shouting at her. She didn't go alone. Although, I would not have done so if I had known what I know now."

Reginald stared wide-eyed at his wife.

"You what?"

"I asked Mom to go with me. I had hoped to get it done and over with."

Reginald turned back to Regina. "Why would you think he would accept responsibility for the boy?"

"Rapu has been calling and asking for his child."

"Oh, that's the reason," the man hissed.

"Reginald, please calm down. Let's request their presence before Raymond proceeds with the test." Rose's calm tone reigned in her husband's temper despite the tension between them.

"It's good the child is with us. Regina will stall on giving consent for the test till they come over." Reginald's words irritated Richard.

"And then what?" Richard said.

"You have been against every move we have been making and yet you have not provided an alternative?" Rose asked. Richard quieted down and sat on the arm of a chair.

"He's angry with me," Regina added. "I have disappointed everyone."

"Understatement," Richard chimed in.

Regina wished Ruby had stayed back with her. She was gaining a better understanding of the extent of her bad actions and character but her friend had gone home to her family.

"I have not been a good parent." Rose's statement made her husband frown. "If I had paid attention to her more and curbed her excesses maybe her fantasies would not have resulted in all this."

"You raised us well enough. Surely you cannot claim responsibility for her wild imaginations and delusions." Richard's words stung Regina but she kept quiet.

"Stop that. If we are to dwell on how we got here, everyone in this room has a role they played and thus some level of guilt to bear." Reginald said. "We need to stop dwelling on faults and face how we will forge ahead."

Everyone watched him pull out his phone and after staring at the screen, he dialled a number they could only assume was that of Robert Luoye. He excused himself and retreated to the privacy of his study.

Richard finally turned to Regina. "I hope you are happy. The amount of stress and strain you have put us through is one for the books. They fought last night, just so you know." He got up and was out the door. Regina turned to her mother.

"Every marriage has its strain to bear. We will be fine."

"Not when the strain is because of their child's foolishness." Regina started to cry, breaking her mother's heart. Rose moved closer, taking her daughter's hands in hers.

"We will be fine and you will too. Things will change but you will adjust, as long as you have learned your lesson."

Regina knelt in front of her mother and welcomed the embrace that followed. She gave in to it, not realising until then how much she had missed it.

8
ONE MORE THING

If not for restraint, Robert would have pounced on Regina and maybe ripped her head off. He had thought that their invitation was an olive branch to his family but could not shake off the feeling that there was something more. He was grateful that Raymond had not accompanied them. Raymond had instead opted for Rita to be there in her right as her brother's legal counsel.

It had been for the best.

Rita's hands were balled up in fists as she listened to the additional truths that Regina revealed. Ropo started crying, but not in anger or sadness. It was more of frustration. Robert Luoye tapped his fingers on the arm of the chair he sat in, his eyes fixed on Reginald.

And then Regina was done.

"Is that all?" Robert asked. "Or will there be more?"

"Nothing more, sir. I assure you of that."

He leaned forward, resting his elbows on his thighs and burying his face in his hands.

"Reginald, what did I do to deserve this?" he asked, pain evident in his voice. "Did you send your daughter to my family to ruin us?"

"I would not dream of such, Robert," Reginald said in his most assuring tone. "On behalf of my entire family, I am sorry. We invited you here to clear all this up once and for all."

"How? Where do you want to start? How do I face my son? I have not spoken to him in a month since that horrid Sunday and now this!"

"We want to help. We are in this together." Rose said first to Robert and then to Ropo. "Ore mi, I am sorry. For my actions and lack of. Please."

Ropo stared at Rose for a while. She was not sure of how to react to all she was hearing. "Where do we start? I fear for Raymond. This may break him."

"It would be best if we tell him as soon as possible." Rita's words stirred up worry in all those present.

"Why do you say that?" Rose asked.

"He plans to pick up the boy from school next week so he can take him to the hospital for a blood draw for the DNA test." Rita's eyes met Regina's and the latter felt the cold stare pierce her soul.

"We will do it tomorrow," Robert said. "Any other time would be a day too late and truthfully, I for one want to get this nightmare done and over with."

Everyone except Regina nodded.

Relief dared to flood her system but she had to hold it back. A foreboding of the next day's events hung over her.

***

Rita's call woke Raymond from a much needed nap. She told him that she was calling ahead of her visit because she wanted to respect his space and privacy. Big Lie!

Her call was a setup. He should have suspected that something was up because Rita never called before coming but he had chosen to believe her excuse of wanting to respect his space and informing him ahead of her subsequent visits.

She showed up with not just their parents but Regina's parents as well and once in the house, his folks asked for a chance to speak privately.

Seated in his room, he waited. His father looked edgy while his mother's face was flushed and tense, evident since she was light-skinned.

"I am having an unpleasant sense of Déjà vu." He looked from one face to another.

"That is to be expected," Robert said. He sat on one of the two single seats while his wife sat in another. Ronke was perched on the bed and Rita remained standing at the door, watching everyone intently.

"I hope you are not all here to try and convince me to give Regina another chance."

"No way."

"God forbid."

"Impossible."

"Heck no." rang out from each person at the same time. Raymond's eyes narrowed.

"Then what is it?"

"There is one last detail to all this madness that needs to be cleared up and we need you to calm down and listen," Ropo said. The confusion on Ronke's face mirrored her brother's.

Rita and her mother glanced at Robert who nodded and leaned forward in his seat.

"Reginald invited us over to his place the other day and something was revealed to us. We felt that in light of what you have been through, it would not be fair to not inform you on time so here we are.”

“And?” Ronke asked.

Robert took one deep breath and let it out slowly while saying a silent prayer that the outcome of what he would be sharing would not be catastrophic.

***

Raymond’s anguished screams echoed through the house and Regina hoped the neighbours did not hear it.

Goosebumps surfaced on her skin as bile rose to the back of her throat. Silence fell and was quickly followed by rushing and running footsteps, causing everyone downstairs to look up in the direction of the stairs that Raymond was running down.

He ran up to Regina, breathing heavily and staring her down. She in turn got up from her seat, took a step back, and met him head-on.

“Is it true?” he asked, “My father just told me something about Ralph. Is it true?”

Regina held back her response. Not because she had nothing to say but because at that moment she needed to stop shaking. She was not sure if she would pee on herself, pass out, or both.

“It is,” she finally muttered. “He is yours and Royal’s.”

“And Royal came to you and you paid her?”

Regina nodded.

“She told me she had an abortion.” His voice trembled and Regina’s heart ached.

"You knew she was pregnant?" Ropo asked.

Robert frowned. He ached for his son and eyed each of the Ajiwes causing Richard, who sat closest to him, to shuffle away.

"She told me before the party. It was one of the reasons she could not make it." he paused and his voice fell. "I was so happy that I was going to be a father but before I could share the news with any of you, Royal told me she had an abortion." Raymond managed a sad smile at the memory.

Ronke let out a sound comparable to a war cry and charged at Regina. Richard rushed forward to hold her back, prompting Rita to surge into their midst.

Both sets of parents watched the three vying for a fight while keeping an eye on the other two before Reginald yelled for everyone to stop.

"This will not get us anywhere. We came here to close this chapter and try to see how we can move ahead," he said. Raymond let out a dry laugh.

"Move ahead?" he asked, flailing his arms in the air. "My reputation is beyond ruined and I am treated like a leper. How do I move ahead?

"I am a shut-in who is looking for a job because I cannot go back to where I worked. The child I have hated for years, and who does not like me one bit either, is biologically mine and the woman I loved sold him to get rid of anything that would remind her of me."

"She made that decision based on the lies she had been told. That should count for something." Rita said.

Raymond sat down, running a hand through his hair.

"What difference does it make? I thought when someone loves you, he or she defends you even when you are caught red-handed committing a crime. Instead, in my case, everyone ran off at the first sign of trouble." He looked around the room. "I am so tired." He shut his eyes, trying to stop tears from falling and failing.

"No friends and no family. The child I thought I had lost." His voice hitched, "Has been here all along and hates me." Ropo rushed to her son and he allowed her to hold him. He sank into her embrace and cried.

Regina wiped her tears. "I wondered why you wouldn't give me a chance. Why couldn't you love me? Why didn't you accept me? After all, everything I had done was because I loved you." she paused, taking a few seconds to comport herself. "But I came to understand that it wasn't love I had but an obsession."

She knelt by Raymond's side, placing a hand on his knee and another on his mother's.

"I am so sorry, Raymond. From the bottom of my heart, I apologize for everything. Sign the papers and hand them over to my lawyer. I will give you a wide berth from now on, I promise. You can hate me all you want but I hope you can let that go so you can heal."

She got on her feet and left. One after the other, the Ajiwes followed without another word.

Ropo sat there holding her son. Her daughters had started crying while their father initially paced the room before sitting down.

"I missed his first steps, his first day at school. I shunned his smiles, hugs, and requests to play." Raymond's muffled voice pushed Ropo to tears. "The boy hates me."

"Children forgive easily. He will forget in time. I am sure he will be glad to have you in his life." Ropo said, looking to Robert for some form of backing.

"And the woman he knows as his mother?" Raymond asked. He finally raised his bloodshot eyes from his mother's lap. "When he asks about her, what do I say? How do I explain her sudden disappearance or the fact that she isn't his mother?"

"When we get to that bridge, we will cross it," Robert said firmly. "For now, let's order food to eat. I am hungry."

The man turned to Ronke who nodded and pulled out her phone to do as her father instructed.

An hour later they were all seated at the dining table, cajoling Raymond to eat.

The quiet was not because there was nothing to say. It was a welcome peace that everyone needed. Raymond felt calm despite the turmoil that raged inside him. Everything seemed right in his world again.

***

On the ride home, Regina asked to be dropped off at her place. As she made to get down, Reginald called out to her.

"You will be attending therapy as soon as we can find a good therapist."

She nodded. There was nothing more to say. She knew she needed it badly.

Inside the house, Regina reached for her phone. In all the madness, she reminded herself that there was one more person she had to clear things with. Biting down on her lower lip, she scrolled through her contact list and tapped lightly on Rapu's number.

He picked up and spoke harshly.

"It's about time. What took you so long to get back to me?"

Regina took a deep breath before speaking.

"I will make this brief and get straight to the point," she paused, "The boy is not yours. Yes, I was pregnant for you but I had a miscarriage."

"You are joking right?" Rapu laughed at the other end, "You think I will believe that rubbish? Haven't you lied enough?"

"For the first time, in a long while, I am not lying. I am sorry, Rapu."

"What are you saying?" Rapu asked. His tone fell a notch.

"I had a miscarriage, Rapu. I didn't carry our baby to term."

"And the boy? Ralph?"

"He is Raymond's, but not mine. It's a crazy story I would like to explain if you would be willing to listen."

Rapu fell silent for a few seconds. "Go on."

By the time Regina was done, all she heard was Rapu's heavy breathing and he started cussing.

"So much for feeling guilty for abandoning you. I came back to fight for you and the kid but nicely done, Regina. I should be thankful though. You stopped me from making a fool of myself.

He let out a dry laugh before ending the call.

Left with her thoughts, Regina sank to the carpet at the foot of the bed and hot tears streamed down her cheeks.

9
FOR RALPH

"Next time you have that surge, you have to consciously call yourself to order." The words of her therapist echoed in her mind when she was filled with excitement over the text that Raymond sent her.

How could she have had butterflies because Raymond asked to meet her? How could she dare harbour an iota of hope? Her excitement waned when she stopped to think and to reason as she had been told to do.

She started therapy a week after her last reveal and facing her delusions head-on scared her. She sat back and reigned in her thoughts before she put the phone down after responding to the text.

Leaning back in bed, she reflected on the chat she had with her father after dinner.

"I will try my best to make it up to you and Mom."

She had sounded like a secondary school girl making a promise to her parents and had felt equally embarrassed.

She was back home as her concerned father requested. Despite his anger, he had insisted that she move back and had gone as far as helping her pack up for the move. There was no doubting it, she felt good to be back home.

Rose had gone to bed early leaving Father and Daughter alone in the semi-lit sitting room. Regina had spoken in hushed tones, a bit afraid of getting a bad reaction from her father because of her words. Reginald was not a man to show emotion but in that moment, his child's words cut him deep.

"I am trying to think of what went wrong when you were growing up for you to end up like this," he said, his face half hidden in the shadows of the corner where he sat in his favourite chair. "I thought I raised you to be strong and independent but now it seems like there was a whole lot more happening that I didn't notice or pay attention to."

"You and Mom fought often. I used to think I could make it all go away by playing house. I would come to you once I noticed any tension, forming activity of all sorts to distract you. I did all my chores, got good grades, and didn't get into any trouble."

"How does it lead us to what you did?" he asked.

"I thought I only needed to maintain a perfect look, and that all I needed to do was fake it long enough for everything to slip into place," Regina sighed. "Instead, things got worse. I dug my heels in deeper because I believed that one day Raymond would look at me, and poof, we would be okay."

Regina smiled a little. Coming to terms with her flawed reasoning felt good. She slept better without the stress of always thinking of how to manipulate people's perceptions. She was happier.

"I thought I was doing the best thing for myself, for Raymond, and my son," she paused and sighed a little, "But all these sound like excuses now and I see them for what they are, evil."

"You aren't evil darling," Reginald said warmly.

"I was not all there either." She pointed to her temple as she spoke, and her sad smile evoked one in her father.

"Your mother and I were strong-headed. You and your brother were smack in the middle. I too promise to make it up to you as we go on."

Father and Daughter fell into a comfortable quietness that embraced them both.

Minutes later, Rose came to check on them only to find them asleep.

Instead of waking them up, she left and returned with blankets which she used to cover each of them. As she left, she lingered in the doorway, smiling at father and daughter.

***

"Thank you for letting me see Ralph."

Raymond nodded. They were watching their son and other children in the play area of an eatery close to Regina's home.

"He has been asking for you and a teacher of his suggested that we set up a few visitations like these till he is old enough to understand."

"You told his teacher?"

"She knows we are divorced. That's the simplest way to put it." His voice was steady and he avoided eye contact. Regina nodded, turning her attention to the boy who looked over at them as though trying to make sure she was still there.

"How have you been?" she asked.

Through her peripheral vision, she saw that he looked over at her, his face devoid of emotion. "I have been good," he paused. "And you?"

"Doing okay." She hesitated before continuing. "Have you heard from Royal?" It was not what she wanted to ask but she did not want to stir up trouble.

Raymond turned to her. "Why do you ask?"

"Just curious. I know it's a chapter you would want to close."

"I have not."

Regina turned to look at Ralph and a smile spread across her lips, catching Raymond's eye.

"You can see him anytime. All you need to do is call ahead to schedule it."

"I think I better not. He shouldn't get more attached than is necessary. It would only make things harder for him." Regina shook her head as she spoke, and sipped her drink.

Ralph ran over to her, falling into her arms, giddy with laughter. They played a little while Raymond watched. The boy grabbed a drumstick out of the pack of crispy chicken Regina had in her hands and then he ran off, laughing.

"He needs you." He hesitated. "I need you, too."

"How?" She gave him a quizzical look that made Raymond smile a little.

"You are better at parenting. I am still learning the ropes. It would be good for you to be there for him when I goof."

Regina laughed softly. "I am sure you will do fine. We can work on it when I get back from my trip."

After a sip of his drink, Raymond cleared his throat. "Why did you do it?"

Regina's brow furrowed in confusion and Raymond pulled back a few seconds before clarifying his inquiry. "The interview."

"You listened to it?"

"No. Rita told me about it."

"I needed to clear the air and quell fake news," she turned to him smiling a little, "Also to get them to leave you alone."

"Why do you care?" His tone was flat, an act he had learnt over the years with her. "Was it out of pity?"

"It's part of my efforts to make up for what I did, no matter how little it may seem."

Raymond looked away. "Should I be grateful?"

"No. I don't expect anything from you. I have taken too much already."

She turned to the playful child she called hers. She would miss him a lot and decided to take in as much of their interaction as she could before her planned trip.

"Thank you," Raymond said, startling Regina. "I appreciate your effort."

Regina nodded. "I wish we had gotten to know each other under better circumstances."

Raymond turned to her, frowning lightly. "You think we would have been better as a couple if we had?"

"We may not have been a couple but, maybe, best friends." Regina had a little smile on her lips.

"I guess we would never know."

Regina's face fell at his response. Raymond stared at her a little longer before looking away.

***

Rita and Ralph were engaged in the most ridiculous conversation about monsters and superheroes that Raymond had ever heard. The hearty laughter across the dining table at his parents' house filled him with joy, a feeling that had taken him time to get used to.

"So much for not talking while eating," his mother said. She and her husband welcomed the liveliness in their home after all the recent chaos.

"We will let it slide. Service was awesome and how else would we continue to frolic in that joy if not by having family over." Robert said. He grinned, glad to have his family in one place, particularly his son. They were having another Sunday lunch but a more befitting one than the last one.

As his thoughts wandered, Robert maintained his smile while dreading the upcoming discussion he was going to have with Raymond after lunch.

***

The silence in the air was thick yet welcomed. Father and Son sat in silence for the first time in months and indeed years. It was long overdue.

A glass of juice sat half-forgotten beside Raymond while an empty glass of whiskey sat beside Robert. The latter sat patiently, waiting for his son to come to him first, for him to open up. The fact that Raymond honoured his invitation was a step in the right direction.

"Did the board finally agree on who to make MD?" Raymond asked.

"They are opting for an external person and are conducting interviews," Robert answered. "I am leaving them to it and will only get involved when they drill down to the final five."

Raymond nodded. He was picking through his thoughts, musing on what he wanted to discuss.

"Have you decided on what you will do for work?" Robert asked. "I cannot ask you to come back to the company even though I would love it if you would."

"I have a few offers already. It's looking good."

Robert nodded. "You are capable and I do not doubt that you will make it no matter what you get into." he paused, taking a deep breath before continuing. "I am sorry for how badly I treated you over the last few years."

Raymond stared at his hands and pursed his lips.

"I appreciate the apology," he said, looking up at his father. "And you can always reach out if you need any help." He had enjoyed working with his father even if it had been under unpleasant circumstances. He hoped he could maintain some form of rapport on that front.

Robert smiled. "I would like that."

The corner of Raymond's lips curled up briefly before he spoke up again. "I heard from Mom that you and your friend are mending fences."

"That is between us, son. It should not concern you what we old men get up to. You concentrate on your life." After a few minutes' silence, Robert added. "How are you and your son doing?"

"It gets better each day. He avoids calling me daddy but we have agreed that Ray-ray is okay."

Robert's heart lightened when Raymond smiled at the mention of his child.

"How about Royal? Have you been able to reach her?" Robert asked. It was a sore topic but he needed to know. There was a lot to catch up on and make up for.

Raymond shook his head. "I was told she travelled after giving birth and her parents have been a bit reluctant. They say they do not want any trouble for her over what she did." he paused before adding. "They were apologetic and asked to meet their grandson."

"Really? Did you agree?"

"I wouldn't expose him to such. I don't know how the kid would react if Regina travels and doesn't return."

"I heard she's travelling. I am here. Just tell me when you need anything and I will be there for you."

"I appreciate that." Raymond picked up the glass of juice. After a mouthful, he looked up at his father. "I asked Royal's parents to tell her I came around but I do not know if I would be contacting her any further."

"What if she wants to meet her child?"

"The agreement she signed was foolproof. Regina saw to that. Even though the decision she made was based on falsehood, I have the sole legal right to decide as his parent."

Robert watched his son closely as he spoke. Despite being only thirty-two, he looked older. His heart ached for his son, regret rising again.

"For now, it'll be just us. Maybe over time, when Ralph is older, I will change my mind."

"It's not just the both of you. You have us." Raymond watched his father fidget before leaning forward, fingers interlocked. "Your mother wants me to ask if you would move back in. The house is big enough for you to have a whole wing to yourself and still be close enough to have us support you."

Raymond smiled, shaking his head. "I am trying to find myself for the first time in a long time. We'll be fine."

"Anyway, your sisters are also there and you don't stay too far. You will have your space but you know how family can be."

With that, he was on his feet and walking to the bar with his glass. He returned empty-handed and stood for a bit before turning to his son.

"Would you like to play a game of chess?" Raymond saw a glint in his father's eyes and he recognized that spark when he challenged him to play. He realized he had missed it.

"Erm, I am a bit rusty on that front."

Robert retrieved the board game and set it out on the table between them. Laughing, he rubbed his palms together before setting out the pieces.

"Well then, I should be able to beat you easily."

In minutes they were laughing and casually discussing varying topics.

10
MOVING FORWARD

"You want to close out on this." Rita sat across from her brother who was reading through the documents for the house he wanted to buy. He had decided to sell the house he shared with Regina and she feared that her brother was moving away, essentially distancing himself from them.

"This house is full of memories I don't want to revisit daily. My therapist suggested it and it made sense."

"At least you are getting into your sessions more."

Raymond could hear a tinge of sadness in her voice.

"I am not moving that far. The new house is still close by." He passed the documents to her to look through. He chuckled when Rita's face lit up as she caught a glimpse of the address of the new house. She returned the papers to him.

"Okay. Good then. I don't have to inform the folks that you moved away." she added. "Congrats on the job too."

"Thanks. I am a bit skeptical though."

"Why? The Company is a good one even though it's a relatively new startup."

"It's not that. I know someone there. Someone from my former circle of friends."

"Oh really. Do you think he will cause trouble for you?"

"On the contrary, I think he put in a good word for me with the co-founder he works directly with and it's not like I will be working directly with him either but it feels weird."

Rita flinched. The topic of her brother's friends was a bit sensitive for her. "I understand what you mean. I am sure that recent developments have made their rounds in the rumour mill. I am happy you aren't having any issues."

"Yeah, I guess. Things are clearing up. In time, some other gist will make the rounds and mine will die down."

Rita smiled. "Are we good bro? I mean we may not be where we were before now but we are getting there, right?"

There was a longing in her voice that made Raymond slightly uncomfortable. "I haven't indicated anything different, have I? We have made a lot of progress."

"It's just that," she paused and sighed, "I sabotaged you a lot. I contributed to a lot of your friends writing you off. My conscience has been heavy. I reached out to many of them, you know, to get them to know the truth."

She retrieved her phone. "They needed to know the truth."

"And how is that playing out?" Raymond asked. He knew his twin was stressed and Rita sighed at her brother's knowing question.

"I have gotten blocked and yabbed. A few didn't respond."

Raymond moved to sit beside her on the settee and drew her close. It was still an uncomfortable interaction for him but he needed it as much as she did. He pushed past the discomfort and sat with her in silence for a few seconds before taking a deep breath.

"A few of them reached out via texts and DMs and I have not replied. I blocked one or two 'cos I could not cope. In all, it's okay."

Rita turned to her brother, teary-eyed and pouting a little. "You don't hate me anymore?"

"I never could." He wiped away her tears. "No matter how I tried. I think at one point I didn't have the strength for it."

"You tried to end it. I would not have survived that." Her tears flowed freely and Raymond pulled her in for a hug.

"I am sorry you had such thoughts. We are good now." His words calmed Rita and they remained in each other's embrace until Ronke's irritated voice startled them.

"You people are annoying." The twins pulled apart, each eyeing their younger sibling as she stood at the door.

"Why are you like this?" Rita asked, tossing a throw pillow at her, which Ronke dodged with ease.

She plopped down on the nearest seat and hissed.

"On a serious note, thank you Ronke. I for one am glad that you stayed by his side. You too try."

Ronke eyed her older sister and smiled at Raymond, eliciting laughter from him.

In time they were chatting over drinks. It was almost as if there had been no rift in the first place.

***

Ruby watched her friend as she packed her clothes and other items while reviewing a list. Regina was scheduled to fly out in the next two days and Ruby had visited intending to help her pack. Instead, she found herself dreading her friend's departure.

"Must you?" she asked, "Seems like you are running off."

"I am and I need it," Regina said as she opened a suitcase. "I need time to detach and distract myself. I will be back though."

"Are you sure?" Ruby asked. She looked around the room and shook her head "You are packing as though you are relocating."

Regina laughed. "Ruby, I am coming back. I can't run from my shadow and besides I need to consider Ralph in everything I do."

Ruby smiled excitedly as she lifted one of the empty suitcases and placed it on the bed.

"I can't believe Raymond allowed visitation rights. That's wholesome."

"He's a good person. He is willing to co-parent for Ralph's sake."

Ruby pulled out an item from the suitcase closest to her before Regina snatched it back.

"I am happy that everything has calmed down. Everyone gets to move forward with their lives in the best way possible." Ruby was a bit distracted by a few items she noticed amongst the mess on the bed.

Regina agreed with her friend. "The agreement states that there would be limited or no interactions with him when it came to my boy and I understand. I am glad that he allowed me to see him."

"Aren't you concerned that he could become hostile to you?" Ruby asked, a frown creasing her brow as she spoke. Regina smiled a little.

"He's not that kind of person but I know I need to be observant in case his mood changes." Regina fidgeted with a dress.

"And Royal? Any word from her since he visited her parents?"

"I heard from Momsi that she sent a message saying she was sorry and regretted her action. She wants to meet up when she gets back into the country but only if Raymond is willing. He hasn't responded."

"How do you know this?"

"My mom and he are mending fences. They are cordial and exchange updates once in a while. They were friends for years and they do share a grandchild." Regina sighed deeply, lying on the bed. "I wish I can take it all back. I am happy our parents can make up even though the relationship I will have with Raymond will only be based on tolerance."

"You want more?" Ruby asked, her tone daring her friend to answer foolishly.

Regina laughed. "A cordial friendship maybe but I'll settle for not being walked out on when in the same room."

"Better."

The friends were soon engaged in a different kind of banter which involved Regina struggling with her friend who was trying to claim some piece of clothing.

***

Regina lingered outside the door for a bit longer before knocking. It felt wrong not to say her goodbyes before leaving for her trip even if she had informed Ralph days before.

After multiple knocks, Regina pulled out the copy of the keys she still had and hesitated before opening the door. She could have left and called Raymond but something nudged at her. The quietness inside the house bothered her even more and she made her way up the stairs.

Their former bedroom was empty and the bed looked as though it had not been slept in. Memories of Raymond choosing to sleep in the spare room made Regina frown. Next, she checked Ralph's room and there she found them. Ralph was asleep in his race car bed and

Raymond was curled up beside him albeit uncomfortably from what she could see. But that was not what piqued her curiosity.

They looked peaceful, cuddled together save for the fact that it was two p.m. and with a closer look, Regina realized that Ralph was sweating. Moving closer she placed a hand on the child's forehead and was shocked to find that his temperature was high. Raymond woke up at that moment and the slight confusion on his face prompted Regina to check his temperature too.

"How long have you both been sick?"

Raymond coughed in response and a light cry escaped from Ralph.

"I thought it was malaria. Got him some meds and he fell asleep. Didn't want to leave him here so I laid down for a bit."

"Since when?"

"Last night, I think. My head hurts."

"You seem to have caught whatever he has." Regina turned back to Ralph, taking off the covers. "Where is Ronke? Or Rita?"

"Ronke had to go back to school and Rita had to go to work." As though just registering her presence, he looked her over. "Why are you here and how did you get in?"

"I still have a key and I wanted to see Ralph before my trip." She looked both of them over again. "Thank God I did. We are going to the hospital."

Initially reluctant, Raymond quickly changed his mind when, after standing up to prove his mettle, a wave of dizziness and nausea almost knocked him out. Minutes later, Regina drove out of the house with Ralph in the arms of his father in the back seat of the car.

"You should head back home. Your flight is tomorrow."

Raymond was reluctantly lying in bed while Regina fussed over him. Both he and his son had caught an infection. Rather than stay in the hospital, he had requested to be sent home and Regina had assured the doctor that she would care for them.

"I rescheduled my flight for another two weeks. I am sure you'd both be better by then."

"That's too much of a bother. Ronke will be back in a few days and Rita will be here tomorrow." He coughed a little and accepted the glass of water that was offered.

"Till they are here, I am not leaving. You are in no position to take care of yourself, not to mention a child. Anything can happen between today and tomorrow."

Raymond watched her through heavily lidded eyes. He was too weak to argue and was soon asleep. Regina left the room and returned with Ralph in her arms. She tucked the boy in beside his father, having decided that it would be better to care for both of them in the same room.

She watched over them for the rest of the evening till a worried Rita rushed into the room at past nine p.m.

"Why are you here?"

Regina ushered her out and explained the situation. Rita eyed her and peeked into the room at her brother and nephew.

"Thank you, I guess," she said and Regina smiled. Without another word, Rita retreated to the sitting room where she made a call. She did not hide the fact that she was speaking to her family and not wanting to eavesdrop, Regina returned to the bedroom and sank into the two-seater couch.

She was tired but grateful. For a moment, they were a family. By the following morning, Raymond was much better and saw Regina off to her car.

"You should have stayed in bed."

"I'm okay. Thank you for helping out."

"I am still around if you need any help," Regina said.

"I am sure Ralph will be happy to see more of you before you leave."

Raymond watched the face of the woman before him brighten. "I would love that."

"You should rest and come over tomorrow."

Regina nodded in agreement and he watched her leave before heading back into the house where a displeased Rita waited.

"Tomorrow? You want her back here tomorrow?"

"Look, she cared for us. I was down and out for the count, sis. Something worse could have happened to the both of us if she didn't show up."

"She had a spare key. Will you be giving her one for your new place?"

"Give it a rest, Rita. She is trying and yes, if I think she should have a key, I'll give her." Raymond gestured up the stairs. "She raised him and I need to recognize that. She raised Ralph when his mother wanted to do away with him."

Rita fidgeted. "Fine. I agree with your decision." She pulled her twin in for a hug and watched him take the stairs.

11
THERAPY

Raymond absentmindedly caressed the soft leather of the couch on which he sat. He knew his therapist was watching him, waiting for him to open up instead of prompting the discussion.

Her technique, and patience, had won him over and helped him unwind, without any pressure.

"To think that you were giving me the silent treatment during our first few sessions," she said.

Raymond smiled at the lady seated in the swivel chair across from him. He had opted for that chair when he first started.

It had been placed closer to the door, an easy escape for him when he felt overwhelmed or uncomfortable. She had accommodated his anxiety and had not rushed him in any way.

"I am glad I didn't stop coming."

"So, how are you?"

"Good. I have been sleeping better since I moved to the new house. No night sweats and urges for alcohol have reduced drastically."

The lady nodded. "What about your relationship with your son?"

Raymond lit up. It was a stark difference from the man who once turned white while talking about his son.

"He is ecstatic at the thought of designing his room and has not asked about his mother much. When he asks, I tell him she travelled and he does not react for too long."

"Children can sense animosity between their parents and when that is removed, they are relieved and grateful that there is no more tension, even if they can't express it."

"You mean he, subconsciously, recognized that there were issues, even when we thought he was too young to know?"

"Oh, they know. They are quite perceptive. I would still advise you to take him to see the child psychologist again. I believe that is also helping him come to terms with all the changes. We can gauge how he is coping and not assume." She smiled, revealing her dimples. "But I am glad to hear that you are doing well."

"He talks to me more. Sometimes I think it's too much." Raymond laughed. "But then I caution myself."

The therapist nodded. "How did you feel when Regina came over and cared for both of you when you were sick."

"Grateful. I was clueless and could have put both of us in so much more trouble. She took care of us."

"You were not uncomfortable with the interaction?"

"My sister asked me the same thing and if I am being honest, it felt good knowing she was there. She postponed her flight and checked in practically every day."

"Has it ever crossed your mind to see if both of you could work?"

Raymond cocked his head to one side and squinted.

He stared at her as she smiled softly. "Why would you ask that?"

"It's just a question."

"No. It hasn't. All I wanted was to get away and get my life together."

He watched her nod and smile again. "I asked out of curiosity. You said it felt good having her there. It means she wasn't such a bad person despite her misguided actions."

"She was a good mother and all other things being considered, a good wife, even if it was mostly to the world." He looked away, staring at nothing in particular.

"Was there anything about her that you liked, no matter how little?"

"She was responsible and took care of the home. I do feel bad for her, 'cos she got stripped of a lot and continues to try to make it up to me."

"How?"

"She refunded what my father sent her as compensation, with interest, and still paid me compensation. I know of at least one interview she granted and I heard she lost a lot of friends and her business is suffering too."

"Sounds like she is or has become a more reasonable person." The therapist watched him closely. She wanted to gauge his reaction to speaking about her for an extended period.

"So you suggest that I consider her?"

"Not at all. I was trying to see how much you have let go of your hate towards her. You gave her more visitation rights and it shows you are moving past a lot and that is good."

"She is the boy's mother and he doesn't have to suffer for her decisions." He shrugged. "There is no reason why we should not be civil for his sake."

She nodded and took down a few notes.

"So would you say that you would rule out having something more with her?"

Raymond fell silent. "She once said that she wished we had met under better circumstances." He shook his head. "A lot has happened, too much even. So right now, my answer would be no."

"You mean there is a possibility in the future?"

Raymond shrugged. "I honestly do not know. I want to take things one day at a time and leave the future for the future. It may hold something different but for now, I need to find myself."

The therapist nodded. "What about your parents and siblings?"

"They are good. I recently started thinking about going back to work with my father under certain terms but not anytime soon because I am still enjoying my job."

The therapist scribbled down a few things and smiled when he looked up at her.

"Any other new developments?"

Raymond nodded. "Ralph's biological mother came to see me. I thought I would have had a ton to say but, right there and then, I could not cope with looking at her."

"Lingering affections?"

"No, not at all. She came with her fiancé who happens to be from my old friend group. We spoke briefly, and they apologized. She asked to see Ralph but I declined."

"Have you reconnected with any of your old friends? You are doing much better with your family, and even your ex-wife, to a degree." the therapist asked, intentionally changing the topic.

"Right now, the only one I speak to is the one at my office. I'd like to think that we have rebuilt some form of rapport, but I am still cautious. I don't speak to anyone else even though several have reached out."

"Friend circles are a good thing even if you keep them small."

Raymond shook his head as he spoke. "I know. Maybe over time or maybe I'll make new friends. I am still a bit wary of my family so the thought of friends is scary."

"Keep trying. You need such social circles."

"As you once said doc, one day at a time. I'll get there someday."

The therapist nodded and closed her notebook.

"Today may be our last session but you are always welcome here."

"I will reach out if I need to. I promise."

They shook hands and Raymond was out the door.

Outside, he took a deep breath before heading to the car. The first time he had walked through the doors of the therapist he had been certain it was in vain. He had made up his mind that he would end it all and that it was the only way to find peace.

Now, months later, he regretted his thoughts but understood that they were born out of despair, depression, and isolation. As he mulled over a few things in the car, his phone beeped and a text notification from his mother caught his eye. He smiled.

Raymond was grateful that he was finding his way back and glad he had not taken the road he had mapped out for himself. Things had gotten better and he was gradually regaining his old self. He would never be the same person he had been before, his experiences would not allow that.

He was hopeful and grateful for every new day.

EPILOGUE
A BIRTHDAY WISH

"Happy birthday, Ralphy!" The choruses filled the air as the celebrant blew out the candles on his eighth birthday cake. The front yard of the Luoye family home was filled with children and adults alike.

Confetti irritated Ronke's nose and she, along with her guest, retreated to a corner choosing to watch the party from a distance.

Raymond and Regina fussed over the birthday boy, having become experts at caring for their child. Both sets of grandparents watched them from the garden chairs arranged for the guests. Robert laughed a little at the antics of a group of boys causing Reginald to nod.

Their wives kept an eye on Rita and the caterers, occasionally catching her eye when she threw puff-puff in her mouth. Her mother shook her head at her, puffing up her cheeks and pointing at Rita's very visible baby bump.

"As if that will work. Remember how much chicken you consumed when you were pregnant with the twins." Rose teased. Ropo eyed her.

"Whose side are you on?" she asked and they laughed. The occasional squeal of a child filled the air, livening up the event a little more.

Hours later, Raymond tucked his son into bed as Regina watched him. At the boy's request, Regina followed them home and waited for him to fall asleep. Retreating to the sitting room, both of them sat down, exhausted from the day's activities.

"I am so tired," Raymond muttered. Regina laughed lightly.

"Next time, maybe we should have a small party instead of such a grand one," she added.

"That will be when he is thirteen, and no, I will not be doing this again," Raymond said, shutting his eyes and sighing again.

They laughed and fell into a comfortable silence.

"How have you been?" she asked.

Raymond hummed.

"I have been good, and you?"

Regina nodded. "I am okay. Thank you for allowing me to plan this with you."

"I would not have it any other way. You are his mom and I can't deny that."

An awkward silence followed. Theirs was still a struggling relationship, but one that seemed to be improving.

"You know you don't have to avoid me like you do. I don't bite."

Regina shrugged. "I can't feign familiarity with a history like ours." She looked over at Raymond. "I hurt you."

"It's been two years." Raymond stifled a yawn. "I don't hate you, at least not anymore, and for Ralph's sake, we can be friends."

"Can we? You want us to be friends?"

"Why not?" He turned to her.

"I didn't think you would want to have anything more to do with me other than taking care of Ralph."

"Look. We are adults and can have an amicable friendship." Raymond smiled softly. He became a bit fidgety. "For the boy's sake and that way, we could get to know each other better."

"Despite our unpleasant history?" He watched her face fall.

"Stop beating yourself up so much. What happened, happened."

Regina smiled. She liked this version of Raymond that sat with her. He was more pleasant and friendlier, and happier too.

"You barely smiled back then," she added. "And now, I get to see your dimples."

They both laughed. The subsequent silence was more comfortable.

"I should leave. It's getting late."

"You should stay. There is a spare room and I am sure Ralph would be happy to wake up to his mom."

"Really?"

Raymond nodded. He held her gaze till she looked away.

"Why?" she asked. "Are you okay with me being here with you?"

"Look, I have had time to mull over it all." He sat up and leaned forward. "You aren't a bad person despite everything that happened between us. We can try to be friends."

"Friends?"

"You want more?"

Regina stalled. "Truthfully, I wouldn't mind. I know that would be foolish thinking on my part but I am being honest."

Raymond nodded. He didn't say anything else and instead got up and walked away. Regina bit down on her lower lip, mentally berating herself. She had started gathering up her things when Raymond returned and sat down.

"I do not know how this will play out or if it's even wise." He held out a key on a chain and smiled. "But I guess this would be a good way to start so you can, at least, be here for Ralph."

Regina collected the key and stared at it for a few seconds.

"Your parents are going to flip," she stated.

"Let's not forget my sisters," he added.

They laughed a little and Regina looked up at him.

"It's not too late for some cocoa." She offered and Raymond nodded.

He watched her walk to the kitchen with the key in her hand as though she feared it would be taken back.

Something caught his attention and he turned around to see his son peeking around a corner, grinning from ear to ear.

Raymond smiled and shooed him away. It had been the boy's birthday wish that his mother be around and he had been wondering how best to make it happen. He felt at peace with his decision and only needed to plan how best he would explain it to his family.

He listened to the light footsteps of his son on the stairs just as Regina returned with their drinks. In time both of them were catching up. Neither could deny that it felt good to be in each other's company, and on much better terms.

They were still recovering but there was no reason why they could not do it together.

The End.

About the Author

Temitope Omamegbe is a creative writer, scriptwriter, developmental editor, proofreader and writing coach driven by the desire to help people achieve their goals of getting published.

An occasional poet, Temitope is also the convener of the **Amethyst Short Story** contest as well as a member of the Black Female Authors Collective.

Her works are **Twice a Bride, Hell Hath no Fury** (a collection of short stories), **The Night Masquerade** and **Of Good Destiny** (both of which are Alphabetical Novellas). She is also published in the 2024 second edition of Brittle Paper's Festive Anthology **Recipes, Rituals & Resolutions.**

When she is not writing, she is a Customer Service Excellence Officer and Card Payment Specialist.

Catch up with her via her social media as Tajmao, on Instagram and Twitter platforms.

THE SABBATICAL

Freedom could be a different kind of chain.

By

TIMILEYIN OKUNLOLA

Dedication

To you who seek rest,

May you find it in the embrace of the One who never lets go!

When it comes to yearnings,

You pine and pine,

Yet it's nowhere to be found.

But when it comes to curveballs,

You are just about your business,

And there it is,

Dropping right in your laps!

Surprise, Surprise!

Iretiola

It's 10 a.m. and I'm hurrying up the stairs that lead to Shots. It's the last Friday before my long overdue leave and boy, am I happy? 3 years without a breathing space in Shots is enough to make anyone run mad. That is 36 months of endless errands, 156 weeks of shouting and cursing all around me and 1095 days of helping adults de-clutter the mess in their lives and be at their very best. I've spent over 26,000 hours of my life setting up appointments and fixing a broad smile on the face of everyone. It's time to set up an appointment for myself as well. It's high time I also smile genuinely and this will start from today!

Today, I become a free soul unburdened with cares and queries, with bills and rings. Today, I gain control over my empire for the coming weeks. Just imagining the freedom at my fingertips has me skipping like a bird. Indeed, nothing beats a well-deserved break and this time around nothing is going to tamper with my plans. Not Mr. Thomas, not family issues and not even a monetary offer.

Of all days to be cranky, the staircase chose today. It seems to grow longer with every step and my lower back aches like hell. *Aaarrgh.* Just 10 more to go. 8...6... 4... 2...And we're here. Finally.

The entrance door is firmly locked which is quite unusual. Goldie is almost always at work by this time and if she isn't here, Sandra, the walkie-talkie is here. I push all thoughts of my co-workers to the back of my mind as I rummage in my bag for the spare key. Getting into the reception, the cool temperature was a welcome relief from the early morning sun.

As with every other morning I've been to work, I am once again amazed at the spotless beauty looking back at me. Shots sits majestically on the last floor of a five-storey building. There is the main studio room where we have our major shoots, the inner studio where we hold exclusive interviews and of course, the reception area which serves as my little haven. Like most mornings, my space has been tampered with during Goldie's cleanup yesterday and I set about rearranging it to my satisfaction. Starting with the pen holder, I clean it out and replace my pens, carefully arranging the colors with the dexterity of *Aso Oke* weavers. After that, the napkins went back into the safe, my snack platter came out and now, I'm fully set for the day.

Soon enough, the first call of the day comes in. It's Mr. Thomas and he wants the new camera in the studio packed before his arrival. With the price tag weighing heavily on my mind, I open the door gingerly to pick up the camera and stop dead in my tracks. The sight before me sends me back to the fortress I've long abandoned. What in the name of God is this?

The Night Comes

It's been hours since that horrible moment at the studio. For all it's worth, it could have been days, months or even years. I really can't tell. I've just been left in the lurch.

It all feels like a terrible, terrible nightmare. The events are blurry and the last I remembered was being bundled into a Black Maria like a murderer.

Funny how your whole life can spiral down right in your presence and you're left feeling naked as if you are in the middle of the harsh desert with nothing but your grief to cover you.

You Can't Shame The Shameless, Can You?

"Oga! Wetin dey sup nau? Una just abandon person for here like banana peel. Nawa for Una ooo. "

"Be like say your craze don start again? Who be your mate for hia?" Officer KK responded. He is a small-sized man who is known for his sharp mouth. It is believed that what he lacked in stature, he made up for with his razor mouth.

"Alaye, park well make we see road. If no be rain wey carry pigeon join body with chicken, who you be? If you comot this uniform wey dey your neck, you fit face me?"

"See, I no get your time today. Carry your fallen chest go meet another maga. No be me and you go dey trade words. "

"Aboki! Oloshi! Leave my fallen chest and go face your family problems. No be me say make you no get wife for house. Odaran!"

That was Kulubu.

One of the most eccentric fellows I've ever laid my eyes upon. Built like a matchstick yet possesses enough strength and vitality to last 2 able-bodied men for a lifetime. Kulubu had been thrown into Cell F for months now and she was kind enough to give me a rundown of how the cells work.

Officially, there are 4 cells in the enclosure. A, B, C and D. A for the Hardened Criminals, B was for the Petty Criminals, C was for Condemned Criminals and D was for those on Life Imprisonment. However, due to the cracks in the system, other cells started springing up and before one could say Jack, the enclosure became a steady side gig for the officials.

Cells like ours, Cell F, is for those who have not had any access to a court hearing and those still in the process of their hearings. Sometimes, it could also house those who were wrongly accused, arrested unlawfully or in my case, people who had no one turning up for them. They keep these lots in separate cells and threaten them while milking their families and loved ones.

Just like me, Kulubu had no access to a fair hearing. She was thrown into Cell F on account of a deal gone south and has refused to be cowered into a false statement or mindless spending. She is maintaining her ground on proving her innocence and has grown a thick skin against the prejudice and unfair treatment that abound in the enclosure. She carries her fallen breasts with pride and proclaims to anyone who cares to listen that they can't shame the shameless. As such, no one can shame Kulubu.

Interrogation

"Miss, can you start talking?"

Silence.

"I said, 'Get Talking!'"

Deadbeat Silence.

"I'm losing my patience here! What is wrong with you, young lady? How many more minutes will I waste on this or are you hell-bent on destroying your chances?"

"Air."

"I beg your pardon?"

"I'm claustrophobic. I need air. I'm suffocating. "

"This is not a vacation home and you're not here to be pampered."

"I'm sorry but my face itches. I can barely breathe."

"And I'm supposed to give you the kiss of life or what?"

Silence

"Can you hear me?"

Nod. Nod.

"Phew! All right, we'll have it your way. See you in 5 minutes and you had better be ready to talk by then."

And with that, he walks out as I struggle to maintain an even breathing. He leaves the door open and stations 2 of the fiery-looking officers at the entrance.

Gust by gust, I feel the air trickling in and it feels better. Way better than all I've breathed these past hours. It feels just like the days when the nightmares haven't started.

Days when I don't wake to the sound of boots walking the floor and of angry men yelling at bitter men. Days when I never fully appreciated the little pleasures of life. Just when I plunge into my daydreams, his deep voice interrupts me once again and this time, I take a good look at him. He is tall and firmly built with a well-chiselled face that has no strands of hair on it.

"I'm back."

"Okay…. "

"Yeah. I'm sorry, it seems we got off on a wrong note. I'm Ethan Wells, the Detective handling your case. I would need you to cooperate as much as you can as this will aid the investigations. So now Miss, CAN. YOU. GET. TALKING? We don't have all day. Matter of fact, I have just 7 minutes left here."

"I'm innocent, please. I don't know anything about this. I'm… I… He…. I urm."

"Hey! Relax. Take a deep breath and calm down. I'm not going to bite. I'm harmless unless you start acting funny. Let's start with you. Tell me about yourself."

"I urm…I'm Ireti. Iretiola Kunfoye. A graduate of Petroleum Engineering and an entrepreneur."

"You studied Petroleum Engineering. What are you doing with Shots?"

"I am a Studio Assistant."

"Studio Assistant? Petroleum Engineering? This still isn't syncing. Mind shedding some light on it?"

"I couldn't get a placement and I had to get something to do so I won't become redundant."

"Simply put, the nation happened to you?"

"Yes."

"What are your job descriptions at Shots?"

"Fixing appointments, attending to customers, handling the overall day-to-day activities of the studio and every other job Mr Thomas apportions to me per time."

"So why are you here?"

"I was brought here."

"Brought here? By which Convoy?"

Definitely, if looks could kill, this man would be dead by now.

"Excuse you, Miss. I'm expecting your answer."

"I was arrested when I raised the alarm at the studio. I wasn't allowed to say a word and this is the first time anyone is hearing me out."

"What made you raise an alarm?"

"I saw a body and I was scared. I've only seen a dead man once and I couldn't hold it again."

"You couldn't hold what again?"

"What?"

"You said and I quote … *and I couldn't hold it again.* So, I'm asking what it is that you couldn't hold again."

"The sight. It was horrid and nothing like I'd ever seen before."

"What do you know that can further the course of our investigations?

"Nothing."

"Nothing?"

"Yes. Nothing. Absolutely nothing. I'm totally blank."

"Okay. I'll see you around and for your own good, you had better fill in the spaces before our next meeting. Goodbye Miss Kunfoye. I'll see you around."

I watch him leave with mixed feelings. I am happy I finally got a hearing and I wish all these can be over.

One - Zero

I've been happy before. Very, very happy. I was gay and full of life. I graduated with flying colours and was eager for what life after school held. I dutifully presented my resume to the top guns day after day but was rejected from office to office. I slept after reading the rejection emails for the day and woke up to the sound of yet another rejection. Everyone thought that was a really tight corner to be but I was cosy in my corner. I had no job but I had a man and that should count for something.

I was young, energetic, beautiful and most importantly in love. In love with the man my heart craved for and who loved me better than I had ever been loved. Life couldn't get any better for me. Doudou and I were a jolly couple until my *white got stained.*

It was our 'indoors Saturday' and I was excited at the prospect of what lies ahead. Games, fun, food and of course some quality time together. I got to his apartment in good time and set to work immediately. The menu for the day was grilled chicken, veggie Sauce, and spaghetti. Although I wasn't financially buoyant, Doudou covered that angle perfectly well and we fitted each other like hands in gloves. Besides loving Doudou, cooking for him was one of the things I lived for. I surfed the net day after day, bought cookbooks, attended classes in my free time and literally created my own recipes just to build a kitchen dynasty for my King.

For Doudou and I, food wasn't just to quench our hunger or prevent an ulcer, it was an avenue for us to consummate our love and solidify our bond. He never allowed cooking to become burdensome or a needless chore I needed breathing space. We did it all together and I couldn't have asked for a better man. Life was all rosy and smooth till disaster struck.

On this particular day, we had just finished our *lovecheon* when there were repeated knocks on the door. Unperturbed, I opened the door and was surprised by the blend of jasmine, orange and bergamot scents that hit my nostrils. Standing before me was one of the most beautiful women I have ever set my eyes on. She was the perfect replica of those glossy ladies from the magazines. She looked and smelled like a billion bucks. Instantly, I felt subconscious in the chiffon dress I got from Dazzy's thrift hub.

"Michael!" she screeched.

"I beg your pardon! Who are you looking for?"

"Mike!" She barged in and kept on screaming like a deranged woman giving me no notice at all.

"I'm sorry. It seems you…"

"Luc. What the heck are you doing here?" he asked.

Wait.

That was Douglas. My Douglas.

"What won't I be doing here? You left me hanging for days and now you have the temerity to question my presence here! Gosh! I can't deal with this now. Can you tell your housekeeper to get me a cold glass of smoothie? I'm so thirsty."

Wait. Where the heck is that coming from? Housekeeper? Me?? How?

"Douglas, what's going on here? You didn't tell me we will be expecting a visitor?"

His silence told me all I needed to know. In all the years I had known Douglas, he had never been that uncomfortable so I sensed a rat. My man would never stay quiet unless he was in big soup.

Like a joke, all our dreams evaporated before my eyes. The plans. The dream family. The vacations. The Games. The naughty nights. The kids. The Names. All down the drain.

Once again, I can feel the now familiar comforting hands of rejection enveloping me and like the dutiful daughter, I go in for the embrace and stay right there.

Men - 1, Me - 0

Kukuruko

It is early morning and I am baffled at the summons. In all my days here, I've never seen the officers come for anyone this early. My breath quickens as I wonder why I have to be the trailblazer for such calls. Soon enough, I am face to face with Detective Ethan and his demeanour is far from being good. I wonder what else has gone wrong.

"How well do you know this man?" he asks, holding up a picture. I stare at the picture and feel no flicker of emotion. I can't remember ever seeing that face smiling at the camera. I look at the dark-skinned man with a goatee again and felt no light bulb moment. No Eureka episodes. Nothing. I am blank.

"I don't know him."

"At all?"

"Yes, at all. I've never seen him before."

"You've never seen him? He wasn't a client? An acquaintance? Your neighbor? Anyone at all?"

"This is the first time I'm seeing him. I've never laid my eyes on him till this moment."

"Can you think deeply? Think back to a few years from now. A few months from now. A few weeks from now. A few days from now."

"I DON'T KNOW HIM! Who is he? And why is he coming up now? What does he have to do with my plight?"

"That's the man who died."

"Oh my! I didn't know. The body I saw looked nothing like this."

"He is lying cold in a mortuary and you're facing a judge in a couple of hours to tell your side of what led to his death."

"I didn't kill him. I've never even seen him till that morning."

"Prepare to tell that to the judge. I'll see you in 3 hours, Miss."

One Step Forward, Two Steps Backwards

The hours preceding the court session were the worst since this nightmare started. I sat huddled up in the Black Maria with sweaty palms. I was scared, afraid and angry. Scared I will be convicted for a crime I know nothing about, afraid of what will follow - an eternity behind bars and angry that God was comfortable seeing me go through all this. So much for Everlasting Love. I couldn't wrap my head around the fact that a few hours from now would seal my fate forever.

After what seems like ages, I find myself before the judge and the teeming crowd.

Indeed, people are *tafia* and they love *aproko*. I spot my coworkers and business owners around the studio among the spectators. They've all been released from the enclosure after a few days of back and forth. The officers insisted I was the major suspect and thus had to be kept under close watch. They all look at me with sympathy.

I've never seen them look at me with that much pity before and it makes me feel more miserable.

Soon enough, the judge comes in and the court proceedings begins. Never in my life have I felt so naked and vulnerable. My life is up there like an object on an auction ground and the haggling is so fierce!

I watch with bated breath as a rotund man introduces himself as my lawyer and fights tooth and nail to get me out. I can feel his disappointment and I lose hope as soon as the judge hit the gavel.

I need no soothsayer to inform me that I am going back to Cell F for good this time.

Who Do You Think Did This?

01

"Why were you not at work on the morning of the incident?"

"I was held up in traffic. By the time I got to work, there were police all over the place."

"So tell me, how well do you know Miss Kunfoye?" Ethan asks, looking straight into the eyes peering at him.

"I met her at work and she has always been a delight to everyone. She helped me get settled in my routine easily and I'm eternally grateful for her recommendations."

"What do you think could have motivated her to kill the young man?"

"Well, humans are complicated beings. So I guess her dark side is just coming up."

"Her dark side? What do you mean by that?"

"You know everyone has one or two unknown habits and most times when we're under pressure, these sides tend to come up."

"I see. So that is what you think this is?"

"I'm just saying, Sir. I mean no harm."

"Has she ever been involved in a physical altercation with anyone before?"

"I don't know o."

"Never???"

"Officer, I've told you all I know please."

"I see. We'll see you around, Miss Sandra."

02

"When did you start working with Shots?"

"Four months ago."

"So how would you describe Miss Ireti?"

"Punctual, Formal and Easy going."

"Did she ever pose a threat to you or any other worker?"

"Not to my knowledge."

"You've never seen her violent?"

"No."

"Unruly?"

"No."

"Do you think she is innocent?"

"I'm not her lawyer."

"You don't need to be a lawyer to answer my questions, Mister."

"I'm sorry. I'm just an IT student and all of these are too much for me to take in."

"It's a lot for us all too and a lot is at stake here. So now, is there any other thing you know or remember that can further this investigation?"

"If I remember anything that can help. I'll do well to tell you sir."

"Okay, we definitely are not done with you yet. Thank you for your time. Mr. Tegbo. You can take your leave now."

03

"Miss Ireti Kunfoye has worked with you for 3 years. In all these years, has she ever been linked to a crime?"

"None that I know of."

"If this turns out to be her first, how would you feel?"

"I don't know."

"Won't you be surprised?"

"Well, I will but as the saying goes, there is nothing new under the sun. Everyone is a walking suspect and in matters like this, I try my best to be safe and tread carefully."

"Mr. Thomas, have you ever been involved in a scenario like this before?"

"I beg your pardon."

"It's a straightforward question that requires a straightforward answer, Mr. Thomas. Yes or No??"

"Mr. Police Officer or whoever you are, what are you trying to insinuate?"

"I'm Detective Ethan and I'm not insinuating anything. I need you to give me a Yes or No answer."

"Okay. No."

"Have you ever been involved in a murder crime?"

"No."

"Has anyone died in your studio before?"

"No."

"How well do you know the deceased?"

"I do not know him at all. Seeing his dead body was the very first time I saw him."

"He wasn't a part of your customer base?"

"No."

"He didn't book any appointment with you?"

"No."

"How then did he have access to your studio?"

"I don't know."

"Who could have let him in?"

"I have no idea."

"Do you have any other information that can advance the course of the investigations?"

"No, I don't."

"All right. Thanks so much for your time, Mr. Thomas. We'll keep in touch with you. Please ensure you do not leave the city without informing the authorities."

"So, I'm now a criminal or what?"

"Everyone is a walking suspect and in matters like this, we also try our best to be safe and tread carefully."

04

"So, Miss Kunfoye, who do you think did this?"

"I don't know."

"What do you mean you don't know?"

"Detective, I don't even know what to think. My brain is muddled up.
I can't think. I can't sleep. It's like I'm dying. I… "

"Do you think this could be a setup?"

"By who?"

"Anyone."

"Really, I can't say… "

"Who among your colleagues do you think can do this?"

"None."

"None?"

"I can't point out anyone."

"Mr. Thomas?"

"No. He can shout and all but kill, nah. Not him."

"Goldie?"

"No, too. She's reserved but not capable of murder."

"Sandra?"

"Nah. She's just a walkie-talkie and nothing more. Can't hurt a fly."

"Tegbo?"

"The poor boy is just hustling for his daily bread."

"You're sure you do not suspect him or any other person?"

"Yes, let's just spread our tentacles wider."

"So, who do you think did this?"

"I think that's your job. To fish out the culprit!"

"Well, yes, but I can't do that without your help. If you keep having shallow thinking, I'm afraid you might just make room for yourself here as you prepare for your last days."

"Am I going to die? Will…. will… they kill me? I…."

"Well, the ball is in your court, Miss. You decide what it's going to be."

Lean On Me

It is midnight and as usual, I'm finding it difficult to sleep. Tossing from one end of the hard floor to the other, I can't help but wonder why I've been sidelined and discarded like a piece of trash. Shots have stylishly washed its hand off the case and I've been left to dance to a discordant tune I never knew its motif.

My vision is clogged as hot tears burn my throat. It's been a hard year and I can't find the strength to push on anymore. After moments of heart-wrenching cries, I feel a strong grip around me and in that moment, it feels so right.

"Mama. Everything go *bam*. No worry. "

"When? I've been here for weeks without any hope and I can't even think straight. I'm just tired. So tired!"

"Eei, no go kolo for here o. These ones are mad people oo. See, you don dey suffer in silence since. If you wan cry, cry make your eyes clear. See, sometimes when person neva cry, e no fit think straight."

That is all the nudging I need to let it all out and after what feels like centuries after, I feel the relief to my bones.

"Thank you. Thank you. Thank you very much."

"Haba, why I con dey here?"

"Still, thank you. You could have ignored me. You could have slept. You could have just left me. You could have......."

"E don do oo. I no run. I no leave you alone here. I still dey with you. No shaking. No Retreat. No Surrender. "

"Awwnn Kulubu. Aren't you just a sweet, sweet human?"

"Well, you could enjoy more sweetness by shining your eyes make you see the plenty sugar wey dey for here."

"Sugar? What sugar could possibly be in this dungeon?"

"You wan dey disguise abi?"

"Haba! How I go dey disguise for my person?"

"You wan tell me say you no know that policeman wey dey always come for here dey eye you?"

"Kulubu!!! For God's sake. Not him. What on earth brought that thought into your heart?"

"Abeg, no dey disguise for here."

"But there's nothing really. And he's also not a policeman. He's a Detective."

"Mama, forget that thing. Na here we go dey when everywhere go clear."

"Oh please. Just go to bed already." I dismiss her but the seed she planted refused to die.

Aromatherapy

It's another day for rounds after rounds of interrogation and I am tired in advance. Tired of it all. I saunter after the constable with bated breath not knowing what to expect next. We arrive at our destination and he leads me into the waiting room almost graciously.

The room is more spacious than previous arenas and there is a soothing smell I can't place my hands on. I look around furtively till my eyes rest on him. I can see him quite all right but my heart seems to be on another rung of the ladder. Being around him always seems to have a calming effect on me.

"I can see you like this better."

"What?"

"The Venue. You like the venue change. I can see it all over you."

"How?"

"Your eyes. They say it all. "

"I can't place this smell though. I've never smelled anything this good. "

"It's Lavender. It will help your episodes."

"Episodes?"

"You're claustrophobic right? The smell will prevent you from getting worked up."

"Oh. Thank you."

"Not to worry."

"Why are you going through all this stress for me?"

"Because I need you alive. It won't do me any good for my suspect to kick the bucket while we're nowhere near the finishing line."

"I see. Has there been any update?"

"Yes. The autopsy is out and it's not looking too good. There were traces of harmful chemicals in his bloodstream and the doctor also pointed to arsenic poisoning. So, it's quite a dicey situation."

"I don't even know this man."

"You don't have to know him to kill him. Acquaintance has never been a saving grace from murderers."

"I swear on my life I do not know this man. I just got to work as every other day and there lies a corpse in the studio."

"I hear you, young woman but if nothing concrete that can exonerate you comes out. You are well on your way to the gallows."

His words bring to the fore the reality of my situation. The soothing scent of the lavender evaporates and all I smell is death.

This Thumping Of My Heart

Ethan

I watch as she is led away and wish I could do something to this thumping of my heart. Never in all my years of practice have I felt this much tenderness for a suspect. From the first day I heard about the murder case at the studio, I was intrigued by the perplexity of the case and was further dumbfounded by the persona of the person involved.

I knew from the first moment I saw her that there was more to this lady than a murder case. The helplessness around her seems palpable and I knew I had more to do than prove her innocence.

Holdincation

Iretiola

According to the radio blaring from the corridor. Today is Tuesday. The 34th day of my nightmare. This day would have been my Tasty Tuesday back home. A day for merriment and movie-binging. All the preparations, list building and all was a waste. A huge waste. I can't help but think back on how it would have been had the plans not been scattered.

With the current situation of things, I decided to make use of what is available and enjoy the vacation with Kulubu. On some days, I read the pamphlets they generously drop in each cell. On others, I discuss with Kulubu and on some others, I stare at the sky and enjoy the ambience.

However, this Tuesday, Kulubu has managed to smuggle in a board game and my excitement can't be over-emphasized. Really, I can't fathom how on earth she was able to smuggle in a Monopoly board but she ignores all my probing and questions and concentrates on acquiring much property and avoiding jail time. I drop the subject and focus on enjoying the moment. I mean, it's Game time and we're sure rocking it!

Right from the tender age of 8, Monopoly has held such a great appeal for me. I've dedicated over 15 years of my life to learning the twists, turns, and strategic actions required to be the last man standing and here in Cell F, I hold nothing back as I pour all the knowledge into Kulubu. That is the least I can do for a woman who has taken me as her very own blood. I only wish we can apply the knowledge and save ourselves from the mess we are in.

Whispers

It's midnight and I'm all alone as I wished but now under different circumstances. I look out of the window deep in regret. I never should have gone to work that day. Something should have happened. Anything at all. Cramps. Typhoid. Broken lock. An accident. Something. Anything. Anything at all!

The two security guards at the cell entrance are at it again. Just that this time around, there are no angry arguments, no jab at Kulubu, and no lewd talk about women. Tonight, it's just whispers. Whispers so fleeting you never would have heard and what I heard did make my hair stand on end.

A Burst Of Fresh Air

Ethan

I study her as she walks out of the court building. She looked even worse than I noticed earlier. With each step, the unease becomes more palpable and my heart aches a bit deeper.

"Thank you, Detective. I never expected this would be possible." She says as she gets to my side.

Indeed, getting her bail has been a herculean task but I wasn't about to bore her with the details. Her being out here is enough reward for the back and forths of getting her bail.

"Let's be grateful it's a done deal now. At least, you can rest a while while we figure out things and spread her net wider."

"To think I wanted a couple of free weeks just to clear my head. Now, I'm stuck with proving my innocence and I don't even know where it will all end."

"Don't worry your pretty head about that. It will all end beautifully. There is nothing to be worried about."

"I hear you but there is something I'm concerned about though. I.. "

" You've had a long day. We'll discuss all about your concerns much later. For now, let's get you home"

I take her hands amidst her protests and walk her to the junction where she can get a cab home. All talks on concerns and worries can wait.

Iretiola

I know waiting can be exhausting but today was on another level. As I sat in my small room, I couldn't help but stare at the clock ticking away on the wall. I was eagerly waiting for 5 o'clock, the time Detective Ethan and I had agreed to meet for an outing. I'd been out on bail for barely a week and this was the first time I would be stepping out of my door for any reason at all.

Finally, the clock struck 5 and I stood up, slipped on my footwear and set out for the venue. It was quite a smooth ride locating the place and just as I was digging in my bag for my phone, I heard his voice.

"Hello Miss" I heard behind me and upon turning round I saw him walking up to me with his signature bright smile.

"Good afternoon Detective. Please lead the way."

"Sure"

I followed him and we walked up to a secluded spot in the garden where we could have a bird's eye view of everything going on. It was indeed a perfect spot!

"Please give me a few minutes. I'll be back shortly" he said walking away and I released the breath I'd been holding.

Ever since I got back from custody, I've been very paranoid and being in such close contact with him wasn't helping matters. I wonder what more sad news he will be breaking.

"A penny for your thoughts, Miss"

He is back and I am surprised at what he brings.

"What are you doing with this?" I asked.

Ignoring my question, he set about arranging the items in the basket he brought - A pack of Rice, Spaghetti, Chicken, Plantain, fruits and chilled drinks.

"So what's the occasion? What are you celebrating?"

"I'm not celebrating anything. I just figured we could do with some food while we converse."

"Some food? This is a spread!"

"Thank you. I'll take that as a compliment. Now please, help yourself."

He passes the plate to me and I dish out some rice, plantain and chicken. I was about to dig in when he interrupted.

"Are you sure you don't want to add to that?"

"No, why will I?"

"You might want to try some spaghetti with the mix."

"Spaghetti? With all of these?"

"A little adventure doesn't hurt anyone"

His smile deepens as I dish some spaghetti and I smile as well. We enjoy the meal in silence for a while and his next question makes me pause.

"So how have you been?"

I shrug. "I've been good."

He didn't smile. Instead, he leaned forward, his eyes boring into mine. "Are you sure about that? I would love to know how you've been handling this whole situation. Are you truly fine? " he asked again.

I have no answer for him so I take a spoonful of my meal, chewing silently.

Ethan leaned back, his eyes fixed on me. "I know this is tough, trust me," he began, his voice smooth and calming "But you need to take care of yourself. The more settled you are, the better you can reflect on information that can aid the investigation and the quicker we can wrap this up. You want this over, right?"

I nodded, lost for words once again.

"Look," he continued, his tone softening, "I understand. You're overwhelmed by all of these which is understandable but please don't just pile it up. You're human, not a robot. Please, Iretiola, don't lose yourself while trying to vindicate yourself."

I knew he was right but didn't know how I was to cope with this new reality. If the culprit isn't found, I'll be thrown into jail and that may be the end of my life, my dreams. Everything.

"I just don't know how to navigate this," I said, my voice already shaking. "What if we don't find anyone? Won't I just rot in jail?"

He reached for my hands, gazing intently at me. "You won't. I promise. I'm here to ensure that never happens. I'm with you in all of this. Every step of the way!"

His words diffused the tension I'd bottled up and I could feel them seeping out gradually giving way for a wave of relief.

Ethan

I watch as her shoulders sag in relief and my heart constricts a little. Only heaven knows how much tension she has built up in her. She appeared frail and vulnerable but there was a strength in her eyes that belied her appearance and I'd been drawn to that resilience from the day I set my eyes on her.

I watch her as she gathers the plates, her fingers trembling slightly. I wanted to reach across the table and hold her hand, reassuring her again and again that this will pass and she will smile genuinely again. But I wasn't sure if that would still be within my official scope or if I would be venturing on personal ground.

The line between the two is blurring with every passing hour.

***

I switched on the lights and walked straight into the bathroom. All through the drive home, I couldn't get my mind off her. Iretiola, such a puzzle. I only hope she will indeed keep being hopeful. The memory of her eyes, a mix of anxiety and feistiness, always brings a smile to my face.

Done with my bath, I pulled out a copy of the case facts which I had brought home with me. It was filled with photographs, witness statements, and diverse reports. I'd gone over it countless times, searching for a fresh perspective which I might have missed earlier. The meeting with her today had rekindled a fire within me and I was determined to get this over and done it as soon as possible.

I picked up the phone and dialed Chuks. Chuks has been my partner since the beginning of my practice and he is always my go-to whenever I'm faced with dicey situations such as this. He picked on the second dial.

"Guy, road don clear?" I greeted in our usual manner, cutting straight to the chase.

"Abeg, I need your help."

Back To The Jungle

Iretiola

I take measured steps towards Cell F and imagine the surprise on Kulubu's face when she realizes I'm back in this hellhole. I could almost hear her laughter seeing the goodies I've smuggled in for her. I waited eagerly as the officer opened the door. He seems to be new around here and I can't wait to get all his gist and other news flying around from Kulubu.

I stepped into the room and stopped. Something is not right. I looked back at the officer but he had already left and I moved forward to the figure huddled up in the corner of the room wondering who they'd brought this time around. Ethan had assured me Kulubu was still here but I don't seem to understand who this figure huddled up was.

"Hello," I called out but didn't get any response. Moving closer, I touched the figure and was shocked at who I saw.

It was Kulubu quite alright. But this wasn't the Kulubu I knew. This can never be the Kulubu I left a couple of weeks ago. She was different. Gone was the fierce and agile Kulubu I know. This is someone entirely different.

"What happened?" I croaked.

She looked up, her eyes vacant and distant. A shiver ran down my spine. Something was terribly wrong.

"They eventually broke me. That bastard broke me!" she said, her voice barely a whisper. The words hung in the air, heavy with despair. I don't want to believe I understand what she is trying to say. Mere thinking about it repulses me.

"What do you mean? Who are you talking about?" I asked, my voice trembling.

She looked away, her face a mask of pain. "He came here. None of the others were here. I cried, I pleaded, I begged….." She trailed off, unable to continue.

A wave of rage and disbelief washed over me. How could this even happen? Right under the nose of the authorities? This should not be and we've got to do something about it. We can't let it slide.

"I've accepted it," she said, her voice surprisingly calm. "It's a norm in this place, a matter of when and not if. There's nothing we can do. We just have to take things in stride and survive it. I only pray you don't get to experience the same my dear friend. It's too awful to recount."

This is strange. Kulubu is giving up and it breaks me to see this side of her. I wonder how many more women the system has broken. I sat beside her and hugged her close to me. Perhaps, the closeness will give her some warmth and comfort.

Talk To Me

"Iretiola! Your attention is needed and you have 2 minutes to get here."

The warder kept on shouting his announcement and I wish I could stuff his mouth with a pillow. I've been enjoying a nap till his shrill announcement intruded my space and put an end to my timeout. I shrug off the uncertainty in my heart and step out to meet the officer who is to take me to where my attention is needed.

I slowed upon seeing who needed to see me.

"Surprised?"

"I already told you all I know, Detective. There's nothing else I know. If they want to kill me in return, they should go ahead, please. I'm tired *abeg*."

"Relax Ireti, I'm not here to hound you about the case. At all."

"So why are you here?"

"I'm just here to talk."

"About?"

"See, Ireti. We all…"

"Please don't patronize me, sir. What do you want?"

"Ireti. Your name signifies hope….."

I looked at him, trying to keep the exasperation out of my voice. "Detective Ethan, I understand your concern for me, but right now, I'm more focused on getting all of these over and done with. I need answers and a way out, not sermons and platitudes."

"Why are you this uptight and cynical?"

"Uptight?"

"Yes! Why do you tend to believe the worst about yourself and your situation? Why do you…"

"Because there's no point! There's no point in believing in what's not sure or trying to hold on to something you can't see. No. This is reality and I've faced it squarely."

"For how long?"

"For as long as I need to. For as long as it will get me away from stupid pretenders like you. I never requested you to help me. You did it out of your own volition and I don't even know what you have up your sleeves. You all are just wolves in Sheep's Clothing."

"Ireti I ..."

"Don't Ireti me. Save all your sorry words for the stupid people who need them. You all keep on repeating the same script. You must be stupid if you think I don't know you have an ulterior motive"

"It's okay Ireti. I may be stupid but I have no ulterior motive whatsoever. I'm only here to help you, that is if you don't mind. See Ireti, it's okay to receive help from people and not everyone is out to hurt you. Never die in silence. We humans were not created to live in a vacuum so don't box yourself in. It's totally fine to lean on someone."

"No, it's not."

"Yes, it is. You see......."

I hear him but nothing seems to matter again than the pounding in my ears. I remember all the times I've been down and I reached out for help, I can hear the condescending words even though they were spoken years ago. I can feel the pain of paying back in ways greater than that which you received.

His words shouldn't have affected me. They shouldn't even reach me but here it is tugging at the carefully tied strings of my heart.

So, I'm Stupid?

Ethan

Never in my wildest imagination would I have thought it possible to agree to being stupid. It's probably the most stupid thing I've done all my life. The more I think about it, the more it actually sounds stupid to me and the more my heart aches for this girl called Ireti.

Away from the degree and sophistication, all I see is a little girl who will do anything to save her space and prevent her world from tumbling over. I can't help but notice the hurt that filled her eyes as we converse. I wonder what made her so defensive and I have no other option than to rely on the one way which has always provided me with answers.

Picking up what is left of my dignity, I make my way to the back of the enclosure which is the only place I can have some respite without any distraction.

Showers Of Blessings

Iretiola

I am lost in thoughts in the makeshift church building when I feel a presence around me and stop for a minute to stare. *Indeed God finish work for some people. How can….*

"Hi… Hello…. "

"Go…Good afternoon, Sir."

Focus Ireti. Focus.

"I've been trying to get your attention for a while now. It seems you were in another world."

"No. Yes. I actually get carried away easily."

"Oh, I can guess."

"I mean not all the time but sometimes I can't help thinking of how things could have been…"

"Don't we all? I mean we all wish for better days and all. We pine for the years that have gone and by the time we're done, the current year has gone by us yet again and it's become a hopeless cycle time and time again."

"Uh."

"No one knows it all or has the advantage of undoing the passage of time. All we can do is live in the present and enjoy it as much as we can."

Some Brains. Things I love to hear.

"Speaking of enjoyment, what sort of enjoyment can be in a horrid place like this?"

"Well, young lady. Enjoyment is relative and highly subject to the individual's definition of Pleasure. But if you ask me, there are at least a thousand and one ways to have a jolly time even in this *"horrid"* Place."

"Oh, I see."

"Yes. Being in a holding facility should not deprive you of the little pleasures of life."

"So would you perhaps be kind enough to show me some of these pleasures?"

"Well, maybe some other time."

"Why not now, Mr. Pleasure?"

"I'm afraid Madam Pleasure Seeker, I have to go now. It was nice discussing with you and I'll see you around."

Without waiting for a response, he walks out and I can't help but admire his gait and wonder what just happened. It is very unlikely for the officers to be messing around with the detainees. Many of them prefer to relate with you like you're non-existent and I can't believe I just had a full-blown conversation with one. Perhaps he's a new one or maybe the universe is finally interested in compensating me for my troubles by sending another helper my way.

Good Samaritan

Today is probably one of my happiest days in this facility. Ever since the prolonged silence on the case, I've not been this agile. I've been downcast and depressed. But today, Kulubu finally succeeded in dragging me to join the other females in the facility and it has been worth it.

It turns out they were working on a clothing project where they get to make tiny clothes and sweaters which they send to different orphanages periodically. I am so elated at the prospect of doing something other than moping around all day that I give myself wholeheartedly to the assignment.

For hours on end, we crochet our pains away while making small talk and poking fun at one another. It is good being around people again. The warmth, the laughter, the faces. It all feels so good and I am lost in that euphoria until a cry interrupts the gathering.

"Oh no! We've run out of supplies."

"Wool don finish?"

"Ooooohhh. Why nau? Na just the hand remain make I finish?"

"Wetin be this bayii?"

I understand that the wools are exhausted but I don't get the reason behind the sighs and heavy despair that hangs in the air. Since Kulubu is my link, I tiptoed to her and asked what is wrong.

Her response is another sign of how corrupt the system has become and armed with the sympathetic faces the women wore, I set out to the kitchen to see who I can talk to. I am a few steps away from the entrance when someone grabs my hands. I look up to give the intruder a taste of my displeasure when I see his smile. I calmed down at once. It is the stranger from the Chapel. Hopefully, he'll be able to help me.

"Good evening. I didn't mean to startle you. I'm sorry."

"It's fine. Good evening, Sir."

"Where are you headed all alone by this time? It's not yet time for dinner. "

"Yes. I... We..."

"Hey relax. I won't hurt you. You can talk to me, okay?"

"We were knitting some clothing to be sent as gifts later this month and we ran out of supplies so I wanted to see if I could talk to an officer who can help us with restocking."

"I see. That won't be a problem. I'll discuss with the Head of Resources and we'll see what we can do."

"Oh. Thank you very much, Sir. You just made my task much easier."

"That's nothing. By the way, you speak really nice. What's your name?"

"Ireti. I'm Iretiola."

"Nice meeting you Ireti."

"Same here. Sorry please, can I get to know your name as well?"

"Sure. You can call me T. J. It is nice seeing you once again and I've got to run now. See you around some other time."

This Is More Than A Problem! It's A Calamity

I watch admiringly as he saunters into the room, his familiar cologne filling my lungs while the questions in my head fly out the window. It's been 3 weeks but it feels like 3 centuries. Seeing him again brings so much relief than I'll love to admit.

"Hey. How have you been?"

"Why are you back?"

"Did you miss me that much?"

"You haven't answered me Mr. Detective."

"Alright. I apologize for the long silence but it was due to no fault of mine. There haven't been any new leads on the case and I didn't want to raise your hopes only to have it dashed again."

"It's alright. So what brings you here today?"

"I felt like seeing you. It's been a while and I decided to come check on you. What's up with you?"

His face reflected his genuine concern and I fumbled for words to apologize for my last outburst.

"I.. I've been fine. Thank you. How have you been too?"

"Quite great. Thank you"

"I'm sorry for the last time. I didn't mean to insult you. I was just so angry and upset. Please don't be offended. I even thought…"

"You thought I wouldn't come because of that?" He asked.

"Yes. I'm sorry. I later reflected on our discussion and I realized I was just transferring aggression to you."

"Do you mind sharing with me who made you so upset?"

I hadn't expected this question and now, I'm at a loss for words. How sure am I that he is not also a part of the evil clique.

"It's fine if you don't want to share."

"No, it's not like I don't want to share. I just don't know how best to go about it."

"It's alright. Just start from anywhere. Take it gradually and tell me all about it"

And so I did. I recounted Kulubu's experience, the whispers I hear at night, the tales in the bathroom and how a large number of my fellow inmates wriggle under the oppressive weight of sexual harassment. By the time I was done, he simply nodded his head and that woke a fresh wave of anger in me.

"You're not going to say anything?"

"To be sincere with you Ireti, this is not the first I am hearing of this. It's been a huge issue for us and we've been looking towards apprehending the culprits."

"You know them??"

"To some extent. Yes"

"Wow. None of the ladies want to talk about their assailants."

"Don't worry your head about that. Now that you've mentioned this again, I think I'll have to inform some of the trusted officials so we can get this over with. But I just have to warn you to be very careful. Please be very cautious. You don't know who might be watching"

"I don't care who is watching. They can't go on like this. There should be something we can do about this. "

"So what do you intend to do?"

"There's this officer I met sometime back and he seems like a good one. If we talk to him, he could join your team and help put an end to this."

"Who is this officer and how did you meet him?"

"Well, we met at the Chapel and he was also helpful in sending us supplies for knitting speedily."

"Do you know his name?"

"Yes. Something J…Jo. No T. J. Yes, it's T. J!"

"What? I mean… How???"

"What's wrong? Do you know him?"

"Yes. Wait. Can't be. Can you please describe this T. J?"

"Well, yes. He is of average height, not slim, not chubby, just in between. He is nice, speaks gently and his eyes are probably the most attractive feature about him. They're so soft and fit smugly with his beards."

"Oh No. Oh No. Ireti, no nau. What have you gotten yourself into?"

"What?? Is there a problem?"

"Ah, Ireti! This is more than a problem! This is a calamity."

"Why are you getting all worked up?"

"Iretiola, this is not good. At all!"

Ethan

It's midnight and I can't get to sleep no matter how hard I try. Ever since the conversation with Ireti, I've been so unsettled. Can't stop wondering how she got herself involved in this Mawadi's issue.

T. J Mawadi, the man everyone is carefully dealing with. From a lanky-looking boy in Police College, he rose through the ranks over the years and now he has made himself a demigod and as much as I would have loved to stay clear of his path, I can't just let this slide again. Who would have thought a deadly predator lies behind that harmless facade of his?

I can't imagine the torture Ireti goes through each night as she consoles his victim, or worse, being his victim herself.

It's time for some decisive action!

Torrents Of Trouble

Iretiola

I suppress a smile as he comes into view. Getting to know Mr. T.J. these past few weeks has been a huge blessing. He is always available to hear me out and never ceases to help with meaningful suggestions on the knitting project. He has fast grown to be our own angel in human form. I am shaken out of my reverie by his heavy steps and I can't help but notice the ugly frown on his face. This is the first time I've seen him this way and it's quite frightening.

"What is the matter, Sir? Are you fine? Why are you this worked up?"

"So this is our Mother Teresa?" he asked.

"Sir?"

"Have you suddenly gone deaf?"

At that moment, I realized trusting this man has been a huge mistake. No one knows I am meeting with him and I definitely will not be getting any justice should things go awry. He had promised to help get help for the abused inmates and had requested we meet so I could supply more details.

Before I know what is happening, he has tied me like a goat and all I can do is cry and beg God for another chance at life.

"Please, I'm sorry Sir. In whatever way I have offended you, please have mercy on me. I never intended to cross my boundaries. I swear."

"Shut up!"

"Please…"

"Will you shut the heck up? Nothing you say or do right now will prevent me from eliminating you. You are an integral part of my story and I will be a bad director to leave you unattended to."

"Please can I know my offense?"

"Offense? That's too trivial! What you have done is sacrilege. How dare you put your nose in my business? I've been on this job for over 15 years and a little rat like you can not come at this crucial hour and disrupt my plans."

He was pacing aggressively now and I knew I needed to buy some time.

"You've been digging too deep, haven't you?" His voice was low, a menacing growl. "Asking too many questions." He paused, his breath hot against my skin. "And I don't like being questioned."

"But what exactly did I do?"

"You were pokenosing. You had your face in my business and I don't like that"

"What business?"

"The women!"

"Jesus!"

Now, I understand the hesitation of the women in revealing the culprits. Who would have thought a man like T.J. would be a part of the people I was bent on smoking out?

"You don't understand how this works, Smarty Pants" he growled, his voice low and menacing. "Here, when you mess with the wrong people, you pay the price." He came close, caressing my neck. I shivered, not from the cold, but from the terror that gripped me.

"Too bad you're learning your lessons too late."

I watch with teary eyelids as he cleans his knife. Yes, I have thought about death and how it will come but in all my musings, I have never considered being slaughtered like a goat and the mere thought of it brings more tears to my eyes.

All my efforts at having a great life are about to be poured down the drain.

The sleepless nights at Uni, the tough days at Regal, and the pressure before I finally secured a position at Shots. All down the drain!

I will never experience the freedom I so much desire, I will never know what it means to be in love and be loved in return.

Most importantly, I never got to make peace with my maker. Blood pounds in my ears and the hairs at the back of my neck become erect as he takes calculated steps to where I am, tied up. If this is the way to go, then I had better ask for mercy in these few remaining seconds of my life.

Dear Lord, please....

I did not make it past the first three words before bursting into heavy tears as the full realization of all I have done as well as my eminent fate dawns on me.

Not On My Watch!

Ethan

I intend to take a brief nap before heading for the facility, however, I can't shake off the unusual weight on my chest. I pace the floor, pray, and sing yet this weight is unmoving. It is almost as if it has come to replace my heart. I can barely breathe. All I feel is this crushing weight. Bent under the weight, I press more into seeking God's answer to this quest in my spirit and within the twinkle of an eye, I feel it again.

Straining under the weight of this burden, I see Ireti tied and bundled up like a stack of unwanted clothing. A man is about to set her on fire and then the picture fades away. I know then that the contention upon this life isn't small and the earlier I get to serious work, the better for everyone because this one won't be wasted on my watch.

Tick-Tock

Iretiola

I waited and waited. Has he changed his mind? Did he leave or has he hatched another evil plan? Is he going to set me on fire? A loud laughter brings me back to reality and I struggle to open my eyes. The sight before me is nothing like I ever imagined.

"Well, well, well, who do we have here if not the iconic Detective himself?"

"Mawadi, what is this madness? What has gotten into you?"

"Well, my dear boy. You are welcome to the party! Your dear lady here wouldn't stop pushing her nose in my business and it's quite unfortunate that you have also trailed that path"

"Mawadi…."

"Gratefully, I do not like talebearers nor do I spare them. So you might as well say your last prayers."

"But…"

"Enough of this chit-chat, please. Now, get out of my way. I have other plans for tonight."

"Mawadi! Don't be stupid! You won't gain anything by killing either of us, the only…"

The next thing happens suddenly. So sudden I never would have believed it actually happened.

But it did and I have another unsolicited evidence on my hands—a deep gash and flowing blood. Ethan has taken the fall for me and for the second time in my life, I actually scream my lungs out.

Reflection

The courtroom had emptied, together with the buzz of the day. Everyone had grown enough interest in the case with the arrest of the popular T. J Mawadi and his cronies. As we journey back to the facility, I can't help but reflect on this new twist in my journey. Thinking about that fateful day still gives me Goosebumps.

My scream drew the attention of the squad Ethan brought with him as reinforcement and they had saved the day with their entrance. I was numbed after the whole incident and couldn't leave the cell for days.

How could I walk freely knowing a man almost lost his life for me?

Although it has all been worth it. The ladies were grateful Mawadi was apprehended and one by one, his cronies have also been picked up. Now, they can sleep with both eyes closed and not listen for footsteps.

I haven't seen Ethan since then and none of his colleagues will speak to me.

After much back and forth, the judge adjourns my case one more time and promises to give his final verdict at the next sitting which is 2 weeks away.

So all we have to prove my innocence is fourteen fleeting days. 14 days and this will be over and done with. But 14 days to unravel this mystery without Ethan seems like a death sentence itself.

On To The Express

Like a rollercoaster, I watch the events of my life play before me and I know I can't keep up with the charade any longer. It is time to let go and embrace help. It is time to get into a better place and as the detective does say tomorrow may be too late. I make the final mental preparations as I hear approaching footsteps in the corridor.

"How is my crying suspect doing today?"

"You're…You're…alive?"

"What? You wanted me dead?"

"No. Why would I? I'm just shocked and happy. I've hoped and prayed for your recovery ever since. Matter of fact, I've never prayed this hard since I was a teen."

"What happened?"

"I beg your pardon?"

"Why did you stop praying? Why did you murder your faith?"

"Oh, not again! You're just recovering, Detective."

"Please Ireti, I insist. And don't you worry about my health, I'm fine."

"It was a futile effort. Life was hard. I kept getting rejected and tossed here and there. I cried for help. Called to God with my whole strength but I couldn't see any response or changes. The whole thing was frustrating. I felt stupid so I quit."

"That's quite pathetic! Don't you think you should have a rethink, Ireti?"

"To what extent will that be? I'm barely living on extra time as it is and…."

"Have you ever bothered to think about why I rushed at Mawadi's bullet?" Detective Ethan asked, inching forward and gazing intensely at me.

"You were trying to be a hero? Knight in Shining Armor or a Good Samaritan?"

"Far from it. I simply wanted to shield you from eternal suffering. One way or the other, I knew you couldn't end it all there. That would have been too terrible."

"And you? You were done with your *assignment*?"

"Far from it. But I was sure the Lord was still working on you and I'll be patient as he does His thing."

"I wish I could experience half of this peace you flaunt around so easily."

"Why settle for half when you can have the whole deal?"

"I've drifted far away, Detective. So far I doubt He will ever want to have anything to do with me."

"No matter how far you feel you have gone, He is ever ready to draw you back. He loves you and yes, He is willing to draw you back into His embrace once again."

"How do I get back into this embrace? It's been years and I don't know how it all feels anymore."

"Don't worry. It's still as peaceful as it has always been. Come here, let's get you back home." He extends his hand to her and grasps hers in a firm hold.

I relax and repeat the words after Him.

Word for word.

 Phrase for phrase.

When it is all over, I feel no thrills, no special feelings but I know something changed and I am ready to believe it and stay with that belief all my life.

Now, Let's Build

I've never ever been interested in the idea of bodybuilding from day 1. I never understood why full-fledged adults should set on a quest to punish themselves and drain their account balances while at it. But having much time on my hands now, I decided to give it a try.

With Kagbo as our makeshift gym instructor, many of the occupants of the facility converge under the tree to do some exercises. Most times, these *gym* activities are just running, squatting and boxing.

Boxing became a necessity so harmless inmates could ward off bullies.

In a space of 8 weeks, I've successfully transitioned from a stressed-out studio assistant to a straight-no-miss boxing champion.

While reeling from the praises and accolades after winning 4 bouts in a row, I suddenly remember a heavyweight local champion who often comes around the studio.

The guy barely talks but merely seeing his face is enough to make any sensible human stay away from trouble. Like a flash, I remember seeing the guy sitting on one of the pavements on the street on nights that we closed pretty late. Maybe, just maybe he was there that night and could have seen something. Anything at all, anything that can help me out of this misery. I can't wait for Ethan to get here, probably this is the light we've been searching for at the end of the tunnel…

Eye Witness

Ethan

"So, tell me, who are you and what do you do?"

"You ought to know that, don't you?"

"I beg your pardon?"

"I mean, are you trying to tell me that you brought in a man you know nothing about for *questioning?* So you people just go about the street, manhandle people, treat them like trash and you don't even know a thing about them or what they are supposed to have done? Now if that isn't amazing, I don't know what is."

"Young man, I am sorry for however you have been treated. Please let's put that aside in good faith and get this done and away with. So I'll start again. I am Detective Ethan and you were invited here to help us with an ongoing investigation. So can I get to know you as well and what you do?"

"I'm Cyprus and I'm a bodybuilder."

"Cyprus? Like in Egypt?"

"That's my name."

"I see. So do you know this man?" Detective Ethan asks, holding up a picture to his face.

"No, I don't."

"Not so fast Cyprus. Take a deep breath. Close your eyes if you want. Think back to a few weeks ago, a few months ago. Didn't you see this man walking on your street? Driving a fancy car? Buying something? Talking with someone? Going to......"

"Let me see him closely." He gazes at it and I can see recognition lights up his face. He tried masking it but it was too late.

"What did he do?"

"He didn't do anything."

"So, why are you looking for him?"

"I'm not looking for him. I am looking for who killed him."

"JESUS! Oga abeg, no be me kill am oo."

"I never said you killed him. I'm asking if you recognize him. See, no one is prosecuting you. All we're asking is that you help us with our investigations so we can apprehend the culprit."

"Please, I don't know the man."

"Cyprus, Someone's life is on the line. Just tell me whatever you know and I promise you nobody will prosecute you for helping us."

"Hmmm. Are you sure of this?"

"Yes."

"Double sure?"

"I'm assuring you no one will hold this conversation against you. You have my words for it"

"Okay. I saw him one Thursday night. He was walking towards Shots Studio complex."

"Okay. Do you know if he walked with anyone at all? Or met someone along the way?"

"Ah, Oga!!!!"

"Cyprus, half information won't get us to where we need to finish this investigation. We need all the information we can get please."

"I saw him with Tegbo and he can't do such a thing. He doesn't even have the heart to kill anyone. Na so so small small money him just dey find."

"I see. Thank you for your help, Cyprus. I go see you later."

Why Did You Lie?

"Tegbo, I am asking you for the last time, why did you lie to us?" Detective Ethan asked.

"I was afraid…."

"Of?"

"I… Please… It was not… We"

"Calm down. If you're not coherent, we can't help you. Now for the last time, can you tell us what transpired between you and the deceased?"

"I only knew him 6 months ago and we didn't have much rapport. He was just some random dude who helped me with money every now and then."

"So, what happened?"

"I can't even explain. One minute I bade him farewell and the next I heard he was dead."

"When was the last time you saw him?"

"On the 15th."

"By what time?"

"8 p.m."

"What happened at 8 p.m.?"

"We met at Crux Junction and he was lamenting how badly he needed a break. That they were suffocating him and taking everything he has worked for away from him."

"They? Who are the *They?*"

"He didn't say but I suspected it was office trouble. He appeared to be a corporate guy"

" So what happened next?"

"He pleaded that I help him with the key to the studio that night so he could rest. At first, I didn't listen and tried to persuade him to go somewhere else but he was insistent and I had to give in."

"You had to give in……"

"I'm sorry. I accepted because he gave me money and I was badly in need of funds."

"Weren't you getting paid?"

"No, I wasn't and N150, 000 sounded like a good offer so I jumped at it. I never knew it would end like this."

"What else happened that day?"

"He handed me a bag that I should keep for him till the next morning."

"Where is the bag?"

"It's at home."

"An Officer will take you home to bring the bag. I believe its contents will go a long way in helping our assignment. In the meantime, you'll stay here with us while we wrap this up."

"Please I'm sorry Sir. I didn't…"

"We're done for now, Tegbo."

****

It's been an hour of ransacking the bag and just when I am about to give up, a little note fell.

Upon closer examination, I realize it is squeezed business cards. Maybe, this is the step towards the right direction I've been looking for.

Dawn Is Here

I watch as she makes her way to the room with heavy steps. I can't help but wonder if this will be worth it.

"Are you fine?"

"I can't complain. What's the latest? Any news for us?" Ireti asks, her voice reflecting a lack of interest.

"Well, yes. There have been several updates and I can't help rushing over to give you a heads up."

"Okay. Thank you."

"What's wrong? You're not sounding your regular self and…"

"I'm fine. Thank you."

"No, you're not. This is not the Ireti I know."

She shrugged and turned her face away.

"What is it Iretiola? Why are you this downcast?"

"I'm tired. We've been on this for how many months now? My life has turned upside them and I don't even know what I'm doing anymore."

"Ireti, you've been doing great so far. It's just a little more time to go!"

"Doing great? Really? What else do I expect? After all, you're not the one stuck here."

"Common, you know I understand every of your struggles here. It's almost over by God's grace. And yes, you've done well. If you can't pinpoint any, at least you helped unravel the harassment ordeal and that has helped save several ladies who would have fallen into the same ditch."

"I hear you. What's the update?"

"We've gotten another lead and….,"

"And it may most likely not lead anywhere. See, don't stress yourself unnecessarily. I'm getting quite good at the Crochet thing. I'll just have to live with that."

"No, you won't. I'm persuaded your time here is almost up. Remember, it's always the darkest when the dawn is near."

"Yes Sir. I didn't know you were this much of a Motivational Speaker".

"Iretiola, dawn is here" I assured her, desperately holding on to the assurance as well.

How Do These Things Happen?

Armed with the business card I found and Google Maps, I set out for Ozida Hub and I am mesmerized by the ambience of the Hub. The colors and architectural designs were fitted like hands in gloves.

Everything looks and feels like a piece of paradise and I wonder for the umpteenth time why a young man with so much at his disposal decided to end his own life.

Walking up to the reception, I met the front desk officer, a middle-aged woman with perfectly manicured nails and a bored expression, and showed her the business cards.

"Mr. Nicholas is currently in a meeting," she said, with the same bored expression and indifference. "He won't be done anytime soon so you may have to call back later."

I flashed my ID. " I am Detective Ethan Wells, from the Police Headquarters. I need to speak to Mr. Nicholas urgently."

Her demeanor shifted slightly, a hint of respect creeping into her voice. " In that case, Please have a seat. I'll inform him you are here."

"Thank you"

I sat and surveyed the room once again. One thing is clear - the young man had substantial money at his disposal. Could there be trouble in the company? Or was it a case of bad gambling?

After an hour, I was ushered into a private office and I could barely contain my shock at seeing the man behind the desk. He was a splitting image of the deceased and I wonder what this meeting holds.

"Detective Ethan, I presume," he said, rising and extending a hand. His grip was firm and his eyes remained fixed on me.

I returned the handshake. "That's right, Mr. Nicholas. Thank you for the audience."

"My pleasure. Please what do I offer you?"

"I'm fine, thank you. I just need to ask you a few questions. I promise not to take too much of your time."

"That's fine. I'm done with my meetings for the day."

"Mr. Nicholas," I began, my voice cutting through the silence. "I need to ask you some questions."

His eyes widened in surprise. "About what, detective?"

I took a deep breath. "About your brother, Tony."

His face paled. "What about him? Is he alright?"

I hesitated, choosing my words carefully. "I'm afraid I have some bad news, Nicholas. Tony is dead."

The colour drained from his face. He stared at me, his mouth agape. It was as if he hadn't comprehended my words. "Dead? How? When? Where?"

"It happened some months ago at the other end of town. It appears to be a suicide. His body was found in a studio and we couldn't get any clue about his identity until a few days ago."

Shock turned into disbelief. "Suicide? That's impossible. He wouldn't do that."

I nodded, understanding his reaction. "I know this must be difficult for you. But I need to ask you some questions."

He seemed to come back to reality, his eyes narrowing in confusion. "What do you want to know?"

"I want to talk about your brother," I pressed. "Was anything troubling him recently?"

He sat back and closed his eyes. "I do not know of any. He was a jolly youth and didn't seem to be bothered by anything."

"There wasn't a fallout between you two?"

"No, None at all."

I leaned forward, my elbows resting on the table. "Really? Because I recently discovered these business cards among his belongings and wondered how they came about " I slid the two cards across the table.

His eyes scanned the cards, then back to me. I could feel the fright underneath his composure "What are these?"

"Business cards, Nicholas. Two identical cards, for the same position in the same company. One for Tony, the other for you. It's quite unusual, isn't it?"

His mind was clearly racing. "I don't understand your perspective Detective."

The room filled with tension. Nicholas's eyes narrowed, and for a brief moment, I saw a glimpse of the man beneath the polished exterior. A man consumed by guilt, by a past he couldn't escape.

"Mr. Nicholas, I would love to ask why there are two business cards for your office. Were you perhaps running simultaneously with your brother?"

"I'm sorry Detective but I don't know what you're driving at. I'm the only recognized Director and I have all the documentation to back this up. I really do not know how you came about the cards."

"Alright then, thank you for your time. I'll keep you informed on how it goes."

"Thank you and how can we access the body?"

"You may have to come over to the station for all your inquiries. So sorry for your loss".

I stood up, ending the interview. As I walked out, I knew I was on the right track. The pieces were slowly coming together and I can't wait to get this all behind me.

Old Tales Never Die

Growing up, I never believed in myths or old fables and tales but I find myself gulping them hook, line and sinker now that I am an adult. It has been a trying period for the last few days and I couldn't have been more grateful for the phone call.

I walked in and indeed Nicholas was sitting waiting for me. I couldn't believe my ears when Chuks called to inform me Nicholas is looking for me and willing to wait for me to arrive. Taking a seat opposite him, I watch with keen interest how unsettled he is. His eyes are filled with a haunted look, a world apart from the composed man I met last week.

"Good day, Mr. Nicholas. I'm so sorry for keeping you waiting. Today was my day off so I had to rush here as soon as I got the call that you were here."

"It's totally fine. I'm sorry for barging into you like this but I need to talk with you"

I leaned forward, my interest piqued. "I'm all ears please."

He took a deep breath. "I have to come clean to you. Ever since you left, I've been troubled and I can't bear it any longer."

My eyebrows rose in surprise. "I'm with you"

"Tony's death... it wasn't entirely a suicide. I'm afraid I pushed him to the wall"

"Interesting. Do you mind shedding more light on this?"

He looked down, his face contorted in anguish. "We argued a couple of weeks ago. I had resumed duty as the Director, an act that hurt him deeply as he had lived to see the day he will be the Director. He has always been a straight-A boy. Crossing his T's and dotting his I's. He has been the acting Director for some months now and worked hard to ensure he became the Director."

"So what happened?"

"I worked my way around the board and got their weight behind me. I was made the Director and he wasn't taking it lying down. We had a confrontation at the office where I gave him a copy of my card and that must have been the last straw that broke the camel's back. He left angrily and I didn't hear from him again till you brought the news of his demise."

"Do you both have any underlying issues?"

"Growing up, we were what you would call 5&6. We did all things together and were united. But as we became older, our choices and decisions differed and that was the turning point in our relationship. He became the hero while I became the villain. He was Midas. Everything he touches became gold and I struggled to even have wood. It was a struggle and I became resentful. Too resentful. "

His voice broke, and he covered his face with his hands. "I didn't mean for it to go this far. I never wanted to hurt him."

I sat back, trying to process the information. This was a complex and tragic situation. "Why are you telling me this Nicholas?"

He looked up, his eyes filled with remorse. "I can't live with this guilt. I feel I led him to make that rash decision due to my outburst on that fateful day as well as previous outbursts."

I leaned back in my chair, my mind racing. This was a complex case, one that would require careful handling. While Nicholas's confession was a significant breakthrough, proving his culpability in a court of law would be a formidable challenge.

"Mr. Nicholas," I began, my voice steady. "What you're admitting to is serious. While your confession is a start, we need more concrete evidence to build a case."

He nodded, his eyes filled with resignation. "I understand. I went to his apartment and found his diaries. He wrote it all down. All my actions and confrontation."

A glimmer of hope ignited within me. Physical evidence was crucial. "Will you be able to get these diaries for me?"

He nodded, handing me a bag."Yes, I brought them already. I also have some of our exchanges via recordings and texts. He made a habit of recording our conversation and sending it to our parents while they were still alive. I should also be able to recover those ones."

I flipped through the diaries and indeed, they contain substantial information. However, we still have one more hurdle to cross.

"Do you have anyone who also knew of your toxic relationship with Tony?"

"Yes. Some of our domestic staff have witnessed the exchanges over the years."

"Perfect! One more thing please, why are you so bent on paying penitence for your actions?"

"I understand you have someone in your custody and I wouldn't want to cause more pain than I've already caused."

"Oh. In that case, you may not be able to go back home today. We will need to make some official entry and set about how to proceed with the case."

"I understand. I knew what I was signing for when I came here today."

I watch perplexed as the man before me struggles with tears. Indeed, there is no peace for the wicked. And above all, I'm grateful for the closure he brought to our lives.

Farewell, Sweet Farewell

Iretiola

It's finally Friday, the last day in Cell F and I'm a bundle of nerves. It's been 24 long weeks and oddly, this place feels like home. The smell, the people, the atmosphere and most importantly the lessons. I am grateful for the reflection and I wish I had done this earlier. Way earlier.

It is a wonder how the case is wrapped up. Although I prayed and trusted God just as the Detective advised I never imagined it would be such a smooth sail. Ever since I left off the track of faith, I have never experienced this quick response and I'm super glad I finally got to go back to the haven I've long abandoned.

I haven't had such an eye-opening experience in years and no matter how mad I am that I stayed in confinement for months, I cannot help but be grateful for the gift of Cell F. Funny how Cell F metamorphosed from a blood-sucking demon to a gift I will treasure forever.

On the flipside, today is the last day of the Sabbatical and despite all odds, I couldn't have wished for a better Sabbatical. And the juicy part is that I no longer have to resume at Shots. Having had some deep reflections on the events of the past months, I've decided to start up a business and pick up my life journey again.

"Hello there! A penny for your thoughts." Ethan said as he walked up to me. His eyes held a mixture of relief and something else, something I couldn't quite decipher.

"Oh, Detective. I never knew you'd be around."

"Well, I wouldn't miss your grand farewell for anything in the world. It's really been a long way coming."

"Thank you and although I don't say this often, I appreciate all you did for me. You were a God-sent and I pray the Almighty will continue to preserve your ways."

"Amen. Congratulations Iretiola, It's all over now," he said. "You're free."

I nodded, unable to speak. The weight of the past few months was still heavy on me. He took my hand, his touch once again calming my nerves.

"I know this has been hell for you, but you've been incredibly brave."

I looked into his eyes and I saw a vulnerability I hadn't seen before.

"Thank you. I do owe some of those bravery to you."

He squeezed my hand. "You owe me nothing, Iretiola. You are strong and would have remained strong with or without my help. I've admired your strength, resilience and never give up spirit. You're indeed an extraordinary woman."

He took a deep breath. "I care about you, Iretiola. So much I always want to keep your hope alive and ensure you're out of harm's way for as long as I am alive."

My heart raced. This seems to be leading somewhere. His words hung in the air, heavy with meaning. I looked into his eyes, searching for any sign of a prank or joke, but there was none. His eyes reflected his honesty and raw emotion, which scares me.

"Right from the day I came across your case file, my spirit has been troubled and upon careful search, I realized the Lord will have me step into the case but I never knew His full intent till you complained of being claustrophobic and I knew I had to make you comfortable for the rest of my life."

"But this cannot work…"

"Why, Ireti?"

"Because I'm battered and not quite healed. I'm not even a part of your deep spiritual thingy."

"See, Ireti, you need to let go of all those thoughts. Remember, you've come into a new life and in this life, that baggage is not allowed. Please, I need you to understand that we're all on a journey of healing and if you will, I would love to walk this journey with you. We don't have to get it all right now. But I'm sure we'll figure out our rhythm along the way."

"Why are you telling me this now?"

"Because this is the right time."

With eyes awash with tears, I listen as he pours out his heart and the more I listen, the more I know this is no fluke.

Ethan is not making this up or trying to patronize me. Indeed, he is the rest Abba created for me.

A rest that supersedes every other. One that surpasses a billion sabbaticals!

About the Author

Timileyin Okunlola is a Nigeria-based poet, creative writer, and author. She is a screenwriter who also has her fingers in diverse pies in the creative field.

She is a contributor to **Hell Hath No Fury**, a best-selling anthology of the Black Female Authors outfit, and currently has 8 books to her credit. Some of her titles include **As My Mother's Daughter, Garden of Spices, Dark Pleasure, Oasis**, and **The Wish** amongst others.

She has been published on diverse platforms such as Life Touchers Africa Network, OakBooks, and Peak Radio amongst others. She is also a contributor to the Moveee and EcoPivot.

Just like life often stresses us all, whenever she feels out of touch with the tide of life, she props up a fluffy pillow, grabs a book, and eases the stress away.

To keep in touch with her updates, kindly connect with her across social media handles @TimileyinOkunlola.

Want More?

If you liked these stories and want more of the authors, check out the about the author sections for their works or read through the summaries of some of their other works below.

THE NIGHT MASQUERADE by Temitope Omamegbe - A secret borne by one affects everyone. Chisom's determination to expose her mother leads to the revelation and realization that all is not what it seems.

AYANFE by Feyi Aina - In a land where a questionable potion decides innocence and guilt, Princess Ayanfe and Captain Dehinde work together to reinvestigate a closed murder case. They fight an undeniable attraction to each other that they both must hide or the consequences will be grievous.

RAPTURE by Mobolaji Olanrewaju - Sparks fly between Asher Fabian and Sappirah Wilson when they take a trip to the Twin Bliss Resort. Time, fate and an unknown foe from the past become obstacles to keep them apart. Is there a chance in the future for both or are they doomed to stay apart forever?

YULTIDE SPARKS (*from Hell Hath No Fury Anthology*) By Christiana Agboni - Christmas is around the corner and it seems the universe is conspiring against Victoria in the form of cocky Dr Simon. Can they stock the fire building between them or will they allow it to fizzle out?

AS MY MOTHER'S DAUGHTER By Timileyin Okunlola - explores the complexities of the mother-child relationship, digging into the intricacies of love, hurt, and identity. It documents a journey of self-discovery, connection and bonding through imperfections.

The Girl in The Mirror: How 2020 Became The Year of My Grand Shift by Olamide Agemo – is a heartfelt narrative that chronicles the challenges, revelations, and personal growth that defined the author's journey during a year like no other.